BEWARE OF VIRTUOUS WOMEN

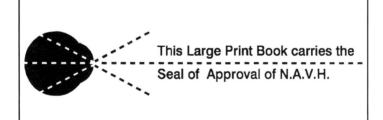

This Large Print Book carries the
Seal of Approval of N.A.V.H.

BEWARE OF
VIRTUOUS WOMEN

KASEY MICHAELS

THORNDIKE PRESS

An imprint of Thomson Gale, a part of The Thomson Corporation

THOMSON

GALE

Detroit • New York • San Francisco • New Haven, Conn. • Waterville, Maine • London

LIBRARY OF CONGRESS CATALOGING-IN-PUBLICATION DATA

Michaels, Kasey.
   Beware of virtuous women / by Kasey Michaels.
      p. cm. — (Thorndike Press large print romance)
   "A Romney Marsh Novel."
   ISBN-13: 978-0-7862-9222-6 (lg. print : alk. paper)
   ISBN-10: 0-7862-9222-9 (lg. print : alk. paper)
   1. Large type books. 2. England — Fiction. I. Title.
PS3563.I2725B49 2007
813'.54—dc22   2006031737

Published in 2007 by arrangement with Harlequin Books S.A.

Printed in the United States of America on permanent paper
10 9 8 7 6 5 4 3 2 1

To Tom and Carol Carpenter

Dear Reader,

It is 1813. England is fighting on two fronts, against both Napoleon and the United States. There is a third, smaller front — but hardly less important in certain quarters — and this front is on England's own shores, the combatants England's own citizens.

Anywhere the smallest boat might land, everywhere the Crown's war-tightened purse has made day-to-day living precarious, there is a chance that the local populace is dabbling in a bit of free trading — smuggling.

The Beckets of Romney Marsh do not engage in smuggling themselves, but they have jumped in with both feet to *protect* those of their neighbors who do. Their Black Ghost Gang has secured the area and operated in peace for two years. But now that peace and the entire enterprise are being threatened by the Red Men, a large, vicious gang whose tentacles reach from France to London's exclusive Mayfair.

And so is born an unholy alliance between Ainsley Becket's business partner and his own oldest daughter, Eleanor, who travel together to London posing as man and wife to unmask the leaders of the Red Men Gang. Trust between the two is paramount if they are to succeed, but one is tightly wrapped in lies and the other has a potentially explosive secret to protect.

It had all seemed so simple. The man Ainsley Becket had been, the family he had built would all die and come to Romney Marsh to be reborn — safe, hidden, hopefully forgotten.

But the world keeps creeping in . . .

Please enjoy Eleanor's story and watch for more Beckets in 2007.

Best,
Kasey Michaels

CHAPTER ONE

1813

Eleanor Becket sat in her usual chair near the fire, bent over her embroidery frame.

Her sisters Fanny and Cassandra, the latter still downstairs only because their papa had retreated to his study and didn't know she'd left her bedchamber, were playing a card game they'd invented together, and neither of them quite knew the rules.

Morgan Tanner, Countess of Aylesford, sister to the three and quite happily pregnant, sat with her legs up on a Chinese hassock, wiggling her slipper-clad toes in delight, for the slippers were new, and she rarely saw them. At least not while standing up and attempting to peer straight down.

A log fell in the large fireplace in the drawing room where they sat, and all four women momentarily looked up from what they were doing, then settled back to passing the time as best they could.

"They're fine," Eleanor said a few minutes later in answer to the unspoken question that had been hanging in the room all evening, and Fanny agreed that of course they were.

"Just enough mist over the water to hide the *Respite,* not enough to hamper them. And the moon couldn't be more perfect," Morgan said, looking toward one of the large windows and the dark beyond. "Callie, stop chewing on your curls. You'll end up with a hair ball in your belly. Odette will pour castor oil down your gullet, and there will be no lack of volunteers to hold you down."

Fifteen-year-old Cassandra Becket used her tongue to push the light brown corkscrew curl from her mouth, then frowned at its damp length. "I can't help it, Morgie. I'm nervous."

"And hours past your bedtime, as it's nearly three," Eleanor pointed out, taking another stitch in her embroidery, pleased that her hands were steady. "You, too, Morgan."

"Me? I'm pregnant, Elly, not delicate. In fact," she said, looking down at her stomach, "I'm about as *delicate* as a beached whale."

Fanny giggled. "Maybe if you didn't *eat*

so much . . . ?"

Morgan reached behind her and drew out one of the small silk pillows she'd placed there to make her comfortable, then launched it at her sister's head.

Fanny neatly caught the pillow, then stood, pressed it against her own flat stomach. She bent her spine back as far as she could, still holding the pillow to her, and began walking across the room, her feet spread wide. "Do I have it right, Callie? Enough of a duck's waddle to look like our dear, sophisticated countess?"

Callie considered this, then said, "Perhaps if you had first stuffed your cheeks with sugarplums?"

Eleanor smiled as she continued to bend over her embroidery. It was so good to have Morgan home with them after so many months away, but if her baby didn't come soon even Eleanor would be harboring a few fears that the girl would simply explode on her own, and not need Odette's midwifery.

"What was that? Fanny, Callie, sit down and be quiet. I think I heard something. Elly? Did you hear anything?"

Eleanor stood and walked over to Morgan, gently pushing her back down into the chair. "We don't want to appear to be too anxious, Morgan. It's bad enough we're all sitting up with you, just as if we don't expect them all to be fine. Ah — now I hear it, too. They're back. Everyone, do your best to appear unconcerned."

Fanny and Cassandra had already picked up their cards again, and Eleanor was once more bending over her embroidery frame as the Becket men entered the drawing room to catch Morgan in the middle of a prodigiously overdone yawn.

"Oh. Look who's back," Morgan said, "and none the worse for wear. Although, darling, could you possibly manage to wipe that ridiculous grin from your face?"

Ethan Tanner, Earl of Aylesford, pulled at the black silk scarf tied loosely around his throat and lifted it up and over his mouth and nose. "Better, darling?" he asked, then bent down and kissed her rounded belly. "Up late, aren't you, infant?"

"Are you referring to me or the baby? Come here, let me hold you. I know you were enjoying yourself romping about playing at freetrader, but I haven't had a peaceful night waiting for you."

Eleanor watched, glad for her sister's happiness and yet somehow sad at the same time, as Morgan yanked down Ethan's mask and grabbed his face in her hands, pulling him close for a long kiss on the mouth.

"At it again, Ethan?" Rian Becket said as he stripped off his gloves and accepted the glass of wine Fanny had fetched for him. "I think I should point out that the damage is already done."

Cassandra giggled, which drew the attention of Courtland Becket. "Been chewing on your hair again? And what are you doing down here at this hour? Get yourself upstairs where you belong."

Eleanor hid a sympathetic wince as Cassandra's pretty little face crumpled at this verbal slap and the child plopped herself down on one of the couches, to sulk.

Didn't Courtland know how desperately Cassandra worshipped him? Or perhaps he did, poor man. "Court? Does Papa know you're back?"

"He does. We came up the back stairs from the beach," Courtland told her, pouring himself a glass of claret. "And, before you ladies ask, the run was completely uneventful."

"You may say that, Court," Ethan said, sitting perched on the arm of the chair, holding Morgan's hand. "If it's uneventful to you that we had to evade the Waterguard and make land two hours behind schedule." He lifted Morgan's hand to his mouth, kissed her fingers. "God, but it makes your blood run, darling. I'll have to do this more often. Can't let everyone else have all the fun."

Morgan rolled her eyes. "Yes, of course. There's nothing like a good smuggling run to liven your exceedingly dull and boring married life. You should go out on every run, really. And don't you worry, I'll be sure to tell our child what you looked like before the Crown hanged you in chains."

"Ha! I think we've all just been insulted, Court," Rian said, pushing back his sea-damp black hair as Fanny looked at him, her heart in her eyes. "As if the Black Ghost could ever be caught."

Eleanor picked up her needle once more, not bothering to follow the lively exchange of jokes and verbal digs that were so commonplace in this rather wild, always loving clutch of Beckets. Like little boys, the men were still riding high on their excitement, and the girls were all more than willing to play their happy audience, even if that meant poking a bit of fun at them.

Was she the only one who saw beneath the surface of that banter? Saw that Fanny believed herself in love with Rian, and that Cassandra's devotion to Courtland was much more than that of a youngest child

14

for her older brother and staunch protector?

This was what happened when you lived in the back of beyond, isolated from most of the world. Siblings in name, but not by blood, as the Beckets had grown into the healthy animals they were, problems had been bound to arise.

But not for her. Not for Eleanor. She was the different one, the odd Becket out, as it were. The one part of the whole that had never quite fit.

Perhaps it was because she had been the last to join the family, and as a child of six, not as an infant or even as experienced as Chance and Courtland had been; already their own persons, older than their years when Ainsley Becket had scooped them up, given them a home on his now lost island paradise. She had landed more in the middle, and had been forced to seek her own identity, her own place.

And that place, she had long ago decided, had been with Ainsley Becket, the patriarch of the Becket clan. She had made herself into the calm one, the reasonable one, the quiet voice of sanity in the midst of so many more earthy, hot-blooded young creatures who eagerly grabbed at life with both hands.

The others would leave one day, as

Chance had when he'd married his Julia, as Morgan had when she'd wed her Ethan. Spencer was also gone, his commission purchased, and he'd been in Canada the last several months, fighting with his regiment against America, much to Ainsley's chagrin.

No matter how loving, how loyal, one by one the perhaps odd but yet wonderful assortment of Becket children would leave Becket Hall. Much as they loved and respected him, they'd leave Ainsley Becket alone with his huge house and his unhappy memories of the life he'd loved and lost before fleeing his island paradise and bringing everyone to this isolated land that was Romney Marsh.

But she'd stay. She and Ainsley had discussed all of that, in some detail. She would stay. As it was for Ainsley, it might even be safer for her to stay.

Eleanor watched now as Rian recounted the night's smuggling run to Fanny, who listened in rapt attention. As Courtland gave in and let Cassandra fuss over him, even try on the black silk cape that turned the sober, careful Courtland into the daring, mysterious Black Ghost. As Morgan and her Ethan whispered to each other, their heads close

16

together, Ethan's hand resting casually on her belly.

Eleanor put aside her embroidery and got to her feet, barely noticing the dull ache in her left leg caused by sitting too long, her muscles kept too tense as she'd held her worries inside by sheer force of will. Her siblings, everyone, believed her to be so composed, so controlled . . . and never realized how very frightened she was for all of them, most especially since the Black Ghost had begun his nocturnal rides to aid the people of Romney Marsh.

She left the drawing room unnoticed, her limp more pronounced than usual, but that would work out the more that she walked. By the time she reached Ainsley's study, it would barely be noticeable at all, which would be good, because her papa noticed everything.

The door to the study was half open and Eleanor was about to knock on one of the heavy oak panels and ask admittance when she heard voices inside the large, wood-paneled room.

Jacko's voice. "And I say leave it go. Cut our losses and find other ways, other people. There's always enough of the greedy bastards lying about, willing to get rich on our hard work."

Eleanor stepped back into the shadows in the hallway, realizing she'd stumbled onto a conversation she wouldn't be invited to join.

"True enough, Jacko," Ainsley agreed, "but we must also deal with this now, or else face the same problem again. Jack?"

Eleanor's eyes went wide. *Jack?* Her breathing became shallow, faster, and she pressed her hands to her chest. He was here? She hadn't known he was here. He must have arranged for a rendezvous with the *Respite* off Calais, then sailed home with them.

Jack Eastwood's voice, quiet, with hints of gravel in its cultured tones, sent a small frisson down Eleanor's spine. "Ainsley's right, Jacko. Someone got to these people, and if they did it once, they can do it again. Two men dead on their side of the Channel, most probably as an example to the others, and the rest now understandably too frightened to deal with us. My connections on this side of the Channel are also shutting the door on me, on us. This is the last haul we'll get, the last we can deliver anyway. Much as I want to keep the goods running — and I can do that, I know of other connections I can cultivate — I want to find out who did this to us, who discovered and compromised our current connections."

"And eliminate them," Ainsley said, his voice low, so that Eleanor had to strain to hear. She could picture him, sitting behind his desk, his brow furrowed, his right hand working the small, round glass paperweight she'd given him this past Christmas. "I thought we were done with bloodshed when we rousted the Red Men Gang from Romney Marsh."

Eleanor heard the creak of the leather couch, and knew Jacko had sat forward, shifting his large, muscular frame. "You think it's them, Cap'n? It's been two years since we trounced them, sent them on their way. You really think they're back?"

"Who else could it be? Perhaps its time to put a halt to all of this."

"Cap'n, you don't mean that." The leather couch protested again, and Eleanor stepped back farther into the shadows as Jacko's large frame passed in front of the open door.

She'd known Jacko since the moment he'd discovered their hiding place, his wide smile and booming laugh so frightening. Julia, Chance's wife, had once confided that her first thought when she'd seen Jacko was that the man would smile amiably even as he cut your beating heart from your chest, and Eleanor knew Julia's description was not an exaggeration.

But Jacko was loyal to Ainsley. Fiercely so. And if Eleanor hadn't learned to love the man, she had learned to trust his loyalty if not always his judgment, even when the memories had begun rolling back to her.
. . .

Ainsley was speaking again. "I do mean it, Jacko. We only began this to help the people here, protect them from the Red Men Gang. A laudable reason, but no one of us suspected the enterprise to grow as it has. We're bringing attention to ourselves, from London, and most probably from the Red Men again. Moving some wool and coming back with tea and brandy, helping these people survive. That was the plan, remember? Now we control most of the Marsh. Someone was bound to notice."

"So you withdraw our protection, leave everyone to find their own suppliers, their own landsmen, their own distributors in London? You watch as they run up against the Red Men on their own, and then bury a few more bodies, add a few more widows and fatherless children to the Marsh. Is that what you're saying, Cap'n?"

Eleanor held her breath. If Ainsley put a stop to the Black Ghost Gang they'd all be safe . . . but Jack Eastwood would never visit

Becket Hall again.

"No, that's not what I'm saying, Jacko. It's what I'm *hoping.* A selfish return to our quiet existence for my sons, our men and, yes, for myself. But we all know that isn't possible, at least not until the war is over and wool prices eventually climb again. Jack? Tell me more of your idea."

Eleanor stepped closer, not wishing to miss a word.

"All right. As I said, someone is trying to cut off both our head and our feet — our contacts both around London and in France. After this last shipment, I have no one lined up to buy our people's wool, and no one to sell the goods we, well, that we *import.*"

"You've been sloppy? How else would anyone know your contacts?"

Eleanor heard the hint of distaste in Jack's tone. "No, Jacko, I don't think I've been . . . sloppy. I think someone else has been very smart. Why confront us here on the Marsh, on the Black Ghost's home ground, when cutting off our head and feet is so much easier than hitting at our well-protected and well-armed belly? And I think it all begins in London, not France. This hasn't happened overnight, our sources have been shrinking for some time now. I've been watching, and I have some ideas, which is why I traveled to France, and why I'm here now."

As Eleanor listened, Jack further explained his conclusions, and his plan.

No one in France had any reason to stop the flow of contraband either into or out of that country. To the French, profit was profit, and they'd deal with the Red Men, the Black Ghost, the devil himself, as long as that profit was maintained, often with much of that profit going directly into Napoleon's war chest. If the French were nothing else, they were always eminently practical.

Which left London. More specifically, Mayfair, the very heart of the *ton*. Bankers and wealthy cits, industrialists, were also suspected of acting as financial backers to the smugglers, but it was common if unspoken knowledge that many an impecunious peer had staked his last monies on a smuggling run and then suddenly found his pockets deep again.

And Jack had an idea where in the *ton* he should look to find the people who had the most to gain if the Black Ghost Gang was rendered impotent.

"I've narrowed my search down to a trio of men," he said. "Three gentlemen friends who have had happy and yet inexplicable reversals of fortune in the past few years. We all know the major profits from smuggling go to people at the very top of society."

"People with the money to put up to buy contraband goods in order to resell them at ten times the price, yes," Ainsley interrupted. "But these men you speak of? You said they've had reversals of fortune, which is not the same as having amassed a fortune the likes of which we know can be gotten. That would put them somewhere in the middle, wouldn't it? High-placed minions, the slightly more public face of the true leaders, but still minions."

"True, none of them certainly is another Golden Ball, but there is money there now, where there had been only debts. If we can get to them, hopefully we can get to the person or persons at the very top," Jack said. "And I'm willing to wager that whoever that is, he's also the brains behind the Red Men Gang. They may not be here in Romney Marsh anymore, but they're everywhere else, like a large red stain spreading over the countryside these past years. No one makes a move without them, and if anyone dares, they're mercilessly crushed. You, Ainsley, you and your sons and Romney Marsh? You are all that stand between the Red Men Gang and complete domination of the smuggling trade in the south of England. The Marsh is too tricky, navigation too dangerous for them to work this area without the cooperation of the local inhabitants."

Jacko spoke up. "All very well, Eastwood, and you've made your point with that pretty speech. But we are here, not about to budge, and you're only one man. Let's hear more of this grand plan of yours."

"I'm getting there, Jacko. You know I've bought a house in Portland Square, to go along very nicely with my estate in Sussex. I'm a fairly wealthy man, thanks to you, Ainsley, and you aren't the only one who sees the merits in planning for a more . . . conventional future, a life after we're done with our adventure. I think it's time I make a rather large but concentrated splash in London society."

"To get you close, have you noticed by this trio of men you suspect," Ainsley said quietly. "You interest me. Go on."

"I think my way in would be through the gambler in the group, Harris Phelps. He's the most reckless, and the most stupid. He's taken to wearing a scarlet waistcoat and always wagering on the red, saying it's his lucky color."

"Damn," Jacko muttered. "Sounds like we're being beaten by an idiot. That stick in your craw as much as it does mine, Cap'n?"

"On the contrary, Jacko. It's always comforting to know you're smarter than your enemy, as long as you don't make the mistake of becoming overconfident. Always remember that even idiots are successful at times, if only by accident. Go on, Jack. I imagine you plan to get close with this Phelps person, and through him, with the others?"

"I intend to lose a lot of money playing at cards with Phelps, yes," Jack said, and Eleanor bit her bottom lip, smiling at the cleverness of the idea. Lose some money, bemoan his shrinking pockets, wish for a huge turn of luck . . . and then appeal to his new friend for some way to increase his fortune.

"You're that sure Phelps is your man? That you'd put your own money on the line?"

"Yes, Ainsley, I am, and I've already begun doing just that. I won't always lose, either, not once I've firmly hooked our fish. Which, if I'm lucky, should be quickly enough to have only a two-or three-week interruption of our runs."

"You've always been a dab hand with the cards, I'll give you that."

"You gave him a lot more than a dab of your money, Jacko, as I recall the thing," Ainsley said, and Eleanor pretended not to hear Jacko's low string of curses.

She remembered when they met Jack Eastwood, and how. A gambler, that was Jack, a gentleman of breeding but little fortune, living on his wits. But that had all changed the day, two years past, when he'd ridden up to Becket Hall with Billy slung facedown across his saddle after rescuing him from a pub in Appledore, where a deep-drinking Billy had the bad sense to accuse a man of cheating when he had no friends present to guard his back. Jack had stepped in, saved the sailor from a knife in the gullet, although both he and Billy had suffered several wounds.

During his weeks of recuperation at Becket Hall, Jack had done more than strip Jacko of five thousand pounds as they'd passed time playing at cards. He also had gained Ainsley's thanks for the rescue of one of his oldest friends, Ainsley's trust and, with that trust, a future.

And never once in that month or in the two years since had he said more than

"Good morning, Miss Becket," or "Good evening, Miss Becket," to Eleanor.

She cocked her head toward the doorway, listening as Jack explained more of his plan. "I'm going to get even closer to Phelps, who will bring me closer to the others, close enough that I can find ways to bring them down, each one of them. But I may need that initial entrée into a wider society, as well. I discussed this with your son-in-law as we crossed the Channel tonight, and he's agreed to give me a letter of introduction to his friend Lady Beresford. I'm now a gentleman who has spent much of his time these past years on his plantations in the West Indies, happily visiting my homeland."

"That should be enough to gain you at least a few invitations. Chance could help you there, too, except that he and Julia plan to remain at his estate with the children until the end of summer, now that he's left the War Office," Ainsley said. "All right. What else? You have the look of a man who isn't quite finished saying what he needs to say."

"No," Jack said, "that's about it. The rest is just details I'll need to handle on my own."

"Such as?"

"I'm thinking I may need a wife."

Eleanor clapped her hands over her mouth, hoping no one had heard her short, startled gasp. Then, once back under control, she stepped closer, anxious to hear what else Jack might say.

"Wives go a long way in making a man appear respectable. It's not enough that I play the rich, amiable fool. I believe I need a wife, as well. Most especially a wife who listens with both ears to other men's wives. Hiring an actress to play the part is chancy, but also worth the risk, I believe. Phelps's wife, for one, has a tongue that runs on wheels. Ask her the right questions, and I may get answers that will help me."

"I can see you believe this Harris Phelps to be the weakest link," Ainsley said. "Who are the other two?"

"Sir Gilbert Eccles is one. But the fellow who most interests me is the strongest of the lot. If he's not the head of the Red Men, then he is very close. Rawley Maddox, Earl of Chelfham."

Before Eleanor could clap her hands to her mouth again, someone did it for her, and she was pulled back against the tall, rangy body of Odette, the one woman in the Becket household who knew every secret, the voodoo priestess who had come

28

to England with the Beckets so many years ago.

"Ears that listen at the wrong doors hear things they should not hear," Odette whispered to Eleanor. "Come away, child."

"But Odette — you heard? *The Earl of Chelfham.*"

"I heard. You want nothing to do with this man. You decided. We all decided."

"I know," Eleanor whispered fiercely as she looked toward the half-open door. "But this is . . . this is like *fate.* And I only want to see. Is it so wrong to want to see?"

"You want the man, *ma petite,*" Odette told her, stroking Eleanor's hair with one long-fingered hand. "He's the temptation you don't want to resist."

"You mean Jack?" Eleanor sighed, realizing protest was useless. "There's no future in lying to you, is there, Odette? *You* see everything."

The woman's face lost its smile. "Not everything, little one. Never enough. But I do know your papa won't approve."

Eleanor wet her lips with the tip of her tongue. "I know. But this is my decision to make, Odette, my chance. If I don't take my chance, I'll have the rest of my life to regret it. Years and years to sit by myself with my embroidery, my paints, my music. Sit and watch everyone else live their lives, while mine just slowly, quietly runs out, like sand slipping through an hourglass. Don't you see? I have to do this."

"Born a maiden, not prepared to die a maiden. Yes, I see."

"No," Eleanor whispered fiercely, then sighed. "Yes, yes, that, too. And why not? I've tried being a paragon, and it's lonely, Odette. It's a lonely life. I want to hold more than other people's children. That's a dream, only a dream. But the earl, Odette? He's real. How can I hear what I just heard, and walk away?"

Odette looked at her for a long time, and Eleanor returned that gaze as steadily as she could, until the older woman sighed, shook her head. "I'll be ordering more candles, I suppose. A bonfire of candles burning for you Beckets."

Eleanor impulsively hugged the woman, neither of them comfortable with such physical displays of affection. Yet Odette put her arms around Eleanor's shoulders and held her tightly for a moment before pushing her away, using the pad of her thumb to trace the sign of the cross on Eleanor's forehead. When it came to asking for divine help, Odette did not limit herself to calling only on the good *loa*.

"Thank you, Odette," Eleanor said, then squared her slim shoulders and walked into her papa's study to confront the man who had been coming to Becket Hall for over two years, and had never noticed her, never noticed the quiet one in the corner.

He'd notice her now. . . .

"A shame Morgan is married," Jacko was saying. "She'd be perfect, you know. Right, Cap'n? Fire and spirit, that's Morgan. Give her a set of balls and — Eleanor." Jacko looked to Ainsley, who had already gotten to his feet.

"Eleanor? I hadn't expected you to be up and about this late at night. Is there something you wanted before you retire?" And that, she knew, was Ainsley's way of reprimanding her. Two quiet, polite questions, both meant to send her scurrying off, because she most certainly wasn't welcome here, at this moment.

She could hardly hear for the sound of her blood rushing in her ears, and she seemed only able to see Jack Eastwood, who had slowly unbent his length from one of the chairs and now stood towering over her.

"I . . . I'll do it," Eleanor said, still looking up at Jack, at the lean, handsome face she

31

saw nearly every night in her dreams. The thick, sandy hair he wore just a little too long, with sideburns that reached to the bottom of his ears. The slashes around his wide mouth, that fuller lower lip. And his eyes. So green, shaded by low brows; so intense, yet so capable of looking at her and never seeing her.

He was a very . . . elemental man, a singular force of nature. Just his physical appearance was so in contrast to herself. Fire to her carefully cultivated ice.

Eleanor felt sure the man was a mass of barely leashed power behind a careful facade, that he had hidden some of himself from Ainsley, which was no mean feat. There was emotion there. He simply kept his feelings deep inside, and Eleanor didn't know if she most longed to know why he hid those emotions, or if she only wanted him to look at her, see her, feel safe to relax his careful shields with her.

So that he might melt her ice and make her *feel.*

"Eleanor . . ." Ainsley said, stepping out from behind the desk. "I'll assume you heard us, but —"

"I said, I'll do it," Eleanor interrupted, still looking at Jack Eastwood, still half lost in her daydream — she, who rarely dreamed, and only about Jack. "I'll pretend to be your wife, Mr. Eastwood. Go to London. Be your ears and eyes around the women. You can't buy loyalty, no matter how high the price. I'm the logical choice, the only logical, safe choice."

Jack quickly looked to Ainsley as if for help, then back to Eleanor, shaking his head. "I don't think your father approves, Miss Becket."

Was the woman out of her mind? Look at her. A puff of wind would blow her away. All right, so there was a hint of determination about that slightly square jaw she held so high on the long, slender stalk of her neck. God, even that mass of dark hair seemed too heavy for her finely boned head. Yet she had the look of a lady, he'd give her that. Refined. Genteel. What was the term? Oh yes, a *pocket Venus.* A sculptor's masterpiece, actually, if he was in a mood to be poetical, which he damn well was not.

The large-eyed, delicately constructed Eleanor Becket reminded Jack mostly of a fawn in the woods. Huge brown eyes, vulnerable eyes. But that limp? London society could be cruel, and they'd smell the wounded fawn and destroy her in an instant.

Would she stop staring at him! Stop making him feel so large, so clumsy, so very much the bumpkin. The skin tightened around his eyes, drew his brows down, and he stared at her, tried to stare through her. Scare her off, damn her. He had enough on his plate, he didn't need any more complications. Certainly not one in skirts.

At last she looked away, to speak to her father. "Papa? You do see the rightness of this, don't you? No one knows me, and when the need is past, I will come back here to live in quiet retirement, as we've always planned. Mr. Eastwood, should he choose to stay in society, can certainly find some explanation for my disappearance. A divorce? Death?"

Eleanor abruptly shut her mouth, knowing she had gone too far. Keep in the moment, that's what she must do, not muddy up the waters with thoughts of consequences.

"We'll speak later," Ainsley said, taking hold of her shoulders, to turn her toward the door.

"No, Papa," Eleanor said in her quiet way, holding her ground. "We'll not speak at all, not about this decision, which is mine. Mr. Eastwood? When do you wish me to be ready to leave?"

Jacko yanked at his waistband with both hands, pulling the material up and over his generous belly. "Always said there was pure Toledo steel there, Cap'n, and you know it, too. She knows what's for. Probably the smartest of the bunch, for all she's a female. I say let her go."

Jack narrowed his eyes once more as he looked to Ainsley, to the grinning Jacko and, lastly, back to Miss Eleanor Becket. Smartest of the bunch? Toledo steel? He doubted that. And yet her gaze was steady on him, and he recognized determination when he saw it. "Ainsley? We could leave tomorrow afternoon. Spend a night on the road while I send someone ahead to alert my staff in Portland Square. We'd be gone a fortnight at the most."

It took everything she had, but Eleanor did not reach out to Ainsley when he retreated behind his desk, sat down once more, looking very weary, and older than he had only a few minutes earlier. "Tomorrow will be fine, Jack."

Jack was ready to say something else, something on the order of a promise to take very good care of the man's daughter. But Jacko slung a beefy arm across his shoulders and gave him a mighty squeeze against his hard body, and the breath was all but knocked from him.

Jacko's voice boomed in his ear. "We trust

you, see? That's the only reason you're getting within ten feet of our Eleanor here. We're all friends here, too, aren't we? Remember that, my fine young gentleman. You saved that fool Billy, and I'm grateful. So don't harm so much as a single hair on our Eleanor's head, because I don't want to have to tie your guts in a bow around your neck."

"No, Jacko, you don't, and neither do I want you to have to try," Jack said when the big man released him, feeling as if he'd just been mauled by a large bear. He shook back his shoulders, bowed to Eleanor. "Miss Becket, with your kind permission?"

She inclined her head slightly, then watched as Jack brushed past her and left the study before turning to her adoptive father. Waiting.

"Rawley Maddox, lifted up to be the Earl of Chelfham," Ainsley said at last, the long, slender fingers of his right hand closing tightly around the glass paperweight. "Of all the names the man might have said . . ."

"Should we tell him, Cap'n? In case he has to watch out for her?"

"No," Eleanor said quickly. "Tell him, and he won't let me go. I *have* to go."

Ainsley nodded his agreement, then added, "We don't know if your memories are correct, Eleanor. We can suspect, but we don't *know*."

"No, Papa, but we've always wondered who I am . . . who I *was*. I know what we decided, what we both felt best, that the past is in the past and won't change, not for any of us. But I can't look away from this chance. I just can't. I've lived too long with the questions, we both have. Why that ship? Why that one particular ship?"

"And you'll take one look at the bugger and have all our answers? Look at him, and nothing more? Not then want to go from looking, to talking?" Jacko shook his head. "Maybe we've all been stuck here too long, if any of us believes that. . . ."

CHAPTER TWO

Jack Eastwood slouched on the velvet squabs of the Becket traveling coach, his booted feet crossed at the ankle, his arms folded over his chest, his chin on that chest, the wide-brimmed black hat he favored pulled down to shade his closed eyes.

He sat in the rear-facing seat, as it was the duty of a gentleman to make any female in his company as comfortable as possible. That, and the fact that he didn't much care for the idea of the two of them sitting side by side, mute, staring into space.

He was tired. Weary as hell, in both mind and body. He'd spent a long week skulking about on the shores of France, buying and beating information out of his contacts there, the men he had helped make rich — that they'd all helped make rich. Greasy, sleazy bastards who'd sell out their own mother for a two-penny profit on a few inches of hand-sewn lace, Lord bless them.

He'd picked up or outright purchased several interesting bits of information about Bonaparte during his trips across the Channel with the Black Ghost Gang these past two years. Information he'd passed on anonymously to the War Office. That eased his conscience some as he continued doing what he was doing.

Because he was not about to stop, walk away. He was still no closer to the leaders of the Red Men Gang, no closer than he'd been when he'd first carefully ingratiated himself to Ainsley Becket.

He allowed himself a small smile as he remembered how he'd done it. How he'd paid a Greek sailor to deliberately fuzz the cards, then quietly pointed out to Ainsley's man, Billy, that he was being cheated. The more-than-three-parts-drunk Billy didn't remember that part, only the tavernwide fight that followed, and his "rescue" by his new friend. Jack's own wounds had come courtesy of the Greek, who hadn't appreciated not being fully informed of Jack's plan.

But Ainsley Becket wasn't the leader of the Red Men Gang. Jack had been so sure, but he'd been proved wrong. Worse, he'd grown to like the man, respect him. Ainsley was a reluctant smuggler, his main concern the people of Romney Marsh, those who suffered because of the low prices for wool, for all their goods, people who didn't smuggle for profit, but to exist. The Black Ghost Gang only rode to lend protection to those they clearly considered to be their own people.

Even more laudable, the man didn't take a bent penny for his efforts, his family's efforts. Not that the Crown wouldn't hang them all just as high if they found out about them.

Jack had been worried as he'd traveled back to Romney Marsh on the *Respite,* concerned that Ainsley and that damnable Jacko would decide to call it a day, shut down the entire operation. But they hadn't, had even offered up Ainsley's strange daughter to him.

And what in bloody hell he was going to do with her was beyond him. She looked, and acted, as if she not only wouldn't, but couldn't say *boo* to a goose. Lord knew she'd said no more than a few dozen words to him since they'd left Becket Hall the previous afternoon. Putting her in a position where she'd be attempting to neatly ferret information out of the wives of his suspects was almost laughable, and could prove dangerous.

He should have said no. Thank you, very generous of you, but no.

But there had been something about the look in Eleanor Becket's huge brown eyes, a hint of both desperation and determination that had affected him in some way he didn't want to examine.

What a mess he'd gotten himself into. Out to catch a smuggler, he'd become one, at least peripherally. Oh, hell, he couldn't persuade himself that he was only acting as an agent, a go-between. He was a smuggler. He'd be hanged as surely as the Beckets if he was caught.

What a far cry from the soldier he'd been in Spain . . . until word had come about his cousin's disappearance. His cousin's murder, most probably, and presumably at the hands of smugglers.

"Mr. Eastwood, are you asleep?"

Jack lifted his hat slightly and looked at Eleanor Becket out of one barely opened eye. "My apologies, miss."

Eleanor watched as he unhurriedly sat up straight, as if he truly cared to listen to what she had to say — but not all that much. "Oh, no, apologies aren't necessary. You've every right to be weary. That inn was abominable. Dirty, the food inferior, and with faintly damp sheets. I should have thought to bring linens from Becket Hall. I only thought . . . um, that is, we're nearing London, I suppose, and perhaps you wish to discuss how we're to . . . to go on?"

"You're right, Miss Becket," Jack said, removing his hat, running a hand through his hair as he wondered what Miss Eleanor Becket would think about sleeping on the ground, in the mud, while being pelted by a cold, hard rain. With his rifle in his arms, at the ready. Faintly damp sheets? Hell, he hadn't noticed. "But the thing is, I really don't know *how* we're going to . . . go on, as you say."

"Really?" Eleanor blinked twice, pushed away the thought that the man surely should have had *some* idea of what would come next, or else he shouldn't have embarked on the plan in the first place.

But that was the practical part of her, the part that had, according to Morgan, sealed her fate as an old maid. Still, she was who she was, and what she was, and clearly someone had to take charge.

"Very well, Mr. Eastwood," she said, unclasping her gloved hands that had been resting in her lap these past three hours, while inwardly she'd longed to use one of them to tip that ridiculous hat off the man's head and tell him to sit up straight and stop acting like Spencer in one of his sulks. But she'd resisted, even lowered the shades and sat in the half-dark so that the sunlight would not disturb him.

"Very well *what,* Miss Becket?" Jack asked, wondering if he should pretend not to notice the twin spots of color that had appeared on her cheeks. The little fawn had a temper. How interesting.

Lifting her chin slightly, Eleanor began to count on her fingers as she rattled off her thoughts with the precision of a sergeant barking orders to his troops. "Number one, Mr. Eastwood, we are married, at least to the world, which includes your staff in Portland Square. Therefore, I am Mrs. Eastwood to the staff, and Eleanor to you. And you are Jack."

"Not *darling?*" Jack asked, the devil rising in him now. "I had so hoped for a love match."

Eleanor dropped her head slightly, lowered her gaze, then looked over at Jack through remarkably long, thick black lashes. "If I might continue?"

Well, that had put him in his place, hadn't it? "My apologies . . . Eleanor."

"Accepted. This is difficult for both of us,

I'm sure," Eleanor said, longing to kick herself for being so formal, for being such . . . such a *stick!* "If you prefer the diminutive, Elly will also do."

"Very well. But you can still feel free to call me darling, *Elly.*"

Eleanor clasped her hands together and pressed her knuckles against her mouth, trying to keep her lips from turning up into a smile. "Now you're being facetious."

"I only sought to ease the tension between us. We'll be fine, Elly, I promise. My staff are very incurious, and that's by design."

"Very well. I really don't look for any problems there, as I've read extensively about the proper running of a large domicile, although I much prefer my experience at Becket Hall. I will, of course, need a maid assigned to me, if I'm to go out in public without you. I also read that somewhere — that ladies do not walk about unaccompanied."

"You plan to do a lot of walking, Elly?"

He kept calling her Elly. She'd really rather he addressed her as Eleanor, that she had not suggested the diminutive. She was not, after all, his sister. "I would like to see some of the sights, if at all possible."

"So I'm right in assuming this is your first trip to the city. You never had a Season when you were younger?"

"Is my advanced age so obvious?"

"Well, that was putting my foot in it, wasn't it? Then you're younger than your sister, the countess?"

"No, you were correct. I am the oldest, already into my majority. I preferred not to have a Season."

"Because of your — damn. I can't seem to say anything right, can I?"

"No, Mr.— Jack. We probably should get past this, as I'm cognizant of the fact that you know little about your new *wife*. I am one and twenty, I never had a Season, and I suffered an injury to my leg and foot as a child that has left me with a slight limp. It pains me in prolonged stretches of inclement weather or if I overexert myself, but is otherwise simply a nuisance. I'm neither ashamed nor proud of my . . . condition, and would prefer you ignore it rather than concern yourself. I am, I assure you, more than capable of the mission I've accepted."

"All but bullied your way into taking. Made a case for yourself against your father's wishes, actually, but who's quibbling?" Jack commented, once more holding back a smile. "I simply want to know why you were so willing to volunteer."

If being a Becket qualified Eleanor for anything, it was the acquired ability to lie smoothly and without suspicion. "I have been no farther than a few miles from Becket Hall since I arrived there as a child of six, which is when I . . . became a part of the family. I know you are aware that only Cassandra is Papa's natural child, and that the rest of us came to him as orphans."

"Yes, I do know that. It's all very intriguing, actually."

"Not really, not if you knew Papa well. At any rate, Morgan's delightful stories of London have intrigued me, and I finally realized I should like to travel to the metropolis. Not for a Season, I don't delude myself into aspirations at that level, but I couldn't pass up this opportunity. Plus," she ended, looking at him levelly, "I am as eager to rid us of our current problem as are you. It's my family, after all, that could be put in danger."

"I see," Jack said, aware that the coach was now riding along well-cobbled streets, even without raising the shade to look out the window. He moved to the front-facing seat, sat beside her. "How do you plan to approach the ladies?"

Ah, good. They had left the subject of her life behind them. As for the rest, she'd simply ignore his proximity. She was almost used to being in his company. Almost. "I don't. I plan to sit very quietly and listen to the ladies. I've learned that most people rush to fill a silence."

Jack considered this, even as he became uncomfortably aware of the silence in the coach and, damn the woman, rushed to fill it. "I begin to feel that I am the amateur here, Elly. Does Ainsley know just how well you've been *listening* as you bend over your embroidery or paints, which is all I can picture of you when I think of my previous visits to Becket Hall?"

"I'm flattered that you are able to recall me at all," Eleanor said, her voice steady even as he actually said what she'd always felt. That she was near to invisible to him, when he had become the center of her life.

"Ouch! I believe I can almost feel the flat of your hand on my cheek for that careless insult," Jack said, then surprised himself by lifting her gloved hand to his lips. "I can promise you that I will do my best to make up for my sins by being an extremely devoted husband."

Eleanor gently tugged her hand free, even as she continued to look at Jack, fought to control her breathing. "I doubt that most of the *ton* behave as Morgan and her Ethan do. Civility will be enough."

He'd hurt her. He'd be damned if he knew how, but he'd definitely hurt her. And, if he had any sense at all, he'd drop this subject completely and get on with the business of how he would further infiltrate the trio of men he suspected of being in league with the Red Men Gang.

Only later, once he was alone, would there be time to think about this strange, fragile-looking young woman who, as Jacko had said, seemed to be formed of finest Toledo steel.

"Tomorrow we'll begin," he told her as the coach stopped, then started off again at a near crawl, caught in the crush of early-evening London traffic. For a woman who'd professed an interest in the London sights, Eleanor Becket seemed content to have the shades drawn tight on the coach windows. Just a naturally secretive little thing, wasn't she? Or she liked sitting in the half dark, which was silly, because she wasn't a bad-looking woman.

"Yes, Jack, tomorrow will be soon enough. How do you plan to begin?"

"With Lady Beresford. We may not be in London long enough to take advantage of the association, get out into wider society at all. I hope not, frankly. But I'll present Ethan's letter to her anyway."

"A bit of honesty covers many a lie, Papa says. At the very least, you could then honestly drop her name into the conversation as you ratchet up your pursuit of the men you mentioned at Becket Hall." Eleanor spoke each word carefully, not wishing too appear too anxious to hear about the men . . . the man.

"Yes. But remember, I've already begun with Harris Phelps, as he frequents several gaming hells on the fringes of Mayfair. Gilly — that's Sir Gilbert Eccles — is more of a cipher, I suppose you'd say, definitely a follower and not a leader. Where Phelps goes, Eccles will follow."

Eleanor wet her lips, swallowed. "And the third? I believe you said he was an earl?"

"Earl of Chelfham, yes. The estimable Rawley Maddox. He's the oldest of the trio by a good twenty or more years, as I already told Ainsley, and definitely the smartest. He's why I'm bothering with Phelps and Eccles at all — they're to be my way in to Chelfham. It's his bride I'd most particularly hope you can cultivate. She's Phelps's sister, which may explain why Chelfham bothers with him. She's also young, probably not more than a few years older than you, in fact."

"Really? How . . . interesting."

"Not really. He's trying for an heir is how I heard the story. His first wife died in a fall down the stairs, the second in childbed. If Chelfham dies without issue, I believe the earldom goes vacant."

Eleanor's head was spinning. "I believe the proper term is *extinct,* if all possible heirs have died. A title is *dormant* if no one claims it or his or her title can't be proved, and *in abeyance* if more than one person is equally qualified to be the holder."

Jack shook his head. Listening to this woman was like being back in class with his tutor as he reeled off dry as dust facts and expected Jack to care. "Is that so?"

"Oh, yes, at least I think so." She smiled at him, and Jack felt an unexpected punch to his stomach. She was such an odd little creature, all prim and proper, yet also so anxious to please. "Papa has a rather large library, and I have quite a bit of time."

"You said *her.* His or *her* title. It would be interesting, wouldn't it, if Chelfham's bride presented him with only daughters."

Eleanor made a great business of inspecting the seam on the thumb of her right glove. "Some peerages can be inherited by females, although their number is very limited. And, of course, private fortunes and land not entailed can be given where one wishes."

Jack sat back against the squabs, more than a little surprised. Then again, what did he care for peerages? And, if he was right, and had his way, the Earl of Chelfham wouldn't have to worry about them, either.

"Rather a fountain of possibly useful information, aren't you? I can see where you are a good choice for my small project, in any case. A lady, and an educated lady at that. I imagine everyone will be wondering why such a fine and refined creature as yourself would agree to leg shackle herself to such a rough character as myself."

Eleanor looked at him quizzically for a moment, then dropped her gaze. What had just happened? What had he just said? How had he said it?. . . *such a fine and refined creature as yourself.*

No, it wasn't actually the words he'd said, but the way he had said them. And he'd said them with this sudden *lilt* in his voice. Why had he suddenly reminded her of Paddy O'Rourke, from the village? He was English, not Irish. Everyone knew Jack Eastwood was English. Born in Sussex was what he'd told them. Yet Eleanor was sure she'd just heard a faint hint of Ireland in the cadence of his last statement.

It had been there, hadn't it? Just for a moment?

She closed her eyes, calling herself silly. A life spent not trusting outsiders had made her skittish, and much too suspicious. Her papa trusted him. Court and the others trusted him. She hadn't even thought about trust, fool that she was, too dazzled by Jack's effect on her.

Well, that particular foolishness needed to come to a quick end. She was a Becket first, and female only second.

Much as she longed to see the Earl of Chelfham, much as she was determined to help Jack Eastwood uncover the identity of the leaders of the Red Men Gang who had threatened the Beckets' very existence, she would remember to keep her faith in herself, and not in anyone else, even Jack Eastwood.

Eleanor's life, that had seemed much too tame to her only a few days ago, was suddenly crowded with too many possibilities for disaster. . . .

CHAPTER THREE

"About time it was you lugged that great big simple self of yours back here, boyo. I was about to give you up."

Jack turned, still in the act of sliding off his neck cloth, to see Cluny Shannon sprawled on the lone chair in his dressing room, a half-empty glass hanging from his fingers.

It was always a half-empty glass with Cluny, who never saw the sunshine without mentioning the clouds.

"My apologies, old friend. I didn't notice a candle in the window. Were you pining for me?"

Cluny finished off his drink, obviously not the first or even the fourth of the evening, and carefully got to his feet, holding the glass in front of him as he advanced on Jack. "Thinking of where to lay off the silver, to tell you the truth. I could turn a pretty penny just for that behemoth you've got sitting on the table in the dining room. Now that I think on it, it's a shame you made it back. Go away again, get yourself lost, and I'll be a rich man."

Jack unbuttoned his waistcoat and shrugged out of it, then began on the buttons of his shirt. "You're getting soft in your old age, Cluny. Ten years ago, and you'd have had the silver before I was halfway to the coast. Have you sold off my clothes to the ragman, or do you think my dressing gown is still here somewhere?"

"I'm supposing you want me to fetch it for you now, don't you?" Cluny put down the glass and navigated his way to one of the large clothespresses, extracting a deep burgundy banyan he then tossed in Jack's general direction. "Here you go, boyo. Cover yourself up before I lose my supper."

"Which you drank," Jack said, snagging the dressing gown out of midair and sliding his bare arms into it, tying the sash at his waist. "I need you sober now, Cluny. We've got us a fine piece of trouble."

The Irishman settled himself once more into the chair. "True enough. I saw her when you brought her in. A fine piece indeed, but what in the devil are we supposed to be doing with her?"

Jack shook his head at his friend's deliberate misunderstanding and headed back into his bedchamber, Cluny on his heels. "That, my friend, is no piece, fine or otherwise. She's Becket's daughter, so if you want to keep your liver under wraps you'll be very careful what you say, and what you do. Understand?"

"Not even by half I don't," Cluny said, pouring wine into two clean glasses. "Becket's girl, you say? So you brought her up to town as a favor to the man?"

"No," Jack said, accepting the glass Cluny offered, "I brought her up here as my wife."

While Cluny coughed and spit, wine dribbling from his chin, Jack eased his length into a leather chair beside the small fire in the grate and waited, pleased to have said something that might have sobered up the fellow at least a little bit. "You all right, Cluny?"

"All right? You go and get yourself caught in parson's mousetrap, and I don't even know about it? I have no say in the thing?"

Jack took another sip of wine, trying to keep his features composed as the Irishman turned beet-red from his double chins to his thick shock of coarse, graying hair. "I suppose you wanted me to ask for your blessing, dear mother?"

"You could be doing worse than putting

your faith in me. And I'm not your bleeding mother, even if you are a son of a bitch. What's she like, this Becket woman?"

Jack considered the question. His first thought was to tell him Eleanor's huge brown eyes were the most beautifully expressive feature in her small, gamin face. That she was fragile, yet seemed to possess a will of iron. That he felt like a raw, too tall, uncivilized golumpus whenever he was near her. That he felt uncharacteristically protective of her, and even more uncharacteristically attracted to her.

But he doubted Cluny needed to hear that.

"Quiet. Smart. Not necessarily trustworthy, but that's all right because I don't think she trusts me, either. Oh, and we're not really married."

Cluny looked at his wineglass, then carefully set it down. "Time to haul myself back up on the water wagon. What did you say? Are you bracketed or not?"

Jack waited for his just-arrived valet to put down the tray of meat and cheese and leave the room, heading for the dressing room to, most likely, cluck over the condition of his master's wardrobe that was much the worse for wear after a week across the Channel.

"What's that fellow's name, again?" he asked Cluny, who'd settled his cheerless bulk into the facing chair.

"Frank," Cluny said, popping a large piece of cheese into his mouth.

"No, not Frank. Francis?"

Cluny shrugged. "I like Frank better, a good, solid name. Why aren't you married? Not that I want you to be, you understand, but why not?"

So Jack explained. For an hour, he explained, as Cluny interrupted almost constantly.

At the end of that hour Cluny had fallen off the water wagon — never an easy ride for him, even in the best of times — and poured himself another drink. "Are you sure that cousin of yours is worth all this skulduggery? I always thought you didn't like the man above half."

"It's not him I'm doing it for, but his mother. Mothers love sons, Cluny, even if the son is a thorough jackass. Besides, even if it all started that way, we've moved far beyond my concerns for Richard. I'm . . . well, I'm *invested* in this now."

Cluny looked around the large, well-appointed bedchamber. "Of course you are, lad. Everything you do is out of the fine, sweet goodness of your heart. I'll be shedding a tear here any moment, I will that."

Jack had told a small fib to Ainsley Becket — the house in Portland Square wasn't really his. It was his cousin's, as was the estate in Sussex. But where his cousin had allowed both places to go to rack and ruin, they were now returned to their former glory. His mother and aunt lived well now on that Sussex estate, not in constant fear of losing the roof over their heads. This house was now furnished in the first stare, thanks to Jack's money. If he found Richard, he'd buy the pile from him, the estate, as well. If he didn't find him, his aunt would surely be happy for the money.

He chuckled low in his throat. "I never said I was applying for sainthood, Cluny. But at least we've a fair division of profits between us and those who take the most risk. Or are you feeling a dose of Christian charity coming on and want to give back your own share?"

Cluny sank his chins onto his chest. "How far two such God-fearing gentlemen as ourselves have sunk. Not that they won't hang us high enough."

"And on that happy note, I think I'll go off downstairs to my study to see if I've anything important to deal with that's shown up in my absence."

"A letter from your mother, that would be the whole of it," Cluny told him, slowly pushing himself to his feet. "She's well, thanks you for the silk, and sends her sister's never-ending thanks for looking for poor old Richard. We're not finding him, boyo, not if we haven't found him yet. My thought is he's moldering at the bottom of a well, or has long since been fed to the fishies."

"I no longer expect to find him alive, Cluny. But I will discover what happened to him."

"Even though he was a worthless bastard who, just like his father before him, begrudged you and your mother every crust of bread family duty forced him to provide his blood kin? Admit it to me at the least, Jack. You're in this for the adventure of the thing. Those Beckets have thoroughly corrupted you."

Jack paused at the door, his hand on the latch. "They're a remarkable family, Cluny. A real family, not bound by blood but by something even more powerful. I admire them very much."

"And they've made you bloody rich."

Jack grinned as he depressed the latch. "Yes. That, too."

He wandered through the mostly dark house, knowing its furnishings weren't a patch on the grandeur of Becket Hall, but pleased nonetheless.

He'd gone from poor relation to foot soldier, from foot soldier to courier, from courier to spy, from spy to trusted aide.

But when an injury had forced him home and he'd learned about Richard's disappearance, he'd picked up his deck of cards and begun his hunt for his cousin. Which had led to Kent, to Romney Marsh, to whispers about the Red Men Gang and, eventually, to the Beckets of Romney Marsh.

"Only good turn the miserable bastard ever gave me," Jack muttered to himself as he made his way through the black-and-white marble-tiled foyer and to the back of the house, where Richard's father had established a reasonable if incomplete library.

It was only when he reached for the latch that he realized that there was a strip of soft light at the bottom of the door. Transferring his candle to his left hand, he eased his back against the door even as he held the latch, slowly depressed it, and pushed it open, turning with it so he was ready to confront whoever was in the room.

"Miss Becket," he said a moment later, battle-ready alertness replaced by anger.

"What do you think you're doing down here?"

Eleanor looked at him levelly, even as her heart pounded so furiously inside her that the beat was actually painful. She held out the book in her hand. "I couldn't sleep, and decided there must be at least one sufficiently boring book in here that would help me."

He took the marble-backed volume from her hand and read, "*A Complete History So Far As It Is Known of That Celebrated English Thoroughbred* — you're interested in horses?"

Goodness, had she really picked that book? She lifted her chin slightly as she answered him. "No, not at all, which is the point of the exercise, is it not, when one is attempting to find something that is so stultifyingly boring it is virtually guaranteed to put one to sleep? Now, if you'll excuse me?"

Or was the man unaware that she was clothed only in her night rail and dressing gown? And couldn't he do something about that expanse of bare chest visible beneath his dressing gown? All that golden hair. Was it soft to the touch? It had to be, just as his chest was undoubtedly quite hard. Thank the good Lord he still wore his pantaloons, because it would be only the good Lord himself who could know what she'd do if the man had been naked beneath that dressing gown. Fainting seemed probable.

As if he was able to hear her silent conversation with herself — hopefully not all of it — Jack tied his banyan more tightly over himself. "I would certainly excuse you, unless you'd wish to talk for a moment? I think we've settled in fairly well, don't you? You're happy with the servant staff?"

Perhaps she should stay, if just for a few minutes. Not act too eager to be out of his company, as if she'd been caught out at something, being somewhere she should not be, doing something she should not do. She'd simply ignore his chest. After all, she'd seen male chests before. Her brothers' chests, that is. Although Jack's chest seemed . . . different. Definitely more interesting.

Eleanor walked over to seat herself on a brown leather couch that was placed against one wall — she would have preferred it against the other wall, but this wasn't her house, was it? "Mrs. Hendersen seems a competent enough housekeeper, yes. Although I'd rather she didn't address me as *you poor dearie*. I'm not sure if that is a comment on my physical state or my choice of husband. Which do you suppose it is?"

Jack leaned against the front of the desk and smiled at her. "I'll speak to her about that."

"No. Don't be silly, Jack. We'll rub along well enough. And Treacle would appear to understand his part in the running of the household."

"Who?"

Eleanor could see that Jack wasn't exactly an attentive employer. Otherwise, the dust on the tables in her bedchamber would not have been so deep she could draw her finger through it. "Your butler, Jack. Treacle is your butler."

"I'm sorry. Cluny takes care of these things. I really don't pay attention."

"Cluny?" Eleanor frowned, unable to recall the name. "I don't believe I remember a Cluny when the servants were presented upon our arrival."

And she thought: *Cluny. An Irish name. There had been a Cluny Sullivan in Becket Village. Dead now, just an old man worn out.*

Jack hadn't wanted to touch on Cluny's existence until the two of them had got their story straight as to who he was, who he would pretend he was as long as Eleanor was in residence. "He's my . . . my personal secretary. Good man, completely trustworthy." Jack stood up again. "Yes, a good man. Was there anything else you needed?"

Eleanor got to her feet and retrieved her book from the desktop. "Thank you, no. I hadn't needed anything when you came in here, and that hasn't changed." *Stick,* she told herself, trying not to wince. *Can't you say something — anything — that doesn't make you sound like a bloodless old maid?*

"Um . . ." she said, holding the book close to her chest, "Cluny is an Irish name, is it not?"

"If it wasn't before, it is now that Cluny's got it," Jack told her, walking her toward the doorway. "We served together in the Peninsula."

"In the Peninsula," Eleanor repeated, longing to kick herself. He'd probably held more scintillating conversations with doorstops. "How . . . interesting. I hadn't realized you'd served."

"I doubt we know very much at all about each other, Miss Becket."

"Eleanor."

Jack nodded. "Elly. Right. I'll have to practice. You don't seem to have any trouble remembering to call me Jack, do you?

Perhaps you're better at subterfuge than I am."

"I'm sure I wouldn't know," Eleanor said, holding herself so rigid that she was certain that, were she to bend over, she'd snap like a dry twig.

She most certainly wasn't going to tell him that when she dreamed of him, she dreamed of Jack. Never Mr. Eastwood. She might be a dull stick of an old maid, but her dreams at least had some merit.

And now she was standing here in her dressing gown, her hair hanging down her back in a long, thick braid. And the man hadn't so much as blinked. Didn't he care? Was she so unprepossessing a figure that this obvious breach of convention hadn't even occurred to him?

Jack, acting without thought (or else he'd have to think he was insane), reached out his hand and ran a finger down the side of Eleanor's cheek. "You're frightened, aren't you, little one? You put on a fine face of confidence, but you're frightened. You'd be skittish, even trembling, if that wouldn't make you angry with yourself. And, right now, you're caught between wanting to run from me, and longing to slap my face for my impertinence."

Eleanor backed up a single step, holding

the book so tightly now that her knuckles showed white against her skin. "I'm certain I don't know what you mean, Mr. Eastwood."

"Jack." He smiled, beginning to feel more comfortable with the woman. Seeing her as more human. He should have realized that Eleanor, living with the Beckets, couldn't possibly be entirely the paragon of virtue she appeared.

"Yes. Jack. But I'm still sure I don't know what you mean. We know why we're here and what we're doing and . . ."

"Do we? I thought we did," Jack said, placing his hands on her shoulders. "But we're damn unconvincing at the moment if we're supposed to be newly married. Having my bride trying not to flinch, run from me, doesn't seem the way to convince anyone, does it? Unless we want to convince everyone that I'm some sort of brute, and I have to tell you, Elly, I'm vain enough not to wish that."

Enough was enough! "Has it occurred to you, *Jack,* that I am not dressed?"

He looked down at her, from the throat-high neckline of her modest white muslin dressing gown to the tips of her bare toes as they protruded from the hem. Bare toes? The woman was walking about barefoot?

"Well, now that you mention it . . ."

"Oh, you're the most *annoying* man," Eleanor said, stooping down so that she could bow out from beneath his hands. "Now, if you'll excuse me, I'm going to bed."

Jack watched her leave the room, her limp noticeable, as if her left ankle simply didn't bend, yet a graceful woman for all of that. Perhaps she was more comfortable barefoot, without the constriction of hose and shoes.

Elly. He'd have to remember to call her Elly, at least in public. And she would have to become used to being in his company. He'd work on that. Find a way to make her relax some of that reserve that was so at odds with the behavior of the rest of the Beckets.

Odd little thing. Pretty little thing.

Jack stepped behind his desk and sat down, opened the center drawer to take out the journal that among other information included a list of French names, the list of those he had used in the past and would not be able to use again — most definitely the two that had been murdered — and noticed that the wafer-thin silver marker he kept on the most recent page was no longer there.

It wasn't anywhere in the drawer. He pushed back his chair and looked down at the floor, then reached down, picked up the thin, hammered-silver piece and stared at it for long moments.

Had he dropped it over a week ago, before traveling to France? No. His mother had given him the marker, had even had it engraved with his initials, then told him he could use it to "mark the pages of your life, my darling." He was always very careful with the thing.

Cluny? Could Cluny have been snooping about in the desk drawers? There would be no reason for him to do so. Besides, if Cluny had been at the drawers they'd be a bloody mess, not perfect except for the misplaced marker.

"More comfortable barefoot, Miss Becket?" he then asked quietly as he looked up at the ceiling, to the bedchamber he knew to be directly above this room. "Or able to move about more stealthily barefoot?"

In that bedchamber, Eleanor now stood with her back against the closed door, trying to regulate her breathing and heart rate.

He'd nearly caught her. God, he'd nearly caught her.

And for what? She hadn't found much of

anything, hadn't even known what to look for, when she came right down to it.

"I wasn't simply snooping," she told herself as she sat down at her dressing table, to see that her face was very pale and her eyes were very wide. "I was being careful."

But now she realized that the lilt she'd heard in Jack's voice for that one moment had probably come to him courtesy of association with his Irish friend. Nothing nefarious at all. What was the man's name again? Oh yes. Cluny.

Jack was allowed to have friends, of course. Gentlemen have friends. There was nothing strange in that.

But so many lives depended on secrecy, on being careful.

"I will *not* allow my heart to rule my head," Eleanor told her reflection.

That resolution made, Eleanor padded over to one of the windows and pushed back the heavy draperies to look out over the mews, as she believed the area was called, and at the few flambeaux and gas street-lamps she could see in the darkness.

At Becket Hall, there was only night beyond the windows once the sun had gone. Darkness, emptiness. The Marsh on three sides, the shingle beach and Channel on the last. Becket Hall was its own world.

Here, she was a very small part of very large city. One of untold thousands of people, thousands of buildings.

How did people live here? How did they exist? For what purpose had they all felt it necessary to jam themselves together cheek by jowl?

She let the drapery drop back into place and surveyed her chamber. It was a lovely thing, but so was her bedchamber at home. She hadn't traveled to anywhere better; she'd merely come to a different place.

Would she be accepted?

Her sister Morgan had seemed to believe that an introduction to Lady Beresford would open many doors, at least enough doors to help Jack insinuate himself further with Phelps and Eccles . . . and the Earl of Chelfham.

The earl and his young bride. Would the woman know anything, or was she a silly creature whose main concerns were balls and gowns and petty gossip? Would Eleanor like her? If she did, would it pain her conscience to then use the young woman for her own ends? And could she do it in such a way that Jack never suspected what she was doing, then asked why?

And she might not even get out into society at all, or so Jack had hinted. Because

70

he hoped they would be quickly successful, so that he could have her back at Becket Hall as soon as possible? Was he that anxious to get her gone? Did he think her limp would be a detriment if he took her into society? Had he even noticed the limp? Lord knew he'd never noticed anything else about her in two long years. . . .

Eleanor pressed a hand to her forehead, feeling the beginnings of the headache.

Everything had happened so quickly, perhaps too quickly.

And she was alone here. Very much alone here.

She came out of her reverie at the sound of a knock on the door. She looked at that door for a few moments, reminding herself that she couldn't see through the thing, so either she had to open the door or pretend she was already in bed and fast asleep.

Which was ridiculous, for the chamber was lit by at least a half-dozen candles. Unless she wanted the household to believe she'd be reckless enough as to go to sleep with them ablaze, and possibly burn down the house around their ears, she'd have to at least go to the door and ask who was there.

The knock came again, along with Jack's voice calling out her name. Well, now at least she knew who stood on the other side of the thick wood, didn't she?

What on earth did he want? Had he discovered that she'd been snooping in his desk? No. She'd been very careful. She'd looked in all the drawers, then through the papers in the wide center drawer. Then the personal accounts book he'd marked at the page that listed several French names . . .

He'd marked the book. There'd been a thin silver marker. A pretty thing, with his initials pressed into it. She'd lifted it, held it, looked at it — his personal possession. What had she *done* with it?

Eleanor squeezed her eyes shut, trying to remember.

She'd opened the book. Taken out the marker. Looked at it. Laid it in her lap. Looked through the pages.

Heard footsteps.

Replaced the book.

Stood.

She hadn't replaced the marker.

She'd stood, and the small marker must have slipped to the carpet, unnoticed.

Had he noticed?

"Just a moment, please," she called out, bending to the dressing table mirror to assure herself she no longer looked so pale which, unfortunately, she still did. She pinched her cheeks hard enough to bring tears to her eyes, then pulled a face at herself before opening the door.

Just a crack.

"Yes? I was just about to retire."

Jack tipped his head to one side, looking down at the sliver of face that was all Eleanor seemed willing to show him. With any luck, she wasn't holding a pistol behind her back, cocked and ready to blow his head off if she was so inclined and who could know what all the Beckets were inclined to do?

"I hesitate to disturb you, as you were probably already half dozing over that book you chose, but I believe I might have found something that would be of more interest. May I come in?"

Eleanor nervously wet her lips, then nodded, stepped back so that he could push open the door and enter her bedchamber. He now had on a white, open-necked shirt beneath his banyan, and she wondered, just for a moment, if she should be flattered that he'd tried to make himself more decent for her, or lament that she could no longer see his bare chest.

Dear Lord. She'd never expected to see a man in any bedchamber she inhabited, not in her entire lifetime.

Stop it, stop it! Stop thinking like that!

She stopped thinking entirely when Jack held out the "something of more interest," and she saw it to be the journal she'd been reading downstairs. Then he held out his other hand, palm up, and there was the silver marker, the damning marker.

Eleanor lifted her gaze to him. May as well be hanged for a sheep as a lamb, as the ruthlessly practical Jacko always said. "You maintain very orderly records. But I might suggest the benefits of keeping them under lock and key."

She hadn't even blinked. Jack had thought she'd pretend ignorance of what he was showing her, deny what she'd done.

But not little Eleanor Becket. Not the large-eyed fawn with the spine of Toledo steel. He should have known better.

He slipped the marker between the pages and put the journal down on a nearby table. "You're probably right, and your honesty in the face of discovery is commendable," he said carefully. Then he turned to look at her, his eyes narrowed in that way he had, and probably didn't know he had — but that Eleanor found particularly unnerving. "Now, do you want to tell me what in the hell you were looking for?"

Eleanor refused to back down. But she didn't consider herself brave, only practical. After all, she had nowhere to go.

"It is important for us to know who we deal with, especially at the moment. You live very well, Jack."

"Ah, now I understand. You think I've been keeping more of the profits than I report to Ainsley? Is that really why you're here?" Then he shook his head. "No, Ainsley wouldn't do that. If he had any questions about my honesty, he'd have Jacko ask them for him."

"You make Jacko sound like a terrible man. A brute."

One side of Jack's mouth lifted in a rueful smile. "I'm wrong?"

Explaining Jacko wasn't Eleanor's priority. She really wished she knew what was, but she'd examine that later. For now, she knew she couldn't betray any weakness. Papa had told her that years ago: *always deceive with confidence.* "I apologize for looking through your desk."

"And it won't happen again? You won't decide listening at keyholes is a grand idea? You won't sneak a peek at my mail, or send someone to follow me when I'm going about in the city?"

Eleanor didn't know quite where to look,

so she continued to look straight at him. "Now you're being facetious. I apologized."

"But with no promise to mend your ways." Jack stepped closer to her. "Why, Elly, I do think I've just been warned."

"No! That is . . . oh, go away. I did a stupid thing, and I'm sorry."

"Ah, that's better. Except, I think, for the part where you were backing up just now, as if I was going to bite off your head. I've given this some thought. We don't look very married, little one. Not if you're going to flinch every time I'm near you."

"You're in my bedchamber, Jack. What sort of behavior were you expecting of me?"

Well, that stopped him. Her words, and the way she stood there, her spine so straight, looking at him with those huge brown eyes. What *did* he expect from her? What did he expect from himself?

He knew what he *hadn't* expected. He hadn't expected to be interested in this quiet female who apparently had depths he'd never considered. He hadn't expected to be so curious as to what went on behind those wide, seemingly frank, ingenuous brown eyes. He hadn't expected to feel quite so protective of her, or so attracted to her.

And now, once more, and knowing it,

damn her, he was going to rush to fill the silence. And fill it by saying something he'd probably regret. "You're free to look at anything in my desk. Anything. You're free to ask me any questions, and I'll do my best to answer those questions. You're Ainsley's daughter, and I consider you to be his agent here and, in some twisted way, my partner."

Now he fell silent, waiting for her to fill that silence with a similar promise of her own.

He may as well have been waiting for Hades to freeze over.

At last she said thank you, and then inclined her head toward the door, which was as close as a refined young lady probably could get to "Now take yourself off, you bugger!"

"Elly . . ."

"Eleanor," she corrected. She had enough on her plate. She might as well be truthful on this one small thing. "I'd much prefer you to address me as Eleanor, if you don't mind."

That was as good as a slap to the face. She'd said her family called her Elly. He was back to being an outsider. "Certainly . . . Eleanor. I didn't wish to presume a familiarity you might not like."

"No, that isn't what I — that is, we are

77

supposedly husband and wife."

"And newly married, too," Jack said, happy to have the conversation steered back to territory that seemed to discommode her more than it did him. Not that he could recall a time when he'd been nervous around a female.

Until tonight.

"Yes, and newly married, as well. We should discuss that, just so that our stories match. Where we met, for one. I'd prefer you did not mention Becket Hall."

Jack nodded. "That makes sense. If I'm exposed, you can disappear. And with no one knowing about Becket Hall or those who live there. So, wife, where did we meet?"

Eleanor was becoming more uncomfortable by the moment. "I'm merely being careful, Jack. No one has to know that I am a Becket at all, that Morgan is my sister. Ethan was careful to keep any of that out of his letter to Lady Beresford."

"You read it?"

"Certainly. Didn't you? As I said, we need to keep our stories consistent."

Jack was beginning to think he was in the presence of a master. That his days as courier and spy had been relegated to amateurish at best. Why, he should be surprised to still be alive, and not have been long since put up against some French wall and shot.

"Do you have a plan?" he asked when yet another silence yawned between them, a silence he'd have to fill sooner or later anyway.

"I do, yes. Sussex is too close, too easily checked for the truth. Your story for Mr. Phelps, as I remember it, is that you have an estate somewhere in the West Indies and are only visiting here, correct? I should say that we met there, in Jamaica to be more precise, and that I am the child of a moderately wealthy landowner there."

"Splendid. Then you came to me with a considerable dowry? That should please our gentlemen. Yes," Jack said, beginning to pace the carpet. "That would work well. I've run through my fortune, and now I want to purloin my wife's fat dowry and use it to invest in something that will very quickly make me very rich, put my near-bankrupt Jamaican plantation to rights." He turned to smile at Eleanor. "You should write novels."

Eleanor twined her fingers together at her waist. "Yes, thank you. This also negates any necessity for ours to be seen as a love match."

"In other words, I'm to be cast in the role of unmitigated cad. Charming. You know, woman, when you eventually disappear the world will think I've buried you under a rosebush. Or haven't you thought of that? Ah, by the look on your face, I can see you haven't. Then it's settled. Ours is also a love match. We have Ethan's reputation to consider here, too, remember, as he's the one who has ostensibly introduced me to the *ton*."

Eleanor, who now knew the full story of Morgan's titled husband and his unconventional parents, smiled at this. "I don't think Ethan is overly concerned about that, Jack."

Why this one point was becoming so important to him, Jack didn't know, didn't want to know. But, damn it, he couldn't spend the next weeks squiring about a woman who cared less for him than she did the dirt beneath her feet. It was just unnatural, that's what it was.

"I think I must nevertheless insist. I want a love match. The appearance of a love match."

Eleanor knew when a battle wasn't worth the fight. Besides, what difference would it make, as they'd both know they were playacting? "For the sake of your male pride, yes, I understand. My brother Spencer would probably feel much the same way. Even if, as you may recall saying, we never set foot in society at all. Very well. If we are in company, any company at all, I hereby promise to make mooncalf eyes at you at every opportunity."

He longed to shake her, shake away some of that quiet reserve that, he felt increasingly sure, hid a whole other Eleanor Becket. The real Eleanor Becket.

"Sarcasm to one side, I accept," Jack told her. He retrieved his journal, then approached Eleanor once more . . . and she stepped one step backward once more. "And *that* will have to stop. We have to practice." He reached for her hand, lifted it to within inches of his mouth. "No flinching now, Eleanor, I'm not going to bite."

She stood very still as he bent over her hand, pressing his lips to her skin for one brief moment that nearly turned her knees to water. She'd rarely had her hand bent over, let alone kissed, so she didn't know if her reaction to the act was usual. But she didn't think so.

Still bent over her hand, he lifted his head to smile at her. "See? Completely painless. I will do this from time to time, as a man does."

It was time to put a halt to this exercise before the man suggested he kiss her cheek, just to make sure she wouldn't scream in maidenly fright. "Claiming his woman, yes. Every animal marks its territory in one way or another."

He narrowed those intense green eyes as he looked at her as if she'd just spoken to him in some unknown language. "You are a piece of work, Eleanor Becket."

"Eleanor Eastwood," she corrected, wondering when on earth her common sense would wake up from its nap and stop her from saying anything else ridiculous. Now was *not* the time to correct the man. Not when he was standing so close to her. Not when he was still holding her hand.

"Eleanor Eastwood. Alliterative, almost rolls off the tongue. And now, wife, good night."

Before she could pull her hand away he lifted it once more, this time turning her hand so that he could press his lips against her palm. For an instant only, he lightly slid the tip of his tongue against her skin before letting her go.

Because he was not a nice man.

He liked the way her eyes grew wide for a moment before she carefully composed her expression — that mix of strength and vulnerability that had begun to tease at him almost unmercifully. He smiled at the way she drew her hand close against her midriff, her fingers curled around the palm he'd kissed.

It wasn't until he was back in his own bedchamber that he began to wonder what in hell was happening. Not just to the mission they'd undertaken, but to him, personally. That little wisp of a woman, seemingly without humor, without much in the way of emotions, had begun to creep beneath his skin, into his consciousness. And he didn't like that. He didn't like that at all.

"Something stuck in your craw, Jack?" Cluny asked from his seat beside the fire.

Jack turned to look at his friend. "Strange, but I seem to remember this pile being large enough for you to have your own bedchamber."

"And that's true enough," Cluny said, leaning his head back against the soft leather. "So? I heard voices through the connecting door. Couldn't hear what you were saying, much as I tried, no shame to me, but I heard the voices. You two settle anything between you?"

Jack stripped off the shirt he'd donned before confronting Eleanor in her bedchamber and slipped his arms back into the silk banyan. Then he said out loud what he'd suddenly realized. "She's frightened out of her mind, Cluny, and probably second-guessing why she's here at all."

"Ah, there's a pity. So you'll be sending her off home, then?"

Jack sat himself down, picked up the snifter of brandy he'd left warming by the fire. "No. I don't think I could blast her out of here with cannon fire."

"Would that be a fact? Scared, but standing her ground. Well, you know what that is, my friend, don't you? That's courage."

Jack looked toward the door that connected his chamber to Eleanor's. "Is that it? Is that why I'm . . . intrigued by her?"

Cluny laughed into his own snifter, a hollow sound. "Lord love you, no. I seen her from the top of the stairs when Treacle was taking her down the line, introducing the staff just like they do in fine houses, or so I'm told. Face of an angel she's got, and a fine, fine figure for such a small dab. Courage? Who looks to a pretty woman with an eye out to see courage?"

"Or, Cluny, who looks to courage and expects to see a pretty woman," Jack murmured quietly. "We'd better get this right, old friend, or Miss Becket in there will be very disappointed."

Then he sat and looked at the door for a long time, picturing Eleanor untying the bows on her dressing gown, climbing into the turned-down four-poster bed, looking small and vulnerable as she lay half-swallowed by the pillows and coverlet.

She barely came up to the top of his chest. He was a tall man, he knew that, taller than most men, but even taking that into consideration, Eleanor Becket was a small woman. He was certain he could easily span her waist with his hands, yet there was no denying her womanly shape. A small bit of perfection he'd actually not noticed during his visits to Becket Hall.

Now she filled his head, and he couldn't seem to get her out again, even knowing he had to concentrate on his plans for bringing down these three men and, more importantly, through them, finding the leader of the Red Men Gang.

Oh, yes, and then there was Richard.

He had to avenge what he was sure was the murder of his cousin. Why did he have to keep reminding himself of that part?

"Cluny?" he asked as the fire burned lower in the grate. "Do you think he was in on it, had been a part of the Red Men?"

Cluny didn't pretend not to know who Jack was talking about. "He was a weasel,

I'll give him that. Could be. Could be. And wouldn't that be a fine kettle of fish, eh? The pair of us sticking our necks into a noose to get some of our own back for a weasel. Besides, we're beyond that now. Your cousin is only a part of this. The rest is us and for us. Wrap your head about that one, boyo. Why, we should be putting down our pennies for Masses for that cousin of yours, he did us such a good turn. We're bad, bad men living a good, good life."

"I don't think Eleanor sees the thing that way, Cluny," Jack said, then drained the remainder of his brandy. "I think she sees us as helping the people of Romney Marsh."

"Ah, then it's going to Heaven I'll be, once they're done gutting me and hanging me in chains? A good thing to know."

Jack grinned. "Isn't it, though?"

CHAPTER FOUR

After two days of travel, but mostly after two nearly full days spent in close approximation with Jack Eastwood, Eleanor had welcomed the rain that had fallen incessantly for the past three days. Ladies, she'd read, do not move about out of doors during inclement weather, and so she'd told him. She did not add that she needed time to recover her mental equilibrium before heading into Society on his arm.

He'd already presented himself to Lady Beresford alone, before Eleanor had even risen from an exhausted sleep that had held her until nearly noon, and she was more than happy to have missed the interview.

She actually had seen very little of Jack, who had once more taken up with Harris Phelps and Sir Gilbert Eccles, making the rounds of several gaming halls each evening, well into the morning, actually, and then sleeping away half the day.

As for Cluny? After a cursory introduction the man had taken to his rooms as if he was ailing, not even appearing at meals. When she'd asked Jack if the man truly was ill he'd explained that Cluny came and went by the servant staircase, and was actually out and about more than she knew.

Jack had also told her he had yet to encounter the Earl of Chelfham, but that this was nothing to worry about, as the earl preferred to do his gaming in the card rooms of his *ton* hostesses, or within the exclusive walls of White's or Watier's. "But," he'd told her, "once the earl learns of the small fortune to be made playing at cards with the inept Jack Eastwood? Then he'll show his face, or we'll be invited to meet him. I only hope his greed doesn't take too long to goad him into action. I'm more than ready to begin winning again, which I plan to do the moment Chelfham joins us at the table."

After that first late morning she still couldn't muster up any shame for indulging in, Eleanor was up near enough to the crack of dawn the next two days to have seriously discommoded Mrs. Hendersen and her maids. Most especially when she'd walked into the kitchens this morning after waiting an hour for her morning chocolate the day before, sat herself down at the newly scrubbed wooden table, and politely asked if she might have a coddled egg and a dish of tea, thank you.

Mrs. Hendersen had explained, gamely attempting to be civil, that the lady of the household should ring for a servant.

Eleanor had then pointed out the illogic of such a plan. "A servant whom, I've now learned, would hear the summons, run up two flights of stairs to hear that I would enjoy a coddled egg and dish of tea. She would then run back down those stairs to have someone procure both, labor back up those stairs, undoubtedly carrying a heavy silver tray, run back to her post, run back when I rang to have the tray taken away."

"Yes, ma'am, but that's the way it is," Mrs. Hendersen had interrupted, which did her no good at all, because Eleanor hadn't quite finished. And, as her siblings could have told the housekeeper, when Eleanor had something to say she could be like water on a rock, calmly coursing along until she'd worn that rock into a pebble, just from steady, low-keyed persistence.

As at that particular moment. "Oh, and then return the tray here, to the kitchens. In other words, Mrs. Hendersen, the simple matter of dealing with my coddled egg and dish of tea would necessitate a half-dozen trips either to or from my bedchamber. Much, much more sensible to move *me,* at least for today."

"But . . . but . . ." Mrs. Hendersen had said, still unaware she might be seeing a slim, petite young woman with an unfortunate limp (the "poor little dearie"), but that she was in reality listening to a quiet verbal assault that would have had Napoleon cowering in a corner and whimpering, "*Assez! Plus qu'il n'en faut!* Enough! More than enough!"

"Beginning tomorrow morning, I shall be taking my breakfast at eight each morning in that lovely small salon next to Mr. Eastwood's study," Eleanor had told the woman — much to the delight of a red-haired freckled young girl Eleanor now knew to be Beatrice, who had been assigned to serve the new mistress.

"That'd be the breakfast room, ma'am," Mrs. Hendersen had told her, her face rather splotched in unbecoming puce as she fought to keep her tone deferential.

"And called so for a good reason, wouldn't you say, Mrs. Hendersen?" Eleanor had responded with one of her gentle smiles, believing that matter settled, and then had immediately moved on to the next subject on her mind.

As Mrs. Hendersen sputtered, Eleanor had then called all the servants together and explained life as it would be under her direction. Life as it was at Becket Hall, where everyone helped with any bit of work that might present itself, and nobody was asked to do what a person could reasonably do for him or herself.

Which, as Eleanor realized almost from the moment Jack came storming into her bedchamber shortly before the dinner gong was to sound that evening, had been a horrible mistake.

She'd been sitting at her dressing table, extremely content as a clearly adoring Beatrice pulled a pair of silver-backed brushes through her hair — the girl had *insisted* — when she'd heard the slam of the connecting door and her "husband's" near bellow.

"What in bloody hell have you been about, woman?"

Beatrice gave out a small yelp and ran from the room, taking the brushes with her, so that Eleanor could only sigh, then lift her hair with her hands and let it all fall down her back, nearly to her waist.

Which seemed to stop Jack, who had been

advancing on her with a fury she hadn't seen in several years, in fact, not since Courtland had discovered Cassandra hiding in the drawing room after filling his riding boots with mud because he'd refused to take her out riding with him.

"How in blazes do you hold all that mess of hair up on that fragile neck of yours? No, don't answer me. That's not my question." Jack kept his gaze on Eleanor, however, as he pointed in the general direction Beatrice had taken moments earlier. "Do you have any idea of the anarchy you have unleashed out there?"

Eleanor searched in one of the drawers of her dressing table, unearthing a deep blue grosgrain ribbon that matched her gown, then tied it around her hair at her nape. "I beg your pardon?"

"It's not my pardon you'll be begging, *wife*. Mrs . . . Mrs . . . whoever she is, is downstairs in the kitchens, crying into the cook's apron." He raised his eyebrows as he glared at her. "And do you want to know *why* she's crying in the cook's apron?"

"Mrs. Hendersen."

Jack was losing control, and he knew it. "What?"

"Your housekeeper. Her name is Mrs.

Hendersen. And, no, Jack, I don't know why she's crying into Mrs. Ryan's apron. Is she ill?"

Jack jammed his fingers through his hair. "She didn't look all that good when I saw her but, no, she's not sick. She's at the end of her rope — and that's out of her mouth, not mine. Did you really tell the servants they only had to do what they wanted to do?"

Eleanor sat down, frowned at him. "No, that's not quite it. At Becket Hall we all help each other. But there are duties, everyone has the duty to help. At Becket Hall they're . . . well, I suppose you could call them the crew. Yes, that's it. There are general assignments, even preferences, but everyone lends a hand where it's needed. It's all rather — what's the word? Oh, yes. Democratic."

"Is that right? Well, don't look now, madam, but *our* crew has instituted a mutiny."

"Now you're exaggerating. It will take a little time for everyone to understand that they're being asked to responsively think for themselves, employ initiative, but —"

Jack let out a short laugh. "Oh, they're already thinking for themselves, Eleanor. According to Mrs . . . damn!"

"Mrs. Hendersen."

Jack glared at her. "According to the housekeeper," he pushed on doggedly, "two of the footmen have thought for themselves that they should be taking in the sights at Bartholomew Fair today, while the cook — ha! Mrs. Ryan — has thought for herself that something called bubble and squeak would make for a fine dinner for the master of the house. Who would be *me,* Eleanor, who doesn't have the faintest damn idea what bubble and squeak is, but I'm damn sure I don't want it served up in my dining room. And then there's that maid of yours —"

"Beatrice? She's been here with me for most of the afternoon, cleaning this chamber and yours, both of which more than needed a good polish."

"Well, good for Beatrice," Jack snarled, dropping into a chair. "That also explains why there's some pathetic little thing sitting beside *Mrs. Hendersen* and also crying up a storm because now she has no dusting to do and she'll soon be on the streets on her back and men with no teeth will be taking their pleasure on her. And that's another direct quote."

Eleanor put a hand to her chin, looked around as if there might be something to see. "Oh. Dear. They don't quite under-stand, do they?"

Jack stood up again. He couldn't seem to stay still for more than a moment. Probably because he wanted to *strangle* this strange, irritating woman. "Yes, I think you could safely say that. I think you could also safely say that you're in no danger of my house-keeper addressing you as *you poor dearie* ever again. Now, what do we do? Correc-tion, what do *you* do, because this is your mess, Eleanor, and it needs cleaning up before Eccles and Phelps come to dinner tomorrow night."

Eleanor, who had been mentally review-ing Thomas Paine's *Rights of Man* in her head as she wondered what she'd done wrong, was suddenly all attention. "You've invited them *here?* But why?"

"I don't know, Eleanor. Perhaps I've become disenchanted with spending my nights attempting to find new ways to lose my money to a fool as thick as Phelps when others are watching and wanting into the game. You'd be amazed at how popular a bad card player with plenty of money to lose can be in London society. Besides, I told them to bring anyone else they wished to bring with them, as my cook is one of the best in Mayfair and my new bride is a real beauty who hasn't recovered enough from our wedding trip to go into Society yet."

Eleanor could feel a flush of color reddening her cheeks. "You make that sound as if — well, never mind."

Jack found himself feeling embarrassed, as well, which was a very uncommon feeling for him, so that he immediately resented it. He began pacing the carpet, still longing to hit something and hoping to dissipate some of his angry energy. "Be that as it may, my new friends, and whoever they bring with them — please God let it be Chelfham — aren't the sort who expect to dine on *bubble and squeak*."

"Yes, whatever that is," Eleanor said, also beginning to pace, only stopping when she realized what a ridiculous pair they must look, each of them marching up and down the carpet in different directions.

Jack paused in front of her on his trip up the carpet, and just looked at her.

As she looked at him.

And then, much to the surprise and amazement of both of them, they began to smile. Their smiles turned to laughter, and Eleanor actually reached out to lay a hand on his arm, to help support herself as her mirth threatened to overcome her.

"I really have to do something, don't I?" she asked at last, looking up at Jack . . . who was looking at her rather strangely. "Um . . . about the servants."

"You have a pretty laugh," Jack heard himself say, wondering where the words had come from. "And your eyes . . . they light up when you smile. I've stayed at Becket Hall several times. Why did I never notice you?"

Eleanor nervously wet her suddenly compressed lips with the tip of her tongue. "I'm sure I have no idea. I . . . I really should go downstairs and . . . and apologize to Mrs . . . um, that is, to Mrs . . ."

"Hendersen," Jack told her, his smile slow as he placed his hands on Eleanor's shoulders. "Fine name, Hendersen."

"Oh yes," Eleanor said, rushing into speech. "A fine name. Um . . . do you think you could let me go now?"

Jack considered this for the length of a second, if that. "No, I don't think so. I'm rather enjoying myself at the moment. Are you aware that there are small golden flecks in those huge brown eyes of yours?" He tipped his head to one side, leaned down lower. Closer. "Yes, I can see them. I can also see myself reflected in your eyes. Your most amazing eyes."

Eleanor would have blinked, but she seemed to have forgotten how to do that, and her body wasn't responding to any commands save the ratcheting up of her heartbeat and breathing. "Are you going to kiss me now, Jack?" she asked him because, obviously, all her usual good common sense had taken French leave so that all she was left with was a curiosity that she was powerless to deny.

Jack smiled. "Would you like that, Eleanor? Would you like me to kiss you?"

"As purely an experiment, you mean?" *Would she just shut up and say* yes? *What was* wrong *with her? The man wanted to kiss her, for goodness sakes.*

"An experiment in precisely what, Eleanor?"

"I . . . well, I was thinking about what you said that first night we were standing here. Precisely here, as a matter of fact, although why you are always in my bedchamber rather than calling me down to the drawing room I've yet to fully fathom. You said that you couldn't have me flinching, drawing back, when you showed the most mundane of husbandly attentions. I've begun to realize that you may be right, especially as we'll have guests right here, at your own — our own — dinner table."

As she spoke, Jack watched that expressive little face. "You know what it is? You've never been kissed, have you, Eleanor Becket? One and twenty and living isolated at Becket Hall — you've never been kissed."

"I don't see where that has to enter into the — please let me go."

Jack lifted his hands, that had been only lightly resting on her shoulders. "I haven't actually been holding you, Eleanor."

"Oh."

"But I could be," he suggested, replacing his hands, this time curling his fingers around her upper arms. "It's not often a man has the opportunity to taste a woman's first kiss. I'd be honored. As an experiment."

"Now you're making fun of me." Eleanor was mortified. But she wasn't moving. She'd noticed that, that she wasn't moving away from him.

Jack was suddenly ashamed of himself. She was probably right. At least partially right. He slid his hands down her arms and took hold of her left hand, leading her over to the chairs flanking the fireplace. "We should talk."

Eleanor was more than happy to sit down, as her knees were shaking. She watched as Jack took up the facing chair on the other side of a low table, lounging in the chair with an ease she couldn't muster for herself as she sat perched on the edge of her own seat. She must look like a hopeful applicant wishing for employment; back ramrod straight, feet close together, hands folded in her lap. And, if not the applicant, then the prissy old maid about to ask to see any letters of recommendation.

But if she sat back in the large chair her feet would no longer touch the floor, and that would be just too embarrassing. Did people really think she *liked* sitting in the small, straight-backed chairs she always gravitated to, for pity's sake? Tall people, and everyone in her world seemed to be tall, didn't have to consider such things the way people who barely topped five feet in height did.

She remained silent as Jack sort of slouched sideways in his seat, his elbow on one arm of the chair, his chin in his hand. *Looking* at her.

She waited for him to speak, fill the silence.

And waited.

Inside Jack's head, he was counting: . . . *twelve . . . thirteen . . . fourteen . . . I'm not going to do it . . . fifteen . . . sixteen . . . come on, sweetheart, your turn . . . seventeen . . .*

"You . . . um, you mentioned that you have visited Becket Hall a few times. After your first stay while you were recovering from . . . well, you know that part. But I doubt you paid much attention to the general running of the household. After all, men don't, do they? So perhaps I should explain more about how we . . . how we go on." She stopped, sighed as she realized what had just happened, how he had tricked her into filling the silence. "You really are the most annoying man."

"Yes, so I've heard. But you're both right and wrong, Eleanor. I have been to Becket Hall, and I'm not so dense or unobservant that I haven't noticed that it's a rather unique establishment. That you're a rather unique family."

"I find us to be quite natural, but that's probably because I really can't remember anything else."

"I thought you said you'd arrived at Becket Hall at the age of six. That's when Ainsley . . . found you?" Jack didn't know if there was another term for what Ainsley had done. Found? Adopted? Accumulated? A man with eight children, seven of them not of his own blood, could be said to have accumulated them, couldn't he?

101

Eleanor was silent for a moment. "I said that? Yes, I suppose I did, in passing. You have a very good memory, Jack."

"And more questions than I'd imagined," he answered truthfully. "Beginning, I suppose with one — how much are you willing to tell me?"

Eleanor looked at him from beneath her lashes. "There really isn't much to tell. Papa and the rest, including the crews of both his ships, decided to move themselves to England after Cassandra's mother died. Papa had no heart to remain on the island home he'd made for everyone, you understand, and it seemed that most everyone felt as he did, that it was time to come home."

"Home? I've met many of the people who live in Becket Village and work at Becket Hall, Eleanor. Not half of them are English."

Eleanor lifted her chin slightly, proud of Ainsley Becket. "Anywhere my father is becomes home to those loyal to him."

"I stand corrected. If everyone else at Becket Hall is as loyal as you, Eleanor, I imagine they'd follow Ainsley into hell if that's where he was headed."

No, they'd all already been there, their hell had been where they'd died on that island, then come to England with the hope of living again, Eleanor thought, lowering her gaze.

"I believe I told you that I never saw the island. I remember none of it, but I've been told there was a storm at sea as they were making their way here to England, and the ship I was traveling on capsized. Fortunately, that ship was within sight of Papa's ships. Jacko himself saved me. Jacko, and then Chance."

Jack frowned. "And that's it? That's what happened? Your ship went down but you were saved? Only you?"

"Only me," Eleanor said, keeping her gaze steady on Jack as he believed her lies . . . most particularly the lie of timing. "Eleanor is the name Papa chose for me, as I was ill for a long time and, as I said, remember nothing, not even my given name. In truth, I don't even know how old I am. Odette decided I was six."

She was lying to him. Lying through those straight white teeth. Jack knew it. The gaps in her story were huge, as if an elephant had just been tossed into the middle of the room. But Jack knew if he pressed for details, made mention of that great, hulking elephant, if he pushed Eleanor, he'd lose any trust he may have gained.

Still, he felt he'd be expected to ask some questions. "Was it an English ship? Do you at least believe you're English?"

"Yes, I'm English."

Jack was learning more about Eleanor. For one thing, he was learning that she answered parts of questions, not the whole of them. She was English, that she acknowledged. She did not say that the ship she'd been sailing on had been an English ship.

"Did Ainsley ever try to find your family here?"

Eleanor looked at him, head-on as it were, when she answered. "There were attempts, yes. But time passed, and I was content. I had a new family, and since I didn't remember anything of my life before the shipwreck I didn't wish to leave that family. And . . . and I'm very content at Becket Hall."

Jack looked at her closely. *More lies. But what sort of lies? And for what reason?* "So content, in fact, that you volunteered to come to London."

"I haven't abandoned Becket Hall, Jack."

"True enough," he said, rubbing at his chin. "But don't tell me you're not . . . curious."

"Curious?" Eleanor folded her fingers together more tightly in her lap. "About what?"

Jack shrugged. "I don't know. About the

rest of the world, what lies beyond Becket Hall and Romney Marsh? About your . . . your *other* family, be they dead or alive? I know I'd be curious."

Eleanor wanted to tell him, tell him everything. Not even her younger brothers and sisters knew the whole of it, but only pieces. Papa knew most of it, of course, but not all. Chance knew quite a bit, because he'd been there with Jacko, had snatched her up when . . . when it was over. But that was all. She'd never felt an overwhelming urge to confide in anyone else. For Jacko's sake, she supposed, since Papa cared for him.

Everyone at Becket Hall seemed satisfied that Eleanor was content.

But Jack seemed to know that no matter how happy she was at Becket Hall, there was always that not knowing . . . that question: who was she? Really? He couldn't, of course, know the rest. Nobody could. Nobody could even imagine the rest of it in their worst nightmares.

"No, Jack," she said now, getting to her feet, "I'm not curious. I'm anxious that we proceed as we are, and hopeful you're right, that these are the men and that we can put a stop to their ambitions. That is why I've come to London with you."

Jack unbent himself and stood up, as well, watching as she distanced herself from him. "Put a stop to their ambitions," he said to the back of her head, to that bewitching fall of dark hair. "What a lovely way of saying that we wish these three guilty and dead, probably by my hand, now that I really think about the thing."

Eleanor turned to look at him in surprise. "Kill them? You're not serious."

Jack chuckled low in his throat as he shook his head. "What do you suggest, Eleanor? That we politely ask them to stop trying to destroy us?"

"Don't be facetious," Eleanor said, almost without thinking the words, and then began to pace, her slight limp not detracting one whit from the enjoyment Jack felt, watching her.

He folded his arms and leaned against the side of the high, wingback chair he'd just vacated. "Ainsley knows, Eleanor. We all do. Ferret out whoever is causing us trouble and eliminate them. You were listening at the keyhole, weren't you? You heard Ainsley say the word? *Eliminate*."

Eleanor stopped pacing. "Yes, but I thought that meant that . . ." She hesitated, her breath releasing in a quick, hard sigh. "Is there no other way? What if . . . what if you found ways to ruin them? Socially? Financially?"

"Make them so unappealing even the leaders of the Red Men Gang will turn their backs on them? Is that what you mean?"

Eleanor frowned. "No, that wouldn't work, would it? Once they're of no further use to the Red Men, the Red Men have no reason to let them live, and perhaps talk, say the wrong thing to the wrong person." Then she looked at Jack. "But then *you* wouldn't have eliminated them, would you?"

Ah, now he saw her problem. She didn't seem to want blood on his hands. Or hers, for that matter. "I see. You want me to destroy them — socially or financially — but let the Red Men actually eliminate them."

"Yes. *No.*" Eleanor sat down on the low chair in front of her dressing table. "Perhaps I'm not as prepared for this . . . mission, as I thought I was. Does Sir Gilbert have a wife, children? You said the earl and Mr. Phelps are both married. God, Jack. I'm to be with these women, *cultivate* them, knowing we could be planning the deaths of their husbands?"

"I don't know about Gilly. Married? I

don't think so. Phelps? Just his wife, I believe." Jack stopped, realized what was happening. "Damn it, woman, I can't be concerned about any of that, and neither can you. A soldier going into battle goes in already a dead man if his mind is full of worries about the enemy's wives and children."

"I know," Eleanor said as she nervously fussed with the handle of a hand mirror on the dressing table. "And I know our first concern is the families we help, and everyone at Becket Hall. I was . . . I was reacting, not thinking clearly."

And if I kill any of these three men, you'll carry the guilt for the rest of your life, won't you, little fawn, Jack thought, looking at her as she bent her head, avoiding his gaze.

He reached down, putting his hand over hers for a moment, stilling her fingers as they pushed at the mirror handle, then went down on one knee beside her, inches from her face. "Eleanor. I'll try, all right? Maybe there's a way to stop them without eliminating them completely, or at least managing things so that the Red Men Gang does our job for us. But I can't promise anything. You understand that, don't you?"

He looked so earnest. He was so close to her.

"I should go home, shouldn't I? I thought I could help, but now I'm being missish, and shortsighted, and definitely not rational. This isn't a game where we can best them, defeat them, then everyone shakes hands and goes on their way, is it? This is life and death. I *know* that. I've always known that. I . . . I just never wanted to really *believe* that."

Jack watched, fascinated, as tears welled in Eleanor's velvety brown eyes, even as she kept her chin high, refusing to give way to her emotions. "Please stay, Eleanor."

"But I've been nothing but trouble to you. I've made a shambles of your household, and now I'm interfering with your plans rather than helping you with them." She smiled wanly. "You know, Jack, I once prided myself on how well controlled I am, how in charge I am of my emotions and most any situation. I've been deluding my-self."

"No," Jack said, amazed that he meant every word he was about to say. "Ainsley wouldn't have allowed you to come here if he didn't trust you completely, trust your judgment. You're a civilizing influence, Eleanor, whether you know it or not. We

109

men tend to think in terms that are rather absolute. Kill or be killed, for one. There may be another way."

Eleanor lifted a hand and cupped his cheek, reacting again, not thinking. "No. There is no other way, and we both know it. Either these men lead us to the head of the Red Men Gang or their own leaders will destroy them for allowing us to even get close. Either way, assuming we succeed, these three men are already as good as dead. When I meet them, I will be speaking to dead men and widows." She dropped her hand to her lap once more. "Rationally, I understand that."

Jack put his hand on her cheek, returning intimate gesture for intimate gesture. A sort of bonding, merely physical, that would mean an agreement to so much more than that. "And you'll be able to live with those consequences?"

"We all live with the consequences of our decisions. Papa has schooled us all to know that. Yes, I can live with the consequences."

Eleanor slowly blinked, and one huge tear escaped, to run down her cheek. Jack wiped at it, gently rubbing his thumb over her soft skin.

He'd never understood war as it had been described to him by fellow soldiers trying to fill the night before a battle with thoughts of home, of wives and sweethearts. How they swore they were there, to kill or be killed, in order to protect those they'd left behind. He didn't understand any of that now. You killed to protect yourself. Yourself and the person next to you, who hopefully felt the same way.

Now he was all but promising to *not* kill in order to protect this woman? This made no sense to him. Violence he understood. Swift, decisive action. And yes, you lived with the consequences. Gentleness, however, and mercy, had never been any part of his equations.

"I'll do what I can, Eleanor. We'll put our heads together, think of something. We'll at least try."

"Thank you." Eleanor pressed her head against his hand, caught between gratitude that he understood and some shame at her female reaction to a male game she'd thought she was equipped to play. Her sister Morgan could have played the game without a thought, without a blink, without a moment of remorse as she did what she believed to be right. But she was not Morgan, even if in her dreams she'd occasionally believed she could be.

Jack leaned in toward Eleanor, and surprised himself by putting his lips to her cheek. "No, Eleanor. Thank you," he whispered, then got to his feet and left the room, wondering how one goes about becoming a better man. . . .

CHAPTER FIVE

"*Handle* them? Are you daft, man?"

Jack handed Cluny a half-filled wineglass, then sat down behind the desk in his study. He'd avoided his friend all day, but at last he'd told him about the previous night's promise to Eleanor. "I didn't know what else to say, frankly. She was looking down at her hands, folded in her lap, as if they already had blood on them."

"Ah, now I understand. 'Out, damn spot! Out, I say!' "

"You're not amusing, Cluny," Jack told him, then drank deeply from his own glass.

"Just remember, boyo, that Shakespeare bloke you're so fond of was penning himself a bloomin' tragedy with that *Macbeth* of his. This is *war,* boyo. You remember war, don't you? We skewer them before they can skewer us?"

"I think she's resigned to that, Cluny. She simply doesn't want *me* to be the one doing the killing."

Cluny spread his arms, some of his wine splashing over the rim and onto his fat fingers, which he then licked, for the Irishman made it a point to never waste a drop of spirits. "What's the difference? Either we go through them to get to the Red Men — that makes them dead, boyo, when we go through them — or we get the names we want and then let them go. In which case, unless we act quickly enough, the Red Men do the killing for us. Blood on our hands either way, boyo, because it's not as if we can just turn them over to be tried and hanged, not without exposing ourselves. Has your little lady figured that out yet? Those men were dead the moment you first looked at them. They just don't know it yet."

"She's not my little lady."

"I say all of what I'm saying and that's your only answer? She's not your little lady? Better your little lady than your little tyrant, boyo. She looks like butter won't melt in her mouth, but she certainly knows how to get her way. What did she do, boyo, weep all over your shoulder?"

Jack shifted uncomfortably in his chair. "No, Cluny, she didn't. I don't think she's seen life before, ridiculous as that sounds."

"Oh? So what's she been doing at this

Becket Hall you wax so poetic about all the time? They had her wrapped up in cotton wool?"

"In a way, yes," Jack said, considering the thing. "Everyone else at Becket Hall is . . . very alive, almost boisterous. And, looking back on it all, I think they all go out of their way to protect Eleanor, try not to ever upset her. I don't know. Maybe it has something to do with the limp."

"If what she did to this household is any indication, boyo, turning everything upside down, I'd think they all need protection from *her.* There's a will there, a strong will. And some very strange ideas."

"I know. I think she reads. Quite a lot. Something filled her full of ideals and high-flown notions, that's for sure. I mean, she's living with a gaggle of smugglers, yet she's the lady, always the lady." He drained his glass. "A lady who longs to be adventurous."

"Until the itch turned to the scratch, you mean," Cluny pointed out, as only Cluny could. "Send her packing, boyo. It's the only answer."

"I can't do that. She even suggested I send her home, but I can't."

"*Won't,* you mean. It's not romance you're thinking about here, is it, boyo?"

Jack was genuinely shocked by the question. "Romance? *No*. God, man, I've no time for romance. Besides, this is Ainsley Becket's little chick. I like my guts where they are — inside, so I don't have to look at them while Ainsley's man Jacko ties them around my neck in a bow. One thing I know for sure, Cluny, Jacko is not the boasting sort. He says something, he means what he says, and then he does it."

Cluny shrugged. "Don't say I didn't try bringing you back around to sanity, boyo. So. You have a plan?"

Jack shook his head. "Not yet, although I'm definitely leaning toward putting a pistol to Chelfham's head and just demanding names from him. Do you think that would work?"

"It could. Simple. Direct. Of course, if he won't tell you then you'd have to shoot him, just to show him you meant your threat, and where would that put us? You've already told me you don't think the other two are worth more than warm spit when it comes to knowing much."

Jack was listening to his friend with only half an ear, as something else had occurred to him. "Chelfham," he said quietly. "Eleanor seems to worry about all three men, but there's something . . . something *more* in those eyes of hers when she makes mention of the earl. Something in her voice. Damn, Cluny, do you think Becket's been holding something back from me?"

Cluny sat forward, interested. "Such as?"

"I'm not sure. Something on the order of perhaps having already heard Chelfham's name. He did agree rather quickly to my plan, now that I think about it. Even about sending Eleanor here with me when she offered to come — when she quietly demanded she come, now that I consider the exchange between them. Ainsley Becket is a very smart man who plays his cards damn close to his chest. Cluny? Do you think he already suspected Chelfham?"

"I've never met the man, Jack, remember? What do you think?"

Jack laughed shortly, ruefully. "I'll be damned if I know *what* I think anymore. He could be using me. I'd even accept that. But why toss his daughter into the mix? That's what makes no sense. Cluny, I need you at my back."

"Never been anywheres else these past seven years, boyo."

"No, Cluny, I mean literally. I want to know if I'm being followed."

"Becket?"

"Becket, yes. Remember, I work for him, but that doesn't mean he's *accumulated* me as he did his so-called children. I don't know who trusts whom here, or if anyone trusts anyone else. Not even Eleanor. I think she's sincere, but how can I be sure?"

Cluny was quiet for some moments, then said: "Bed her."

"What?"

"Now, now, boyo, don't be climbing over that desk to clamp your hands around my neck. Think on it, that's all I'm saying. Pillow secrets, that's what I'm talking about. Women have been doing it since the dawn of time, since Adam and Eve, I suppose. Only you make sure it's *her* does the talking, whispering the secrets. Little thing like that, living in books, living in the back of beyond? And a cripple, too, into the bargain? Couldn't ask for easier pickings. She'll fall into your arms like a ripe plum. Sweep her off her feet, boyo, give her the fairy tale she's been dreaming about, and you'll soon know everything she knows, maybe even more than she thinks she knows."

Jack rubbed the wineglass between his hands. "And then what, Cluny? What do I do with her then?"

Cluny laughed, his large stomach moving up and down. "Well, hell's bells, boyo, how should I know?"

Jack got to his feet and came out from behind the desk. "I don't know why I even listen to you, considering that the last time I did we were in Badajoz and I ended up explaining to the major about how three local chickens had unexpectedly impaled themselves on a stick over our campfire."

"And hanged right then you'd have been for stealing, if I wasn't smart enough to offer the man one fat hen for himself," Cluny said with a smile and a wink. "I never did figure out how you got jumped up to lieutenant while I stayed just a lowly foot soldier, when it's obvious I'm smarter than you by half."

Smiling at the memory, Jack held out a hand to his friend, to help him to his feet. "It's almost seven. Come on, Cluny, I've had an extra place set for you. Phelps's note this afternoon said he and Eccles will be bringing three guests with them. I'm hoping that means Phelps's wife and sister, and Chelfham himself. I'd value your impressions of them all."

"Don't need to see them to do that," Cluny said, allowing Jack to help him out of the deep leather couch. "Two fools and their

119

keeper. You already know who to watch. You just don't know who's watching you."

Jack had nothing to say to that, so he simply left his study, stopping in the hallway to check his reflection in the glass and be momentarily pleased with the jacket he'd had tailored for himself at Weston's. Just like a real gentleman, which he supposedly was, from birth, if not from inclination, experience and, for a long time, the size of his pocketbook.

He passed a pair of maids in the hallway, both of them moving quickly with their heads down as they walked toward the dining room. He smiled, knowing his Portland Square mansion had been a veritable hive of industry all day, and every surface sparkled and shone as it had never done before in his memory. Eleanor had said something right to the staff. But, as he was beginning to understand, it was very difficult to say *no* to Eleanor Becket. Small, quiet, *determined* Eleanor Becket.

And there she was, already in the Drawing Room, sitting on a backless carved wooden chair he last remembered seeing in the Breakfast Room. "Good evening, wife," he said as he strolled across the room, then bowed over her hand.

Eleanor waited for him to turn her hand,

tease at her palm with his tongue, but his lips had barely skimmed the back of her hand before he released her. "It's nearly seven," she said as he crossed to the drinks table, holding up a decanter of wine. "Thank you, no. I'm too nervous, and need to keep my wits about me."

Jack poured some of the wine in a glass and took it to her. "All the more reason for this," he told her. "You look delightful, by the way. Red very much becomes you."

"Thank you," Eleanor said, accepting the glass as well as the compliment. Then she smiled, and there was new life sparkling in her eyes. "I thought it would be interesting to match Mr. Phelps's waistcoat."

Jack laughed, inwardly amazed. "That's the spirit. As long as we're here, in the middle of this, we may as well enjoy ourselves. As Cluny would say, good on you, Eleanor."

"Then I thank both you and Cluny." Eleanor could feel heat and color rising into her cheeks. She'd had a long, stern talk with herself, reminded herself of both her stated mission and her private hopes, and had decided that displays of maidenly missishness were a thing of the past. Weakness was dangerous, as was too much thinking. Thinking about how handsome Jack looked in his evening clothes was most dangerous of all.

Jack looked about the room, at the sparkling mirrors and gleaming silver. "I'm not in residence often, Eleanor. I hadn't realized how lax the staff had become. If our meal is half as fine we should impress our guests all hollow."

"I just spoke with Mrs. Hendersen and Mrs. Ryan in the kitchens and, although they were not precisely delighted with my appearance there, I'm happy to say that everything is running along quite smoothly. We can only hope our guests are on time, as Mrs. Ryan very much dislikes allowing her poached salmon to sit."

"It usually stands?" Jack asked, hoping to put a smile on Eleanor's face, that was looking rather pale and pinched once more. "Relax, Eleanor. You'll be a marvelous hostess here, just as you are at Becket Hall. Do you suppose that place will fall into rack and ruin without you there to make friendly, unannounced visits to the kitchens?"

"You give me too much credit." Eleanor's features relaxed in a small smile. "But, again, thank you. I'm so nervous."

Jack pulled over a chair and sat down beside her. "Yes, I'd noticed that." He took her hand in his, lightly squeezed her cold fingers. "Believe me, none of them is worth your worry. They'll arrive, we'll talk inanely about nothing as I pour drinks for everyone. We'll be called to dinner by Treacle — see, I've remembered his name, at least. And if Mrs. Ryan — another remembered name for which I congratulate myself even if you don't — if Mrs. Ryan happens to have served up green peas we'll get to see Eccles try to balance a half dozen at a time on his knife while Phelps asks us all to lay odds he won't be able to slide them in his mouth without at least one falling off onto the tabletop."

Eleanor giggled, actually giggled. "You're making that up. Nobody does things like that."

"Really? Eccles does, I've seen him do it," Jack said, pleased with Eleanor's reaction to his banter. "After dinner, you ladies will come back here, where you will *listen* as the ladies fill the silence, and the gentlemen and I will retire to the card table set up in the breakfast room, where I will proceed to fleece said gentlemen like sheep on the Marsh."

Eleanor's smile felt more natural now. "You really intend to fleece them?"

"Absolutely. Chelfham will have come

here because Phelps has told him what an easy mark I am. Nothing like breeding discontent among your enemies. Besides, I'm down more than three thousand pounds and it's time to get that money back, no matter whose pocket it was in last."

"We want them to turn on each other? Why?"

"Not turn on each other, Eleanor, not precisely. Just not be quite . . . happy with each other. *Divide et impera.*"

"Divide and rule," Eleanor translated easily, a woman who may have read extensively but had yet to discover the oft-written admonishments to young ladies that they were, by and large, to behave in front of gentlemen as if they had no more learning than a watering pot.

Jack looked at her in open admiration. "You know Latin?"

Eleanor shrugged. "Not precisely. There is a slim book of Latin proverbs, I believe you'd call them, in our library at home. Machiavelli was fond of quoting that particular maxim, as I recall. Papa agrees, in theory, but much prefers *Actus non facit reum, nisi mens sit rea.*"

Jack pondered those words for a few moments, as his days with his cousin's Latin tutor were far behind him. "The act is not criminal unless the intent is criminal?"

"Yes, exactly. It's an ancient legal maxim, but one that eases Papa's soul whenever he begins to question himself."

"Because he tells himself he's helping the people of Romney Marsh, while not pocketing a penny for himself."

Eleanor studied the contents of her glass, amazed to see that half of those contents were gone. "Jacko lives by that maxim as well," she heard herself say as she turned to place the wineglass on the small table beside her. "And he sleeps very well."

"You don't like him, do you?" Jack asked, suddenly very curious about Ainsley Becket's best friend.

"We . . . understand each other. He's a man who thinks simply, and acts impassively," Eleanor answered, tempted to lift the glass to her lips once more before she could blurt out *I liked him more when I knew him less.* She lifted her head, looked toward the open doors to the foyer. "Wasn't that the knocker downstairs? They're here, aren't they?"

Jack stored away what Eleanor had just said, and the way she'd looked when she'd said it, not knowing what the devil any of it meant. "Treacle will deal with their wraps, then show them up, announce them." He squeezed her hand. "Listen to me, Eleanor. This is *your* house. You are the gracious hostess, but you are also in charge, understand? Deal from those strengths."

Eleanor returned the squeeze of his hand. "I'm truly terrified about meeting these people, Jack."

Jack leaned in, lifted her chin with his bent index finger, smiled into her huge, heartbreakingly beautiful brown eyes. "Then don't think about them. Think about this instead."

He pressed his mouth to hers. Lightly, but at least marginally insistent; withdrawing for less than the space of one heartbeat, then slanting his lips against hers again, sliding his tongue over her soft, full bottom lip before he sat back, looked at her.

Damn Cluny and his ideas.

Eleanor's eyes were closed, her lips slightly parted, as if in anticipation of what would come next. Jack knew what he *wanted* to have come next, but the idea of nailing shut the doors to the drawing room, keeping their unlovely guests out so that he could further explore his swift, unexpected reaction to what had just happened wasn't possible.

He watched as Eleanor opened her eyes wide, then blinked, looked at him, raised a hand to her mouth. He forced a smile. "I'm now supposed to tell you that our guests will be announced at any moment, and you're supposed to respond *what guests?* At least that was my plan. Did it work?"

"Until you pointed out your strategy, yes, I truly think it did," Eleanor told him in all honesty and not a little disappointment. "I suppose you might have slapped me just as easily in your effort to calm me, so I'll thank you for the kiss."

"You're welcome," he said, and Eleanor's stomach did one last small flip as those marvelous slashes appeared in his lean cheeks and the sun-squint lines around his eyes made him look momentarily mischievous, not at all dangerous.

But then, as he stood up, those amused green eyes turned hard and unreadable, and Eleanor sensed the leashed power of the man. Where his kiss had done nothing but transfer her anxieties from one subject to another, Jack's confident, intelligent look at this moment worked where the kiss had failed.

And, for the first time, she realized how like Ainsley Becket this man was. What she admired in Ainsley Becket she admired in

Jack Eastwood. More than admired in Jack Eastwood. No wonder her papa trusted Jack. He must look at the man and see himself, once again young, once again with the world before him, not tragically behind him.

Eleanor would have liked time alone to think about this, think about her reactions, even her motivations for feeling toward Jack as she did, but Treacle was standing just inside the doors now, announcing their guests.

First to enter the room, *sweep* into it, actually, was the Earl of Chelfham and his countess.

And nothing. Nothing happened.

Eleanor looked at the man without a flicker of recognition, with no immediate feeling of kinship. Instead, she found herself rather amused, for the man had the appearance of an overdressed peacock, his blue coat cut of some nearly iridescent material, his neckline and sleeve cuffs dripping lace, his spotted waistcoat spanned by at least three golden chains hanging heavy with beribboned fobs. He carried a large white lace-edged handkerchief he was actually holding up to his nose, as if leery of encountering a stench.

And he was short. And more than faintly

128

plump. The top of his head shone in the light from the chandeliers, his only hair in an overlong half circle of fringe bordering his bald pate.

He was a cartoon figure, resembling drawings she'd seen when Morgan brought them from London, telling everyone that the drawings were exaggerated, but sometimes not so much so, for London was fairly thick with posturing idiots.

The woman on his arm, however, was gorgeous. Taller than her husband by a good three inches, her height accentuated by the tall feathers in her hair, and younger than he by more than two score years, she was a blond angel with huge blue eyes that matched the color of her fashionable gown.

The only thing marring her perfection was the look of utter boredom and disdain on her beautiful face.

As Jack went to meet his guests, Eleanor sat primly, her hands in her lap, and watched as a man entered the drawing room alone, ahead of one other couple.

Sir Gilbert Eccles, obviously, the bachelor of the group. He was tall, reed thin, and had somehow missed out on a chin somewhere along the line, poor fellow, while being overly blessed in the area of his Adam's apple. He had the nervous air of one who hopes to please, even if no one is looking his way. Eleanor tried to imagine the man attempting to balance peas on his knife, and found that easy to do.

And there was no mistaking Harris Phelps. He was the only other gentleman to enter the room, for one, and in looks he much resembled his sister, tall and blond, although the feminine features had not transferred well to the man, who looked more weak than handsome. He was wearing a bright scarlet silk waistcoat under his dark blue superfine, so that he looked like a more nattily turned-out Bow Street Runner, those gentlemen often referred to as Robin Redbreasts.

Phelps had gone directly to Jack, leaving his small, somewhat pudgy wife to stand just inside the doorway, looking rather lost.

Eleanor remained seated when Jack brought their guests over to be introduced, and she felt she did very well, lifting her hand for each man to take in turn, and only feeling slightly nauseous when the earl bowed over her fingertips while positively leering at her before his eyes narrowed and he turned away from her, his interest obviously not engaged.

Lady Chelfham then sat down in the very middle of the blue-on-blue striped satin couch nearest Eleanor, spreading her skirts around her so that Miranda Phelps had no choice but to take up her own seat on the facing couch.

This left Eleanor, sitting on her uncomfortable bench positioned at the end of the low table that divided the couches, squarely in between the two women.

And she was the hostess. That meant she was in charge of at least beginning the conversation. Or so she thought.

"My lady, are you comfortable?" Miranda Phelps asked nervously. "Perhaps you're cool? Or warm? Yes, it is warm, isn't it? I believe you left your fan in the coach, but I could go and —"

"Miranda, please stifle yourself," the countess said in a lazy voice. "If I should require my fan, my woman will fetch it." Then she turned to Eleanor. "We have two other engagements this evening, Mrs. Eastwood. You will be serving soon?"

Eleanor might have been flustered at first, but she did not much care for the way the countess treated her sister-in-law, and cared less for the crushed look on the latter woman's homely face. "Perhaps, my lady, if you felt yourself overencumbered with social engagements you should have cried off from our small party? I'll call my husband over here and explain your difficulty."

"Oh, no," Miranda Phelps said, looking panicked. "You can't do that, Helen. Harris distinctly told me that we had to come because his lordship wanted to see — that is . . ." She looked around rather wildly before her sympathetic gaze landed on Eleanor. "I believe they're going to pass an hour playing at cards after dinner, at Mr. Eastwood's invitation."

"Really," the countess replied, her voice dripping venom. "Is your husband an idiot then, Mrs. Eastwood? Or just so deep in the pocket he doesn't mind losing to my husband, arguably the best player in London?"

"Is he, indeed?" Eleanor responded, her chin lifted slightly. "I assure you, I wouldn't know, having always considered my husband to be quite proficient at . . . games."

"Do you play, Mrs. Eastwood?"

"No, Mrs. Phelps, I do not," Eleanor answered, smiling at the woman who had begun to perspire visibly. "My accomplishments, I'm afraid, run more to the ordinary. Embroidery, watercolors. Singing. Do you sing, Mrs. Phelps? I would think you have a lovely singing voice."

Thankfully, Mrs. Phelps hadn't needed more than that one question to set her off into a long, rambling, stultifyingly boring recitation of some of her favorite songs, songs she and her sister used to sing for their papa on cold dark nights in Lincolnshire.

From there she went on — with the countess yawning into her hand — to say that she, too, dabbled in watercolors, although not well. "But now that we reside for months of the year at Chelfham Hall, I'm encouraged to better myself, as the prospects and vistas there are lovely and I long to do them credit."

"A fruitless yearning, alas, as I've been forced to view your renderings," her ladyship slid in, then snapped her fingers twice above her head, an action that — remarkably — had his lordship scurrying to her side like an obedient puppy. "I've yet to be holding a glass, Rawley."

The earl took hold of her upraised hand and brought it to his lips, kissing her fingertips one by one. "A thousand pardons, my darling. I'm afraid we were talking."

"Miranda was also talking, Rawley. You know how her inane prattling fatigues me."

And so it went. Throughout the uncomfortably lengthy minutes before Treacle called them to supper, throughout the five courses of the meal, and without a moment's break once the ladies left the men to their cigars and cards.

Helen Maddox, Countess of Chelfham was, in a word, nasty. She bullied her sister-in-law, badgered her husband, and after one particularly uncomfortable interlude where she positively *stared* at her, totally ignored Eleanor.

Which, when she thought about it, pleased Eleanor straight down to the ground, especially after the one time the countess *did* speak to her, and that was only to say, "Oh, you're a cripple. Rawley didn't tell me or I should certainly have begged off. I loathe infirmities, they make me queasy. I'll lie down, now. Miranda, fetch my woman."

And so, while the mantel clock seemed to have stuck on the quarter hour, the countess reclined on one of the couches, her summoned maid standing behind the couch wielding an ivory-sticked fan and looking daggers at Miranda each time she opened her mouth to speak.

Eleanor and Miranda retired to the music room to look through the song sheets shelved there.

"She isn't really mean, you know," Miranda told Eleanor as she sat with a stack of song sheets in her lap. "I mean, she is, usually, but I think that's because she's not happy. I mean, not that she's not thrilled to be a countess. Lord knows anyone would be delighted, I know I would, but she can't quite care for his lordship, you understand."

"She seems to have no trouble ruling his lordship," Eleanor said, hoping to keep the conversation alive and on point even as Mrs. Phelps's candor surprised her.

"Oh, yes, definitely. Harris says that's because she's going to give him an heir."

"The countess is pregnant?" Eleanor felt suddenly ill herself, knowing she and Jack, one way or the other, were probably going to make this unborn child fatherless.

Miranda leaned closer to Eleanor, who sat beside her on the small couch. "Harris says he wonders whose baby it is, because his sister was rather . . . rather wild when she first made her debut last season. Oh, I know I shouldn't say such things, but I cannot like her, and as we're residing with them, I'm always in her company. I've begged Harris to leave London, take us home to Surrey, but he refuses. Too busy, he says. I don't see how he could be busy. All he does is to go off without me to gamble all night and then sleep until two in the afternoon. Oh, I'm doing it again! Mrs. Eastwood, forgive me. I shouldn't have had that second glass of wine. Harris says my tongue runs on wheels when I imbibe."

"Shall I ring for the tea tray? It's rather early, but you might feel better with some nice hot tea and cakes." Eleanor figuratively patted herself on the back for her offer, as she'd much rather press another glass of wine into that pudgy little hand.

"Oh, no, no thank you. No more cakes for me for a while. Helen gives me her castoffs, you understand, and I simply must be able to wedge myself into the green velvet by Christmastime. I've already planned to use the extra material for a lovely shawl — she's so much taller than me, you understand. But I am thirsty, so perhaps just one teeny, tiny bit more wine?"

Eleanor rang for a servant and within moments, it seemed, Miranda Phelps was swallowing down a full glass of wine as if it were water, fresh and cold from the pump.

With a look toward the hallway, Eleanor decided to dare more questions. "Your husband and the countess are brother and sister. Were he and the earl acquainted before the marriage?"

Miranda frowned, thinking back, or just trying to think clearly. "Harris and his lordship? No." She leaned closer, as she'd done earlier, with the air of one imparting something important. "We were poor as church mice before his lordship clapped eyes on Helen. I'm not saying we're swimming all that deep in the gravy boat now, but things have most definitely been better for us since their marriage." She rolled her eyes. "Except for Helen being even more toplofty now than she was, thinking herself better than anyone else."

"Well, she *is* a countess," Eleanor pointed out, then dug in a little deeper. "But I must say she doesn't treat you very nicely, does she?"

"Ha! If you knew the half of it, dear, kind Mrs. Eastwood! I know why Harris married me, for my father's money, certainly not because he . . . well, the miller's daughter can't be choosey, can she? Especially one who looks like me."

"I sure he cares for you. Deeply." Eleanor hoped she sounded sincere.

"No, he used my small dowry for Helen's Come-out last Season, figuring she was the way to our fortune. We'd still be hiding from creditors if it weren't for Helen and her advantageous marriage, as she constantly reminds us. *Her* sacrifice, she says it was, as if she hasn't benefited mightily from the marriage. *And* the title. Lording over us, over me." She lifted Eleanor's own untouched glass in a sort of mock salute, then drained that, as well. "Here's to a painful labor and breech birth for *her ladyship*."

Then Miranda blinked, hiccupped, and made a valiant but vain grab for the song sheets that began sliding off her lap and onto the floor. "Oh! Look what I've done!"

"Don't worry, Mrs. Phelps," Eleanor assured her, going to her knees on the carpet. "You just sit and compose yourself while I gather these. No harm done."

"Thank you, Mrs. Eastwood," Miranda said, then made a not quite straight line toward the drinks table and the wine decanter Treacle had deposited there.

Eleanor sat back on her haunches and sighed as she watched the woman navigate the music room, full glass in hand, picking up figurines, running her fingertips across the silk panel draperies, nearly knocking over a music stand . . . bending to pick up Eleanor's large leather portfolio of watercolors.

"Here," Eleanor said, hastily getting to her feet, the song sheets fluttering to the floor once more. "Let me take that for you, Mrs. Phelps."

"No, no, that's all right. Is this yours? You did say you paint watercolors, didn't you? Or was that me? I think I said something of the sort. That I paint watercolors. But I'm sadly ham-fisted when I pick up a brush. Let's see what you do, shall we?"

Eleanor may not have been in society for more than a few days, but she was fairly certain that physically wresting her portfolio out of Miranda Phelps's hands would not be considered polite.

Polite, however, was for those who had nothing to hide.

"Mrs. Phelps, forgive me, but I'm afraid I must insist," Eleanor said, taking hold of the portfolio with both hands — one more than Miranda had, as she wasn't about to give up her wineglass. "I'm a terrible artist and cannot bear to think of anyone else seeing my poor efforts."

"Very well," Miranda said with a shrug, giving up the battle without a blink. "Oh, and look, still that mess on the floor. Shame on me." Her features crumpled and she began to cry. "I can't do anything right. Harris says so, and he's right."

Now Eleanor was exasperated. Really, the woman was a total loss, wasn't she? Sad, spineless. And tipsy into the bargain. "There, there, Mrs. Phelps," she said through gritted teeth. "I'm sure that's not true."

Miranda sniffed, brightened as she made

another grab for the portfolio. "Then I can see your paintings?"

Eleanor's mouth dropped open. Why, the conniving woman — in her own way she was as bad as the countess, except she used pity to get what she wanted. "No, I'm afraid not. I really don't feel comfortable showing my watercolors to anyone."

"Gracious, wife, what's been going on in here? The floor looks as if there's been a snowfall."

Eleanor turned about to see Jack walking into the room, stopping when he encountered the mess of song sheets scattered over the carpet. "Jack," she said, hoping she didn't sound too desperately happy to see him. "I had a slight accident, that's all."

"Ha!" Miranda Phelps shouted, successfully grabbing the portfolio from Eleanor's relaxed fingers. "Now I've got it! You're too modest, Mrs. Eastwood. You'd made me so curious, I *must* see your watercolors."

Eleanor nearly slapped the woman's hand, but she restrained herself. She'd only ever seen men drunk, never a female, and she wasn't sure how to handle the woman. But slapping her held enormous appeal. "Mrs. Phelps, I said no," she said evenly, in a tone that would have warned her siblings to stop what they were doing or else Eleanor would be disappointed in them. Miranda Phelps, however, didn't seem to be worried about her disappointment.

"Here, I'll take that," Jack said, neatly stepping in and removing the portfolio from the grasp of both women. "Eleanor, Treacle has brought out the tea tray but the countess has decided she'd rather forgo the niceties and push on to their next engagement."

"Really," Eleanor said, thinking she'd like to slap the countess, too, as long as she was in the mood. "Then we shan't keep her, shall we?"

"I know I don't want to," Jack said quietly, winking at Eleanor as he handed her the portfolio, then took Miranda's arm, carefully maneuvering her past the spill of song sheets and out of the room.

Leaving Eleanor to tuck her portfolio back where it was, propped against the side of a chair, then take a deep, steadying breath and steel herself to remain civil until their guests had departed.

And never had an exodus been accomplished so quickly, as Miranda was fairly roughly grabbed at the elbow by her husband and dragged out onto the landing behind a red-faced Earl of Chelfham and his now smugly smiling countess.

Only Sir Gilbert tarried long enough to

bow over Eleanor's hand. Then, with a slight, almost awed nod to Jack, he, too, was gone.

Chapter Six

Eleanor made her way over to the couch lately vacated by the countess. Not caring what Jack might think, she toed off her evening slippers and drew her legs up onto the cushions, tucking her skirts over her feet. "What uniformly unlovely people," she said, shaking off Jack's offer of tea. "Thank heavens they had another engagement."

Jack smiled at his "wife," who certainly seemed to have no problems with the idea of making herself comfortable in his presence. And, if that was good for the goose . . .

Untying his neck cloth, Jack sat down on the facing couch, tugging the starched cloth out from around his neck, then opening the top button of his shirt. He could think of worse places to be than London society, but few that were more personally uncomfortable.

"What *was* going on when I found you?"

Eleanor leaned down and began absent-mindedly rubbing at her left calf. "Mrs. Phelps was . . . in her altitudes, I'd suppose would be the kind way of saying it. Goodness, she drank so much wine I was surprised she didn't forgo the niceties of a glass and simply drink straight from the decanter. She's a very unhappy woman, Jack. But, fortunately, she does seem to enjoy the sound of her own voice."

"Meaning she filled the silences for you?" Jack asked, watching as Eleanor rubbed at her leg through the material of her gown.

"Well, to put it as succinctly as possible, Harris Phelps married her for her dowry, which he then used to present his sister to Society, hoping for an advantageous marriage that would feather all their nests. I can't know for certain, but I'm sure they made a dead set at the Earl of Chelfham when the man showed an interest."

"And it worked," Jack said, nodding his head. "I doubt you missed that finger-snapping call to heel earlier, before we went in to dinner?"

"I most certainly did not. But that's because she's increasing, according to Miranda Phelps. I believe the earl is jumping through hoops because his wife carries the heir you told me he desires so much."

Jack was fairly certain the heir wasn't the only reason an aging, mud-homely man would willingly put himself at the beck and call of a young, beautiful woman who allowed him in her bed, but he refrained from pointing that out to Eleanor. "You'll not be surprised to learn that Chelfham treats Phelps as badly as his wife does her sister-in-law. And Eccles? I'm beginning to think the man has no idea what's going on, even as he reaps some of the benefits. However, when you're as low as Phelps, it's always comforting to have someone lower than yourself standing at the ready when you feel the urge to kick something."

"Why would he need Eccles for that? Wouldn't his own wife be sufficient? It's painfully clear that he despises her."

Jack could stand it no longer, so he moved over to sit at the bottom of the other couch, to put his hands on Eleanor's calf.

"What are you — no, Jack, don't do that," Eleanor protested, attempting to push away his hands. "I'm perfectly fine."

"I know you are," he said, careful to keep her foot covered as he held on to her knee with one hand, began rubbing at her calf with the other. "God, woman, your muscle's in a cramp. Tight as a drum. Lie back and let me help you."

She wanted to say no, but the spasm, rather than easing, seemed to be getting worse. So she sat back, closed her eyes. "I think I must have overdone today. I must have been up and down the stairs a dozen times." She winced as Jack's fingers pushed at the knot in her muscle.

"Just relax, Eleanor," Jack said, keeping his hands moving, easing his left hand down to the hem of her gown, then reaching beneath it to take hold of her silk hose–clad foot. "Do you get cramps like this often?"

"Not this bad, no." Eleanor bit down on her bottom lip, shook her head. She didn't know which was worse, the pain of the cramp or the knowledge that Jack had both hands beneath her gown now, holding her foot steady, massaging her calf.

Jack was careful to keep his eyes on Eleanor's face, seeing the pain registered there in the way a white line had formed around her mouth. Her foot was so small and slim, fragile in his large hand, but her ankle seemed to be all hard bone, and not very well aligned. To ease the cramp, he tried to bend her foot up toward her shin, keeping the heel down . . . which was when he realized that Eleanor's ankle did not bend. Not even an inch, as if the bones had all fused, frozen together.

"What happened, Eleanor? You were injured when your ship sank? Is that what you said?"

Eleanor could feel the cramp begin to ease and tried to move, but it was too soon. The mere action of straightening her knee caused the cramp to seize her muscle again. "I don't recall saying that."

"Perhaps I assumed," Jack said, amazed at the way she lay on the couch, stoically soaking up the pain he was sure must be considerable. He moved both hands to her calf, doing his best to coax the muscle out of its rock-hard spasm. He wanted her to relax, think of something besides the pain. "But am I right?"

Eleanor nodded, purposely took a deep breath, then released it slowly. "The ship was sinking and . . . and I was hiding belowdecks when Jacko found me. A frightened child, hiding."

She hadn't seemed to notice that Jack slid one hand up to the back of her knee. The feel of her, through the silk hose, was doing things to him that he should be ashamed of — and he might be, later. For now, all he knew was that if her calf felt good under his fingers, her thigh would feel even better. "So Jacko found you, saved you. But you were injured."

She longed to tell him the truth. Tell *somebody* the truth. But what would that serve? Nothing and no one. "Jacko passed me to Chance — you've never met him, I don't think — and he was holding me as he ran up the stairs to the deck. There was fire everywhere, and things were falling and people were shouting. . . ."

"Fire? But the ship floundered in a storm," Jack said, then wished he'd kept his mouth shut, because Eleanor's eyes suddenly went wide and panicked.

"I . . . I was very young and very frightened. Perhaps a lantern had smashed? I don't remember. I've been told that Chance put me down, just for a moment, and I ran away from him. Perhaps I was looking for my . . . my parents. They tell me something fell on me, trapping my leg. I really don't remember anything much after seeing Jacko, to tell you the truth, and nothing of my life before that moment, either. He frightened me with his smile. I think I already told you what happened then. I screamed at the sight of him, then fainted, only rousing once Chance had me up on deck."

"I'm not a child, and screaming occurred to me as an option when I first saw the man," Jack said, hoping to encourage

Eleanor to continue her story.

"He's fiercely loyal to Papa," Eleanor said, as if that explained everything there was to know about Jacko. "I . . . I think the cramp is easing," she added, sitting up more against the cushions, holding down her gown at the knee. She'd said too much, most of it without thinking, because her mind was too filled with sensation, the sensation caused by the feel of Jack's hands on her leg. Her pain was only secondary.

Jack reluctantly slid his hands out from beneath her gown, fairly certain he should borrow Cluny's beads and ask the man how to say a rosary in penance for unclean thoughts. He put out his hands to help Eleanor to a sitting position. "Slowly, Eleanor. You don't want that cramp to come back. Here, I'll help you with your shoes."

Eleanor smoothed down her gown, very aware that she now sat so close to Jack that their limbs were touching. "Thank you, but if you could just, um, hand them to me? At times like this, I've found that I'm more comfortable without shoes."

"Did your leg pain you very much the first night we arrived here?"

Eleanor remembered that she'd been barefoot when he'd found her snooping about in his study. In a moment of daring, she smiled at him. "Shall I lie and say yes?"

Jack put his crooked index finger under her chin, and eased closer. "What a bundle of contradictions you are, Eleanor Becket. I believe you're honest to a fault, right up until the moment you look at me with those innocent fawn eyes and lie to me without so much as a betraying blink. I only wonder if I'll ever be able to sort the lies from the truth before you finally decide to trust me."

It was the fire. How could she have slipped so badly as to mention the fire? "I do trust you, Jack. I wouldn't be here, in London, most certainly not in this room, if I didn't trust you."

"Then you'll trust me to do this?" he asked just before he pressed his mouth to hers, gathering her against him as he did so.

Eleanor was stiff in his embrace, but only for a moment, as she realized that she was where she'd wanted to be for nearly two years. She opened her mouth on a sigh as she slipped her arms beneath his, to press her hands against his back, and Jack deepened their kiss, taking her mouth in a mix of gentleness and hunger that shook Eleanor to her core.

She didn't protest as he eased her against the cushions once more, this time following her down, cradling her with one arm as his hand slid down her hip and onto the thigh of her uninjured leg.

They were fused together now, both of them on their sides, as Jack felt sure he'd crush her if he dared to put his full weight on her small body.

This was madness, Jack knew, but she tasted so good. Insanity, pure and simple, but she felt so good. Jacko's smiling face and deadly mirthful eyes flashed into his mind, and were just as quickly banished, as were his promise to Ainsley Becket and possibly even his already scant hope of Heaven.

"Eleanor," he whispered against her ear as he broke the kiss so that he could hold her more closely. "I'm not hurting you, am I?"

Eleanor felt his breath, warm against her throat, and that warmth, curiously, sent a shiver straight down her spine. "I've always known you could never hurt me, Jack," she heard herself tell him, at which time her eyes opened wide as she realized what she'd just admitted. *Always. Always known. Because she'd always been thinking about him. Oh, God . . .*

Jack felt her body stiffen even as Eleanor tried to withdraw from him, which would be impossible until he removed himself from the couch. He was a bastard, an unmitigated bastard, a rotter, plain and simple. The woman was infatuated with him. But how was he to have known that? He *should* have known that, damn it! Hell, he had to be the only gentleman ever welcomed to Becket Hall, ever accepted by Ainsley Becket. It would only be natural for the lonely spinster of the household to begin weaving fantasies about him.

He had to give her a way out, get past this awkward moment without embarrassing her more than she'd already embarrassed herself.

Jack levered himself to a sitting position once more, bringing Eleanor up with him, as he still had his arm around her. "Well, I've gone and done it now, haven't I?" he said, reaching down to pick up her small silver slippers, place them on his lap. "Do you think we can say the blame lies on both sides? You for being so appealing, me for taking advantage of my good friend's daughter."

"Yes, I suppose so," Eleanor said, drawing on years of holding back her emotions, of behaving, of hiding, of sitting quietly while longing to run, to scream, to even hit something if the spirit took her. "We had a . . . um, a stressful evening. Allowances should be made, as well as assurances that nothing remotely like this shall happen again. Now, if you'll excuse me?"

Before Jack could say anything else, Eleanor had gotten to her feet and was on her way out of the room in her stocking-clad feet, her limp barely noticeable.

"She should never wear you," he said once she was gone, glaring at the silver slippers in his hands, then frowning as he realized that the left slipper had been modified so that its heel was higher than the other one. Was that a help, or a hindrance? If she was more comfortable without shoes at all, why would she wear one with a higher heel?

"I'll be glad when this is over and she's back in Romney Marsh," he muttered aloud as he got to his feet, still holding the slippers. Then he looked toward the foyer and the staircase Eleanor had just climbed to the bedchamber that adjoined his, that was no more than an unlocked door away from his. "Glad? Let her lie to you, Eastwood," he told himself, rhythmically slapping the soles of the slippers against his leg as he headed for his study, "but don't start lying to yourself."

He hesitated as he reached the music room and looked inside, as candles still burned in their holders, and the song sheets remained where they had somehow been scattered onto the carpet.

"Penance," he suggested to himself out loud, entering the room to pick up the song sheets himself. A paltry penance, but Eleanor, he felt sure, would be appalled to think she had made extra work for the servants. He didn't know much about her, was sure he knew less every day, but he did know that.

Down on his knees, Jack reached for song sheets, stacking them in front of him, only pausing as he noticed Eleanor's portfolio tucked in between a chair and table. Miranda Phelps had certainly wanted to take a look at Eleanor's watercolors, and Eleanor had been just as adamant that she didn't.

"That was as close to a catfight as I've seen in a while, as a matter of fact," he said, picking up the song sheets and placing them on a table before gathering up the portfolio and carrying it to his study.

He laid the portfolio flat on his desktop, then sat down behind the desk and looked at the thing. Simply looked at it.

Eleanor's portfolio.

So? The journal in this desk drawer was yours.

She's modest, that's all, and has a right to

her privacy.

She knows more than she's telling and you have a right to be suspicious of anything she does that seems out of the ordinary, unusual. It's your neck on the line.

Watercolors, Eastwood. What in bloody blazes do you think you'll find in there? All the lost secrets of the world?

"Oh, the hell with it," Jack said at last, and reached for the leather strap holding the portfolio closed, then opened the thing before he could change his mind.

The papers inside were of varying sizes. The very first one made him smile, for it wasn't a watercolor at all, but a small charcoal drawing of Cluny dozing in a large wicker chair in the conservatory. There was little detail, as if the sketch had been made quickly — probably before Cluny could wake to find out he'd become Eleanor's subject.

There were more small sketches, all of them rather broadly drawn, yet all of them perfectly capturing the likeness of the subject.

Mrs. Hendersen sipping tea at the large wooden table in the kitchens.

Mrs. Ryan, stirring a pot.

One of the young maids, up on tiptoe,

wielding a feather duster over the front of a piece of furniture.

Treacle simply being Treacle.

And himself. Jack smiled as he looked into his own face, to see that Eleanor must have sketched him from memory, and the memory hadn't been a happy one for her. His mouth was open, his eyebrows slammed down over his eyes, and he was holding up what had to be the journal he waved in her face a few evenings ago.

"Well, then, not blind adoration at least," he muttered, noticing the small horns she'd placed on top of his head. "Maybe I was flattering myself."

"Flattering yourself, is it? I know you're talking to yourself, boyo," Cluny said, sauntering into the room.

Jack laid down the drawing and picked up the next one, that he believed most probably depicted the view from Eleanor's bedchamber window. "You're home early."

"Ever been to a cockfight where the cocks are all devout cowards? Makes for a damn dull evening. What have you got there?"

Jack smiled as he kept turning over pages, some of them larger now, all of them watercolors of the exterior of Becket Hall as seen from several angles. "Watercolors of Becket Hall, Cluny. Here, you've never seen the place. This one? That's how the place looked the first time I saw it, in the middle of a rainy winter."

"I would have kept on riding, myself," Cluny said, squinting down at the watercolor. "Looks a good place for ghosties and suchlike."

"Not really," Jack told him, turning over another painting. "Here. This one is of the sun shining on the large terrace that faces the Channel. Look at that, Cluny. Eleanor's very talented, isn't she?"

Cluny tipped his head from side to side. "Eleanor, is it? These are hers?"

"Yes, and you should see the sketch she made of you."

"Thank you, no, boyo. I know what I look like, and I'm not proud of the fact. Now, could she be drawing me without the belly, I'd be pleased."

"Then you won't be pleased," Jack said, smiling as he kept carefully turning over the sheets, only to lose that smile as he looked at the next rendering.

"And the chins. Could do without the chins, too, now that I think on it. Do you think she could — what are you looking at, boyo?"

Jack turned over the sheet, looked at the

next watercolor. Then the next. The next. "Damn."

Cluny came around to Jack's side of the desk to look more closely at the paintings. "Thought you said our little girlie never set foot away from this Becket Hall of hers. You know what that is, don't you, boyo?"

"Oh, yes, Cluny, I know what that is, because we've both already reconnoitered the place, haven't we?" Jack said, caught between anger and an unexpected disappointment that only increased his anger. "No mistaking it. That's Chelfham Hall."

"You getting the feeling you've been taken up for a ride by these Beckets of yours, boyo, and they're the only ones what really know where you're going?" Cluny asked, looking at his friend, who was already glaring at the ceiling over his head.

"You know that idea you had, Cluny? About pillow secrets."

"I remember," Cluny said, heading for the drinks table, but keeping one eye on his friend. "What of it?"

Jack sat quietly, feeling the sting of betrayal as he accepted a full glass of wine and lifted it to his lips. Before draining its contents, he said quietly, "What of it, Cluny? I don't think you're the only one who's thought of that game. . . ."

CHAPTER SEVEN

At some point during the evening, amidst all her other chatter, Miranda Phelps had mentioned that, missing country air, she made a point of walking in Hyde Park every morning around eleven if the weather was fair.

The countess, as Eleanor recalled, had countered this statement with a rather sarcastic remark about her sister-in-law feeling more at home with the nannies and encroaching cits that clogged the area at that unfashionable hour than she ever would in the Promenade in that same park at five.

Doubting she would meet the countess, which suited Eleanor down to the ground, four days after the disastrous dinner party she and her maid, Beatrice, entered the park at precisely eleven o'clock, Jack's town carriage remaining outside the grounds for them.

She hadn't told Jack of her plans, mostly

because he seemed to be avoiding her as studiously as she was avoiding him. She'd been closer to him in her dreams in her bed at Becket Hall than she was now, only one unlocked door between them.

So, just last night, she'd locked the door. At least now she didn't feel as if he had a standing invitation to repeat what he'd obviously regretted doing in the first place. It was bad enough that she did *not* regret it.

In fact, if she was to be a help to Jack at all, she would have to take steps on her own, and the only one she could think of was to further her acquaintance with Miranda Phelps.

"Oh, dear, this is so much larger than I'd thought," Eleanor said as she surveyed the green landscape unfolded in front of her. "I've read that the park consists of well over three hundred acres, but as I've nothing to compare that size with in my head, I didn't realize how very vast that is."

"Yes, ma'am," Beatrice said, waving to someone Eleanor didn't see.

"A friend, Beatrice?"

The maid blushed very red as she nodded. "I suppose he is, ma'am. He was just standing there the other morning, three days ago as a matter of fact, when I stepped outside to fetch the milk for Mrs. Ryan, because you said we should help where we can because that's what we want from everyone else. He said his master forgot something here the other night and he was sent to fetch it."

"Really?" Eleanor was scarcely paying attention up until that moment, but now she was listening closely. "His master, you say. And who would that be?"

"Why, his lordship, the nob what was to dinner, remember, ma'am? Gerald is a footman for him over in Grosvenor Square, ma'am, an *upper* footman. We've . . . um, we've been walking out every night ever since. Not in the park, ma'am, because that's too dangerous after dark."

While Beatrice spoke, Eleanor was busy looking at the people coming and going along the paths and across the well-scythed lawns. She saw no one in livery, no one who could be a footman. "I don't see him, Beatrice. Point him out for me, please."

Beatrice shaded her eyes with her hand and looked around, then dropped her hand to her side. "Oh, he runned off, didn't he? I suppose I shouldn't have oughta waved, being here with you and all. Not that he'd be in any trouble for a wave, would he, ma'am?"

"No, of course not," Eleanor said, thinking over the maid's admissions. "You said you walk out in the evenings. But it's not evening, Beatrice, so what do you suppose your Gerald is doing here now?"

The maid opened her mouth to speak, then shut it, furrowed her brow. "Why, I'm sure I don't know, ma'am."

"What did he forget?"

"Ma'am?"

"His lordship. You said Gerald told you his master forgot something."

"Oh, that. Not forgot, exactly. Lost. Well, we looked, Gerald and me both, but we couldn't find it nowheres."

Eleanor was doing her best to control her temper, and her sudden anxiety. "You allowed Gerald to enter the house, help you *search* it?"

"Well, yes, ma'am," Beatrice answered, beginning to look worried. "You said we was to use our in-in . . ."

"Initiative. Yes, I did, didn't I. So, Beatrice. Where did the two of you search?"

Beatrice screwed up her face as if the contortions could help her concentrate. "The drawing room. The dining room. Mr. Eastwood's study . . ."

"Mr. Eastwood's study? Beatrice, I don't believe the gentlemen ever left the dining room, but chose to play cards there for the little while our guests remained after dinner. I'll ask you again, what were you looking for?"

"A stickpin, ma'am. A diamond stickpin. But we didn't find it, hard as we looked."

"That's too bad," Eleanor said. "So, you searched together?"

"Oh, yes, ma'am, I'm not such a looby as to let just anyone walk about my master's house willy-nilly. Except when you rang for me, ma'am, o'course. But that was just for a few minutes, because all you were wanting was to have me button up your gown, remember? The blue one?"

Eleanor remembered. She'd rung for Beatrice, and had kept her for a good ten minutes, as she'd also asked her to help with her hair, that had been proving particularly unwieldy that morning.

She put her hands on Beatrice's upper arms, trying to remain in control. "Where was Gerald when you were called upstairs?"

"Oh, ma'am, he wouldn't have nipped anything, if that's what you mean. Gerald's a good man, he is."

"Yes, and I'm sure you're a sterling judge of character. Where was he when you left him, Beatrice?"

The maid began to sniffle. "In . . . in Mr.

Eastwood's study."

Eleanor closed her eyes for a full second, then looked very intently at Beatrice. "And when you came back downstairs, Beatrice? Where was he then?"

Beatrice rolled her eyes up toward the sky, then down toward her toes, her mobile face contorting once more before she smiled and looked at Eleanor. "I remember now! He was waiting for me, just there, at the bottom of the servant stairs. Said he was hoping for a peek at m'ankles. Cheeky thing, but then he asked me to go walking with him, so that was all right."

Eleanor considered the logistics of the thing as she let go of Beatrice's arms and began walking aimlessly down one of the paths. Jack's study was at the rear of the main living floor of the large house, as were the servant stairs leading both up to the bedchambers and down to the kitchens. The whole thing could be perfectly innocent.

So why was she suddenly fighting a nearly overwhelming urge to look over her shoulder, to see if anyone was watching her?

"Ma'am?"

Eleanor took a breath, smiled and turned to her maid. "Yes?"

"I shouldn't have oughta done that, should I, ma'am? Are you going to turn me off with no notice?"

"No, Beatrice, I'm not," Eleanor said, turning around to retrace her steps to the street and her waiting coach. "I am, however, going to ask you to try to remember as much as you can concerning any questions Gerald might have asked you about the house or Mr. Eastwood or myself. Can you do that, Beatrice?"

The maid nodded furiously. "Oh, yes, ma'am, I can do that."

"Very good, Beatrice. But before you do, are you walking out with Gerald again tonight?"

Beatrice was wiping away tears now, whether still in fear of her position or worried that she'd be denied her Gerald, Eleanor didn't know, and did not especially care.

Beatrice colored again. "Yes, ma'am. Right at eleven o'clock. If that's all right by you, ma'am?"

Eleanor stood quietly as the maid quickly stepped in front of her to open the coach door and pull down the steps even before the footman could jump down to do the job himself. Beatrice was using her initiative again.

Then Eleanor took one last, hopefully casual look around, still feeling as if something were boring between her shoulder blades, and told the maid, "I should be the last person to interfere in matters of the heart, Beatrice. Now, come along, and tell me everything you and your Gerald talked about, all right?"

CHAPTER EIGHT

When Jack walked into his study at two that same afternoon, rubbing at his temples where a drink-induced headache still lingered, it was to see Eleanor sitting behind his desk and quite obviously waiting for him.

And looking at him steadily, too, without a hint of nervousness or shame . . . and definitely not with longing or desire, damn her. Her coolness exasperated him, the way she seemed able to function at so many different levels without any of them somehow melding together. Colliding, to explode in the sort of confusion he'd been feeling for days.

"Wife," he said tightly, heading for the drinks table, then thinking better of the idea. It was bad enough he drank deep when at cards with the Unholy Trio, then again when he finally returned home to sit in his bedchamber and stare at the door leading to Eleanor's rooms.

"You didn't take my advice," Eleanor said without preamble, doing her best to ignore how weary Jack looked, how vulnerable in those first unguarded moments before he'd realized she was in his study.

"And what advice would that be, Eleanor?" he asked, sprawling on the leather couch on the opposite side of the large room that was, in fact, really rather small now that the two of them — and all their secrets — occupied it.

"Locking away your journal," Eleanor said, opening the drawer and pulling the offending thing out, carefully placing it on the desktop. "I believe we must now assume that the earl knows at least something of what we're about, which changes our plans considerably."

All right, so maybe a single small hair of the dog that had bit him last night *was* in order. Jack levered himself to his feet and slowly walked to the drinks table, keeping his gaze on Eleanor as he poured himself a glass of wine. "Would you care to elaborate?"

Eleanor folded her hands on top of the journal, keeping her eyes downcast as she related all that had happened earlier in Hyde Park, then went on to tell him what she'd learned about Beatrice's conversations with the footman, Gerald.

"I won't plague you with what I asked her and how she answered, but will summarize thusly. Gerald inquired about you, inquired about me, asked about how long we've been married. He was remarkably inquisitive about my origins, which is disconcerting at the least, and I'm thankful Beatrice is not privy to that information. Gerald also wondered quite openly about your comings and goings, to which Beatrice answered that you seem to come and go at all hours of the day and night without rhyme or reason, and are often absent for full weeks at a time."

Jack put down the wineglass, untouched. "Christ. Is that all, or did he ask to count the silver?"

"Oh, I'm not done," Eleanor informed him, finally looking up and meeting his narrowed eyes. "Beatrice is a very *talkative* young woman. When I pushed a bit — I think she at last had begun to realize what she'd done — she told me that this Gerald person now knows that your valet is constantly lamenting the damage done to your fine clothing and the fact that in just the past six months two pair of your boots have been lost to what he's convinced is damage from seawater. Oh, and Cluny seems to have been the topic of conversation more than once, although Beatrice knows no more than I do myself, which is that sometimes he's here, sometimes he's not, and nobody's allowed into his rooms to clean them so they must be a fright."

Jack was slouching on the couch again, his long legs outstretched in front of him as he looked toward the open door to the hallway, glad that this was one of those times when the always pessimistic Cluny was gone, if only for the day. "I think I'd rather she'd handed him the silver and the blunt for a coach ride to Dover. I obviously slipped up, Eleanor, tipped Chelfham somehow. But I'll be damned if I know how."

Eleanor felt sorry for him, longed to tell him everything would be all right, that this was all some strange coincidence. But neither of them believed that.

"Perhaps, if we believe the earl to be a part of the Red Men, he is simply very cautious when someone new is introduced into his company?"

"So he sends his man — that was no mere footman, Eleanor — to find a way into my house? I can swallow the first part, but not the second. I think Beatrice was more of an opportunity than a plan. This Gerald was watching the house early in the morning, Beatrice saw him and his plan to gain entry to the house was made up on the spot."

"Does that matter?" Eleanor asked, although she did agree his version of events sounded plausible, that they were merely being watched until opportunity arose in the appearance of Beatrice. "And the earl could just as easily have been curious as to why anyone would so doggedly pursue and befriend his brother-in-law, who anyone can see he believes to be a total waste. We've moved too fast, that's the whole of it, and now the earl knows something."

"Something, yes. But what? He could assume many things, couldn't he? That I dabble in free trading. That I know he does, too. That I want to join him. That I'm thinking of blackmailing him. On and on." Jack swung his gaze back to Eleanor. "That's it then. You're going home."

Eleanor had been expecting this reaction, and had prepared for it. "We can't do that. We can't do anything that will make the earl think we know that . . . well, that we know he suspects something. I have, in fact, just accepted an invitation from Lady Chelfham to attend a ball planned for the end of the week. The countess's note was very kind, profusely apologizing for her ill humor the other night as well as the lateness of her invitation, and blaming both on her delicate condition."

"She actually apologized? Sounds as if Chelfham does know how to put his foot down, doesn't it? I wouldn't have believed his countess does anything she doesn't want to do."

"I don't believe she does," Eleanor told him, looking at him intently. "In fact, I'm beginning to question everything about our strange evening. The countess all but ordering us from the drawing room so that she could be alone, to do Lord only knows what. Miranda Phelps becoming so conveniently intoxicated and whispering nasty secrets to me about her sister-in-law. At first I congratulated myself, but I think I may have been the one who was maneuvered, which is rather disconcerting. You never told me what happened when you all played cards, although from the furious look on the earl's face as he hustled everyone out, I'm assuming you lightened his pockets considerably?"

Jack nodded, still thinking over what Eleanor had said, her conclusion that they were all, men and women both, involved with the Red Men Gang. It seemed a plausible conclusion; the Becket women weren't exactly quiet bystanders in the Black Ghost Gang ventures, were they? "Not considerably, no. But certainly enough to disconcert him when Phelps began to taunt him, pointing out that *he* had clipped my wings without any problems and now he was watching Chelfham lose hand after hand while he still won."

"How did you manage that?"

"It was no great feat, believe me. Phelps switches his cards from hand to hand when they're inferior, as if this will help improve them, and holds on tight when he's been dealt a better hand. I'd raise the bidding whenever Phelps held on tight, and soon Chelfham was matching me bid for bid, so that he lost both to Phelps and to me. I'm still playing much the same game these past few nights, and I thought — no longer think — that Chelfham keeps coming back for more because he believes he can best me."

"I thought the plan was to *lose?*"

"It was originally, until I became fatigued with that idea. Now I'm winning, and talking about how I am looking for somewhere to invest my winnings. After all, it doesn't matter how I get myself in, as long as I get the invitation."

Eleanor shook her head. "I won't pretend to understand all of that. But what of Sir Gilbert?"

"Oh, he doesn't gamble. Eccles is one of those persons who just *is*, but doesn't really *do* anything."

"A cipher. Yes, I thought so myself." Eleanor quickly moved on, feeling the subject of her possibly being sent back to Becket Hall should be left behind them as quickly as possible so they could concentrate on what was more important — what they would do next. "We can ignore him if you are certain, but I don't believe we can similarly discount the countess and Mrs. Phelps. It embarrasses me to think how I disregarded the one and thought it easy to dupe the other. But unless we want them to know we suspect them of knowing what we're about, you need to continue on as you were, and I will have to continue my role as the quiet little cripple."

"And that makes you very angry, doesn't it?" Jack asked, wishing he didn't see the logic of the thing.

"I'm not best pleased, but I'll manage," Eleanor said, then noticed that her knuckles had turned white. She deliberately unclasped her hands and got to her feet. "But everything else has changed now."

"I know. Besides becoming doubly confusing."

"I agree. We have to assume that this Gerald person saw your journal and that the earl now knows you're involved in free trading. Which leaves the next move to him, doesn't it? Either he'll invite you to join him, pool your resources as it were, or he'll consider you dangerous to him and try to . . . to eliminate you. I'll assume that your man Cluny is watching your back."

Jack goggled at her — knew he was goggling — and then threw back his head and laughed out loud. "God. For a moment there I guess I'd forgotten whose daughter you are. Yes, Eleanor, I, too, have come to the same conclusions. And yes, Cluny has my back."

"Good," Eleanor said, praying Jack's confidence in the Irishman was well placed. "What shall we do about Beatrice?"

"If we're to continue to behave as if we don't know we suspect them, I imagine we do nothing."

"No, that can't work. She's bound to tell this Gerald person how I questioned her this morning. We can't let them meet, nor can we do anything to the man without alerting Chelfham."

"I could push her down the stairs hoping

she breaks a leg," Jack said, surprisingly amused to be planning strategy with the gloriously attractive mix of genteel lady and hardheaded general that was Eleanor Becket.

Then Eleanor smiled at him, more than willing to help him break the tension for a few moments. "I've already thought of and dismissed that idea, for she could just as easily break her neck, and then what on earth would we do with her?"

Jack was hard-pressed not to jump up from his seat and kiss her senseless. "That could be inconvenient, couldn't it? Especially for Beatrice. We'll simply have to forbid her to see this Gerald again, much as that seems to put me in the role of stern father, which I can't care for. I'm still wondering how Chelfham knew, what made him suspect me."

"And me," Eleanor pointed out, sitting down beside him.

"Only through me," Jack said absently. "I'm the one who made a misstep somewhere. But again, the only thing he can't know is why I'm interested in him — whether I want to join him or if I think I can destroy him, take him out of the game as I take over his enterprise."

Eleanor's mood, that had been caught

between her fears for Jack and worry for the success of the entire mission — and concentrating more on Jack than any thoughts of the Red Men or Chelfham or even her family — brightened considerably at these words.

"You're right! He can't know that you work with the Black Ghost Gang rather than by yourself or with some other group. Nothing in your journal or anywhere in your desk implicates anyone in Romney Marsh, thank God, but only indicates that you are involved in freetrading. Lists of delivery dates, the cargos delivered, that sort of thing. You could simply be an . . . an opportunist."

Jack grinned. "Why, Eleanor, I think I'd be insulted, except that you're correct. I am an opportunist, and I've prided myself at being damn good at it over the years, too, until this afternoon. I only wish I knew for certain how he tipped my lay, as Cluny would term the thing. I was so careful. *Thought* I'd been so careful."

Eleanor was so excited with this new idea that she put her hand on Jack's as she said, "We were looking at this from entirely the wrong perspective. Let's begin again. *We* know what we're about, but all the earl can know is that you keep a journal that reveals you are somehow involved in the smuggling trade, whether that be in financing ventures or some other area, and that you have taken great pains to be introduced to him. Correct?"

"Correct," Jack said slowly. "He doesn't know about the Black Ghost Gang, knows nothing about you or your family — again, thank God. And now we've been invited to Chelfham's ball, haven't we?" He turned and put his hands on Eleanor's shoulders, pulled her in for a quick, hard kiss. "Maybe, wife, just maybe, all our worrying is for nothing, and I'm about to be invited to quite a different party."

Eleanor sat there, stunned by the kiss, Jack's words only slowly penetrating her brain. She'd been worried for no reason. "It's . . . it's exactly what you wanted, what we planned, no matter that nothing happened quite in the way we planned. The earl is going to invite you — and your money — to become a part of the Red Men Gang. We almost have him!"

Jack rubbed his thumbs against Eleanor's upper arms, wondering if he could dare kiss her again. "Don't forget the other possibility, Eleanor, in which case you could be a widow by the end of the week."

The complete panic that flashed in her eyes was like balm to Jack's soul. Could he believe that Eleanor was more worried for him than she was dedicated to exposing the Red Men Gang?

"You're not amusing, Jack," Eleanor said at last, shrugging free of his hands and getting to her feet, her back turned to him as she hugged her arms to her waist. "We're playing a very dangerous game here and we can't assume or dismiss anything."

Jack got to his feet and stepped close behind Eleanor, his hands once more on her arms as he bent his head to whisper in her ear. "Why, Mrs. Eastwood, I do believe you're worried about me."

Eleanor closed her eyes, longing to lean back against him, give herself over to him even if he was only teasing her. "Jack . . . I —"

"Or are you only worried about yourself, your family?" he asked her, damning himself, but unable to hold back the question that had been burning in his brain for days. "Are you here to help me, Eleanor, or were you sent to watch me?"

She wheeled about in his arms, shocked to the core by his words. "What? What are you saying to me, Jack? We *trust* you. Don't you trust us?" *Don't you trust me?*

"Ah, there she is, the sweet innocent Eleanor. Butter wouldn't melt in her mouth." Jack wanted to stop. Stop talking. Stop destroying the little he thought there might be between him and Eleanor, the much more their association might become. "I'm a fool, Eleanor, a damn bloody fool, and I very nearly let myself care for you, let myself believe you might care for me. Hell, I was idiot enough to think maybe you'd *been* caring for me for a long time, before I at last opened my eyes and finally looked at you."

"Jack, I don't know what you're —"

He smiled bitterly, shook his head. "This is all a game, isn't it, just as you said? A dangerous game. You, me, Chelfham, Ainsley, even Jacko. All a game of who trusts whom. And now I know. I'm the employee. I should have remembered that. I'm not a Becket. Tolerated, but never quite accepted, never quite trusted, never quite one of you. I could have lived with that, Eleanor, if you'd just stayed the hell out of my way, kept me from having ideas I never should have had."

Eleanor's heart was pounding furiously as she saw the pain in Jack's eyes, knowing she had put it there. Was amazed that she could put such pain there. "Jack, you're wrong.

Papa trusts you, we all do. There's nothing . . . nefarious going on here, I swear it. And we're getting close now. We'll soon know everything Chelfham knows."

He felt incredibly sad. Looking in those huge, innocent brown eyes, knowing she was lying to him. It would be so easy to say he trusted her. Kiss her. Take her to his bed. Open that damn last door between them. "I saw your portfolio, Eleanor."

She tried to step back, run, but his grip on her arms was too tight, even painful. "You . . . you had no right."

"We're not going to debate rights here, Eleanor. How long did you and Ainsley and the rest know we were dealing with Chelfham? If I hadn't guessed it myself, would you have eventually told me? You were even *there,* Eleanor. Poor little cloistered Eleanor Becket, she's never set foot off Romney Marsh. And I believed it. I believed it all. I'm a damn fool."

Eleanor could feel herself shutting down as she withdrew within herself, within her memories. "I should have told you. I was going to tell you."

"What? Did you say something, Innocent Eleanor? You whispered, but I think I heard it. You should have *told* me? Yes, Eleanor, you should have. Ainsley should have. But now I've figured it out on my own, haven't I? Well, at least you won't have to worry about sacrificing yourself by seducing the gullible hired help, will you? That should be a great relief to you. After all, there are limits, even for family."

Eleanor swung from her heels, acting, for once in her life not thinking, the flat of her hand connecting with Jack's cheek with a force hard enough to send his head sideways on his neck.

She, Eleanor Becket, who had never so much as raised her voice in her life, had just raised her hand to the only man in her life she had ever believed she could trust with her heart.

She turned and slowly, carefully, walked out of the room.

CHAPTER NINE

"You surely do know how to make a mess of things, don't you, boyo?"

Jack shot Cluny a look that might have terrified anyone who hadn't spent weeks on end in the muddy battlefields of the Peninsula with him. "She lied to me. You saw it, you saw the watercolors. How could I not call her on it?"

Cluny pursed his lips as if considering this, then said, "While you, my good friend and lieutenant, are as pure as the driven snow, with not a secret to you. You, who not so long ago said you weren't looking to apply for sainthood. A good thing, that, because what you'd be getting is fire and brimstone. How hard did she hit you?"

Jack allowed himself a small smile. "Hard enough. There are hidden fires to that woman, although I think she might have been as surprised as I was to find that out." He pushed himself up and out of his desk chair. "This is ridiculous. She didn't even come down for dinner. We can't go on like this. I should go apologize."

"For what, boyo? For peeking at her pretty pictures? Can you do that, and then not ask again about how they came to be in her portfolio? Your questions, her answers, and you'll be back where you started, with only another knock to your thick head to show for your trouble."

"I know that. But I think I've figured out what to do."

Cluny turned in his chair, put out his leg to stop Jack as he headed for the door. "Not quite yet, boyo. What have you figured out? Oh. Oh, no. You're going to trade secret for secret, aren't you? Jack, you can't do that."

Jack retraced his steps, settling one hip against the edge of the desk. "Why not? It seems logical. I show that I trust her, and she returns the favor."

Cluny sighed, shook his head. "Didn't think such a little dab could hit that hard, but she's rattled your brains, hasn't she, boyo? Think, Jack. She spills so much as a word of what you're planning to tell her, and the Beckets will be cutting you up and using you for bait, they will. Not to mention what they'll do to your loyal Irish friend. I have plans, boyo, and they include dying of simple old age."

Jack knew the risks. He'd spent most of the day circling the problem, looking at it from all angles. "I don't think she'll do that, Cluny. I think she was more disappointed in me this afternoon, for questioning her, than she was angry that I'd found something she obviously didn't want me to see. If I show her that I trust her — trust her with my life — she won't betray me."

Cluny pushed himself to his feet. "I think I'm going to be losing my supper any minute now," he said, pressing one hand to his ample belly. "What a bag of moonshine, Jack. Anyone would think you're soft on the girl."

"I respect her, Cluny. She's a very brave woman. Not a girl at all."

"Respect her, is it? What part do you respect most, boyo? Those big brown eyes? Or maybe that trim little figure?"

"Don't do that, Cluny," Jack said tightly. "We're friends, but don't do that, you understand?"

"O-o-o-oh," the Irishman said, holding out his hands as be backed up a few steps. "So the wind truly blows that way, does it? Never thought I'd see the day your good sense went flying because of a woman."

"Don't exaggerate the thing, Cluny," Jack

said, pushing away from the desk. "We've got a mission here, remember? Worm our way into Chelfham's good graces and let him lead us to the leaders of the Red Men Gang, and stop the drain on our purses. That's why we're here, that's why Eleanor is here."

"Even if she and that papa of hers already knew Chelfham was one of them, but didn't see the need to tell you?"

"Even if that's true, yes. We're in no more danger now than we were when we started this thing. Granted, Chelfham seems to be onto me, knows I'm in the same *business* as he, but that's what we wanted. We're close, Cluny, and getting closer. The more I think about it, the more it doesn't matter that Ainsley might have been a step or two ahead of me."

"And the flowers will come again in the spring, tra-la, tra-la." Cluny reached for his wineglass and downed its contents in one angry gulp, then threw the glass at the fireplace. "Then go on. Go! Tell her all your bloody secrets. Am I still to have your back?"

Jack knew his friend was angry, disappointed. "If you're still willing, yes. Now come on. I don't have to make my confession to Eleanor tonight, do I? Let's the two of us call for my coach and take ourselves for a ride down Bond Street, maybe stopping in somewhere for a — *what in hell was that?*"

Jack was running even before he heard the first high-pitched scream, for the sound of shattering glass, followed quickly by a muffled *thump,* seemed to have been right above his head.

He raced up the servant stairs three at time, Cluny already far behind him, and could smell smoke as he made the next landing. "Eleanor!" he shouted, heading straight for her bedchamber. "Fire! Cluny! Sound the alarm! *Fire!*"

He flung open the door in time to see Eleanor on her knees, rolling a screaming Beatrice inside a small rug. Behind her, the drapes were on fire. "Eleanor!"

"Jack!" Eleanor slapped at the carpet with both hands. "Something came crashing through the window and Beatrice tried to stomp out the flames. Her skirts caught on fire. Oh, God, the drapes! Hurry, Jack!"

He was already hurrying, pulling the bedspread from the bed and using it to beat at the flames that were crawling up the velvet draperies. "Get out, Eleanor! Someone will get the maid."

Eleanor's response to this demand was to quickly assure herself that Beatrice was in no further immediate danger, then rip off her dressing gown to use it to beat against the flames at the other side of the window.

"Damn it, Eleanor!" Jack didn't have time to physically remove her from the chamber, knowing that if the fire gained a foothold the house could be fully involved within minutes.

"Stand back from the window, Eleanor!"

Having beaten down the flames somewhat, Jack discarded the bedspread and yanked at the draperies, pulling both draperies and their moorings from the wall.

Eleanor immediately realized what he was trying to do and dropped her now-singed dressing gown in order to run to her dressing table. She picked up the small backless chair and returned to the window, using the chair legs to smash out the rest of the broken glass.

With Treacle's help, as the butler had come running as soon as he'd personally pulled the fire rope in the drawing room, Jack was able to shove the draperies past the window frame, so that they fell to the bushes that lined the rear of the mansion.

"Get some servants down there to douse

those draperies, make sure they don't smolder," he ordered Treacle, then pulled Eleanor away as several servants ran into the room, each of them carrying buckets of water they threw against the window wall and floor, even though the fire appeared to be out now, with the walls streaked with black smoke and only one fairly charred circle on the wooden floor.

In the middle of that charred circle was a brick tied with burned rags.

Mrs. Hendersen and Mrs. Ryan had already unwrapped the sobbing Beatrice, and the two older women helped the maid from the room. Jack could see that half the maid's skirts had burned, and her exposed leg was fiery red.

"You acted very quickly, Eleanor. It wouldn't have taken more than a few moments to turn her into a living torch," Jack said, his mind running in several directions, but that much was clear, and had to be said.

"Papa is very stern about the possibility of fire," Eleanor told him, amazed as she realized what she'd actually done, reacting without much in the way of conscious thought. "We have drills, as he calls them, the idea being that we react immediately to any threat of fire. Fire is a sailor's worst enemy, and a highly respected one."

"It's no less of an enemy here in London," Jack answered as he turned to look at Eleanor, whose face was streaked with black smoke. Beatrice must have been brushing her mistress's hair when the brick came through the window, because Eleanor's hair was loose and . . . "Christ, Eleanor. Your *hair.*"

Eleanor lifted a hand to her hair, but it wasn't there, at least not in the quantity she'd expected, at the length she was accustomed to. And what she did touch was brittle, hard. "I . . . I didn't realize . . ."

No, she probably hadn't. But Jack did. He realized that, in her determination to save Beatrice, Eleanor had put herself in grave danger. "Perhaps it isn't as bad as . . . well, as it looks."

"If it's as bad as it *feels,* it's fairly terrible. I suppose I'll simply have to cut it off, won't I?" Eleanor said, looking up at Jack's soot-streaked face. He seemed so far away. Everything seemed so far away, and faintly dark around the edges. "You're very dirty, you know."

"And now the pot is literally calling the kettle black," he told her, trying to smile as the servants bustled about, now attempting to sop up the water they'd splashed everywhere. "Come with me, Eleanor. You can't stay in here."

"Just one small moment, boyo," Cluny said from behind him. "You see this? Nobody tipped over a candle in here."

Jack took another look at the brick and nodded. "I know, Cluny. Tomorrow. We'll discuss this tomorrow. For tonight —"

"Already done. Two of your footmen on the front, two more on the back. All of them armed, so it's hoping we'll have to be that they don't shoot each other. Still think his lordship is your new bosom beau?"

"I said, tomorrow," Jack all but growled as he led Eleanor toward the connecting door to his bedchamber, only to find the door had been locked.

"I . . . I'm sorry, I . . . I can't seem to remember where I've put the key," Eleanor said, feeling even more vague. Honestly, what was wrong with her?

And then she swayed where she stood and Jack quickly swept her up in his arms, cursing under his breath as he brushed past hovering servants and into the hallway, barking out orders for a tub to be prepared in his chamber at once.

"You can put me down now, Jack," Eleanor said once they were inside his bedchamber. "I'm fine, really. I suppose I was simply . . . overwhelmed for a moment."

"How nice to know you're human," Jack told her with a smile, but not putting her down until she was directly in front of one of the large leather wing chairs flanking the fireplace. "Here, let me put your feet up on this table. Sit back, Eleanor. You've had a shock."

Eleanor watched, bemused, as Jack seemed to be everywhere at once, locating a small pillow he pushed beneath her feet after sliding off her ruined slippers, resurrecting a soft woven throw he tucked at her waist, fetching her a small snifter of brandy and ordering her to sip it slowly.

"Jack, sit down. Please," Eleanor said, embarrassed by his attention. "Look at your hands."

"What about my — oh," Jack said, holding his hands out in front of him, fingers spread, turning them over to get a good look at them. The backs of both hands were very red and, he began to notice, rather painful. "I'm only singed. What about you? Are you burned anywhere? Other than your hair, that is."

"My hair is quite enough, thank you," Eleanor said, holding on to the snifter with both hands, those hands trembling slightly as the enormity of what might have happened began to dawn on her. At first there was nothing to do but react to the sound of the shattering glass, to the sight of flames flaring upward when Beatrice had bravely but shortsightedly attempted to stamp out those flames with her foot.

Jack watched as Eleanor sipped at the brandy, then shivered and made a face, obviously having not experienced the strong taste until that moment.

God. When he'd seen her, saw her silhouetted against the growing flames . . .

"Why do you think he did this?"

Jack shook off his thoughts and looked at Eleanor. "Chelfham? Then we are agreed this was no random act. And here I thought I was such a wonderful fellow and he'd be happy to welcome me as one of his partners."

Eleanor was feeling warm from the brandy, very nearly giddy, in fact. "I suppose I shouldn't have to worry now about just what to wear to his lordship's ball."

Jack smiled at her courage. "But it doesn't make sense, Eleanor. What good is killing me without first knowing more about me? The scope of my . . . business. The routes, my contacts both here and across the Channel. Dead, I can tell him nothing."

"Yes, and if the man was going to take

aim at you, you'd think he'd plan something that held more possibility for success." Eleanor took another sip of brandy, beginning to think it didn't taste too terribly like one of Odette's medicines.

And then she had a thought, a very disturbing thought, one she couldn't possibly share with Jack. *Had he really been the target tonight? Or had she betrayed herself somehow? Had the fire just proved her right, proved Papa right?*

"Eleanor? You've gone white as ghost beneath those smudges," Jack said, putting his hand on her shoulder. "I didn't feel my injuries at first. Do you hurt somewhere? Is it your leg?"

"Uh . . . no. No, I'm fine." She tried to sit up more against the back of the chair. "I really do need a bath, though. Do you suppose someone could fetch one to another bedchamber and I'll —"

Jack gently pushed her back down. "You're staying here. Someone's bringing water for a hot tub and I'll have Mrs. Hendersen find some nightclothes for you somewhere since anything in your chamber has to smell badly of smoke."

"No, Jack, don't be silly. This is your bedchamber. I couldn't put you out. It's bad enough I have to be shifted. And I really should go check on Beatrice. Odette taught me a few things about ointments and such, and I know that nobody should put butter or lard on her burns because, well, I don't remember why, but I should go tell them to —"

"Eleanor, you're staying here," Jack said firmly. "It's settled. Ah, and here comes the first of the water for your tub. And Mrs. Hendersen, good. You'll take charge, please? Don't listen to a word Mrs. Eastwood says, for the poor woman is slightly delirious. She needs a good bath, fresh clothing, and to be tucked up in the bed behind me, all within the hour. And have someone bring some hot water to my dressing room."

"Delirious? Jack!" Eleanor tried to get to her feet but the pillow beneath her legs slid to the floor and she got herself tangled in the knitted throw. "Jack, I will *not* be put to bed like a child. Jack?"

But he was gone, the door to his dressing room firmly closed behind him.

"He must love you very much, Mrs. Eastwood," Mrs. Hendersen said, folding back the screen in the far corner to reveal a large, hand-painted tub. "Now, you just relax and we'll soon have you put to rights. Goodness, what on earth will we do with that hair?"

"Mrs. Hendersen, I have no idea, although I do believe scissors will be involved," Eleanor said on a sigh, then reached for the snifter and drank some more brandy. It probably wasn't what she should be doing, but it was the only thing that she could do at the moment.

Tomorrow, first thing, she had a confession to make. She'd already left it too long. The clear light of day might change her mind on the matter, but for now, the possibility that she, not Jack, had been the earl's intended victim seemed more than slightly plausible. . . .

CHAPTER TEN

Jack, dressed in a clean shirt and pantaloons, sat behind the desk in his study once more, looking appraisingly at Cluny, who was being remarkably quiet for a man whose ability to form an opinion was championed only by his willingness to share it with the world.

That silence, of course, didn't last too long.

"I have no choice. I have to alert Ainsley," Jack said, once the subject of the flaming brick had been discussed from every possible angle.

"Easily enough done," Cluny agreed, nodding his head. "Tuck up a note with our little Miss Becket as you shove her in the coach for her ride home."

"You sink your teeth into an idea and won't let go, don't you, Cluny," Jack said, getting to his feet. He'd had enough of sitting. Enough of thinking, of talking. "She stays here. I couldn't let her go in any event, not unless you and I both traveled with her, and we're not going anywhere."

"You think Chelfham would try to grab her somewhere along the road? Use her to get what he wants from you? Damn, boyo, you are thinking deep, aren't you. Kudos to you. Now, that said, what do we do with her? And don't try to tell me you're still thinking of trading secret for secret. We've no time for that sort of maudlin pap now. Chelfham's too close, and getting closer. And not, boyo, in case you're harboring any cheery thoughts, because he wants to be your new bosom beau."

"Eleanor and I had already figured out that he could go either way — ask me to pool our resources, or decide I was superfluous to his enterprise. He chose a strange way to eliminate possible competition, though, didn't he? I keep coming back to that, wondering about that. And trading secrets is exactly what I'm going to do, Cluny, the fire didn't change that. This house could have burned down around both our heads — it's time Eleanor and I were completely honest with each other, if we've any hope of finishing what we've started. What someone has started."

"Fair enough, boyo, it's your neck, and

I've never thought I'd enjoy an old age anyway," Cluny said, making his way to the drinks table. "You go do what you feel the need to do, and I'll stay here and dedicate myself to this lovely bottle here. Because, after tonight, it's definitely the water wagon for me until we get all this sorted out."

Jack smiled at his friend. "You've never ridden the water wagon for more than a week at a time."

Cluny hefted the bottle. "Exactly. Go to it, boyo, because that's all you've got."

Leaving Cluny with the bottle, Jack climbed the servant stairs, stopping outside the closed double doors to Eleanor's bed-chamber. Someone had rolled up a damp-ened cloth and placed it at the bottom of the door to contain the smell, which Jack considered a very good idea. He was careful to close the doors behind him when he entered the chamber, his nose quickly as-saulted by the lingering smell of burned velvet.

Treacle was in the room, actually holding a raw plank across the broken window as a footman nailed the thing into the woodwork above three others that were already in place. The remaining pair of large windows that looked out over the mews had been opened to the night breeze.

"Treacle?" Jack asked when he didn't see what he'd come to see. "There was a brick, just here . . . ?"

The plank now in place, the butler hurried over to Jack, stripping off his now badly soiled white cotton gloves. "Yes, sir, I removed it before questions could be raised. Shall I fetch it to you, sir?"

Jack shook his head. "No, there's no need. It's not as if our perpetrator scratched his name in the blasted thing before tossing it up here. How extensive is the damage?"

"Well, sir, we've already removed all of Mrs. Eastwood's wardrobe, to give it a good airing tomorrow, hoping to salvage most everything." He looked at the maids, who had hesitated in their work, then said, "A word with you, outside, if you please, sir?"

"Certainly." Jack preceded the butler into the hallway, then waited as the man checked to be sure the damp roll of cloth was once more shoved firmly against the bottom of the door, informing Jack that a similar roll of cloth had been placed at the bottom of the connecting door to his bedchamber. "Thank you, Treacle. I suppose you have a few questions? Possibly more than a few questions?"

"No, sir, it's not my place to ask questions," the butler said, and Jack detected more in Treacle than he'd previously seen. More than just a servant; this man had seen action somewhere.

"Well, I thank you for that, Treacle, because I seem to be damn short of answers at the moment."

"Yes, sir. I should tell you, sir, that Mrs. Ryan, although she wouldn't wish you to know, has a liking for a pipe each night once her duties are completed in the kitchens."

Jack bit back a smile. "Does she now. Good for her."

"Yes, sir, very fond of her pipe, sir. She takes it out in the mews, away from the house. But tonight, sir, she saw a man all dressed in black coming down the alleyway, all skulking-like, sir, and she stepped back into the shadows, thinking she was about to be stumbled over by some housebreaker. But then the man stopped, looked up at the windows, and the next thing Mrs. Ryan knew, there was this flash of fire, and it was heading straight toward one of those windows."

"She saw it all?"

"She dropped her pipe and ran fast as she could, sir, straight into the kitchens. It was me ringing the fire bell, and all of us there so quickly, because of Mrs. Ryan and her pipe. Poor woman. When she went back for it, it was to see it smashed on the stones. We're supposing one of the staff must had trod on it whilst they were gathering up the draperies."

"That, Treacle, or someone was warning her to silence, not that we'd want to point out that possibility to Mrs. Ryan before she tells us everything she knows. Did she get a good look at the man? Would she know him?"

"That she did, sir, and that she does." Treacle looked down the hallway, making sure it was empty of listening ears. "It was Beatrice's young man, sir. Mrs. Ryan saw his face clearly when he lit up that brick like a torch. His sleeve caught fire as he hefted the brick for the throw, Mrs. Ryan says, and he cursed a fair treat as he beat out the flames, some very unlovely words, then ran off. Poor Beatrice. She'll be horrified, sir, to know that her young man did this."

"Beatrice has enough to worry about with her burns. She doesn't have to know anything else, Treacle, if we don't tell her. Can we trust Mrs. Ryan's discretion?"

Treacle smiled conspiratorially. "Her discretion and a new pipe, sir?"

"Done. Now, if that's all? I'd ask if there might be something you'd like, but I don't wish to insult a soldier for doing his duty as he saw it."

"Yes, sir! If I may, one thing more. Beatrice asked for me to tell Mrs. Eastwood that she's very sorry but she thinks she's all done with initiative."

Jack was still smiling as he rapped lightly on the door, then entered his own bedchamber, to see only a single bedside candle burning in the darkness. He approached the bed, and there was Eleanor, smack in the middle of the large mattress, half-propped up against a multitude of pillows.

And soundly asleep. In his bed, just as he'd imagined her. He simply hadn't imagined her asleep. He definitely hadn't imagined her lying there alone.

He didn't know how long he stood beside the bed watching her sleep, and he didn't care if he stood there all night. She was safe. That was all that mattered to him.

Fortunes to be made. Deadly competition. Smugglers. Secrets on every side. None of this mattered, a realization that stunned Jack, as he was feeling something he'd never felt before, hadn't really known existed.

He cared more for this one small, confounding woman than he did anything else in this world. How in *hell* had that happened? How had he *allowed* that to happen?

How could he have avoided it, since he certainly hadn't seen it — whatever *it* was — coming at him. He was suddenly here, in a place he didn't understand, feeling emotions he hadn't known possible.

Eleanor muttered something under her breath, then turned away from him, and in the small light thrown by the candle he suddenly noticed her hair, or the lack of it. Someone had been at it with a scissors, or possibly a very dull knife, as the shoulder-length locks were decidedly uneven. Free of most of its weight, her hair seemed to be attempting to curl, although Jack wasn't sure if that could be called an improvement.

Poor little thing, shorn like a sheep, except that sheep were better treated.

Not taking time to think about what he was doing — why waste time considering options he wasn't going to take — Jack half knelt on the mattress and leaned over to touch a hand to her hair. Her damp, slightly warmed hair.

A few stray tendrils had fallen onto her cheek, and he carefully smoothed them back away from her face.

Slowly, so as to not disturb her — after all, she might send him away if she woke — he levered himself onto the bed and stretched out beside her, his head propped on one bent arm, his left hand free to stroke her hair, watch her profile as she slept on, unaware of his presence.

So this was what was meant by "a full heart." His heart did feel full, even the pain of longing only a pleasant ache, a fullness that actually made him smile.

And then Eleanor opened her eyes and turned, looked up at him. "I . . . I thought I was dreaming."

Again. Thank God I didn't add that. Again. Dreaming of Jack. Again.

"I came to check on you," Jack told her, knowing he'd told a more convincing lie at age five, when his mother had caught him attempting to sneak out of the kitchens with an entire apple tart and he'd said he had planned to share it with his cousin Richard. "Someone's cut your hair."

Eleanor pushed herself up against the pillows, still not quite sure she wasn't dreaming. "There was no alternative, unfortunately. And it smelled terribly. Mrs. Hendersen tells me her cousin is a hairdresser, and she'll summon him tomorrow, to snip at it some more."

"Her cousin? Does he know what he's doing, do you think?"

"Does it matter? I doubt I could look

much worse," Eleanor said, wincing. "It's already starting to curl, which I hate. My sister Cassandra looks very sweet in her curls, and quite young. Curls are for children, don't you think?"

Jack reached out to touch her hair once more, allowing one sleek dark curl to twine itself around his finger. "I don't find your curls to be at all . . . childish," he told her honestly. "In fact, I find them very intriguing. More intriguing by the moment, actually."

"Oh," Eleanor said in a very small voice. Then she realized that the square neckline of Beatrice's night rail had somehow slipped sideways, falling down over her right shoulder. She attempted to pull the material back up and over her shoulder, only to have the neckline gape just at the center, so that she all but slammed her hand against her chest.

"Here. I think this solves the problem," Jack said, pulling up the silk sheet he'd commandeered from one load of cargo from France. "There," he said, once Eleanor had grabbed at the sheet and tugged it up to just under her chin, "more comfortable now?"

"Not really, no," Eleanor admitted honestly. "I . . . I've never had a man in my bed, you understand."

"You're in *my* bed, if we want to be precise about the thing," Jack told her, then dared to finish, "just where I've imagined you these past few interminable nights."

Eleanor shut her eyes, allowed the shiver to wash over her, then looked at Jack. "You shouldn't be saying that. And I shouldn't be listening."

He moved closer. "There are a lot of things, a multitude of things, we shouldn't be doing, Eleanor. Many more we shouldn't have done, either of us. Strangely, at least for the moment, this moment, I don't care. Do you?"

Eleanor raised her eyes to the underside of the canopy over the bed, took two quick, shallow breaths as she pictured herself as she lay there, in Jack's bed. In Beatrice's ridiculously overlarge night rail of simple white cotton. Her horribly butchered hair tumbled around her head. Both her hands maintaining a death grip on the sheet she held tucked straight up under her chin. Honestly, the man certainly did pick his times, didn't he?

"You . . ." She let go of the sheet she'd been using as a shield. "You are the most annoying man. . . ."

Jack smiled, surprised at his amusement

in the midst of the tension that was his building passion. "And you are the most exasperating woman. So controlled, so very *deep*, as in all still waters, I suppose. Can you blame me for wanting to know what lies beneath that serene surface?"

"I'm hardly *deep*," Eleanor protested feebly, thinking she might want to swallow now, except she seemed to have forgotten how one managed that particular feat. She was having enough difficulty trying to control her impatient breathing. "Really."

Jack slowly closed his hand around a fistful of silk sheet and began sliding it down, down. Out of the way, just as he longed for her night rail to be out of the way, his own clothing to be out of the way. Everything that lay between them, both here in this bed and everywhere else gone, out of the way. Unnecessary. Forgotten.

"And I say there's passion there, Eleanor. Hiding deep in those still waters. Hiding there, waiting for someone to bring it to the surface. Shall we see who's right?"

"Please don't ask me," Eleanor whispered. "If you ask me, I'll have to say no."

"Then I won't ask. . . ." Jack breathed against her as he lowered his head to hers, captured her mouth even as she opened it to say something else neither of them wanted to hear.

Her mouth tasted like the sweet tea Mrs. Hendersen had probably fetched for her, sweet and faintly milky, and for some reason he'd never understand, highly sensual. He couldn't get enough of her mouth, would never have enough of it.

He cupped his hands on either side of her head, her curls tangling around his fingers, entrapping him, enslaving him, and with his gratitude.

He kissed her closed eyelids, he suckled on the velvety softness of her earlobes, licked at the sensitive skin behind her ears . . . always returning to her mouth, that wonderful mouth, that soft, warm, welcoming mouth.

She'd been driving him quietly insane, even as he'd denied the tug, the urge, the demand he felt whenever in her presence. From the moment she'd looked at him in the traveling coach and damned him by saying she was flattered that he remembered her at all.

She'd pointed out his blindness when it had come to her, to the oldest daughter of the family, and he'd been kicking himself ever since for having spent two years running tame in the Becket household without once noticing the most intriguing, infuriating, intelligent, exasperating, *exciting* member of the family.

He'd been able to think of little else ever since, even as he tried to rid himself of the woman who could turn his comfortable world upside down, have him questioning his every move, his every motive.

What a fool he'd been! What a gift he held tonight.

He moved now, but not in a calculated way, only reacting to the signals Eleanor sent to him, whether she realized what she was doing or not.

Her soft moan against his mouth prompted him to slide a hand across her shoulder, down the length of her arm, twine his fingers with hers, use the pad of his thumb to draw small circles in her palm. Leaving the next move up to her . . .

Eleanor had never felt this way before, was having trouble absorbing all of her various feelings, all of the sensations warring for her attention. Her breasts seemed to long to be touched. How could that be?

Touch. Touch. She needed touch. She needed to touch as well as be touched. The word became a mantra inside her head. *Touch. Touch. Touch . . .*

She lifted her hand, guiding Jack's hand

to her breast, then gasped when that hand closed over her, as his warmth reached her through the thin cotton of her night rail, as the thumb he'd teased her palm with now moved in small circles just at her nipple. She reached her arm up and around his back.

"Jack . . ."

His name came to him quietly, a whisper in the dark, and he heard the question in Eleanor's tone, as well as the plea. She didn't understand what she was feeling, what was happening to her, yet she wanted to learn more.

He longed to teach her.

But slowly. Slowly. They had all night. Morning would come, and the walls might go back up, the problems, the differences, the secrets all coming back, brick by damning brick. But not tonight. Tonight was theirs. To share. To experience.

For tonight, all the walls had come tumbling down.

He kissed away her clothes, kissed each new revealed marvel of her even as he stripped away his own clothing, even as the bedside candle burned low then sputtered out, with only the small, dying fire to throw soft, wavering shadows over them.

She was so small, so perfect. That she

would entrust herself to him, that she would trust him, penetrated to his core, shook him, even frightened him.

He was not a gentle man. He'd never felt the need, nor even the desire, to be so. Until now. He'd die before he hurt this woman.

Yet he needed her. He needed her so badly. Needed her gentleness, her quiet courage. Her strength, so strong within that seemingly fragile female body.

When at last he entered her, caught her soft cry of surprised pain with his mouth, the need to possess her momentarily overtook him and his gentle assault intensified as he plunged deeply once, twice, before disciplining himself to move more slowly, leash his passion, brace himself so that the full weight of his body didn't crush her.

Eleanor felt herself spiraling out of control even as she lay still, her arms tightly around Jack's back, her palms flat against the rock-hard muscles beneath his smooth skin.

She hadn't known. How could anyone have possibly known? How did someone describe the indescribable? He filled her, he made her complete. She wasn't alone. Until now, she hadn't even realized that she'd been alone.

She wanted more of him. She wasn't sure how she knew there would be more, that there even could be more, but her body seemed to understand. She lifted her hips to him, to take him more deeply.

"Eleanor," Jack breathed against her ear, "are you sure?"

"I don't even know what I'm asking," she told him honestly. "But there's more, isn't there? I feel . . . I feel *hungry.*"

Jack raised his head, looked down at her. "I don't want to hurt you."

"I don't break, Jack," Eleanor told him, desperate to see his face in the dim firelight.

"No, you don't, do you," Jack said, and she thought she saw the flash of his smile before he kissed her, before he lowered himself more fully to her, began to move inside her once more.

Eleanor felt the spiral begin again, taking her higher even while tightening inside her, and she moved with Jack, allowing her body to dictate her response, beyond rational thought, all her carefully built control winging away without regret.

Not a dream. Reality. How much better to live in the world, rather than to simply stand back where she was safe, and observe it.

Jack heard Eleanor's soft cry even as he felt her climax take her, taking him with her, taking him beyond anything he believed he knew possible.

His body was sated, yes, but his heart had never been full before. Not like this. He didn't want to let her go, didn't want to leave her, held on to her tightly, was not amazed when the unfamiliar sting of tears pricked behind his eyelids.

"Eleanor," he said simply as he moved onto his back, pulled her against his side, kissed the top of her head as she lay very quietly.

"Hmm?" she asked muzzily, exhausted and exhilarated at the same time, with exhaustion, to her chagrin, beginning to take the upper hand.

"Nothing," Jack said, smiling into the dark. "Just . . . Eleanor."

"That's nice . . ." She snuggled more closely and was soon asleep. Jack remained awake, suddenly dreading the dawn. The inevitable dawn, the dangers they faced, and the wall of secrets that still stood between them. . . .

CHAPTER ELEVEN

Eleanor woke slowly, reluctant to leave her dreams. Then her eyes shot open wide as she moved into a slow stretch and felt a not uncomfortable awareness of her body, a small soreness that was almost pleasurable.

Jack. Not a dream at all. *Jack.*

She turned on the pillows, to find that she was alone. Thankfully alone.

She needed time. Time to think. Time to consider. Time to — "My hair!"

Eleanor wriggled to the side of the large bed and slipped to the floor, hunting for slippers she belatedly remembered had been ruined in the fire. Worse, she was naked.

"Oh, my God," she whispered, frantically pulling back the covers as she searched for Beatrice's night rail, then slipping it over her head, poking her arms into the overlong sleeves, nearly tripping over the hem as she headed for the large mirror hung over a table between the windows.

"Oh, my God," she repeated, dropping the material and lifting her hands to her head, to the jumble of wild curls that hung in ridiculous ringlets all at odd lengths around her head.

She hadn't cared. Last night. Just cut it all off, she'd told Mrs. Hendersen.

Now, this morning, she cared.

"What will I do? What will Jack say when he sees me? I can't let him see me!" She pushed her hands against her forehead, then pulled back her hair, pressing it to her head as she stared into the mirror. Was that better? No, it was worse. Impossible to be worse, but it was.

Eleanor took a deep breath, turned away from her reflection. "This is *not* important. In the scheme of things, with everything else that is going on, this is *not* important. This is a small thing. There," she told herself, holding her hands out in front of her and pushing down with her palms, figuratively pushing down her mounting hysteria. She, who was never flustered, never shaken from her own disciplined calm.

Except for yesterday afternoon when she *slapped* Jack.

Except for last night, when she'd . . . when they'd . . .

She would not die a maiden.

A giggle escaped her and she quickly covered her face with her hands.

"Ma'am? Are you all right? I knocked, but —"

"Mrs. Hendersen!" Eleanor quickly clasped her hands in front of her, took a deep breath, attempted a smile. "I didn't hear your knock."

"I'm sorry, ma'am. I've come to help you with your toilette, as Beatrice is in her bed and the doctor Mr. Eastwood had brought to her says she's to be there for two weeks, at the least. An entire fortnight, ma'am. I'll be shifting things, sending Mary to you, but I thought, for this morning, I'd tend to your needs myself, if that's all right?"

Eleanor desperately tried to assimilate everything the housekeeper was saying. Simple things, household things. Certainly easy enough to understand. Goodness, she'd been dealing with a household four times this size at Becket Hall. Surely she could manage a simple shifting of staff.

And what else? Oh, yes. She needed to see her bedchamber. Oversee the cleaning, the necessary redecoration. Her clothing! She should ask someone to please find a way to air out her clothing. And sleeping arrangements. She couldn't stay in here. Last night was . . . was an aberration. Possibly. Maybe. But she couldn't simply assume that everything had changed because last night had happened.

She should go into her bedchamber, take up pen and paper, start to make lists, beginning with the most important. What was most important?

"Mrs. Eastwood? You look sort of funny, pardon me for saying so. Are you all right?"

Eleanor raised her head and looked hopefully to Mrs. Hendersen. "My hair, Mrs. Hendersen. We start with my hair."

"Oh my, yes, ma'am, I can see that, begging your pardon again. My cousin will be here directly, as Treacle sent a footman to fetch him. Mary will soon be bringing you something to wear as we've managed to freshen most everything, although the blue silk, ma'am, seems reluctant to give up its smoky smell. But you aren't to fret about that, or about anything, ma'am. Mr. Eastwood was very clear about that. You are to rest, and so he said just before he went out."

"Jack — Mr. Eastwood isn't at home?"

"No, ma'am. He and that Mr. Shannon were tight as inkle weavers all morning, and then they both went off together. Mr. Shannon, he was looking angry and muttering in that Irisher way he's got, or so Treacle says."

"I see," Eleanor said, not *seeing* at all. "Did Mr. Eastwood happen to say when he'd be returning?"

"Oh, yes, ma'am. For dinner, ma'am. He stopped personal to see Mrs. Ryan, and tell her to snap her fingers and create a miracle, as he and Mrs. Eastwood would be dining together this evening."

"He said that? How . . . well, how nice. Mrs. Hendersen, if you will not mind a break in the routine I have set, I believe I'd like to repair to my . . . the bed and eat my breakfast there, resting just as Mr. Eastwood has directed as I wait for your cousin to arrive. Let us only hope that your cousin, as well as the always able Mrs. Ryan, proves capable of a miracle."

"I should hope so, Mrs. Eastwood. Oh, I almost forgot," Mrs. Hendersen said, reaching beneath her black apron and coming out with a folded and wax-sealed piece of paper. "This was delivered for you late yesterday afternoon, Mrs. Eastwood, but somehow did not come into my personal possession until this morning. I do hope it isn't important."

"Didn't come into your possession? I don't understand."

Mrs. Hendersen sighed in a way that said she was a woman overburdened with idiots.

"The person who delivered the note did not also pass over a small, um, remuneration, ma'am, so that the footman felt no urgency in passing the missive along to me. He has been disciplined. I'm so sorry, and dearly hope it is of only small importance."

"Our servants expect *tips* for doing their duties? London certainly is strange, isn't it?" Eleanor said, taking the folded sheet with some trepidation. She looked at the red wax seal to see that it was plain, with no crest imprinted on it. She turned over the paper, decided it probably wasn't an invitation. Yes, Jack had gone to see Lady Beresford, but if this missive was from that lady, surely her husband's crest would be imprinted on the wax.

Staring at the paper wouldn't tell her what had been written on it, so Eleanor thanked the housekeeper again, dismissed her, and crossed to Jack's desk and the letter opener she knew was there because she had been the one to dust the desk a few days earlier. A lifetime earlier.

She slid the opener under the hardened wax, then pulled back one of the draperies so she could have more light to read the letter:

Mrs. Eastwood,

You were so kind. I wish to be kind, also. Your husband plays a dangerous game I pray in my heart he will win. But I overheard them and they are planning something terrible against him. I would not wish to see harm come to you. If, for instance, there were to be a fire late one night? Could you flee fast enough with that unfortunate limp? Or would you be caught, trapped in the flames? I would think that to burn to death would be so very painful.

Your husband brings this danger to you and the danger will follow him wherever he goes. Show him this letter, impress on him that you must go, he must send you away where you will be safe.

I am powerless, but you are not. Leave London now, tonight. Go home, Mrs. Eastwood. I can do nothing else to help you and risk more than you know just in writing this letter. I implore you. Leave now, today! Hurry! Save yourself!

The fairly overwrought letter wasn't signed, but Eleanor knew who'd written it. Miranda Phelps. Who else could it be?

The woman had tried to warn her, and

only a servant's lapse had kept that warning from arriving in time. She'd taken some risk, and she'd betrayed her husband in doing so.

Eleanor read the missive again, and then again.

"Yes. She betrayed her husband in order to warn me. Not Jack, me. I'm the one who is to leave. *Save myself.*"

Eleanor laid the piece of paper on Jack's desk, then wrapped her arms around her waist and continued to look down at it. Read the words again.

Had Miranda conceived those words? On her own? Using her own initiative? Did Miranda Phelps *have* initiative?

Or had someone else dictated the words to her?

That seemed more likely.

Eleanor needed to talk to Jack. Explain to Jack. Now. Today.

He'd be angry. He'd have every right to be furious. With her, with all of the Beckets.

Eleanor looked toward the still unmade bed, longing to return to the dream, knowing reality wouldn't let her.

CHAPTER TWELVE

An early-morning drizzle had finally gone, leaving behind warm damp air and one of those uniquely thick, swirling London fogs that turned the afternoon into a yellow-tinged dusk. The Earl of Chelfham carefully picked his way down the wide stone steps leading from his private club.

He stopped on the flagway, looking about, then frowned and muttered something under his breath, obviously not a happy man.

He was about to discover that Jack Eastwood was a very angry man and, according to Jack's mental calculations, angry trumped unhappy every time. He and Cluny had argued, hotly at times, but in the end Jack had prevailed: he'd had enough of stealth; he wasn't very good at it. He would confront Chelfham head-on. Now. Today.

He fell into step beside the earl as the man approached a narrow alley on his way down the street, and within moments the earl's direction had been changed.

"Here now! Let go of my arm! What's going on? Eastwood, is that you? Is something amiss? God, man, you look so fierce, don't you? So sorry I can't linger, but I'm on my way to White's."

Jack, his hand still gripping the earl's arm just above the elbow, guided him a good twenty steps down the alleyway, to a place the sun hadn't reached in decades, although several generations of cats seemed to have found a use for the area. "Where are your shadows, my lord? You look rather naked without them."

"Harris and Gilly? They're the reason for all this melodrama?"

"Yes. Phelps and Eccles. You don't keep them close for their elegant conversation. They were supposed to meet you at your club, weren't they? They always do, every day at one. But not today. Would you like to know why?"

"You've killed them?"

What sort of question was that? And why did the man seem to be genuinely amused? "No, I didn't kill them. They've merely been detained so that you and I could have a private conversation."

Chelfham continued to rally. "Oh. Well,

more's the pity. Were I you, I would have had the Irisher slit their throats. You would have saved me a lot of trouble, had you snuffed them both out. They led you to me in the first place, after all. What a fine pair of fools."

The earl brushed down his coat sleeves and shot his cuffs. "Tell me, how is your little wife? I heard there was a fire. Terrible thing, fire."

This wasn't going as Jack had planned. The man should be terrified, not behaving as if he knew what Jack was after, and why. "So you admit it? You sent someone to burn down my house, kill us?"

"Don't be any more stupid than you can help, Eastwood." Chelfham removed his curly brimmed beaver hat and stroked a hand over his bald pate. "I *did* have you warned so you could get your wife out of there, poor little cripple that she is. I'm not entirely heartless. The note was very specific. If she was hurt it's on your head."

This was getting worse and worse, the older man somehow turning the tables, putting Jack on the defensive, sending him off balance. "Warned, you said? I don't believe my wife and I received that warning."

"No? Harris bungled that, as well? Your

house was never meant to burn down, by the way, but simply to be . . . singed a bit."

Jack had wondered about that. The fire had come too early in the evening to catch them all unawares in their beds. He realized he had been used, and had responded just as the earl had figured he would. "Did you also plan that I should come straight to you afterward?"

"I couldn't be sure," the earl said with the ring of honesty. "A coward would run away, and you've now proved you're not a coward. A righteous man would have had his knife between my ribs by now. But I'd already ascertained that you're not a righteous man. I'll admit, however, that I hadn't considered that you might remove Harris and Eccles from the board, thus opening me to personal attack. My mistake, I'm sure."

"No. Mine, I think, for not killing you the moment I dragged you off the street."

"Ha! Bravado comes too late, Eastwood. I know your sort, and killing me would be murdering what you believe to be your golden goose. Greed. That's why you're here. It's amazing, isn't it, the power that emotion has over us all? So, shall we stop all of this silly posturing, take the gloves off and get down to business? After all, we both know what we want."

Jack felt perhaps he was beginning to understand. "So the fire wasn't meant to kill me, but to see if a little danger might scare me off. You didn't even consider inviting me in until you'd tested me. But you are going to invite me in now, aren't you? Now that I've shown what a greedy bastard I am?"

"Yes, I suppose I am. Ever since I began eliminating my competition, I've been waiting for you or someone like you to come along, hoping for some sort of compromise — those on the losing side most often would rather compromise than be annihilated. And then, suddenly, there you were. I can't say I don't admire the way you thought you could worm your way into my company through my idiot, red-breasted brother-in-law. That was my suggestion, you know, that he wear those ridiculous red waistcoats. It's red flags that attract bulls, correct?"

Jack felt himself being fascinated against his will by Chelfham's devious brain. "But how? How exactly did you know?"

"That you were the one? Quite easily, in point of fact. You gave yourself away. As if a man with your obvious talents would want to waste more than a moment's time with my deplorably obtuse brother-in-law? Hardly, Eastwood. You're much too good at cards to lose quite so often. And to lose to Harris? Impossible."

Jack couldn't resist a self-deprecating smile. "All right, I'll grant you that. I was perhaps a bit too transparent in my pursuit."

"Don't pretty it up. Slipshod and much too anxious, that's what you were, while thinking yourself brilliant. You're smart, but not as smart as me. I don't intend to hang, Eastwood, and you're the sort who will, sooner or later, unless someone like me takes you in hand. I had to test you, didn't I? As I said, another man would have taken last night's hint to heart and beaten a hasty retreat. Yet here you are, caught between wanting me dead and licking my boots so that I'll invite you to become a part of my small . . . enterprise. Greed. I admire greed, I really do, as it has served me well over the years. Shall we talk terms now? You'd like that, I'm sure. But not yet. Promise to send the little cripple away, and then we'll talk. That was the main point of the exercise anyway, you know, as I was already fairly certain I had a use for you."

This made no sense. He'd damn near burned down the house to get Eleanor out of the way? "Eleanor? Why? What has my wife to do with this? Why would you want her gone?"

Chelfham looked at Jack through narrowed eyelids. "I don't like her, that's why. M'wife doesn't like her. She's deformed, Eastwood, and pregnant women shouldn't look on the deformed, the crippled. Why, the babe may already be marked, thanks to your wife. I had the devil of a time calming mine the other night and, well, she's made certain demands. When I please my wife, my wife pleases me. I don't think I have to be more clear than that, as you've seen the woman. So, do we have, as the tradesmen say, a deal?"

Jack picked his way carefully, refusing to allow himself to knock the man down for his insult. "I'll have to think about that, Chelfham. After all, Eleanor and I are only recently wed. What excuse could I have to send her away? Can't we compromise on this? She stays, but just keeps out of your wife's line of sight? I've got my contacts, both here and in France. I've got boats, men, safe places to store the cargo. I do bring a lot to the bargaining table, Chelfham. Granted, I don't operate on the same scale as your Red Men Gang, but —"

"Tut-tut-tut. We don't bandy that name about, Eastwood, ever. Your life is already worth nothing if I tell him how you have pursued me. Mine, too, for that matter. You have no idea what he could do to you, what he can do to anyone who gets in his way."

Interesting. "He? But you're the one in charge of the Red Men."

Chelfham snorted. "I'm not stupid enough to believe that. There is only one *real* leader, Eastwood. We're all the rest of us nothing but minions, chosen and tolerated only as long as we serve a purpose. Freetrading. That's *my* purpose. Tea and brandy and fine silks. But there's so much more. Tentacles, reaching everywhere, into everything. More than a young puppy like you could even dream."

What was there beyond money? Power? Yes, power. And money buys power. Jack pushed for more information, keeping his expression one of awe mixed with curiosity. "One man? One man controls so much?"

Chelfham seemed to like having an audience, and kept talking. "You have no idea what he controls. Freetrading? The Red Men themselves? A means only, not an end for him. Frankly, I'm growing weary with the whole of it. Working, taking all the risks — you found me, didn't you? — and then handing the majority of the profits over to him."

He shook his head, paused a few moments, then looked levelly at Jack. "Look, Eastwood, I'm a reasonable man. Comply with my demand — not a terrible demand, after all — and send your wife away. Then I will bring you in, and only then. You've got bottom, or you wouldn't still be here. I like that."

"What a twisted mind you have, Chelfham. You call that an invitation to do business with you?"

"Think, man. I had to treat you as an adversary, keep Harris from guessing my real plan. I didn't think you'd run, but I did hope you'd send the cripple away. Two birds downed with the same stone, as it were — or the same flaming brick. Show me you're sincere, send her away. Then it will be just the two of us, without Harris or his simpleton friend knowing, without *anyone* else knowing." Then he added, as if it was an afterthought, "He wants them gone anyway."

"*He* wants them gone. Not you — this other man. You are a minion, out of your own mouth. So tell me, why am I dealing with you?"

"Because I'm as close as you'll ever get. You want to stay alive, don't you? We'll enlarge on your little enterprise, you and I, add my money to it, then split the profits fairly between us. Forty percent for you? That seems fair. Either that, Eastwood, or take the cripple and what small profit you've made and use it to buy passage to Jamaica or some such place. Disappear. Because you already know too much, because this is my only offer, and because those are my conditions."

"And because next time it will be considerably more than a flaming brick. Yes, I begin to see your less than subtle strategy." Jack filed away the earl's mention of Jamaica. Eleanor's story included Jamaica, but no one had as yet heard that story. Coincidence? He thought not. "Or, since I really think I don't like you, Chelfham, I could simply turn you in to the authorities right now, and continue on as I am."

"You could. I'd be very sorry to do it, but I'd then have to turn you and Harris and his friend Eccles over to the hangman. I'd be mortified for everyone to learn that my beloved brother-in-law was dabbling in smuggling with you while under my roof. Damned upset. Why, I'd been quietly gathering evidence of his guilt, but had hesitated to turn it over to the Crown, worrying for my wife's health if she learned the truth. Sad. So very sad, don't you think?"

Jack chuckled ruefully. "So that's why you put up with him? Him and his scarlet waistcoat, his deep gambling? He's your carefully set up sacrificial lamb if anyone gets too close?"

"Sacrificial lamb? I like that. He does rather *bleat* when he talks, doesn't he? And, yes, every smart man has one always at the ready. I should know." Chelfham smiled a greasy smile that seemed almost painful. "You're a smart man, Eastwood. But not smarter than me. I've been playing this game a long time, as both pawn and bishop. I don't know how you figured out that I'm involved with . . . no, we're done discussing him. A man wants to die in his bed, preferably sated and still buried deep inside a beautiful woman, even if he did have to buy her."

Jack watched as the earl sauntered toward the flagway, then followed after him, feeling the fool. An impotent fool. "You're afraid of your own partner?"

"Never equal partners, remember? Not you with me, not me with him. There is only ever one block at the top of every pyramid." The earl looked back at Jack, smiled. "And let's just say I've watched him long enough, so that I've learned how to survive. You could learn that from me as we both get very rich."

"Become your protégé, you mean, as you betray this man you so obviously fear? You continue to work with — for — him, with the two of us quietly building our own private empires. With you in charge, of course, as there is only one stone at the top of every pyramid." Jack gritted his teeth and said the words. "I'd be honored, my lord."

"And there's the answer I've been waiting for. Good for you, Jack! He'll never know about us, as he doesn't dirty his hands with details as long as his profits remain constant. You operate on Romney Marsh, correct? One of those ragtag bands that smuggle small cargos up and down that inhospitable bit of coastline? I've been having some fun there lately, there and in one small stubborn corner of Cornwall, dissuading people from dealing with these smaller gangs. I'm guessing the Marsh. Whichever it is, you wouldn't have come looking for a partner at all if your enterprise weren't already in trouble."

Jack thought it was time for a bit of patently false blustering on his part. "Then you'd be wrong, on all counts. I still maintain all my contacts. Whatever you think you're doing to anyone else, it hasn't affected me. The only reason I found you is because you've been slipshod, not me."

"Oh, please, Eastwood, don't insult me, not when we're only beginning what will be our lucrative association. I know where you operate from because we've *got* everything else. And you've come to me at just the right time. Harris and his friend clearly have outlived their usefulness. I need someone who can do the, shall we say, dirtier work. Last night's debacle proved yet again that my brother-in-law is not up to the task. My God, man, you and your little bride could have been burned up in your beds. You really didn't get the dumpling's note?"

Jack rubbed at his temples, where his head had begun to ache. "You sent a note. You actually did that? Warned me, then set my house on fire? And all to have me understand that I'm vulnerable if you want me to be, and to have me fear for my wife's life, send her away."

Chelfham spread his arms wide. "What can I say, Eastwood? I'm a man besotted by his wife."

"You could be a dead man. I could have killed you back there, and I was tempted," Jack pointed out as the two of them walked along the flagway, toward White's. "I could still kill you for the insult to my wife. In fact, I believe I'd enjoy that."

"No. No, no, no. Don't bother to posture and bluster now, man, because I won't believe you, you've left it too late. Join with me, Jack, just the two of us, and I can protect us from . . . from the man atop the pyramid."

"Just the two of us," Jack repeated, stopping on the flagway, so that the earl also stopped, turned to look back at him. Jack needed to be absolutely clear on this one point. "Does that mean what I think it means?"

The earl's smile beamed through the swirling fog as he walked back to Jack. "See? Not a stupid man. I was counting on that. Get your wife gone, please, before you dispose of them. My wife will have enough on her plate, what with ordering mourning clothes to honor her brother."

Jack kept his features blank. "Just a small question, my lord. How often do you feel this need to . . . change partners?"

"Worried, Jack?" Chelfham clapped a hand on Jack's back. "Good. It's never wise to become complacent, is it? Now, get that wife of yours gone and we'll be partners in earnest."

"That may take a few days," Jack told him,

then asked the question most important to him. "We met in Jamaica, my wife and I. Did you know? You said Jamaica earlier."

"I did? Oh, of course. Your wife told mine," Chelfham said quickly. Too quickly? "Yes, I'm sure that's it. Now you've kept me long enough, and I'm late for an appointment. Damn!"

Jack watched as Chelfham pushed his bulk into a trot, heading toward White's. He didn't go inside, but approached a man just then climbing into a fine black coach drawn by four coal-black, perfectly matched horses.

The opened door of the coach quickly obscured the man from Jack's sight, but he could see that the fellow was well dressed, tall, with quite long legs.

Chelfham piled into the coach behind the man and the door slammed shut, the horses moving off, the coach moving directly past Jack, who had stepped into the mouth of yet another narrow alleyway. There were no markings on the door of the coach, no coat of arms. The driver and footmen wore plain black livery.

The shades were drawn.

"Those tits cost somebody a pretty penny."

Jack looked to his left to see Cluny had

come up beside him and was also watching the town coach and its matched hackneys move off down the street. "Remember that coach. We may go looking for it someday soon."

"And good luck to us then," Cluny said, sniffing. "Could be any of hundreds, save for the tits."

"Then we watch for those horses."

"Yes, and that's just what I've been longing to do with my days, don't you know. Could there perhaps be a reason?"

"Possibly. We might have just caught a glimpse of the top stone of the pyramid, Cluny," Jack said as the two men walked toward the corner, where Jack's own closed coach waited. "Where are Phelps and Eccles? Chelfham would like them weighted with chains at the bottom of the Thames."

"Then it's disappointed the man will be when they both show up again, isn't it? It's a long way from a faulty wheel on a carriage to the bottom of the Thames. What happened with his high-and-mighty lordship?"

"Quite a lot. I'm to send away my crippled wife because his wife thinks the mere sight of her will mark her unborn child, and then I will be taken in as Chelfham's fairly minor partner as he uses me to betray the true leader of the Red Men Gang or whatever the whole is called, if it's called anything. Right after I remove from him the burden of his brother-in-law and the hapless Eccles, both of whom seem to have become dispensable. Our friend Chelfham is a very interesting man, and he believes me to be a greedy and not too bright fool. He also knows about you, by the way."

"He does now, does he? Boyo, have you considered that we may have bitten off a bigger bite than we can easily swallow? You were looking for your cousin, remember? Now we're up to our necks in Red Men and Black Ghosts. I don't like this, boyo, and I find myself wondering more and more about this Ainsley Becket of yours. There's more going on here than we either of us know. I can feel it in my shins."

They climbed into the coach and headed back to Portland Square.

Jack settled himself against the squabs, his weariness having more to do with facing the hours ahead of him than with the fact that he'd not had much sleep the previous night. "Make yourself scarce tonight, Cluny, if you will."

"You still plan to tell her everything? Ainsley Becket's daughter?"

Jack scrubbed at his face with both hands,

then looked at his friend. "Do I have a choice?"

"You do that, boyo. Send her away. I say it, Chelfham says it."

"Yes. But I know *why* you say it. Something else is going on here, Cluny. I can feel it, almost taste it."

"There's nobody following you save me, boyo, not unless whoever it would be is a lot better at the job than I am. The woman is their spy, and a good one, for who would think a little thing like that could be so devious? They just don't trust you, that's the whole of it. You're with them, but you're not a Becket. That's just the way of things in this world."

Jack remembered holding Eleanor in his arms. That was no sham, what they'd done, how they'd felt. How he'd felt. "I think you're wrong, Cluny," he said, then added quietly, "Christ, I hope you're wrong."

CHAPTER THIRTEEN

Eleanor sat in the drawing room with her leather case open on her lap, paging through the watercolors she'd painted from memory, or what she thought to be her memory.

Knew to be her memory . . .

Jacko had taken her portfolio with him when he'd gone off for over a week a few years ago, then come back to her with them. He'd walked into her bedchamber unannounced, handed her the watercolors, nodded his head once, and then left again.

Neither Jacko nor Eleanor nor her papa had ever spoken more than a few times about the watercolors, what they meant, what any of her slow, painful recollections meant. The implications. She hadn't told Jacko that she'd also remembered what had happened that last terrible day, and his part in the horror. All she'd at last said to her papa was that she had decided she would be happiest remaining at Becket Hall . . .

and he had agreed.

Some things, things that could not be changed, were best left alone. Her real name. Her childhood home. Jacko and those last minutes before her escape from Chance's arms and her terrified run across the flaming decks.

And Papa. Always, everywhere, the kind, gentle, guilty Ainsley Becket.

She should have destroyed the watercolors. But how could she do that, when they were all she had of the first six years of her life? She'd actually enjoyed looking at them, or had until she'd come to London.

Eleanor shut the case and propped it next to her seat before rubbing at her left calf, not even realizing what she was doing.

"Another cramp, Eleanor?"

She looked up, startled, because she had been waiting seemingly forever to hear the front door close in the foyer below, been listening for the sound of Jack's voice. "No, er, no, I'm fine, thank you." She sat up straight and folded her hands in her lap. "It's habit, I believe," she said, looking at him as he walked into the room, so very *male,* sending her thoughts slamming back to the previous night: how his body had felt against hers, the way he'd held her, the way he'd breathed her name, the way he'd brought her fully alive.

Now here he was, and she couldn't find any words, was more nervous than she'd been in her life. How could two people share such intense intimacy, then be unable to meet each other's eyes? Because Jack seemed to have developed some sort of fascination with the wine decanter he'd lifted, now held in his hand, still not removing the crystal stopper, filling his glass.

Eleanor felt her throat tightening, wondered where all the air in the large room had gone, because she was having trouble catching her breath.

Jack turned to Eleanor, holding up the decanter. He felt like a raw youth, and the feeling unsettled him, added to the anger he'd carried home with him. "Would you . . . ?"

"No. No, thank you," Eleanor said, then looked down at her entwined fingers. "Um . . . Treacle summoned a glazier and the window is repaired."

"Good for Treacle," Jack said shortly, carrying his full wineglass across the room, to sit down opposite Eleanor, taking his first really good look at her. "Your hair. It's . . . you look wonderful."

Eleanor involuntarily lifted a hand to her exposed nape. "I've been shorn," she said, looking at Jack. "It was all Stanley could do, I'm afraid."

"I hope we paid him well," Jack said, getting up from his seat and, wineglass in hand, walking all the way around the bench Eleanor sat on. Her thick dark hair was sleek, glossy in the candlelight, and none of it seemed to be more than two or three inches long. Spiking around her forehead, onto her cheeks, more spikes curling slightly, caressing her nape. Her eyes looked huge, larger than ever, and her high cheekbones and small, faintly pointed chin gave her the air of a forest sprite, a beautiful, fragile, perfect porcelain statuette.

God. And he'd held her. Made love to her. Gently, carefully, he had roused the simmering fire beneath the ice. Had that been only last night? It seemed years . . .

Eleanor shifted on the bench as Jack continued his visual assessment, feeling heat running into her cheeks. "I feel strangely naked . . . um, that is . . . not myself."

"Where are the curls?" Jack asked, longing to slide his fingers into the near-ebony thickness. "Last night there were curls."

"I know. Stanley . . . he found a way to cut them out, at least that's what he said. Mary, who's taking over Beatrice's duties for now, was taught how to brush it, keep it all from curling, and I'm quite happy about —" Eleanor gave up and turned to look at him. "Where were you all day?"

Jack smiled, wishing he could relax completely. But how could he do that? "You missed me, wife?"

"Stop that," Eleanor said, drawing on long years of riding herd on her siblings. "It was a simple, straightforward question and —"

"I missed you," Jack whispered, having leaned down to breathe the words into one cunningly exposed, shell-like ear. "Every minute. Every second."

She closed her eyes, allowed her body the reaction it would not be denied in any case. "You . . . you were gone so long."

"I know," Jack said, straightening, returning to his seat on the couch. She wasn't as calm as she appeared. Good. Because, God knew, neither was he. "It was unavoidable, I'm afraid. I had to see our friend Chelfham."

Eleanor's heart skipped a beat. "You *knew?* I mean, we both certainly had guessed that — you actually confronted him about the fire? Oh, Jack, was that wise?"

Jack felt another quick, unexpected shaft of anger in his chest. "Was it wise? Was *I* wise, you mean? That sounded very much like a reprimand, Eleanor. Am I supposed to consult with the Beckets on every move I make? Perhaps even beg permission? How remiss of me not to know all the rules."

Eleanor mentally slapped herself for speaking too quickly. "No, of course not, that's not at all what I meant. It's just that there was a note. I'll get it for you."

"No need," Jack said, wondering what was wrong with him. He'd nearly bitten her head off, this woman he cared for, worried about . . . had taken to his bed. "Chelfham said we'd been warned. What happened to the note?"

"Ridiculousness, that's what happened. It seems that whoever delivered it neglected to monetarily reward the footman, so he was in no rush to immediately pass it on to me. Then, of course, there was the fire, and the note was forgotten. The note, the warning, didn't come into my possession until late this morning. It was addressed to me, you see, warning me about the fire, warning me to leave at once because your . . . activities had put me in danger."

"Damn," Jack said, almost to himself, then looked levelly at Eleanor. He hadn't been overreacting, reading too much into Chelfham's words, his reactions. The fire had only been marginally meant for him; Chelfham's assertion he was testing Jack's mettle sounding too convoluted to make real sense. Eleanor had been the real target, probably the only real target. "I don't understand. Why is he so damn hot to get you gone?"

Eleanor sighed, knowing the moment had come for her confession, and much too soon. One night, that's all they'd had. And now that one night would have to sustain her for the remainder of her lonely life. "I should have told you. I didn't consider it possible, none of us could have considered such a thing, but I believe he thinks —"

Jack went on as if she hadn't spoken, still pummeling his own brain for answers. "You're a cripple, the bastard said. A *cripple*. His bitch wife can't stand to look at you. Damn the man, how I wanted to knock him down for that."

Eleanor's jaw dropped, but she quickly recovered. "That's what he said? He actually said that?"

Pulling his temper back under control, Jack explained. "I'm sorry, Eleanor. That is what he said. That he'd had Phelps's wife pen the note warning you, so that you'd leave London. The fire was only meant to bring home the warning, make it real.

Because Chelfham's wife is increasing and she's hysterical that looking on a . . . looking on a person with a limp might somehow mark her baby."

"I see," Eleanor said, her heart pounding. Perhaps she'd been wrong. Perhaps she could keep her secret another few days at the very least. Steal herself a few more memories with Jack before he had to be told. "That was his reason?"

"No," Jack said, shaking his head. "That's what he *said,* what he wants me to believe. I've yet to discover his reason. Does he have a reason, Eleanor? Do you know what it is?"

This wasn't going at all as Eleanor had planned, had even rehearsed the moment. She had been going to work up to what she had to tell him. Slowly, carefully. And now, just as she'd thought she might have gained a short reprieve, he'd put the question to her again. "Why would you think there's another reason?"

At last Jack pulled his full attention back to Eleanor. Something was very wrong. She was sitting quite still, looking as serene and composed as she always did, but Jack knew her better now, watched as she leaned down to rub at her calf, then caught herself in the motion, and sat up straight once more.

"Chelfham mentioned Jamaica, Eleanor,

suggesting I take you there if I felt the need to retire from . . . from the field, as it were," he said, weighing his every word now because he knew each one to be extremely important. "He said you'd told his wife that we'd been in Jamaica. Did you tell her that?"

"No," Eleanor said, squeezing her hands together in her lap. "Our conversation never became quite that personal, what little there was of it. Jack, this is getting us nowhere. Tell me what happened with the earl, and we'll go on from there, all right?"

"Because there's somewhere to go from there, isn't there, General Becket?" he asked, still finding it difficult to believe that the soft, willing, even eager woman he'd held in his arms last night had become the quiet, nearly withdrawn woman he faced now. A creature of secrets. A wall had come up, one he'd hoped gone, and he didn't know what to do about it, how to fight it, beat the damnable thing down again. "Very well, first things first."

He told her all about his conversation with Chelfham, about the man's offer, repeated the man's demand, and ended with his belief that he'd caught a fleeting glimpse of the real leader of the Red Men Gang.

"And not just the real leader of the smugglers, Eleanor. According to Chelfham, freetrading is only one small part of what this mysterious man in the black coach is into — the financing arm of a much larger enterprise, I guess we could call it. In other words, we may have stumbled into a hornet's nest far beyond anything we imagined."

Eleanor only nodded, still concentrating on something else Jack had told her. "He really wants you to *kill* those two men? His own wife's brother? What a horrible man. What did you say to him?"

"I didn't say yes or no," Jack told her, then smiled. "Which, now that I think about the thing, was probably as good as a yes to Chelfham. But to get back to this mysterious head of the pyramid — I think we need to get word to Ainsley about him. If the man is as powerful, and dangerous as Chelfham seems to believe he is, it probably is time we all retired from the smuggling trade. We've had a good run, but we may be in over our heads. This is serious business."

"Papa would never do that," Eleanor told him confidently. "The people on the Marsh rely on us, on the protection of the Black Ghost. They're virtually defenseless without us, even more so now that we know it's definitely this Red Men Gang that's turned its eyes back on us. I had thought the worst of the danger over when —" She broke off, looked down at her hands once more.

Jack got to his feet, alert to her every nuance now, any small betrayal of the secrets that stood between them. "Another secret, Eleanor? Something else that can't be shared with the hired help?"

"Yes. No! I — Jack, we couldn't have known this would all become so . . . complicated. I just wanted to see . . ." She lifted her clasped hands, pressed them against her chin. She took a deep, steadying breath as she looked at Jack. There was no turning back now. "Rawley Maddox is my uncle."

Jack had considered several possibilities as he'd been driven back to Portland Square, but not this one, never this one. He sat down again, leaned forward, his elbows on his knees. "Chelfham's your uncle," he repeated, trying to push the news more firmly into his own head, he supposed. "And you knew this? Ainsley knew this? What am I saying? Of course you all knew. Sweet Jesus."

Eleanor avoided Jack's intense gaze. Sitting on the unyielding bench, she felt like a prisoner in the dock. But when she spoke it was dispassionately, and very carefully. Not all secrets were hers to tell. "Yes. We knew. We didn't, not for more than a decade, I believe, but then I began to have these . . . dreams. I began to remember things, things I'd forgotten, certain events the child I had been most probably wanted very much to forget. Then . . . at about the age of eighteen, I believe, I suddenly remembered my given name. I was reading a novel, you see, and a character in the book had that same given name and . . . well, then after that, everything seemed to come rushing back in strange bits and pieces. Slowly, as they became clearer, I even began painting my memories."

Jack sliced a look toward the portfolio leaned against the side of the bench. "Childish memories. A pond with small boats on it. Trees and rolling hills. Swans. A large white mansion in the distance. Nothing like Romney Marsh or Becket Hall."

She looked at him in surprise. "You looked at my portfolio? When?"

"After our rather infamous dinner party," Jack said, grabbing a straight-backed chair and carrying it over to place it in front of Eleanor, back to front, then straddle the thing as he continued to look at her. He did his best to appear calm, invite further confidences. "And were your paintings correct? I'll assume someone checked."

Eleanor nodded. "Jacko. Once we knew

my name, everything else became relatively easy. My uncle had assumed the title and was even in residence when Jacko ... reconnoitered the estate. My watercolors were extraordinarily accurate. But we decided, all of us. There was no point in pursuing an association with the man. I was ... *am* happy where I am. I have a family."

Jack crossed his arms on the back of the chair, leaned his chin on his forearms, searching her face, watching her every emotion play across her features. He longed to hold her, but she looked so fragile he was afraid, in her tense state, she'd break, shatter in his arms. Better to let her speak, get all the information out where they both could see it, act on it. Then he'd retire to his chambers and punch a wall, or something.

"Assumed the title, you said. Your father was the older son, was the earl? I want to be certain I understand. You're the daughter of an earl? And Ainsley didn't *pursue* this?"

His gaze was unnerving, as was his tone, and Eleanor knew she'd be a fool if she didn't know he was quite upset. "No, Jack, I didn't want him to. In fact, I expressly asked him not to do anything. There's nothing I wanted that I didn't already have, and I possess no way of proving my identity in any case. I'd have to leave Romney Marsh. I'd . . . I'd have to explain my family, and how I became a part of that family."

"Your ship went down in a storm and they saved you," Jack said, frowning. "That's reasonable."

"Yes. Yes, it is. Perhaps I was too hasty," Eleanor said, anxious to move on with her story, not dwelling on any of the details Jack didn't need to know. "That night, when I overheard you speaking with Papa and Jacko? I heard my uncle's name and realized I wanted very much to see him. Not to declare myself, cause him any trouble. But just to see him. It . . . it seemed the perfect opportunity, and now this unknown uncle was possibly an enemy. I had to know, Jack, you can understand that, can't you? That wasn't unreasonable, was it?"

"I don't know, Eleanor. If it was all so *reasonable,* why didn't you tell me? Does Ainsley care so little for you that he'd just blithely hand you over to me so that I could bring you here, put you in danger from what we thought at the time could possibly be the head of the Red Men Gang? My God, Eleanor, sometimes I think all of you Beckets are insane, and that I'm even more insane to be involved with the lot of you."

"You're angry, and I'm sorry for that." She couldn't stand having him look at her that way any longer. Curious. More than a little upset, even disappointed in her, disappointed in the family he'd aligned himself with, not to put too fine a point on the thing.

"Angry is such a mild term, Eleanor, for how I feel right now. But that doesn't mean I can't think. Who else is here? In London. Who else is watching? How many Beckets are monitoring every move you and I make, every move Chelfham makes? If he or they contact you, be sure to invite them for dinner, won't you?"

Eleanor blinked, surprised by the question . . . then realized she shouldn't be. "I . . . I don't know if anyone *is* here. No one contacted me, told me. But that does make sense, doesn't it? Papa would want me to be safe."

"Yes. Which takes more than the hired help, obviously. Too bad none of them saw Chelfham's man about to set my house on fire. I may have to complain to Ainsley when next I see him."

"Oh, Jack, I'm so sorry. What a muddle this is." She got to her feet and walked behind the nearest couch, as if the piece of furniture could somehow protect her. "But, to be truthful, none of us thought anything would come of my being here. And you weren't even positive the earl was involved, remember? Yet you seem to think he knows who I really am. Isn't it much more likely he's telling the complete truth, and I have nothing to do with any of what's happening now? He's involved with the Red Men, we know that now. He'd like you to join your *business* with his. And his wife dislikes . . . cripples."

She was fairly certain she didn't believe the last thing she'd said, and convinced that Jack didn't believe any of it.

Jack got to his feet, pushed the chair away, speaking randomly, as different thoughts struck him. "We could swallow that whole, I suppose. Or we might consider that he could have recognized you here the other evening. You could resemble your mother very much. Something. He might not even realize exactly why he wants you gone, but just that the sight of you somehow make him uncomfortable — and I don't mean your limp, damn it."

"No, I know that's not what you mean."

"Well, thank you for that. Now let's see if we can agree on something else, all right?"

Eleanor wet her lips, swallowed her nervousness. "Such as?"

"Such as, Eleanor, if I were a fanciful man, I'd think a man like Chelfham might have had something to do with the death of your parents, as he got himself an earldom out of it, didn't he? But that's impossible, isn't it, because your ship went down in a storm. With a fire raging on the deck. Fire, in the midst of raging storm. Wasn't that it, Eleanor? And one thing more. You were sailing to Jamaica, weren't you, Eleanor? Either to or from Jamaica?"

She raised a trembling hand to her forehead. He was pressing so hard, too hard, and she was having trouble keeping her wits about her, her lies sorted. "I told you, Jack. I didn't even begin remembering anything until a few years ago. I was only a child, I may have muddled some of those memories."

Jack felt he was getting closer. "Chelfham knew, of course. He knew the ship was lost because it never showed up, either here or in Jamaica. He was the earl, assumed his dead brother's title and fortune. Lucky man. But now, all these years later, along comes a young woman who would be his niece's age, a young woman who looks very much like her mother — we'll just assume that, for the sake of our story — and he begins to wonder. Had his niece somehow

257

survived the shipwreck? And here I am, having just told him yes, I met my wife in Jamaica, which pretty much confirms what he is — possibly is — thinking. He set the trap by mentioning Jamaica, and I walked straight into it. Damn it all to hell, Eleanor! You and Ainsley should have told me!"

Eleanor nearly flinched, but held her ground. "We couldn't know, Jack. Do you really think he recognizes me? That seems fairly far-fetched."

"Why? I'm supposedly the living spit of my dead father now that I'm a grown man, to hear my mother's maid tell the story. It's possible, Eleanor. Anything's possible. And, since he's not exactly falling on your neck, shouting that he believes you might be his long-lost niece, we have to conclude that he's been made very nervous by your appearance here in London. Now, why would he be nervous if he had nothing to fear? Tell me all of it, Eleanor, because I'm beginning to think Chelfham believes I *am* in on the whole thing. Smuggling? The Red Men Gang? Is that really what I'm after from the man? Or am I pushing my wife in his face just before I demand money from him for our silence? Christ, what a confounding bloody mess!"

She couldn't tell him the whole truth. Not yet. Not without Papa's permission. But she could tell him something. "Do you remember when we spoke of the laws of inheritance?"

Jack nodded. "Vacated titles," he said slowly. "Titles in abeyance. Titles where he or she couldn't prove —" He stopped, astounded. "Chelfham's title can be inherited by a female?"

Eleanor's smile was indulgent. "No, that's very rare. I just wished to point out that I've had ample time to investigate everything about the laws concerning such things. I have, I admit, also spent quite a lot of time on this subject where it particularly concerns the Maddox family. It is left to the discretion of the current earl to dispose of unentailed properties and monies, jewelry, any way he sees fit. Papa — Ainsley — has, well, he has ways of finding out things, and it would appear my father had decided he did not much care for his brother, but that he made ample provisions for my mother and me. With my mother also . . . gone —" She paused, then finished. "I was to inherit two small properties and the London mansion, as well as quite a substantial sum of money."

"Having met Rawley Maddox, I can't

believe that eventuality made him a happy man. But if you and your mother had also perished, everything went to him?"

"Exactly. He would have been the only one left alive to inherit, as Papa pointed out to me. Coming to London, confronting my uncle, could only mean long years of struggle in the courts, all without much hope of being able to prove my claim. I chose not to pursue the matter."

"Because Ainsley's rich as Golden Ball anyway," Jack said with a half smile that quickly faded. "And because of the limp? Tell me truthfully, Eleanor. Did your leg have anything to do with your decision? Because, damn it, there's no reason for that."

"Thank you, Jack. My limp is a part of me, and I barely think of it." Eleanor's smile nearly broke his heart. "But I'm not like my sister Morgan. I feel no compelling need to stand up and dare the world. I'm happy as I am. I'm only sorry I didn't say something to you sooner. That wasn't only selfish of me, but dangerous for you."

"And you," Jack reminded her, his anger slowly dissipating, to be replaced by a sadness he didn't want to look at just at this moment. The sadness he felt as the outsider, looking in; invited in from time to time, but never asked to stay. Even now, as they were here, together in the same room, he could feel Eleanor slipping away from him.

It was time to speak of what was to come next. "Yes, it would appear it was dangerous for both of us. Do you want to send me back to Becket Hall? I'm more of a hindrance now, and would most certainly understand."

Jack went to her, took her hands in his; her cold hands. "We're only guessing about why Chelfham is so interested in you, Eleanor, even if I feel confident I'm right. And if I am, we can't take the chance he'd follow you . . . do something. He seems in quite a hurry to separate us. Keep me here, get you gone, out on the road. Unprotected."

Eleanor's eyes went wide. "Do something? Attempt to kill me, you mean?" She pulled her hands free and turned her back on Jack. "Sometimes I wish I'd never remembered. Everything was so much easier when I didn't know, couldn't *really* know. I mean, to actually put it all into words . . ."

Jack slid his arms around her, gently pulled her back against him, feeling all his anger and indignation melting away. All that concerned him now was Eleanor. "So I'm right? It wouldn't be the first time he's tried to kill you, would it, Eleanor? Please. Tell me the rest of it. I know there's more. A fool would know there's more. What happened on that ship? There was no storm, was there? Just the fire. Your ship was attacked, wasn't it?"

She pressed the back of her head against his chest, her eyes closed. "Don't ask me that, Jack, because I can't tell you. Let's just say that you could be right, and move on from there." She turned in his arms, looked up at him pleadingly. "Please."

He stroked the side of her face. "How can I deny you anything?" he asked, because she was right. He knew what he had to know, for now. "But you're not going anywhere without me, do you understand? You're not to leave this house. Cluny and I need a few days, no more than three, to scour London for that damned black coach, and then we're all going back to Becket Hall. Together. I'd like to think I'm a capable man, but this is bigger than any of us thought. Ainsley has to know."

"And you don't want to kill anyone," Eleanor said, trying to summon a smile.

"Phelps and Eccles? No, I have no reason to kill them. They're pawns in this, too. Your uncle, however, is another matter entirely."

"Don't call him that. Please."

"Very well. Chelfham is quite a complicated and nasty piece of work, using his own brother-in-law as his convenient dupe, trying to circumvent his superior in the hierarchy of this damned Red Men Gang in order to increase his fortune — while at the same time admitting his awe and fear of the man." He shook his head. "Enough, Eleanor. I don't want to think about him or any of this, not any more today."

"No, neither do I," Eleanor said, watching in bemusement as Jack lifted her hand, pressed a kiss into her palm.

"So let's think about us," he said quietly, curling his fingers around her hand and leading her into the hallway . . . and up the staircase.

CHAPTER FOURTEEN

Eleanor didn't begin to panic until they'd reached the landing and Jack turned her in the direction of his bedchamber — at which time she remembered that it was still the middle of the day and what on earth did he think they'd be doing, and what if servants were working in her adjoining bedchamber, and Jack's valet could come walking in on them at any time, and then there was Cluny, and only heaven knew when he'd pop up, and . . . and, oh, what was wrong with her? Why couldn't she be more daring?

She wanted this, didn't she? She'd worried that last night would be her only memory as she returned to Becket Hall to live out her lonely days. She longed for Jack's arms around her. She could almost taste his kiss. Her body was singing with anticipation.

So why was she thinking of sunlight and servants? What was there about her that refused to allow her to throw caution to the four winds? Were some people simply born full of *proper* and *prudent?* Why couldn't she be more like Morgan, like all the rest of the Beckets? Why did she have to be so . . . so *Eleanor?*

Jack felt Eleanor's reluctance in the way her body had stiffened and her steps had slowed. Clearly, one night in his bed hadn't banished all her virginal reservations. She looked like a lamb being led to the slaughter, which wasn't exactly a whacking great endorsement of his prowess in bed, was it? "You said Treacle had summoned a glazier?"

"Oh, oh yes, I did, didn't I?" Eleanor responded quickly, hoping she didn't sound *too* grateful for this at least momentary reprieve. "And Mrs. Hendersen unearthed some quite lovely draperies from the attics, but they can't be hung, naturally, until the walls are repaired. I'm afraid that would mean all of the walls, even if only the one was damaged. I know that's an expense, but —"

"I think I'll be able to manage," Jack told her, taking her hand and leading her past the doors to the master chamber. One step at a time, as long as those steps eventually ended in *his* bedchamber. "Let's see the progress, shall we?"

Then he hid a small smile as he heard her relieved sigh. She was such a lady, his small Eleanor. Even when she longed to be a wanton. But that was all right. It was even fine. How he would enjoy watching the petals of her passion open one by one, until she realized the full flower of her womanhood, and even the power she held over him, the power he was increasingly willing to yield to her.

He pushed open the door and reminded Eleanor to step over the rolled rag that was still on the floor, then stepped back to let her precede him into the chamber. Progress, as he could see, was already being made. For all her talk of equality, she seemed very capable of directing the servants, employing them all to their best abilities.

Eleanor Becket could probably quietly *please* and *thank you* and *if you don't mind* entire armies into following her into the very mouth of Hell. For who could say no to those huge brown eyes? Who would ever wish to see them fill with unspoken disappointment, or not long to see approval reflected in those velvety depths?

And she had no idea of her own power, which was amazing, it really was. Almost as amazing as the fact that he'd overlooked her for so long, had looked at her without ever really seeing her. But the Beckets knew. Even Ainsley had wilted, as much as that man could cede power to anyone, under Eleanor's quiet insistence that she come to London.

The Beckets believed in Eleanor. Now Jack knew that it was up to him to show her that she could believe in herself.

"Everything is still rather a mess," Eleanor said, bringing Jack back to attention.

There were now no draperies on any of the three large windows and the harsh sunlight clearly showed the extent of the damage.

"We came very close to a disaster, didn't we?" he said, picking his way across the floor that was now littered with the discarded draperies and a few rolled-up carpets in order to examine the wall and floor nearest the repaired window. "Fire. London's greatest fear."

Eleanor motioned for one of the servants to remove the draperies, then joined Jack at the window. "I've read about the Great Fire of London," she said, frowning at the charred wood at her feet. "To think that only one hundred and fifty years ago almost this entire city burned to the ground. In less than one night, three hundred houses gone, as well several churches and even half of London Bridge. But the Lord Mayor wasn't concerned when he was told, and went back to bed. Imagine a man in a position of power being that irresponsible and cavalier about the welfare of his citizens."

Jack was looking out over the square, mentally picturing the whole of it on fire. "He was forced to become concerned soon enough, when the fire continued to spread. Three hundred houses the first night? Over thirteen *thousand* by the time the fires were finally out, and all because the flames had been allowed to get out of control." He turned to look at Eleanor. "Do you know how it's said the fire started?"

Eleanor bit her bottom lip, nodded. "One baker jealous of another, and trying to burn down his rival's place of business. I had considered the similarities, yes. If Beatrice and I hadn't been in this room when the fire began, who knows what might have happened. The Earl of Chelfham is a very selfish man, and very shortsighted at that. His own residence isn't but two blocks from here."

"Impulsive," Jack said, nodding his head. The wealth of Eleanor's knowledge no longer amazed him, and he enjoyed conversations like this with her more than he would have ever believed he could. He enjoyed the way she used facts, how she came to conclusions. And he respected her opinions.

"Yes, I would agree with that assessment. Impulsive, and exceedingly self-serving. He thinks like a greedy child, and doesn't measure the consequences before he acts."

"Exactly. He acts quickly, often without putting much thought into the thing. He seemed genuinely surprised when I grabbed him off the street, as if that particular consequence of his actions hadn't really occurred to him. He was ready and willing to bargain, but certainly not prepared to defend himself physically."

Eleanor nodded, as Jack had said just what she'd been thinking. "To the earl, after reading the note your next step would have been for you to come to him, hat in hand as it were, ready to abide by any terms he might name. Of course you surprised him. You didn't play the game by his rules, his concept of how life should be for him."

"The man's arrogance is amazing. I agree, Eleanor. Our new friend Chelfham decides in his mind how things should go, and refuses to even think of any variables in how events may fall out. If Chelfham had been the Lord Mayor, London would have completely burned to the ground, because fire wasn't in his plan, therefore, it couldn't happen. Interesting, isn't it? And a failing, a shortsightedness we might be able to put to our advantage."

Eleanor was on safer ground here, discussing not her uncle, but tactics. She'd spent years listening to Ainsley Becket, having lengthy talks with him about the methods, strengths and failings of long-dead generals and ancient wars.

From the Caesars, to Machiavelli, to Washington, to Wellington and Napoleon, Ainsley had taught Eleanor that to understand the man was to have already won half the battle. Strategy was a game, one on which many lives depended, and to play the game a wise leader knew every piece on the board.

Ainsley's mistake, the one he could never forget, was believing that, knowing a man's failings, he could manage them. But how do you manage evil? How does a rational man learn to think like a monster?

Chelfham wasn't a monster. He was a fool. A selfish fool. Eleanor knew she had to concentrate on that . . . but never underestimate the man, either. She knew the price

Ainsley had paid, that all of them had paid.

"We've also learned that the earl will never strike directly, get his own hands dirty, so naturally he didn't think that you would," she said, leaving the servants to their work as they returned to the hallway. "He's the sort who hires others to carry out his crimes while his hands remain clean. Rather the way he wants you to murder his brother-in-law and Sir Gilbert."

"A coward, in other words," Jack said, opening the door to his bedchamber and motioning for Eleanor to once more precede him.

"No," she said, halting where she was as her mind filled with thoughts of her uncle. "Perhaps cowardly in some ways, but also very mean, quite capable of wickedness. His failing, I believe we can safely assume, is that he thinks he knows what will happen — what he believes *should* happen — and then he doesn't make more than one plan, or prepare for more than one avenue of attack."

She looked up at Jack. "In other words, if you lead him to believe something he'll plan accordingly. Then, to best him, you just have to do what he hasn't prepared against."

"Give all indications of attacking by sea,

271

then attack by land," Jack said, nodding his agreement. "Now all we have to decide is what we want him to think."

"Yes," Eleanor said thoughtfully. "And, for now, I imagine that would be to have him think you are more than willing to be his partner?"

"Which, other than to send you out of the city, would mean eliminating Phelps and Eccles. As a show of good faith, you understand."

Eleanor frowned. "We'll think of something else," she said, then walked into the bedchamber, hardly realizing where she was until Jack closed the door behind them.

He suggested Eleanor take a seat by the fire while he rang for a servant.

"Oh, don't do that," Eleanor said without thinking. "Just open the door to my chamber and ask someone in there for whatever it is you want. It's silly to have people running up and down the stairs all the time."

Jack looked at her, realized she was serious. "They are servants, Eleanor. I do pay them."

"Yes, I know," she answered, settling herself into one of the leather chairs that flanked the fireplace. "But common sense is common sense, isn't it?"

Jack scratched at the side of his neck,

considering the thing. "Is the connecting door still locked? I could go back to the hallway, but using the connecting door wouldn't take quite so much effort on my part, would be more direct, right? And common sense is common sense."

Eleanor felt hot color running into her cheeks. "Now you're making fun of me. Yes, Jack, the door is now unlocked. I'd appreciate a cup of tea and perhaps some small cakes, thank you."

Only when he was gone did her nervousness come back. Here she was, in his bedchamber, not ten paces from the bed they'd shared last night. And it was still daytime, the servants were still in the next room. She got up from her chair to draw the draperies at both large windows, casting the chamber into something more approaching evening light, then quickly retook her seat before Jack returned to catch her in the act. Not that he wouldn't notice the difference.

"Well now," Jack said, returning to the room, closing the connecting door, locking it, then tossing the key onto a nearby table, "I do believe we have the happiest servants in all of Mayfair, wife."

Eleanor watched nervously as he walked to the door leading to his dressing room, turned the key in the lock. Did he know how her body shivered each time he called her *wife?* Yes, she was sure he did. "Really? Why would you say that?"

"I informed them that they were free to go about their usual duties because I would hire — well, I'll figure out who I should be hiring — others to finish up in your chamber. There will be a tray of tea and cakes delivered here promptly, and we're not to be disturbed until Mrs. Ryan's special dinner, which I have asked to have served promptly at eight o'clock."

"That's embarrassing, Jack. They'll all know you have sent them away so that we can . . . be alone."

"You are my wife, Eleanor," Jack pointed out as he lit a taper from the fire in the grate, then went about the dim room — he'd noticed the closed draperies — lighting a few candles.

"We both know that isn't true," Eleanor said, loving the way each newly lit candle cast a golden glow on Jack's masculine features. He was so incredibly handsome. They were so incredibly alone.

Jack was about to answer — God only knew what he was going to say, because he didn't — when there was a quiet knock at the door and he settled for calling out "Enter!" then watched as Mrs. Hendersen herself carried in a full tea tray, placing it on the low table in front of Eleanor. "Thank you, Mrs. Hendersen."

The housekeeper curtsied, looked curiously at Eleanor, then all but backed out of the room.

"She seemed rather nervous," he said, once the door had closed. He waited five seconds, exactly, then turned the key in the lock.

"She . . . that is, Mrs. Hendersen may have come into my . . . into this chamber earlier, and noticed that . . . that I might have been slightly upset."

Jack raised one eyebrow as he walked over to seat himself in the facing chair. "Upset? Really. How so?"

Eleanor gave herself a small shake, demanded of herself that she appear in control. "I might have appeared as if I'd . . . as if I'd been upset."

"Yes. Upset. You said that. Shall we try being more precise? Upset. Angry? Frightened?" He paused a moment. "Regretful?"

"Regretful?" Eleanor frowned over that one, then said quickly, "No! No, I don't regret — oh, you're an annoying man."

"I believe you've said that before, too."

"That's only because you really are."

Well, at least she no longer looked as if

she was about to up and run. That had to be an improvement. "I'm sorry, Eleanor. Tell me what had you upset, all right?"

She looked at the tea tray, the thought of sweet cakes all but making her ill. "You weren't there."

She'd spoken so quietly. "I beg your pardon? I wasn't there? I wasn't where?"

Eleanor rolled her eyes. "Oh, for pity's sake, Jack. *Here.* You weren't *here.* I woke up and . . . you weren't here."

Jack lounged back in his chair, his thumbnail caught between his teeth as he looked at her, smiled at her in sudden pleasure. "You wanted me to be?"

Looking down at the tray of cakes, Eleanor had a fleeting thought about how satisfying it might be to pick up the plate and fling its contents in Jack Eastwood's face. But, because she was Eleanor Becket, quiet, reserved Eleanor Becket, she abstained. "I would have appreciated the gesture, yes."

"I did say goodbye," he told her. "I leaned over, kissed your bare shoulder. You smiled, then snuggled back into the pillows. I was very tempted to stay. Very tempted."

"Oh. How . . . how nice. Would you care for some tea?" Eleanor said all at once, even as she reached for the silver teapot. But she'd moved too quickly, and could only watch in horror as the pot tipped, fell onto the floor, hot water splashing into the fireplace. "Oh! Look what I've done!"

"Don't touch that," Jack warned as he pushed her hand away, for Eleanor was about to put her hand on the hot metal. "I'll take care of this."

Eleanor nodded her agreement, then sat back and watched as Jack did just that, righting the teapot, replacing it on the tray. The carpet was wet, but it was only water and would dry. "I'm never clumsy." She glared at him, suddenly more angry with him than she was disappointed in herself. "I'm never unsure. I'm never nervous. I'm *never* clumsy."

Jack picked up the tray and put the entire thing on the floor, figuring that if Eleanor wasn't clumsy again, at least she wouldn't get cake crumbs all over everything. "I suppose this is all my fault? Because I'm such an annoying man."

Eleanor couldn't take much more of this, this *looking* at her, so she got to her feet and put some distance between them. "I wanted to tell you about my uncle. I'd wanted to tell you yesterday, was just about to, but then there was the fire, and then . . . well, you know what happened then."

"I have some vague recollection, yes," Jack said, knowing he shouldn't be enjoying himself quite so much. But Eleanor Becket flustered? This was probably something he wouldn't see often.

"If I might continue?" Eleanor said, beginning to pace. "And then you were gone, and I read the note, and I knew you were coming back, but I didn't know when, or what I would say to you because now that we'd . . . and you'd left without a *word,* so what was I to say, how was I to act? Was I supposed to *say* something, act differently, pretend it never happened, look at you —"

Jack stopped her simply by stepping in front of her and putting his hands on her upper arms. "Eleanor, enough. I thought I'd appreciate seeing you flustered, but I don't, not when I'm responsible, at any rate. It's all right, really. We've already discussed the note. We'll talk more about what you finally told me, what you've still to tell me if you decide to trust me."

"It's not that I don't trust you —"

"*Shh.* I said, we'll revisit all of that later. Right now, I think we need to discuss what happened between us last night."

Eleanor felt panic gripping her again. "Oh, I knew it, I just knew we'd have to do that," she said, letting out her breath on a sigh. "Do we *have* to?"

"If you're going to go back to jumping ten feet in the air every time I come near you, yes, we do. We made love, Eleanor, you for the first time. We didn't do anything wrong, not unless you're sorry about what we did."

"No," she said slowly, looking up at him with those huge brown eyes that held powers she didn't comprehend, or else she'd use them on him more, totally destroying him. "Are you?"

He shook his head, smiled down at her. "I am a little worried about Jacko, though," he said, at last giving in to the impulse to run his fingers into her short cap of hair. "You may not remember, but the man was very clear about the thing. Harm so much as a single hair on your head, and he'd tie my guts in a bow around my neck, or at least I think those were the words. I've harmed considerably more than a single hair on your head."

Eleanor stepped back, raised her hands to her newly cropped hair. And then she did what he'd hoped she'd do. She smiled. "I would have to say that you're in fairly deep trouble, Mr. Eastwood."

"Happily, even you Beckets can't kill a man twice, because I don't even want to think of the punishment Jacko would come up with if he knew I'd taken you to my bed."

They were back to that. They could discuss her uncle, they could discuss the fire in her bedchamber. They could discuss the Great Fire, the Lord Mayor and her uncle yet again. But always, always the conversation came back to *that*.

"Why did you do it?" Eleanor asked him, because the question had been driving her nearly insane all day.

He was going to have to become accustomed to her directness. "Why?" he repeated, momentarily nonplussed. "What sort of question is that?"

"The wrong one, obviously," Eleanor said, straightening her spine. "But we've known each other for over two years, and in all of that time you've never —"

"We've *known* each other only a few days, Eleanor," he interrupted quietly. "I've been an idiot for two years."

"That's . . . that's very pretty," Eleanor said, lowering her eyes, which was a pity, because he really enjoyed looking into those eyes that seemed to mirror her remarkable soul. "Thank you."

"Yes. You're welcome," Jack said, trying hard not to let his amusement enter his tone of voice. "Eleanor, are you ever going to let me make love to you again?"

Well, that did it. She was looking at him now.

"Isn't . . . isn't that why we're here?"

He lightly rubbed at her upper arms. "I'd like to think so, yes. I'd like to think that you've been thinking about me all day, the way I've been thinking about you. I'd like to touch you, kiss you, feel you move beneath —"

Eleanor didn't know how it happened, but somehow she was standing on tiptoe on her good leg, her hands braced on Jack's shoulders, her mouth pressed against his. Her body pressed against his.

Jack's mouth softened in a smile, and something inside Eleanor prompted her to relax her own rather tightly compressed lips. The instant memory of how Jack had taken her mouth last night, *possessed* her mouth with his, threatened to send her reeling, wonderfully off balance.

But she had nothing to fear, because Jack was already scooping her up in his arms and carrying her to the bed. *He's very good at this* her mind registered vaguely as the satin coverlet made its way to the floor, to be followed rather swiftly by their clothing, even as he somehow made certain that her modesty was preserved by the soft, silken sheets.

Not that she'd opened her eyes above once, at which time she'd glimpsed more of Jack's body than she'd seen in the dark of last night. Much more.

Last night she'd been comfortably sleepy when he'd come to her, warmed by the brandy he'd given her, hidden by the dark that concealed them both. Dreamlike. The night had been dreamlike.

But not today.

And yet, when he touched her, when she felt his strong hand close around her breast, it was not the dream that she remembered, but only the *now* that was so much more real.

Jack was amazed at the way he seemed able to gauge Eleanor's every mood, simply from the way her body responded to his touch. Nervous. Curious. Bashful. Yielding. And, as he coaxed her with his hands and mouth, slowly blossoming, flowering. Yearning. Wanting.

He kissed her mouth, her breasts, her soft belly. Taking his time, giving her time, delighting in her every hesitant response. She was perfection under his hands, and he needed to prove that to her, give her the confidence to completely give herself over to him.

He kissed her hip, trailed his lips down the length of her thigh, stroked the tender skin behind her knee with his tongue. He could feel the strength in her slim calf, remembered the taut knot the muscle had become the night he'd rubbed away her cramp.

Half sitting, and careful to keep his gaze on Eleanor's face, he bent her leg and lifted it until he could touch his mouth to her ankle.

"Don't . . ." Eleanor breathed quietly, suddenly not thinking of her nakedness exposed to him, but only of the scars, the awkward way her crushed and broken bones had fused together as they'd healed.

Jack lowered his eyes to look at her ankle, felt a shaft of real pain as he imagined the agony the six-year-old Eleanor must have gone through, the pain she carried with her now. He saw the near-brand on the skin just above her ankle; almost round, as if a large iron bolt had burned into her flesh.

What in bloody hell had done that?

He kissed the scar, and Eleanor expelled her breath in a soft cry as she watched him, then held her arms up to him, silently begging for him to come to her, hold her.

Jack knew he'd dared what to Eleanor must feel like the ultimate intimacy, so that he didn't push, didn't question. Instead, he reassured. Bending to her once more, rousing her slowly with long, increasingly intimate kisses, gliding his hands over her body until her tentative response became more daring, until her eagerness nearly matched his.

Eleanor gloried to the ripple of muscle she could feel as she pressed her palms against Jack's back, and when he at last levered himself over her, into her, the rush of pleasure caused tears to sting behind her eyes.

She held him, held on to him tightly, her untutored body responding to his every move until at last she didn't have to think, but only react. Even initiate.

She felt an unexpected rush of power mixed with her building passion. Power, control. And then, most glorious of all, the giving up of that control at the divine instant there was nothing else in the world except Jack and the moment. . . .

CHAPTER FIFTEEN

If Eleanor was to have only one night in her life, one memory, she knew which she'd choose.

They'd dined in absolute splendor and blessed solitude, then gone back upstairs, Eleanor feeling rather giddy from the small amount of wine she'd drunk — or with anticipation, which was more likely — Jack scooping her high into his arms at the top of the stairs and carrying her back to the bedchamber.

He spread a blanket in front of the fire and told her silly stories about Cluny, poor fellow, and actually peeled and hand-fed her luscious green grapes. She admitted that she'd always wanted to be more daring, like Morgan, and he'd told her he would have to choke her sister within a fortnight if he were to be put in Ethan's boots, and that he liked Eleanor just fine the way she was. Which, he said, was perfect.

And then they'd made love. Long, pleasing, wondrously satisfying love. She learned him. He learned her. There was nothing and no one in the world except the two of them.

A night out of time, a perfect treasure of a memory, to be held close to her like a secret she stored in her heart but would always be able to take out, look at, remember.

But morning always comes, and dawns aren't always peaceful.

"It would work, Jack," Eleanor insisted, not for the first time. This time her words seemed to have chased Jack from the bed, and she watched as he angrily jammed his arms into his banyan.

He turned about, to glare at her. "And if it doesn't? What then, Eleanor?"

"You'll be there. You and Cluny both. You wouldn't let anything happen."

Jack's smile was bitter. "Now you're thinking like our friend Chelfham. One plan, with no thought of failure to complicate matters. Things go wrong, Eleanor. This isn't like one of your damn books. Things go *wrong*."

He might as well have slapped her. "Yes, Jack," she said, levering herself out of the opposite side of the bed, her bare feet slipping to the floor. "I do understand that things can go wrong. More than you might know. If you have another idea, Jack, we'll consider it. But we need this over, we need this done. We don't have time to return to Becket Hall, confer with Papa and the others. Every day we delay is dangerous."

"Is that some quote I don't recognize? Some old general scribbling his own version of events after the fact? The winners write the histories, Eleanor, and the histories are always crammed full of victories. Never the defeats."

Eleanor searched out her slippers and dressing gown, hoping Jack didn't notice how her hands were shaking. "He wants me gone, Jack. He wants, if we're right, to have me out of London, where he can attack the coach, be rid of his problem. Be rid of me. We *believe* that, correct?"

Jack fought to get his temper under control. "We *suppose* it, Eleanor, but don't *know* it. Not for certain. The whole thing could be just as he said — that his pernicious bitch of a wife doesn't want to look at you."

"But then she wouldn't have to, would she? I would not be invited to visit, and she wouldn't visit here. A simple solution. But not simple enough for Chelfham. No, Jack, it's as you said. He knows, or at least he suspects enough to make him willing to eliminate me, just so that he *can* be sure."

"A family resemblance. I never should have put that idea into your head."

"I never should have suggested Jamaica as the place we met," Eleanor said calmly. "But we are where we are, and now we have to move on."

"He won't show himself, you know. He'll hire someone else, and make very sure he's extremely visible at one of his clubs while that someone else is attacking the coach. So what does that gain us?"

"Knowing," Eleanor said quietly. "We'd no longer be guessing, supposing. I'd know then, for certain."

Jack took hold of her cold hands and led her over to the chairs in front of the fireplace, each of them taking up a chair. "Know that Chelfham was behind the deaths of your parents. You've always wondered about that, haven't you? Why?"

"Please, Jack, not now," Eleanor begged him. "When we're back at Becket Hall. You'll know everything then, I promise. But, yes, there has always existed the possibility that . . . that someone wanted us all dead. There were reasons to believe that."

Jack looked at her intently. "How is Ainsley involved? He is involved, isn't he? Not your secret to tell, isn't that what you said?

You were the victim, Eleanor — how is it not your story to tell?"

Eleanor bowed her head for a moment, and when she raised it again, her eyes were calm, her gaze steady. "Have you no secrets, Jack?"

He opened his mouth to answer, then stopped, shook his head. Now was not the time. There would never be a good time. "We could dress one of the maids in your clothing, have her heavily veiled as she quickly enters the coach."

"There's no one else in this household as small as me, save the tweeny, and she's only fifteen. I don't believe anything will go wrong, but if it does, I'd never forgive myself. Please, Jack. We've been round and round for the past hour, and this is the one sure way to bring my uncle into the open, the one thing that will expose him."

At last he saw the gaping hole in her logic. He'd been too angry, too worried for her, to see it at first. "Because we capture his men and they give us his name, lay all the blame at his doorstep. Eleanor, no one will believe a pair of thieves over a peer of the realm."

"Agreed," Eleanor told him. She'd thought about this, long and hard, and was sure she had the solution. "Which is why we convince those men to implicate Phelps and Eccles. *They* will turn on the earl in order to save themselves. Chelfham's arrogant, and will not have thought of that possibility — attack from within. There's little to no possibility he would prepare for such a betrayal, as he believes himself to be very much in charge. Of course, if we're *really* lucky, it will be Phelps and Eccles he sends to dispatch me, since he can't really ask his *new* partner to do it, can he?"

Jack rubbed at his chin, considering this. "I'm an idiot, I know it, but that makes some sort of twisted sense. Either way, Phelps and Eccles will sing like birds once they're in the guardhouse, they won't want to hang alone. Some day, Eleanor, you must show me these books you've been reading all these years."

Eleanor smiled, feeling they'd gotten past most of their problems, and that the argument was now settled. "Will you be able to do it, Jack? Go hat-in-hand to Chelfham and tell him you agree to send your crippled wife away to your estate in Sussex tomorrow afternoon?"

Jack nodded, his mind busy. "He *will* send Phelps and Eccles, Eleanor. Send them, use them, then have me kill them so that they can never betray him — all with me not knowing that they'd murdered my wife. I think Chelfham would appreciate the irony of that."

"Mean, but not stupid," Eleanor said, agreeing. "You know, Jack, the problem with Machiavelli was that he knew how to gain power, but never how to use it once he had it. My uncle is not a good manager of his power. He uses people, then discards them, unwilling or unable to either instill loyalty or offer trust. He'd discard you for someone else eventually, once he knew all that you know, once he had tucked your supposedly small smuggling operation into his own."

"And yet there is someone he is afraid of, remember? This unknown man in the black coach? Even as Chelfham plans to betray him, he very obviously fears him. Once you and Phelps and Eccles are supposedly disposed of, I'll demand to be taken to meet the man, or else I would anonymously lay information about Chelfham's crimes to the Crown."

Eleanor didn't like thinking about this part of the plan. "He'll fume and bluster, declare that he could just as easily implicate you. But then, in the end, he'll communicate with the man in the black coach, say that he has a problem, a man who must be killed or else they all risk exposure. He will have run out of trusted allies, by his own actions, and he'll have no choice but to ask for help."

"He'll see it as his only hope, yes, although I doubt our mysterious stranger will agree."

Eleanor twined her fingers together in her lap. They'd been over this part before. "You'll follow, and watch. The mysterious man in the black coach will most certainly kill him before he goes into hiding, aware that you are too close for his safety. As he unwittingly leads you to this man, my uncle also will be walking straight into his own death. And I'll be partly responsible, although the blame lies with him, and his own greed, his own crimes. It is all rather Machiavellian, isn't it?"

Jack went to his knees in front of her chair, put his hands on hers. "Can you live with that, Eleanor? Once we begin this, we can't turn back. Can you live with the consequences?"

"With Chelfham gone, the entire Red Men Gang would be in disarray, at least for a while. We might even be extraordinarily lucky and learn who the true leader is, and Papa can take steps to protect our people in Romney Marsh. Either way, the Black Ghost Gang will be able to operate in safety again while the Red Men are busy fighting among themselves, all of them jockeying for higher positions once the earl is gone. So many lives balanced against that of a . . . a monster. Yes, Jack, I can find a way to live with that."

Jack rose slightly on his knees and took Eleanor into his arms, holding her tightly.

Had she realized one last thing? Had her clever mind come to the conclusion that success at any level meant that Jack Eastwood would have to disappear from London, quite possibly from England itself, once the man in the black coach had been made aware of his existence?

Yes. She knew. Perhaps that was even why she held him as fiercely as he now held her. Eleanor seemed very adept at imagining actions all the way through to their last consequences.

Chapter Sixteen

Jack obligingly stood still in the drawing room as Eleanor fussed with the folds in his neck cloth. His valet would be appalled, but Jack let her fuss, because she was nervous, and because he liked looking at her bent head as she stood within the circle of his arms.

"Are you quite sure you want to do this?" she asked when she'd patted at the cloth one last time and finally looked up, met his eyes.

"You don't think I can playact, Eleanor?"

"It's not that. I just know that you'd like nothing more than to knock him down, or worse. Do you really trust yourself to . . . well, to . . ."

"Lick Chelfham's boots? Ask him precisely which part of his flaccid fat ass he'd like me to kiss?" Jack supplied helpfully, then grimaced at his crude speech. Eleanor was a lady. "Forgive me. I promise, Eleanor, I'll do everything except gift him with a detailed itinerary of your journey into Sussex. I've had some experience at being devious."

"Oh? And when would that have been, Mr. Eastwood?" Eleanor asked, moving away from him to pick up his curly brimmed beaver hat and soft leather gloves. Their theories — her theory — were about to be set into motion and, once begun, could not be stopped. She didn't worry about herself. She only worried about Jack.

He bent down, kissed the nape of her neck. "And that, my dear lady, is for another time. Preferably when you are in a very, very good mood."

"Really? Or are you working up to suggesting that we trade secret for secret?"

"Is that possible?" Jack asked her, turning her about to smile down in her face. "If so, I'd be more than happy to tell you all about the time I coaxed my cousin into commandeering the brandy decanter from his father's study, and the two of us drank ourselves to sloppy inebriation behind the stables."

Eleanor lifted one well-defined eyebrow. "And you call that devious?"

"I do, madam."

"How is that devious?"

Jack leaned down to whisper in her ear.

"Because I only pretended to drink, while watching my cousin go green as an eel. And he deserved it, as he'd taken my horse out without permission and brought him back lame."

"Well, then," Eleanor said, having witnessed and mediated more sibling quarrels than she cared to remember, "that seems only fair. You never told me you have a cousin. In fact, you've really never told me much at all about your life before you came to Becket Hall. Why is that?"

Jack shrugged, mentally kicking himself for bringing up his cousin. Now was not the time. There would never be a good time for that discussion, that disclosure. "Because my life was so bloody boring until I met you Beckets, I suppose. Was that the knocker?"

Eleanor blinked, a thought that was trying to surface slipping away. "Was it? Who would be calling on us? Surely not the earl."

In answer to her question, there came the sound of booted feet taking the marble stairs at least two at a time, followed by a shout: "Elly? Elly, where the devil are you?"

"Rian?" Eleanor turned wide eyes on Jack. "It's Rian," she said again, unnecessarily, then lifted her skirts and raced toward the hallway, only to be scooped up by her brother and swung around in a circle, just like a sack of flour, she supposed.

"I've got news, Elly," he told her when she begged him to put her down. "It's Morgan. She's gone and had *twins.*"

"Well, that would explain the sheer size of — twins? Really? Tell me all about it. Oh, Rian, it's so *good* to see you. *Twins?* Leave it to Morgan never to do the ordinary."

She took his hand and led him over to the couches, pulling him down beside her, and only with great effort refraining from pushing back his dark curls that were, as always, overlong, nearly hiding his remarkable Irish green eyes.

Rian, she'd always thought, had the face of a poet. Of all the Becket brothers, Rian had the slightest build. Not as tall, not as broad, everything about him drawn with a finer hand. He may have been nearly nineteen, or at least if the age Papa had given him when he'd come to the island had been correct, but he looked so much younger, so much more innocent than that, so that Fanny, his constant companion, seemed more an unasked-for protector than a sister. Even with a good two days' growth of beard, Rian much more closely resembled an aesthetic than a warrior. How he'd always hated that . . .

"Hello there, Jack," Rian said, sliding his fingers through his hair, pushing it back off his forehead, only to have it slowly begin sliding front once more. "You been taking good care of our Elly?"

"He's taking perfectly good care of me," Eleanor said impatiently, grabbing Rian's hands in her own and shaking them in order to regain his attention. "Morgan. Tell me about Morgan. Is she all right? Was it a long confinement?"

"Some wine, Rian?" Jack asked, and the younger man nodded gratefully. "You look as if you've been in the saddle for a long time."

"I only stopped to rest Shamus, and to snatch a few hours sleep in a fairly ratty inn. But London is magnificent, Elly. The sheer size of it. I never imagined!"

"Rian," Eleanor said in her most determined tone, "I want to hear about Morgan. That is why you came here, isn't it?"

Rian accepted a glass from Jack and downed its contents in three long, fairly inelegant gulps. "She's Morgan, Elly. She stood up from the table two nights ago, said *oops* and made a terrible mess on the floor, and the next thing we all knew Odette was tripping down the stairs with two babies in her arms. Court nearly had to prop Ethan up, I tell you, because his knees buckled where he stood. Morgan's fine. The babies are fine. Even Ethan is fine, once he stopped worrying about Morgan and realized he's now father to both a son and a daughter all at one and the same time. It's Odette who's not smiling all that much."

"Odette's ill? Why do we always forget she's growing older?"

"It's not her age that's made her ill, not that she's really ill. She's just walking around muttering about twins being very powerful and Morgan and Ethan's twins being probably strong enough to rule the world or ruin it. You know Odette, full of voodoo and superstitions. Can I have another, Jack?"

Rian held up his empty glass, but Eleanor snatched it from him before Jack could take it. "What you need, Rian, is a bath and a bed, and probably a good meal. Papa really allowed you to come to London. I'm amazed."

"Why? You're here. Morgan was here. Even Chance. Nobody's recog—" He shut his mouth, looked at Jack, who had sat down on the facing couch.

"I'm not really here," Jack said, smiling at

Eleanor's brother. "And my ears don't work."

Rian grinned at his sister. "I like him," he said, then grabbed the empty glass from Eleanor and trotted off to pour his own wine.

Eleanor looked at Jack, shrugging slightly. "I don't know why he's here," she mouthed to him.

"Rian," Jack said, getting to his feet, his tone casual. "Did you volunteer to bring the news about Morgan, or did Ainsley single you out for the mission? I mean, it wouldn't have taken that much longer to dispatch a letter, would it? Not that we're not delighted to see you. Aren't we, Eleanor?"

"Yes, we're delighted to see you, Rian," Eleanor repeated, looking at Jack as she said the words, her face not giving away what he was sure was her unhappiness with his blunt statement. But that was too bad, because Jack Eastwood didn't like surprises, and Rian Becket was a surprise. Not to mention a damn inconvenience.

"And wasn't that heartfelt. I suppose a fatted calf for dinner is out of the question?" Rian said, looking at both his host and hostess. "What am I interrupting?"

"Nothing," Eleanor said, patting his hand.

"You've interrupted nothing. How long can you stay?"

"I was hoping for a week," he told her, but this time he looked only at Jack. "More, if you need me. What's going on? Court and Papa can be damned closemouthed when they want to, and we won't even consider Jacko."

"Rian, dear, you just answered your own question," Eleanor told him, very much the older sister. "If Papa wanted you to know, you'd know. Now, did Papa send a letter with you?"

Rian's expression closed. "No."

Now it was Eleanor's turn to look at Jack. "Because Papa didn't send you, did he? This was all your idea."

Rian jumped to his feet, once more reminding Eleanor of a poet, a rather intense, hot-blooded poet, unfortunately. "Damn it, Elly, how do you always know? Chance is gone to hell and married life, Spencer's off to war. Court's playing at Black Ghost. What am I supposed to do? *Knit?*"

"He could be useful, Eleanor," Jack said, feeling a little sorry for the boy, who certainly had a point. "He's not incompetent."

"Well, thank you for that, Jack," Rian bit out. "And now go to hell."

"Rian," Eleanor said, getting to her feet

and placing a hand on her brother's arm. "We've . . . that is, we're in the middle of something rather important, which is why we're in London in the first place. Now be truthful. Is that why you're here? Because you know something's happening and want to be a part of it? Because if you're here to see gaming halls and cockfights, you'll be on your way home the moment you've rested."

Rian immediately calmed down. "This is about the Red Men Gang cutting off our suppliers, isn't it? I knew it. What else could it be? After all, Jack, you're in charge of that end. Of both ends. Tell me what you need me to do."

Eleanor instinctively knew that it was time she retired from the field, leaving it free to Jack and whatever he decided to tell Rian.

"I'll go upstairs and pen a letter to Papa," she said, heading for the doorway. "He's either half out of his mind with worry, or enjoying the joke. But since I can't know which, we really need to tell him Rian is here with us, and safe."

Jack waited until Eleanor had left the room before taking hold of Rian's rather dusty and disheveled neck cloth and rapidly backing him up across the room, all the way to the wall. "Now, halfling, why are you here? No more lies."

"I told you. Morgan's babies. I . . . I thought Eleanor would want to know as soon as possible. And . . . and to help, yes. But I already said that. Jesus, Jack, what else could there be?"

Jack gave the younger man a quick shake. "Jacko. There could be Jacko. Couldn't there?"

The boy should never play at cards unless he wished to be thoroughly fleeced. "Jacko? No. Why would you say that?"

"Because, my fine young spy, London is a rather large place, and because I don't believe Ainsley sent you here alone. But if Ainsley didn't give you my address, someone did, and the only other someone who knows it is our good friend Jacko. Now, do you agree to talk, or do we stand here like this until your sister comes back to ask why?"

"Let go," Rian said, then shook back his clothes when Jack did just that. "I could have fought you, but Elly would have heard."

"And how would we have explained your bloodied nose?" Jack shot back, indicating that Rian should sit down once more, then fetching wine for them both. "Talk."

"There's not much to say. After the babies

were born, Jacko pulled me aside and said this is the excuse we needed to have someone sent to London. To keep an eye on you if you'd begun having any thoughts about Elly that you shouldn't be having. Jacko's very protective of Elly, you understand. We all are, but Jacko even more so, God only knows why. Maybe it's because he's so big, and she's so little?"

"She's stronger than most of you think, and a grown woman, as well," Jack informed him coldly.

"Elly's a mother hen," Rian said, not without affection. "Somebody's got to mother her, too. She's never set foot off Becket lands."

"While you are world-traveled, I suppose?" Jack said, unable to help himself. "At least, unlike Eleanor, you were on the island, weren't you?"

It was amazing, the look that came over Rian's handsome face. An instant shuttered look, almost as if someone had snapped their fingers and he'd responded like a well-trained dog. "I don't know what you mean, Jack. God, I'm famished. Do you suppose I could have something to eat?"

"Cut the line, Rian, I know about the island. Ainsley was in business somewhere in the islands. Merchant trading. Shipping.

Something. Near Jamaica, I figure. And then he brought you all here, back to civilization. Except that he stuck you all in Romney Marsh, which many might say is not civilization at all."

"If you know, why ask?"

Because I'm nosy as hell, because I want to know what happened there, what happened to Eleanor, and how. "You're right," Jack said aloud, then smiled. "Back to Jacko, if we can? He actually sent you here in the way of a chaperone? No other reason?"

Rian shook his head. "Just that, and telling me to make myself useful, get some of the wet out from behind my ears. Oh, he did tell me to be sure to remind you that he ties very good bows, whatever that means. Come on, Jack, my ribs are shaking hands with my backbone — I truly need something to eat, the wine's going straight to my head. Where's the kitchen? Or I'll find my own way?"

The younger man was already on his feet once more and, knowing the Beckets' approach to taking care of themselves whenever possible, Jack only vaguely waved him toward the back of the house, and the stairs leading down to the kitchens. By now his servants were probably becoming accustomed to such behavior.

Rian got as far as the doorway before Eleanor appeared once more, looking slightly harassed, so unusual in his calm, composed, determined Eleanor. "I forgot, Rian," she said, shaking her head at her own folly. "Their names, dear. I completely forgot to ask the names of Morgan's babies."

"Oh, that. Caused something of an upset with that, I'm afraid. She named them Geoffrey and Isabella."

"And Papa was upset?" Eleanor asked quietly, her heart somehow singing and breaking at the same time. Geoffrey, the man Ainsley Becket had been. Isabella, the woman he'd loved and lost.

"You know Papa. He went very quiet, and then excused himself for several hours. Jacko finally ran him to ground in the dressing room next to Morgan. It's serving as the nursery for now, you understand. He was just standing there, looking at the babies. He must have been there for hours."

Eleanor pressed a hand to her mouth as she blinked back sudden tears. "And he's happy?"

Rian nodded his head. "I'd say so, yes. Jacko took him off to bed, and then came downstairs, whistling. If Jacko's happy, Papa must be happy."

"What am I missing here?" Jack asked, confused. "Are those special names?"

"Oh, yes, Jack," Eleanor said, leaning against his side. "They're special names. Very special names, very special people. It's like a circle, closing." She shut her eyes for a moment, as if seeing something only she could see, then stood up straight, looked at her brother. "You've been on the road all day, Rian. Aren't you hungry? Come along, I'll introduce you to Mrs. Hendersen."

Jack stayed where he was, watching them walk away, arm in arm. A circle closing? Yes, he supposed so. And he was standing on the outside of that circle . . . and damned if he knew why.

"No more secrets, Eleanor. One day, and very soon, no more secrets . . ."

CHAPTER SEVENTEEN

"I don't much like delays. They usually mean trouble," Cluny grumbled as Jack walked into his study long after midnight, leaving Eleanor only reluctantly, as he enjoyed holding her sleeping form in his arms very nearly as much as he did making love to her. Especially tonight, when their time together had seemed stolen, as they'd had to wait until a travel-weary Rian had finally gone off to bed.

Not that he'd expected the boy to go on some sort of nocturnal rounds, checking on his sister's sleeping arrangements — but try telling that to Eleanor.

"And a good evening to you, too, Cluny. I take it you at least found my note warning of our delay and to make yourself scarce. Where were you earlier?"

"Having a jolly time, of course, tramping about in the rain and mist with my eye out for a perfectly matched team of black horses." Cluny lifted his glass, tipped it to show it was empty. "Have you any idea the sheer number of black coaches drawn by black horses that exist in London? Not counting the rented hacks and hackneys, of course."

"No," Jack admitted, a small smile tickling at the corners of his mouth, "but I'll wager you have a fairly good idea."

"I thought I spotted it the once, just at the end of Saint James's Street, but by the time I hoofed myself down there it had driven off. Useless, my boy, useless. We're definitely going to have to goad Chelfham into contacting the man, then follow him to their meeting place. We've run out of time to use that Lady Beresford you were chatting up the other day, when you still thought to dip yourself into society."

Jack handed the Irishman a full glass of wine, then retrieved his own from the drinks table. "True enough, although her ladyship did manage three invitations for us. It's a shame it's not safe to have Eleanor traipsing all over Mayfair. So it's either push Chelfham into running to the man, or hold a knife to his throat while I convince him to simply tell us the man's name and location, as I believe you've already suggested. That idea, by the way, is beginning to hold some appeal."

Cluny sat forward eagerly. "Now you're making some *sense,* boyo! And about bleeding time, too. It's what I've been saying all along. Quick, to the point — the knifepoint, that is."

"And yet, we're going to do this my way," Jack said, settling himself behind his desk.

"The little lady's way, you mean. And for the life of me, I don't know why you've agreed to such nonsense."

"You don't have to know that, Cluny," Jack told him, then realized that the man deserved an answer. After all, he would be sticking his neck out, too. "All right. Listen, and kindly fight back the urge to interrupt me the way you always do."

"Damn your eyes, I do not interrupt!" Cluny said belligerently, so that Jack laughed and pointed at the man. "Often," the Irishman added grudgingly, then sank back on the couch.

"Thank you, friend. The story is long, involved, and I don't know the half of it — I think I do, but I'm not positive — so I'll say this quickly. What I didn't tell you earlier is that Chelfham is Eleanor's uncle, and may have had a hand in the death of her parents. Her death, as well, except something went wrong — right, actually — and she was spared, rescued, and somehow became one of the Beckets."

"Humph," Cluny grumbled. "Who else has Ainsley Becket got stuffed out there in the back of beyond? The rightful king of England? We surely could use him, and that's a fact, seeing as how the one we've got has gone all batty."

"You're interrupting, Cluny," Jack pointed out, then continued his truncated explanation. "Neither of us believe Chelfham's story about his wife's aversion to cripples —"

"I don't know, boyo. I had an aunt once. Sadie was her name. She'd run screaming whenever she saw Colm Divine making his way into the village, saying he was bad luck. Walleyed, Colm was. Never knew where he was looking, which was enough to spook poor old Sadie, let me tell you. She ran smack into a tree, the once. Smashed her nose, then blamed poor Colm for her new crooked face. Myself, I thought it was a whacking great improvement."

Jack coughed quietly, then folded his hands together in front of him. "Are you quite done now? Or is there a second verse?"

"I liked you better when we were on the

Peninsula. You laughed at all my stories then, and asked for more."

"I was trying to stay awake so I wouldn't freeze to death," Jack told him, grinning. "Besides, anything was better than listening to you snore. Look, Cluny, either Chelfham sends someone to attack the coach, or he doesn't. But it's the only way Eleanor feels she can determine if her uncle is a killer, in addition to being a general bastard and one of the leaders of the Red Men Gang."

"A good question, I suppose, but I have a better one. How does your little lady know Chelfham's her uncle? You've been keeping secrets from me, boyo, and I can't like that."

In fits and starts, which was the only way anyone accomplished anything with Cluny, Jack explained everything, including his necessarily delayed plan to call on Chelfham, to tell him Eleanor would be leaving the city the following day. An entire day lost to Rian's arrival.

"We follow, catch the villains and hide them safely away, then you go to the earl and demand he take you to this fellow in the black coach."

"Very nearly correct, Mr. Shannon."

Jack and Cluny both turned to see Eleanor standing in the doorway in her dressing gown and, of course, bare feet. "Jack and I *both* will confront my uncle."

"The bloody hell we will," Jack declared, getting to his feet.

"Ah, and now isn't this going to be jolly," Cluny said on a smile. "Will you be needing a referee, boyo?"

"No, I will not," Jack said, coming out from behind the desk and grabbing Eleanor's wrist, tugging her after him into the hallway and not stopping until they were closeted together in the drawing room.

"Jack," Eleanor began earnestly, "you can see that I'd want to be there."

"No, I damn well can't see that, Eleanor," he told her, his temper running hot. No. Not his anger. His fear. Who knew what all could go wrong when he pushed Chelfham into a corner. He couldn't lose her now.

But now was not the time for a declaration. Especially since, at the moment, he wanted less to kiss her than he did to shake some sense into her hard little head.

"Please, Jack, think about my feelings for a moment. I lived more than half my life not knowing who I was or even how I came to be a Becket. Oh, they told me what they believed I needed to know," she said, sighing. "They told me I was shipwrecked and that Jacko had saved me. They told me that. They told me simple things, and very

313

simply. It was only when I began to remember on my own, when I at last remembered my name, that I learned more."

"I understand that, Eleanor. You were only a child. What I don't understand is how this seems to translate into you personally confronting your uncle. No, it's too dangerous."

Eleanor's hands closed into fists at her sides. "I need to hear him say the words, Jack. I didn't know that, not until you mentioned his name nearly in the same breath as the Red Men Gang, not until I came to London, not until I saw him. The pieces are fitting together, yes. But I have to hear the words. I have to hear him say them to my face."

Jack took a quick turn on the carpet, pushing through his hair with both hands, then stopped in front of Eleanor once more. "There's no great mystery here. If you're right to think he had something to do with your ship going down, it's because your uncle wanted the title. Greed, Eleanor. Greed, and the need for the power and prestige of being the Earl of Chelfham. I can understand you wanting to know the *how* of it, how he arranged the whole thing — whatever the hell it was — but not the why. The why is obvious."

"Perhaps to you," Eleanor said, standing her ground. "But there's more."

She had his attention now. "More than wanting the title? What else could there be?"

Eleanor knew the time had come for truth, no matter how horrible. "Papa doesn't know any of this."

Jack went very still. "Any of what, Eleanor?"

She rushed into speech. "If I told him, he might have felt it necessary to seek the earl out himself. No, that's not true. He most definitely would have sought him out, years ago, when I first remembered my name. I couldn't allow that any more than I could stop him. I'd never risk Papa. I just couldn't. He may have his suspicions now, see a connection now, but if you hadn't mentioned Chelfham's name I never would have told him the rest. What else I'd remembered."

"The Becket loyalty never ceases to amaze me, or impress me. Tell me this much, Eleanor. If Ainsley knew what you're damn well going to tell me now — would he have allowed you to come to London?"

"Never."

"All right. I needed at least that much clear in my head. I can't blame Ainsley for something he didn't know. Now tell me."

"The first nightmare," she began quietly,

wetting her lips, then swallowing down hard on the words that begged to be said. "The first nightmare was words. Only words. Angry words, terrible words I couldn't quite grasp, couldn't quite understand."

Jack led her over to one of the couches and sat down beside her, keeping her hands in his. She looked ready to crumble. "Eleanor, if you don't want to tell me right at this minute, I'll understand, and we can talk again tomorrow." A single tear slid down her cheek and he wiped it away with his finger. "It's that bad?"

"I'm sorry," she said, lifting her chin, reaching deep inside herself for all the strength she could muster. "The nightmare wouldn't go away, kept returning every few months, and slowly became clearer in my mind. Perhaps I needed to be older, stronger, before I could really remember or make any sense out of those memories. The voices? I was hearing my parents. Screaming at each other as two sailors held my father by both arms, dragging him toward the railing of the ship. He was wrapped nearly head to foot in heavy chains."

"Pirates?" Jack asked, then realized he was doing just as Cluny had done — interrupting. "I'm sorry, go on."

"Not pirates, Jack. I wasn't supposed to

see, to hear anything, but I'd slipped out of the cabin and was on deck the entire time, watching. Perhaps all the commotion woke me. In any case, I know I was dressed in my night rail — Odette kept it for me, as it was all I had of my life before . . . before that day. I know it was dark, I can even remember the feel of the rough planking beneath my bare feet."

Eleanor closed her eyes, and the vision of what she'd seen appeared in her mind's eye as clear, and as terrible, as ever.

"He was accusing her of playing him false, and she wasn't denying it. She . . . she seemed to be *taunting* him, calling him the worst sort of cuckold." She hesitated a few moments, then said, "I watched as he was thrown overboard, still cursing her. I listened as she laughed. When I screamed, and she saw me, she told me it was all a dream, then hustled me back to our cabin."

"Sweet Jesus." Jack hadn't known what he thought he might hear, but he certainly hadn't expected that.

Eleanor tugged her hands free and wrapped her arms about herself, rocking slowly. "The next day, she told me that my father had died and what I'd seen was his dead body being lowered into the sea. She kept insisting what I *thought* I'd seen was only a dream."

"You'd want to believe that, wouldn't you, Eleanor. A child would want something like that to be a dream."

"Yes, I'm sure, and that's probably one reason it took me so long to remember."

"Then what happened? But only if you want to tell me."

"I do want to tell you, Jack. We weren't on our way to Jamaica. We had only just left there, were perhaps only one or two days out, at the most. We were traveling with other ships, on our way back to England. Back to my mother's lover. But first it was necessary to remove her husband. A terrible accident at sea, you understand. At least that's what I believe now," she ended quietly.

"And the storm?"

Eleanor gifted him with a small, watery smile that nearly broke his heart.

"There was no storm, Jack. You already knew that, didn't you? You tripped me up in my lies. Papa . . . Ainsley, was a privateer, not a merchant ship owner, plying the waters all up and down the islands. You knew that, too, or at least guessed as much. The very next day after . . . afterward, our ship was attacked and sunk. It was a mistake in some ways — that attack — but it happened."

"Sunk? Ainsley didn't try to save your ship, sell her as a prize?"

"No," Eleanor said, realizing she'd said too much yet again. The rest wasn't hers to tell. "I told you, it was a mistake. But Jacko saved me. I was badly injured, and by the time I was recovered I was in England, just another one of the many Beckets of Romney Marsh. That part you know."

"I know some of it," Jack said tightly. Eleanor's story was horrific and still full of holes, yet he knew one certain thing had to be stored away in his mind, one question he needed answered: why would a privateer deliberately sink a fully loaded merchant ship?

"When we see Papa —"

"I know, Eleanor. And Ainsley damn well is going to tell me the rest, since you persist in believing you'd be betraying some sort of trust. There will be no more secrets, sweetheart, no more lies. Not between us. At least now I suppose I know why you want to confront Chelfham. You want to ask him if he knows about what your mother did, and how she was able to accomplish it, get the crew to kill her husband."

"Not only that, Jack," Eleanor said, at last

succumbing to the need to lay her head against his strong chest. She'd been carrying her secrets so long, too long, and it felt so very freeing to share them with him.

Jack gently stroked her hair, waiting for her to continue.

After a few moments, she did. "Before he was thrown overboard, my mother told her husband how she'd betrayed him, and with whom. I firmly believe Chelfham helped arrange his brother's death. I've never thought otherwise. You already think so, too, as Papa would have if I'd told him what I've just told you. Yes, I would like to hear the words from Chelfham's own mouth. But if we're right, and my coach is attacked, what I'd really need to know now would be how that same man could, years later, order his own daughter killed."

Chapter Eighteen

"Ah, good, you're up and about," Rian said as he entered the breakfast room, clearly dressed for a day on the town. He lifted a silver lid and plucked out a slice of ham he then began to gnaw on. "So, what do I see first, Jack? The Tower, you suppose? I hear there are lions in the Tower. And tigers."

"Don't bother, Rian," Jack said wearily, indicating that the young man should take up a seat across the table from him. "The morning post has arrived, and I took the liberty of opening your sister's letter to Eleanor. Morgan's babies were born the day after Eleanor and I left to come to London. Not three days ago."

"Fanny. Blast the girl."

"Cassandra, actually. Someone needs to sit that girl down with a primer. Her spelling is atrocious. So, Rian, how long have you been in London on Jacko's orders? How long have you been following me?"

Rian didn't seem the least upset that he'd been found out, which made him not only young but either supremely stupid or exceedingly confident. Or both. "Not all that long. First I went to — who says I was following you?"

"Not my good friend Cluny, that's for certain," Jack said, not without a trace of humor. "Now, do you want to tell me why you've been following me? And why you decided to show up here, of course."

"Well," Rian said, speaking around a second mouthful of ham, "the second part's easy. The inn was terrible, and the food worse. I figured you and Elly were living higher than that, so why didn't I take advantage of that fact. I'd show up, bearing good news, and with no questions asked. Morgan wanted the babies to be a surprise for Eleanor when she came home. Didn't count on Callie feeling she couldn't wait, though. I should have, shouldn't I?"

"Apparently, yes," Jack said, leaning his chin on his hand, rather fascinated by the young Rian Becket. "Now the first question. Why have you been following me?"

"I'd still say it was Jacko's idea that I should protect you, watch your back. But you wouldn't swallow that crammer again, would you?"

"No, I don't think so," Jack admitted, grinning.

Rian popped the last of the ham slice into his mouth and wiped his fingers on a serviette he lifted from the table. "Very well, the truth it is then, although you're not going to like it much. I'm here to make sure that — if you somehow managed to get yourself dead — there'd be someone close by to spirit Elly off safe back to Becket Hall."

"The confidence you Beckets have in me is nearly unmanning. I'll have to thank Jacko when next I see him," Jack said, watching as Rian picked up the plate in front of him and returned to the large buffet table, to begin lifting silver tops and choosing his next course.

"I told you, Jacko's especially protective of Elly, and always has been. Like an old woman, that's what we say. And I really was all hot to come up to London in any case."

"To get some of the moisture out from behind your ears," Jack said, recalling what the boy had said when he arrived.

"Exactly. I wasn't insulted, seeing as how I know I'm still fairly wet, and a chance was a chance. Who's the Irishman, by the way? You might want to tell him to suck in that belly of his when he's trying to hide between doorways. It was always sticking out like a wrapped thumb. I didn't have to follow you, Jack. It was easier just to follow him."

"No wonder he never saw anyone following me," Jack mused aloud, appreciating the humor of the situation — not that he'd mention the joke to Cluny. "I suppose now that you're here you'll want to be of some use?"

Rian returned to his seat, dishes in both hands, a piece of toast clenched between his teeth. "Any yamm?"

"Jam? Certainly." Jack passed him the small crystal container.

"Strawberry. Famous! What was that you asked? Oh, do I want to be of some use? I'd be delighted. How?"

Jack knew his life wouldn't be worth a bent penny if anything happened to Rian, but the boy still could be helpful. "Your sister's shoes are a disaster with those odd-size heels on them."

"Really? We have our own bootmaker in Becket Village you know. Ollie. A good man." Rian shoved back his chair and lifted his right leg high into the air. "Made these boots, Ollie did, and they look as fine to me as any I've seen since I've come up to London. What did you say he did wrong with Elly's shoes?"

"As I said, he put different-size heels on

each shoe, with a higher one on her . . . affected leg. I've noticed that she's much more comfortable barefoot, which leads me to believe she shouldn't have a higher heel on one shoe, even if it makes her gait smoother. I don't like that she hurts."

"Well, hell's bells, no, neither do I. So you want me to take Elly where? Bond Street, isn't it? Today?"

"Today, yes. See if someone can manage to put new heels on at least one or two pair of her shoes, then order several pair to be delivered here. I can always have someone send them along to Becket Hall if we're no longer in residence. A dozen pair, Rian. Slippers, half boots, whatever she needs and a few she doesn't, with the bill coming to me."

"She'll give me trouble there, Jack, you paying and all."

"Ah, but you're the brother, you're the *man* here. I have all confidence in you." Jack got to his feet. "I'll be going out now, probably not returning before you leave. Don't go until at least noon, Rian, you understand? That's important. At least noon."

"No, I don't understand," Rian admitted honestly. "Elly's always up and about early. Don't know why she isn't this morning. Not like Elly to be a slugabed."

Jack knew why, but he wasn't about to tell Rian how his sister had held on to him last night as he'd carried her upstairs. How he'd held her as she cried tears too long held inside over a secret she'd hidden from everyone for too many years. How he'd loved her gently, then more fiercely, deep into the morning hours.

"London hours are different from country hours," was all he said.

"I suppose so," Rian answered, obviously not that concerned. "But we don't ever have anything sent directly to Becket Hall, Jack, you know. Elly will give the shopkeeper the direction for the first place the shoes will go. After that, they'll go elsewhere — the places always change — and then finally to Becket Hall."

"Amazing," Jack muttered upon hearing of yet another layer of careful Becket secrecy, then added, "Watch her, Rian. I don't expect any trouble, but don't let her out of your sight. Take my coach and two footmen with you. All right?"

Rian's mouth was full yet again, so that he just waved a hand in Jack's general direction and continued eating as if one of his legs had gone hollow and he needed to fill it back up immediately.

Jack smiled to himself as he left the breakfast room, remembering when he'd awakened every morning, starving, and only losing that smile when the bitter memory of his uncle's recounting of the cost of eggs and kippers each time he dared to refill his plate took its place.

Thinking of his dead uncle led immediately to thoughts of his missing cousin, and the secret he still kept from Eleanor.

Did it matter anymore? His reasons for meeting the Beckets seemed like ancient history, only his aunt's pleading to please find her son, or what had happened to him, holding any importance now.

He was one of them now. A Becket. Or as close to a Becket as any outsider could be. Ethan had been accepted, that was obvious, or he wouldn't have been along on their last smuggling run. If Ethan could be accepted, so could he. Not just tolerated, not just used for his expertise. Accepted. One of them.

He wouldn't betray the Beckets because he wouldn't betray Eleanor. The Becket secrets, whatever they all were, were safe as houses with him. It was that simple, and that complicated, because he could no longer rationalize the *why* of his continued association with the Beckets and their, frankly, illegal activities. Treasonous activities, some would say.

The rights and wrongs of what he was doing, who he was becoming, the depth and reasoning behind his loyalties, accompanied Jack all the way to the three shallow steps leading up to the front door of the Earl of Chelfham's town house.

He hesitated for a moment, pulled out his watch and checked the time. Ten o'clock. More than enough time to say what he had to say, and leave Eleanor safe as she and Rian shopped in Bond Street. After all, why risk abducting her in full sight of the world, when a traveling coach on an isolated roadway made for much the easier target?

Now all Jack had to do was swallow down the bile that threatened to rise in his throat as he thought of the coming interview with Rawley Maddox, the murdering Earl of Chelfham.

Eleanor's father. Sweet Jesus . . .

"Mister Jack Eastwood to see his lordship," he announced forcefully when the door was opened at his knock and he was ushered inside the black-and-white tiled foyer of the house that, he silently noted, was not furnished half so well as his own. A silly thing, even petty, but he would take his pleasure where he found it, so that he would be able to resist taking his pleasure in breaking Rawley Maddox's fat neck.

"His lordship is still at breakfast, sir," the bewigged butler informed him archly, keeping his gloved hands at his sides rather than holding them out to receive Jack's hat and gloves.

"I'm aware of that, my good man," Jack lied smoothly as he turned his hat upside down and carefully dropped a gold coin into it. He neatly covered the hat with his gloves, then held out both to the butler. "His lordship expressly asked that I join him. I'm sure he informed you of our appointment."

"Why, yes, sir," the butler said, accepting the hat, the gloves and most definitely the coin. "Mr. Eastwood, of course. My apologies, sir. If you would be so kind as to follow me?"

Jack was feeling anything but kind, but he certainly did follow, remembering the night Eleanor had declared, "You can't buy loyalty, no matter how high the price." He'd have to remember to tell her how inexpensive *disloyalty* was in London.

The Earl of Chelfham was at the trough — the breakfast table — when Jack was announced, a large white linen serviette tucked into his collar, three full plates spread out in front of him. "Eastwood! I knew you'd show up. Splendid! Come,

come, sit down. Eat!"

"I've already broken my fast, thank you," Jack said, pulling out a chair a small distance down the table. "I'm still slightly confused. Are we chums now, Chelfham?"

"Ha! As if a man like you had any choice. I don't mind a bit of bluster. I've done some myself from time to time, truth to tell. But I knew you'd come around. So, when does the cripple leave for your country house? Sussex, correct?"

It was bad enough that the earl called Eleanor a cripple, but seemed even worse now that Jack knew all that he knew. "Her name is Eleanor, Chelfham."

"And her place is *gone*. That was part of our deal," the earl said, his expression going from jovial to solid marble in the space of a second. He pulled the serviette from his collar and looked levelly at Jack. "So?"

Jack attempted to look subservient, as the earl seemed to expect him to, but it wasn't easy. "My wife departs tomorrow at noon. I would have sent her sooner, but she feels slightly ill and the journey was necessarily delayed. I know what you demanded, and I'm complying with that demand. Now it's time you show me some measure of good faith in return."

Chelfham popped a last bit of kipper into his mouth and spoke around it. "A show of good faith, is it? Very well. I suppose a hearty handshake wouldn't be enough for either of us. But, first, don't you have something to show me? I've already heard about it, you understand, but I really do need to see it for myself."

Jack pulled a slim journal from his jacket pocket and tossed it onto the table. He'd spent long hours yesterday making up a false set of names, delivery dates, monies collected from his freetrading operations. All the earl would need to know once he *eliminated* Jack as his new partner. "As you can see, I anticipated just such a request. I'm not stupid. We share now, Chelfham, or this association is over before it's really begun."

Chelfham's smile all but screamed *Oh, yet you* are *most certainly stupid, Eastwood, and very nearly dead.* But when his mouth moved, it was to say, "Very well, you drive a hard bargain, Eastwood, but fair is fair. It's only fitting that I should show you some proof that I know what I'm about. Shall we adjourn to my study?"

For the next half hour, Jack allowed himself to be content with the few pages of several different journals Chelfham agreed he could see. Mostly, he saw long columns of figures alongside coded explanations. The earl was kind enough to decipher those for him, so that Jack ascertained that massive amounts of tea, brandy and silk made up most of the "imports," while the "exports" were not the raw materials Europe always craved, but gold coin.

Jack knew he should not try to content himself with degrees of guilt, but helping the people of Romney Marsh by selling their wool for a profit somehow seemed less reprehensible than sending the King's actual coin across the Channel to eventually help fatten Bonaparte's war chest.

Not only that, but Chelfham had shown Jack pages from only about half of the thick stack of journals he kept locked in his desk, each journal covering a different smaller "gang" that made up the whole. Each gang had it's own name. The Green Men Gang. The Yellow Men Gang. But, above them all, the Red Men Gang. Red, the color of hell-fire. There was nothing the least bit ragtag about these operations; Wellington's troops may not have been so well organized.

"And you're in charge of all of this? I'm impressed, truly. Your profits must be staggering," Jack said at last, when his mind became too full of information to possibly hope to remember any more details.

Chelfham had been lounging on a green leather couch below the study window overlooking the back gardens and mews. There was even a door on that wall, leading out to those small gardens — a fact Jack had been happy to commit to memory. "Yes, but they are not *my* profits, sad to say. I do believe your small enterprise yields you nearly as much as riding herd on this entire vast operation does me."

"But I take all the risks," Jack pointed out as Chelfham gathered up the journals and locked them into the drawer once more. "It would seem, pardon me, that you're nothing more than a glorified bookkeeper."

"To someone like you, yes. But I have my uses, and my talents."

Jack pretended surprise, as if some great revelation had just struck him. "You're the one who arranges for the funds needed to purchase goods in France, aren't you? You're the one who moves in society, who picks and chooses just who gets to *invest* in your schemes. Yes, I can see your usefulness now."

The earl's smile faded. "Enough of this. All you need to know is that I supply the funds, and you supply the rest. The mules, the men, the boats. Within a year, our enterprise and our profits will grow tenfold. Agreed?"

"Agreed," Jack said, getting to his feet. "Just one more question if you don't mind. What happens if the *real* leader of this rather marvelous enterprise finds out what we're doing behind his back, discovers that you're diverting some of the investor's funds to feed and grow our own, separate enterprise on Romney Marsh?"

"That's simple enough. Then we're dead, Eastwood, both of us."

"Yes, I thought as much. You're risking quite a lot, Chelfham, and all for a few extra pennies. Is no one ever rich enough?"

The earl's smile returned. "No. Never. But don't rush off, Eastwood. If you'll recall, there's still the matter of my *former* partners."

Jack was finding it more and more difficult to play the fool. "In my own good time, Chelfham. And in my own way."

"And no need, actually. I could tell that your heart wasn't really in it, you know. That you actually might have felt the task distasteful. So, when an opportunity presented itself to me last night, I took it. Just to prove to you that you are my partner now."

"Meaning?" Jack asked, yet again trying to reconcile this evilly grinning man with the notion he was Eleanor's father.

"Meaning, Eastwood, that early yesterday evening I presented them with a cask of fine brandy from one of the runs — delivered to me straight from France. I told Harris that I had sent it directly on to Gilly's rooms in Half Moon Street, where they could drink it without bothering about Harris's wife nattering in his ear."

"Straight from France, you said?"

"Absolutely. French brandy as pure and clear as water itself. Yes, a very rare and special gift, you understand. There was a note included with the gift, informing them that I was also increasing their share of the profits. So much to drink to, so much to celebrate. I imagine they're dead drunk by now. Literally."

Jack understood immediately. For ease of shipping, brandy was often put into small casks just as it came out of the still, and massively overproof. Unless heavily diluted with water, and perhaps some burned sugar for color, what came from the cask was nearly colorless, fairly tasty, but fatal in any quantity. "You sent Eccles a cask straight from France? You did warn him to dilute it, didn't you?"

"And defeat the purpose of the gift? Hardly. I expect we shall be hearing the sad news by tomorrow. So, what say you, Eastwood? How long do you think convention will force me to continue to house my brother-in-law's appallingly boring widow? No, no, never mind. I can be magnanimous. A fortnight, at the least. Now, if you'd be so kind as to take yourself off to Half Moon Street and retrieve my note before Eccles's maid arrives tomorrow for her weekly clean and dust-up? That should make everything all nice and tidy."

Jack set his jaw. "I'm not your servant, Chelfham."

"No, you're not. We're partners in our sure to be brilliantly profitable merge of your rougher talents and, well, and of my brains, Eastwood — face it, you know I'm speaking the truth. And we're now both beholden to each other, in some way, so that we're more than happy to perform . . . favors for each other."

"We each hold something over the other's head, you mean, and can pull it out at any time we need something," Jack said, noticing that while Chelfham's smile was still as wide, it had lost its cheerfulness.

"Yes. A lesson I learned years ago, as a

matter of fact, to my chagrin, as it only works when both parties are beholden to the other. So be frank with me, Eastwood, is there anything you might want from me? Just ask it."

Jack was more than willing to test the man. "Very well. My wife remains in London."

Jack had grown heartily sick of Chelfham's smile, his smug attitude, and to see both desert him now both pleased him even while it made him more concerned for Eleanor's safety. "No, Eastwood, absolutely not. You've already agreed that she must go."

"Yes, I forgot. Partners, but not quite equal partners," Jack said, at last revealing a portion of the depth of his anger.

"Oh, don't sulk, Jack. We'll find you someone else," the earl said, regaining his smile. "God, man, look at the piece I found. You'd be astonished at what money can buy."

CHAPTER NINETEEN

Eleanor had returned from shopping with Rian and had been waiting for Jack for more than two hours — and her temper was none the better for the wait.

How dare he send her off with Rian acting as her grand protector? And to purchase shoes? At a time like this, all Jack could think for her to do was to purchase *shoes?*

Still, she thought, holding her legs out in front of her as she sat in their shared bedchamber, she had to admit these were very pretty shoes. Ollie certainly had never suggested soft kid slippers with matching black ribbons wrapped cunningly around her ankles. The ribbons even covered her scar, something she hadn't realized was possible.

She'd earlier stood a good distance from the large mirror in the bedchamber, then watched her reflection as she walked toward the glass. It was upsetting to her that her limp seemed more pronounced now, but she couldn't deny how much more comfortable she felt. She'd been on her feet most of the day, and yet her calf did not ache even a little bit.

Perhaps she'd forgive Jack for sending her off while he went about plotting the earl's downfall. . . .

"Mrs. Eastwood, ma'am?"

Eleanor broke from her reverie to see that Beatrice had entered the bedchamber. "Beatrice," she said, getting to her feet. "Whatever are you doing here? I believe the doctor ordered you to your bed."

"Yes, ma'am, he did," the maid said, nodding her head. "I couldn't do it, ma'am. You need someone more than that silly Mary watching over you, that's what I thought when I was laying there, all like some useless lump. What if someone tried to hurt you again, ma'am? And there I'd be, tucked up in the attics, and no use to your dear self at all. I'd never forgive myself, I wouldn't."

"Why, thank you, Beatrice," Eleanor said, flattered. "But what about your leg?"

Without hesitation, Beatrice pulled up her skirts, revealing bandages on her leg from thigh to ankle. "Mrs. Hendersen wrapped it all up nice and tight for me. Can't bend my knee for asking, though, ma'am, so now I'm gimping about, just like you." She let go of her skirts and clapped her hands to her cheeks. "Oh, ma'am, I'm that sorry."

"Don't be," Eleanor told her, walking across the room to give the woman a brief hug. "And I'm very nearly overwhelmed, dear Beatrice."

"Then I'm still your lady's maid? You won't be turning me off? Mr. Treacle said as how you'd be turning me off, seeing as how I'm not doing nothing but taking up space and eating my fool head off."

"Treacle said that, did he?" Eleanor was amazed at how angry the butler's words made her. "Beatrice, I want you to go back upstairs to bed, and stay there until Mr. Eastwood's physician says you are allowed to return to your duties. As for Treacle, you're not to worry your head about him, do you understand?"

"Oh, yes, ma'am, thank you, ma'am," Beatrice said, curtsying, and at last allowing a wince of pain to appear on her round, homely face. "God bless you, ma'am!"

Once Beatrice was gone, Eleanor returned to her seat on the chair in front of the desk, and tried to resume her indignation over Jack's order that she be hauled off to Bond Street. But she couldn't do it, hard as she tried. She loved her new shoes, almost as much as she loved the fact that Jack had cared enough about her comfort to see that she had them.

Small acts of kindness. Isn't that what her papa had told her? Small acts of kindness led to great rewards, most usually in the form of loyalty, or acts of kindness returned.

Beatrice, for all that she'd been burned in an effort to save her mistress, seemed to truly believe she owed Eleanor a loyalty far greater than Eleanor could have expected or even hoped for . . . because Eleanor had showed her *kindness.*

And now here she was, certainly justified in being angry with Jack, yet feeling nothing but kindness for him because he had showed kindness to her.

Eleanor picked up the letter opener as she thought about this, turned everything over in her mind before saying quietly, "Either he really, truly cares, or he is very, *very* clever. . . ."

The small brass clock on the mantel struck the hour of six, bringing Eleanor back to the fact that, no matter what else Jack Eastwood was or wasn't, he wasn't *here.*

And she wanted him here. She needed him here.

Eleanor didn't know how to react to that

knowledge. She'd always been so private, so self-contained. Even with all of her love for and long talks with her papa, she had been careful to keep her own counsel on her most private thoughts.

Now, all she wanted to do was share those thoughts, those secrets, even those fears, with Jack. She wanted to let go of the tight reins she'd always kept on herself and her emotions.

When he touched her, loved her, she wanted to cry out, move beneath him with all the heat she felt inside, give herself over to him in every way possible.

She didn't want to be Morgan. She no longer envied Morgan's freedom, her willingness to share herself and her joy with the world. Her willingness to *dare.*

Eleanor simply wanted to be Eleanor. Be herself. *All* of herself. Even if she hadn't realized there could be more to her than the quiet, dutiful daughter, the calming one, the rational one, the *good* one. The *forgiving* one.

And, yes, she wanted to dare. But in her own way. She longed to confront the Earl of Chelfham, tell him what she knew, then walk away her own person, free of him, free of her sordid legacy.

She wanted to go to Jacko, release him from his guilt, the guilt whose source she'd long pretended she did not know.

She wanted to shout to the skies: *I am me! I am Eleanor Becket! I have made myself!*

This was the gift, the real kindness, that Jack Eastwood had given her. Not the dreams of a silly, shy virgin, but the hopes and confidence of a woman.

And when he finally decided to drag himself back here to her, she'd damn well tell him!

CHAPTER TWENTY

Jack sat in the dimness behind a table situated in the rear of a nameless tavern at the bottom of Bond Street, looking into a mug of ale rather than drinking from it.

Cluny had been with him until a few minutes ago, the two of them discussing the events of that afternoon. The actions of that afternoon. The disgust of that afternoon.

But now the Irishman was gone, heading back to the small inn and the locked room where their prize snored away his drunkenness. Cluny would stay with the man until he was recovered, until he was needed, and Rian Becket would have to take Cluny's place tomorrow when Eleanor drove out in the coach.

Rian was young, but he'd plenty of experience, riding the Marsh with the Black Ghost. Jack had no worries on that head; the boy would obey orders.

Unless that plan was no longer necessary.

He already had his man, and he only needed the one. Two men betrayed, one of them dead — Chelfham had made himself an enemy Jack could use. Now to discover exactly *how* to use him. Draw Chelfham out, bring him face-to-face with Eleanor at a time and place better suited to keeping her safe. If she felt she had to confront him, hear the words from the man's own mouth, Jack would by damn find a way for her to safely hear them; put the past in the past, where it belonged.

There was a way. There had to be a way. He simply had to find it . . .

Jack was so intent on his thoughts that it took him a moment to notice that someone had slipped into the chair across the table from him. He looked up slowly, taking in the sight of the well-tailored but not flamboyantly dressed man. A sophisticated gentleman of means.

Yet not many London gentlemen had such startlingly intelligent eyes, or moved quite so quietly. The stranger sat at his ease, but Jack could feel the tension in the man, the alertness born of a soldier . . . or at least of someone accustomed to having to deal with unexpected attack. Accustomed, and un-afraid.

He was a handsomely put together man. The intelligent eyes were darkly green, his thick light brown hair long and tied back at his nape. His hands, that he'd been careful to rest on the tabletop where Jack could see them — to show that he was harmless, Jack supposed, and which Jack had already sensed was a misnomer — were well shaped, the fingers long, almost artistically formed.

But most of all, more than anything, there was this *air* about the stranger. A certain unexplainable aura of confidence and danger that was no longer any stranger to Jack.

"Good afternoon to you, Mr. Eastwood," the man said, his voice low, pleasant.

"Yes, thank you. Good afternoon to you. Please allow me to hazard a guess here, my good sir. As you're the only one left, at least as far as I know, you're Chance Becket, aren't you?"

"Ainsley told me you were sharp as a tack. Yes, I'm Chance Becket. A pleasure to meet you at last, Jack."

Jack's mind was racing furiously. "Of course, and a pleasure for me, as well. Rian nearly gave you away, didn't he? He told me he'd not come straight to London, but had first gone somewhere else. He went to you, didn't he? To tell you about the countess's new babies. To tell you Eleanor was in

London, and so much more. I should have realized. And here I was, deluding myself with the notion that Ainsley trusts me."

"He does trust you, Jack, or else we wouldn't be having this conversation. You would have been dead two years ago," Chance Becket said amiably as he lifted his hand to a passing barmaid, signaling that two more mugs of ale were needed at the table.

"Yes," Jack said, smiling. "There is that, isn't there. So, if you'll allow me to refresh my memory? You'd be the oldest, correct?"

"Correct, if that matters to you."

Jack was in no mood for evasive banter, so he went straight to the heart of the matter. "It does, if you are willing to believe that I'm in love with your sister. Madly, deeply and irrevocably in love with Eleanor Becket."

Chance raised one well-defined eyebrow. "Well, you're direct if nothing else. I have a wife like that. Go on. You're going to ask me for her hand in marriage?"

Jack sat forward, rested both arms on the tabletop. "There's nothing I'd like more, but first things first. You're not Ainsley, but you are the oldest, and you are here. There's something I have to say."

Chance picked up one of the heavy mugs

of ale the barmaid slapped down on her way to another table, and held it an inch from his lips. "That sounds ominous. Does this have anything to do with Chelfham and the Red Men, or are you about to complicate things further with some sort of confession I'd then be forced to deal with?"

Jack smiled. He liked this man. This man might soon slit his throat, but he liked him. "I'm going to complicate things, I'm afraid. As you've already pointed out, I've been with Ainsley for about two years," he said, as it was always best to begin at the beginning. "But I came to be with him under false pretenses."

"Really. More than ominous." Chance put down his mug, untouched, and tossed two coins onto the table top. "Shall we walk?"

They were out on the flagway before Jack spoke again. "I tricked my way into Becket Hall because I was fairly certain you Beckets had something to do with the smuggling trade in the area."

Chance smiled. "Well, shame on my dear brother Courtland. I warned him about his flair for the dramatic. The cape, the mask. Overdone. I told him so. But I interrupt. How did you decide that?"

Jack stole a look at Chance Becket, who was walking with his hands clasped behind his back, and looking no more dangerous than any other gentleman passing up and down the flagway. If anything, he seemed genuinely amused. "Your father's friend Billy is a talkative drunk."

Now Chance laughed quietly. "Such is his reputation, yes. As I'm sure you heard."

"I asked the right questions, and only guessed at the rest. He didn't betray you," Jack said, defending the older man. "I was with Wellington for a time, and learned how to ask the right questions, then make reasonable deductions. But that's another conversation for another time, and what I'm trying to do now is confess. I was a gentleman of little means, as I portrayed myself to Ainsley, but I was not earning my daily bread after returning from the Peninsula by traveling about England, playing at cards."

They stopped at an intersection, waiting for a break in the crush of town carriages on the roadway. "No. You were looking for freetraders, isn't that what you said? Were you — are you — working for the Crown? Because that would be a bloody pity, my friend."

They moved on, carefully skirting a large puddle in the middle of the street, then joining up together on the other side of the road. "No, not really. And before I tell you anything else, I want to say that what happened with Ainsley was a complete surprise to me. Being accepted that way, taken in, made a part of the entire enterprise. My reasons for being in Romney Marsh at all are no longer important, but I feel I must reveal them before I can be comfortable asking for Eleanor's hand in marriage."

Chance stopped, looked at Jack. "And will you tell her, as well?"

Jack grinned. "If I'm still alive to do so, yes."

"An honorable man. What *will* we do with you, Jack Eastwood?"

"Hear me out, I suppose. Only after I found myself a part of . . . of your family business did I dismiss the idea of turning you all over to the Waterguard. You should know that. My loyalty lies with Ainsley Becket, who I consider to be one of the most amazing, and amazingly intricate men I've ever met, and I've dined with Wellington and his staff."

"You'll have to tell my brother Spence all about that dinner when he's finally home again. I enjoy watching him go green with envy at times."

Jack smiled at that, as the remark eased some of his tension. If he was to see Spencer Becket again, the odds were good that Jack wouldn't be finding himself dead before nightfall. "You should also know that I have forwarded the occasional anonymous note to the War Office, warning of rumors I'd heard about French spies being transported back and forth across the Channel. I did this both before and after I met Ainsley. I think, know, I did this to salve my conscience, as I was now a freetrader myself, and not about to walk away from either the excitement or the comfortable living I was beginning to enjoy very much."

"Honorable and refreshingly honest. An adventurer with a conscience. No wonder you admire Ainsley. Please, continue."

"You'd like to wring my neck, wouldn't you? Right here, in the middle of Bond Street. But I never put your family in danger, I can swear to that."

"I'd say thank you," Chance told him, "except for the fact that you'd be hanging just as high as the rest of us if you did. I believe I read one or two of those anonymous notes of yours, when I was still with the War Office. You signed them *A Friend of the Crown,* correct? We were of course very interested in the idea of information crossing the Channel to Napoleon. In fact, I was sent to Romney Marsh to poke my nose about, looking for spies, thanks to what was probably the first of your little notes. I believe we missed each other by mere weeks, as a matter of fact."

"You actually worked in the — God, that's rich, and rather brilliant. Serve your country and at the same time keep your ear to the ground to learn if your family ever came under suspicion."

For the first time, Chance's smile left him. "I served the Crown as my choice, Jack. There was nothing devious or self-serving about it. Now, are you done?"

"With my confession? Yes, I think that's it."

"Then I suppose it's my turn. While I appreciate your honesty, we already knew what you told me just now, Jack, except, I'll admit, for that *Friend of the Crown* business. Ainsley has known from the beginning."

Jack turned to him in surprise. *"What?"*

"Oh, my, now you're upset. Ainsley said you'd be upset. Think about this for a moment, Jack. Knowing Ainsley now, as you think you do, is this a man who carelessly opens his home to strangers? A man who would risk his family by embracing that stranger?"

"Christ. No. No, he isn't. God, I thought

I was being so clever. But Ainsley still holds to the charade, and so does Jacko. Hell, Jacko came to my room and played cards with me nearly every day and — Christ, I'm an idiot! So you already knew?"

"I received a few communiqués from Ainsley about you while you were recovering from the wounds you invited in order to impress us, yes. And, as I was still at the War Office, it wasn't difficult to investigate your background. So, if you feel better now, having confessed your . . . sins . . . shall we get on with it? I want to hear more about Chelfham."

"Not yet. What about Billy? Did I use him, or did he use me? While I was thinking I was learning secrets from Billy, was he actually just feeding me information, reeling me in like some fish on a line?"

"You were asking too many questions in the area, Jack, and, sad to say, not being quite as discreet as you thought you were. You came to our attention. And Billy? Oh yes, definitely, he was sent from my employ to Romney Marsh to do exactly what he did. As well as Demetrious, once our ship's chandler, who you paid to help start the fight that night in the tavern. You shouldn't have fought so well, Jack. Demetrious had the devil of a time avoiding your fists and keeping his knife directed at . . . nonfatal areas. We needed you injured and helpless. Down, but not out. Billy's injuries, of course, weren't real at all, as every last man and barmaid in the tavern that night was ours, all of them playacting quite convincingly. So yes, I think you can say you were reeled in like a fish. My apologies, I'm sure, but we needed a closer look at you."

"Well, I'll be damned," Jack said, at last seeing the rather twisted humor in the whole episode. "I'm also probably very lucky to be alive, aren't I?"

"You've proved yourself loyal," Chance said, gifting Jack with a companionable slap on the back. "Now, finish it, because I know there's more, unfortunately. In fact, that's why I'm here, rather than anyone else. To answer what we knew had to be your rather burning questions so that we can all move on. Ainsley, in his infinite wisdom, thought it might be time, that after more than two long years you were probably suffering from increasingly annoying attacks of conscience."

Jack shook his head, ridding it of the rather embarrassing remnants of Chance's earlier revelations. "Since I have little choice, I suppose I have to accept that, although if you're hoping to hear me thank you, I don't think that's going to happen. So, yes, let's finish it. Tell me, while at the War Office — did you work with the Dragoons along the coastline?"

"Ah, and here we are, at the heart of everything. Not directly, Jack, no. Now I'll be helpful yet again — my wife tells me it's only polite to be helpful when possible — and ask you why you want to know, so that you can tell me."

After all that he'd already admitted, mention of his cousin was only the last hurdle Jack needed to jump over before he knew whether or not he was accepted, or was about to become a dead man. Or at least that's what he'd thought a few minutes earlier. But Chance Becket already knew what he was going to ask.

"Then let me tell you what you already know. Tell you why I came to Romney Marsh in the first place. I was there to find out what happened to my cousin, a lieutenant with the Dragoons patrolling the marsh until he dropped off the edge of the earth a little over two years ago. My mother and I live with my widowed aunt, and she'd begged me to find out what happened to him."

Chance was all seriousness now. "You couldn't get that information from his commanding officers?"

"No, not enough to satisfy me at any rate. They were rather curiously closemouthed, and the most I could get anyone to say was that he'd disappeared the morning after intercepting a smuggling run. Their evasions made me more curious than I'd been when I first asked my questions, so I thought up the idea of passing myself off as a traveling gamester, always carefully listening for any information about smugglers in the area. Richard wasn't much of a son, and I doubt he was much of an officer, but my aunt deserves some sort of answer as to what happened to her only child. Did he desert? Is he dead?"

Jack looked at his companion as they walked along through the early evening in silence for nearly a full minute before Chance said, "We're speaking now of Lieutenant Richard Diamond."

Jack stopped walking, peered at Chance with some intensity. "Yes. Diamond. And you know what happened to him. You knew him personally?"

Chance had also stopped a few paces along the flagway, and now he made his way back to Jack, not stopping until he stood directly in front of him. "I knew him. And, I'm sorry to say, since even the worst of us is often loved by a mother, your cousin is most definitely dead."

At last, an answer. At least part of an answer. "How do you know that?"

"Because I was there, Jack. Because I watched him die," Chance Becket said flatly, looking straight into Jack's eyes.

"You watched him die?" Jack took a deep breath, let it out slowly. "Enough. I've heard enough. And you picked this moment to tell me?"

"I'll tell you the rest if and when you ever want to hear it. But we knew it was more than time you heard the truth from me, especially once Treacle saw which way the wind was blowing between you and Elly."

Jack stepped back against a brick storefront and laughed out loud; a release of tension, he supposed. "Treacle, too? My own butler?" Then he just as quickly sobered. "Does Eleanor know about Treacle?"

"No. He was installed long before Elly bullied Ainsley into letting her come to London. I would have loved to have been there for that, you know. Jack, I'd be as angry as you must be, but we felt Treacle necessary. We're very used to protecting ourselves."

"Fine. I understand," Jack said soberly, pushing himself away from the wall. "But it ends now. Treacle, and anyone else you've got spying on me. Either I'm trusted or I'm not."

"I agree. Ainsley agrees, which is why I'm here, and why I'm going to tell you about your cousin's death, both the why and the how of it. There's a coffeehouse just down this street. Confessions are thirsty work, on both ends. Shall we?"

By the time another hour had passed, Jack and Chance had come to terms with each other, and with the unhappy coincidence of their shared association with Lieutenant Richard Diamond.

They had, in fact, come along far enough in their association to begin to form a tentative friendship. This in no small part had to do with the fact that both men loved Eleanor Becket.

And, because speaking of Eleanor could only lead to why she was in London, at last Chance asked Jack if, loving Eleanor as he said he did, he was aware that the Earl of Chelfham was her uncle.

"Not her uncle, Chance. Her natural father," Jack said quietly. "She told me that no one else knows, so I'm aware I'm breaking a confidence. But I think you need to know this one, most especially if we decide to remove Chelfham from the playing board.

Eleanor's mother cuckolded her husband with his own brother. Imagine the burden of carrying that knowledge with you for at least the last few years, since her memory began returning to her."

"Her *father?*" Chance put down his mug and leaned in closer over the tabletop. "That's not possible. Is it?" He held up one hand. "No, I didn't mean that. Anything's possible, especially, God knows, here in London. And Ainsley doesn't know?"

Jack shook his head. "Eleanor was afraid if Ainsley knew everything he'd come to London to ask the earl some very pointed questions, and she wasn't willing to risk that."

"Yes, that sounds like our Elly. She's protective to a fault. Damn, you're right. She shouldn't be here. Not if we're going to be eliminating the earl in some way. Bad enough when we thought he was her uncle. What else have you discovered? How deeply is he involved with the Red Men Gang?"

Once again Jack found himself handing information over to Chance Becket, but he no longer had any reservations in doing so. Besides, he could use the man's help.

"Set herself up as a target?" Chance said when Jack finished his explanation. "No.

That's not going to happen. Not with Elly. I don't want her to so much as see that bastard again, let alone talk to him. The whole thing is too . . . hell, I'll say it — too sordid for her. She's got such a pure heart. She won't be able to handle anything like that. She'll take it all on her own shoulders, even if the man isn't worth a single worry."

"I agree, although I think she can handle a lot more than you give her credit for. A spine of Toledo steel, that's what Jacko said. I didn't believe him then, but I believe him now," Jack told him, happy to have an ally. "That said, which one of us is going to tell her she's already seen the last of Chelfham? She's determined, Chance."

"She can be as determined as she wants to be, it's bloody not happening. You're in love, Jack, which makes you vulnerable to her pleadings, but I'm the brother, and I can be more forceful with her. We'll put our heads together, think of something else. Especially now that you've got your man safely stowed away. You're certain he's going to live?"

"Cluny thinks so, although when I left him the poor bastard looked three-parts dead, nearly as dead as the other one. If we have to, we'll prop him up in front of Chelfham, I suppose."

"Yes," Chance said slowly, rubbing at his chin. "We'll both think about this some more, but first I'd like you to tell me what Elly has told you she remembers about her . . . well, the events of her rescue. I know her, and she would never tell you more than her own story. There might be something the man who loves her still needs to know."

Jack was more than willing to do just that. "You're right. She's holding something back, Chance, saying it's not her secret, which makes me believe she's protecting Ainsley in some way. But she keeps getting tangled up in her own lies and evasions, and I know she wants to tell me. It could wait until I see Ainsley, speak to him directly, but I won't say I'm not willing to hear what you have to say if you think it's important."

Chance held his mug with both hands. "She never told us what you've just told me, so I honestly don't know how much she actually remembers. God, I hope she never remembers the worst of it. That's always been Jacko's greatest fear, and I don't think he'll appreciate me telling you about it. But, in a way, this does concern you, as some of it concerns our friend Chelfham. We never had a name, you understand, until Elly's memory started to return, but it wasn't until you brought up the same name in connection to the Red Men Gang that we began to consider the impossible. And it does seem impossible, even now, with your mention of the man you saw entering the black coach. I don't know how I'm going to tell Ainsley this one, frankly. I damn well know I don't want to tell him."

"You're a fine fellow, Chance," Jack said with a wry smile, "and I'm happy to know you. But if you don't get to the point soon I may have to reach across this table and choke it out of you."

Chance returned Jack's smile, his just as wry. "Sorry. I'm trying to sort out what you need to know from what we only suppose, what I sincerely hope isn't true."

"Let me see if I can help," Jack offered. "Ainsley, your entire family, were privateers. I guessed as much, and Eleanor finally confirmed that for me. Privateering is allowable under English law. You did have a Letter of Marque from the Crown, didn't you?"

"We did," Chance answered, then smiled in remembered amusement. "We also had Letters of Marque from Spain, one from America, and another from France — although that last was a clever forgery, I will admit. And *that*, my friend, was not *allowable*. Some might say that wasn't *sporting*, and others, probably with good reason, could even have called us next door to pirates. However, we considered ourselves English at the bottom of it, and never attacked an English ship. Never, Jack."

Suddenly Jack understood. "Until you attacked the ship Eleanor and her family were traveling on from Jamaica to England?"

Chance nodded. "We were misled, betrayed by Ainsley's partner — in more ways than you can imagine. And yes, a part of that betrayal ended with us mistakenly attacking an English ship. From that moment on we were finished, we couldn't stay where we were, even if we wished to, and God knows we had no reason to remain. Ainsley had been about to move us to Becket Hall in any case. We no longer needed adventuring to survive and, besides, it was time to get the girls to civilization. Morgan, Fanny. Cassandra, who was just an infant."

His hands closed into fists on the tabletop. "But we were talked into one more adventure, and a bounty that would make us all wealthy beyond our dreams. Four merchant ships traveling together, each of them loaded to the gunwales with treasures and heading for Spain, and with only two slow-moving escort ships we could outmaneuver with half our sails gone. Too much to resist, you understand, the way our *partner* laid it all out to us. Besides, Ainsley was ending the partnership by retiring to England, and his partner argued that he deserved one last large haul. Ainsley decided we'd do it. One final hurrah, as it were."

"And all hell came crashing down around you," Jack said quietly, the sudden bleak look in Chance's eyes more than enough for him. He didn't need to hear any more, except as it affected Eleanor. "Eleanor said you sank the ship she was sailing on, and I wondered about that. As privateers, you were allowed to take the ship, sell it. You sank it to hide what had happened, didn't you?"

Chance seemed to be having difficulty bringing himself back from a most unpleasant memory. "Yes, we sank the ship with a broadside right at the waterline. We came out of the fog bank at midmorning, believing our *partner* and his ships to still be with us, to find him gone and ourselves surrounded by a damn armada. It was chaos, Jack. We had been thoroughly betrayed. Outflanked, outgunned, outmanned. And damned desperate."

"He left you all out there to die? *Bastard.*

Where was he?"

A small tic began to work in Chance's left cheek. "Elsewhere. Let's just say he was busy elsewhere." He shook off the memory and leaned his elbows on the tabletop. "But here is what you need to know. Eleanor and her mother were still on the ship, hiding. Nobody realized that until we'd hit her with the broadside. But Jacko was still onboard, the last man to swing over to the Black Ghost — he had a flair for the dramatic back then — and he heard the woman cry out. He yelled to us what he was doing, and then disappeared below decks."

"That took some courage."

Chance smiled. "Jacko is invincible, or so he believes, and he was a lot younger then. If you think he's formidable now, you should have known him then. But to get on with this, and get it said as quickly as possible. I swung over to help Jacko and found him belowdecks. Eleanor and her mother had hidden themselves in a deep cupboard in the captain's quarters, probably placed there by the captain himself. He's also the one who most likely armed the mother and told her what she had to do if the battle was lost."

Jack felt suddenly cold in the pit of his stomach. "Kill the child. Kill herself. Anything's better than two women, even a female child, in the hands of pirates."

"Yes, I'm sure that's what he told her. I want you to understand this, Jack. There was fire everywhere by now. We knew the ship was going down. The woman had poor little Elly in a death grip at the very back of the cupboard, and she was holding a pistol to her head, screaming for us to leave, that she'd kill the child before allowing us to ravish her. She already had the damn thing cocked. There was another pistol beside her, obviously for herself."

"You couldn't reach her?"

Chance shook his head. "Each time I tried, she turned the pistol on me. She didn't believe the ship was sinking. Nothing we said could convince her to let go of Elly, drop the damn pistol. Jesus," he said quietly, "I've lived the moment over and over in my head, trying to remind myself that I was only seventeen, that there wasn't all that much I could do. But I should have done more, I should have done *something*."

"Yes, but what? And all while the ship was sinking? You had to get them out of there, or leave them there to save yourselves."

"Exactly. And Jacko was not going to leave a child to drown. He . . . uh . . . he told the woman as much, over and over, even as the ship began yawing badly and we knew we only had another few minutes before the damn thing was going to roll. But the woman wouldn't listen. She just wouldn't . . . listen." Chance hesitated a moment, sighed. "Jacko shot her very cleanly between the eyes, so that she'd immediately drop the pistol."

Jack sat back against his chair as if a bullet had just slammed into his own body, staring at Chance. "He *shot* her?"

"He warned her. If she wanted to die she could, but he was by damn getting the child to safety." Chance put a hand to his forehead. "I was half in the cupboard, and Jacko had the pistol directly next to my ear when he fired. Jesus, the sound of that pistol going off . . . the sound of Elly's screams. I'll never forget either one. At any rate, I was able to get inside the cupboard now, and I grabbed Elly up, raced her up on deck, where she got away from me, began running across the deck. That's when a piece of falling rigging got her and her leg was injured."

"I've seen her ankle, Chance. Seen where a piece of iron burned into her skin, seen the mess that was made of her bones."

"We were lucky Odette was able to save her foot, lucky that she ever walked again.

But she doesn't remember any of that, Jack. She has, as you already know, remembered other things in the last few years. Her name, vague memories of her home. Obviously she also remembers what happened to her father the day before the attack — the man she believed to be her father. But not the attack itself. Thank God, not that. We lived in a terrible world, Jack, and I don't think it's gotten any saner in the past fifteen years."

Both men sat quietly, Chance Becket undoubtedly reliving yet again a scene that no one should have witnessed let alone been a part of, and Jack mentally going over past conversations with Eleanor.

She had quoted something to him in Latin. *Actus non facit reum, nisi mens sit rea.* The act is not criminal unless the intent is criminal. She'd said Ainsley used those words to help ease his soul, but that Jacko *lived* by the maxim, that he was a man who thought simply and acted impassively . . . "And he sleeps very well."

Jesus.

At last Jack said, "She remembers, Chance. From the few conversations we've had where Jacko's name was mentioned, I'd have to say she knows. She remembers everything."

Chance sighed deeply. "Then I pray to God she never tells him. He thinks of Elly as his daughter, you know, and loves her past all reason, in the only way he knows how to love. He'd die for her without a second thought."

"And kill for her, as well. Yes, I actually was already aware of that. Thank you, Chance, for being so honest. I know telling me couldn't have been easy. One more question, though, please. You say you were half inside the cupboard. Do you remember what Eleanor's mother looked like? Does Eleanor look anything like her?"

"As if cut from the same cloth," Chance said, once more shaking his head. "I'd think that must drive Jacko nearly crazy whenever he pulls out his conscience for an airing. Why?"

"I think Chelfham flat-out recognized her, that's why. I appreciate all you've told me, but now *I'll* tell *you.* Keeping secrets damn well nearly got Eleanor killed. And if that had happened, my friend, I would have come after all of you Beckets, and you would have had to think up a whole new definition of hell on earth."

"And I believe you." Chance chuckled low in his throat. "Jack, friend, my Julia is going to adore you. Shall we go?" He got to his feet, this time Jack tossing down some coins, and they walked out into the rapidly gathering twilight.

"Eleanor is undoubtedly wondering where I am," Jack said, feeling much like a husband about to have a peal rung over his head, and smiling happily at the thought. "I suppose I'm going to have to get used to keeping her informed of my comings and goings."

"If you value your head, yes, you are. And I say that from experience. Now, are we finished? No more lingering questions, no more heartfelt confessions?"

Would Jack be pushing his luck? He decided to find out. "Two more questions, actually. One, Morgan named her twins Geoffrey and Isabella, and Eleanor told me they were very special names. Why?"

"Sorry, Jack. You'd have to apply to Ainsley for that answer. Which, by the way, I wouldn't do if I were you. Eleanor will tell you when she thinks it's time. What else?"

Jack hesitated, then decided he'd already pushed, so why not push one more time. "Ainsley's unnamed partner. The one who betrayed him all those years ago. Can I assume he's dead?"

Chance put on his hat, tapped it down at an angle on his head. "We have, for a little over fifteen years. We were given what we believed to be credible proof."

"And now?" Jack asked, remembering the man in the black coach. "Now that you know that Chelfham most probably had something to do with murdering his brother on the very ship you were tricked into attacking — with the help of the ship's captain, apparently — and that he's now a part of this Red Men Gang which is apparently led by the mysterious, dangerous man in the black coach? After all, you Beckets were privateers turned freetraders. Do you still think Ainsley's partner is dead? All these threads, Chance, slowly weaving together. Can this all be coincidence?"

"No, Jack. I don't think this could all be mere coincidence, and neither will Ainsley. Not that I'm going to tell him about the man you saw — and neither are you. Not yet. He already may have his suspicions, but that's all he'll have for now."

"Because we need to wreak some small havoc here first, with the Red Men Gang. With our mysterious stranger's flow of income?"

"Exactly." Chance slammed his fist into

his hand. "It has to be him. He betrayed us while calling us friends. He took Chelfham's money to rid him of his brother aboard ship — and then betrayed him, as well, setting up that same ship for attack. That's just the sort of thing that would amuse him. Everyone loses but him."

"Except that Eleanor lived," Jack said, soaking up information and sorting it in his head. "Not only did she live, but she remembered. I suspected Chelfham, and when I mentioned his name, the pieces all began to tumble into place, didn't they? But it all began with Eleanor. I want her out of London, Chance, as fast as we can get her gone."

"I agree. Let's get this done, destroy as much of the Red Men Gang as we can, cut off the supply of funds to our mysterious stranger. Then we'll get you and Elly safely to Becket Hall and me back to my domestic obscurity. Because once we're done here, Jack, it will be time for the Beckets to keep their heads lowered, tend to their own sheep for a while, and proceed very slowly, very carefully."

"You're talking about years, aren't you? If you go after him at all. Is that what you're saying?"

Chance Becket's handsome face looked

now as if it had been chiseled out of finest marble; cold, and unyielding. "Years? Yes, Jack, I think so. But if it's truly him, if he's alive, if he's out there, we'll find him. In our own time, and on our own terms." He looked at Jack, his green eyes dark as a stormy sea. "And then we'll introduce him to the deepest level of hell."

"When the time comes, I want to be a part of it," Jack told him. "For Eleanor."

"For Elly. For the man who was Geoffrey, and for his Isabella. For all of us. For more than you can ever imagine. *God.* If I thought I understood Ainsley then, when it all happened, I understand even more now, now that I have my own wife, my own children." He touched a hand to Jack's arm. "I think I have an idea, one that will make Elly's arguments moot. If you're game?"

"Let's hear it."

CHAPTER
TWENTY-ONE

Eleanor, half asleep, lifted her hand to push at the lock of hair that tickled at her neck, then sighed, curled more deeply into the chaise lounge that had been aired and brushed after its exposure to the smoke, then placed in Jack's bedchamber.

The slight tickle came again, and she frowned, flicked at it once more before thinking: *Spider?* Spider!

Her hand came up a third time, this swipe much more forceful, and the back of her hand came into sudden, hard contact with something much larger than a spider.

"Ouch! Damn, woman, that was my nose. Are you trying to maim me?"

Eleanor at last opened her eyes and turned onto her back, to see Jack hovering above her in the dim light. "Jack?"

"And who else where you expecting in your boudoir, madam?" he asked, lifting the dragging cashmere shawl and pushing it out of his way as he sat down beside her. He longed to crush her in his arms, protect her from all possible harm, and yet was at the same time in awe of her, and all she'd silently carried on her shoulders for so long.

"Someone more punctual, obviously," Eleanor said as she sat up, pushing at his arm. "You're still sitting on the shawl. Get up, so that I can."

"Why? I rather like you where you are. All soft and warm and . . . well, no longer pliable, I suppose." He grinned down at her. "All right, all right, don't pull faces at me. I'm getting up."

He was trying to be amusing and boyishly endearing, Eleanor supposed, and she, she also supposed, was to respond by forgiving him the fact that he had been gone all day and late into the evening, without a note, without an explanation.

But, although her relief that he had returned to her safely was very nearly overwhelming, Eleanor was not feeling quite that charitable.

"You sent me off with Rian," she told him once she'd slid her legs over the striped satin and pushed herself up to a sitting position. "Do you have *any* idea what it is like to have that boy running amok in a millinery shop?"

Jack had retreated to the drinks table and now held a glass of wine in his hand. "I sent you to a bootmaker. What were you doing in a millinery?"

Eleanor rolled her eyes. Men, even if you loved them, could be so terribly obtuse. "The milliner's shop was just a few steps down from the bootmaker, and I saw a bonnet in the window that I felt sure would be perfect for Fanny and — who are you to ask me to account for my time? Where *were* you?"

"In a moment, Eleanor," Jack said, putting down his glass and taking her hands in his. Delaying the inevitable? Yes, that was it. He'd faced the French in battle, but telling Eleanor what he and Chance and Cluny had done? He'd have to slowly work himself up to that particular bravery. "Tell me about Rian. I'm not sure how somebody runs amok in a millinery shop."

Eleanor rolled her eyes even as she tugged mightily, withdrawing her hands from his grasp. "He insisted upon offering his *opinion,* that's how. And I can tell you honestly, Jack, that there are a multitude of utterly brainless young girls in Mayfair whose mothers would be well advised to keep them on firm leashes. The giggles were bad enough, the constant applying to Rian for his thoughts on each bonnet tried on. But when I saw one of them slipping a small scrap of paper into Rian's hand? Well, Fanny has one less bonnet, and Rian can tell her why."

Jack covered his mouth with his hand, to hide his smile. "What was in the note?"

Once again Eleanor rolled those huge brown eyes, and Jack longed to grab her, kiss her senseless. "The time and place for a clandestine assignation, of course. Lady Sylvia Barnsthorpe should be leg-shackled to her bed until she grows some sense."

"You're delicious as a dragon of maidenly virtue, Eleanor. I imagine all your sisters and brothers shudder when you're displeased with their behavior. But tell me, isn't Rian in love with Fanny? They're both very young, but they're not related, not really, and I always thought that —"

"Fanny fancies herself in love with him, but nothing will ever come of it," Eleanor said, wondering why they were pursuing this inane conversation, why *she* was pursuing it, when all she really wanted to talk about was Jack, and where he'd been all day. "Rian is war mad, and won't be happy until he's on the continent and someone is shooting at him. His greatest fear in life is that Wellington will have won before he can get there. Where *were* you?"

Jack held up one finger. "In a moment, Eleanor. Before you grabbed hold of Rian's ear and dragged him back here, did you happen to actually visit the bootmaker's shop?"

Eleanor was immediately embarrassed. "Oh, yes. Yes, I did. I was angry with you for demanding that Rian take me there, but you were right. Mr. Bodkin was able to remove the higher heel on my shoe and replace it with one matching the other shoe. I'm much more comfortable now. I . . . I *list* rather more to one side when I walk, but I do feel much better this way, and I thank you."

"You're welcome," Jack said, then put out his arm and made a circling motion with his finger. "Show me."

"Show you? Walk about like some prize pig on parade? No, I most certainly will not," Eleanor said, wondering if she might still be lying on the chaise lounge, still very much asleep, and dreaming of this new, rather belligerent Eleanor Becket.

"Very well," Jack said, retrieving his wineglass. "Then I suppose there's nothing else but for me to tell you where I've been all day."

Finally, Eleanor thought, primly folding her hands in front of her. "You did go to see Chelfham, didn't you?"

Jack actually had to jog his memory on that one, as it had been a long, eventful day. "I did, in fact, early this morning. He knows you'll be leaving London tomorrow, which is why I knew you'd be safe today."

"Yet you sent Rian and two footmen with me, all of them rather conspicuously armed. People were all but goggling at me, and openly wondering who I was. I longed to tell them I was the princess of some fantastical foreign land, but I restrained myself."

"That's a shame, you should have done it. Now, is there anything else you're angry about, Eleanor?" Jack asked, grinning, and adoring her. "Just so we can get it out of the way, you understand."

Eleanor looked down at her clasped hands. "Mrs. Ryan prepared a rather lovely trifle for you because you'd commented favorably on her last offering. I instructed her to divide it up amongst the staff before it was ruined. And that is by way of a warning, as I wouldn't be surprised if bubble and squeak returned to the menu tomorrow." She smiled up at him. "There, I think that's it. Am I a shrew? I feel like a shrew, but I've been so worried all day . . ."

"I'm sorry, Eleanor," Jack said, lightly clasping her upper arms. He'd already decided not to tell her about Chelfham's murder attempt on his partners, one that had been only partially successful. She had enough information about her natural father, without adding more sordidness into the mix. "Chelfham told me something that sent me off at a run, and that one thing led to another, and another. I thought about you all day. You're all I think about, which is why I want this over. It's gone on too long as it is. The damn man is interrupting my wooing."

Eleanor longed to melt against him, but held herself back. "And it will be over tomorrow. Even if we're wrong, and he doesn't attempt to attack my coach, we'll go to him, confront him, make him confess to all of his crimes. I know just what I want to say to him, what I want to ask."

Jack knew he had to tell her what he'd done, the plan he and Chance had not only decided upon, but had already acted upon. Now to see how angry she would be at him, and be very glad Eleanor wasn't the sort who threw things. "We don't need to hear him confess to his involvement with the Red

Men Gang, Eleanor. The fool showed me where he keeps his records, most probably because he doesn't plan on me living out the week, once I've done his dirty work for him."

"Killing his brother-in-law and Sir Gilbert."

"Phelps and Eccles, yes," Jack agreed carefully. "He most definitely wants them both dead. At any rate, Cluny and I visited Chelfham's study earlier tonight, once he'd left for the evening, and relieved him of the records of his dealings with the Red Men. And before you say anything wonderfully caring, like how I shouldn't have put myself in danger, let me assure you this was nothing I hadn't done before. So, frankly, Eleanor, we no longer need Chelfham to say much of anything, and he won't be saying it to us."

She'd speak with him later about his prowess as a housebreaker but, for now, Eleanor wanted to be very clear about what she believed it necessary she still learn. "Except for him to admit to me that he is my real father. Except for him to tell me if he was involved in the murder of the man I thought was my father. Except to tell me how he knows who I am, and to ask him why he wants me dead."

"No," Jack told her, in real sympathy with her desire to hear what Chelfham had to say. "It's over, Eleanor. That part is over. You already know most of it, and learning more won't change anything. He can only hurt you if you confront him. Let it all go, Eleanor. You have your family, your real family. And you have me, if you want me."

Eleanor blinked back sudden tears. "I don't understand a man like that. If he loved my mother at all, why would he want me dead?"

"I don't know, sweetheart, except to say that your mother died a long time ago, that Chelfham has a wife now and a possible heir soon, and you could be nothing more to him now than a complication he doesn't want," Jack said. "There is something I *do* know. I know that it has been nearly a full day since I last kissed you."

Eleanor allowed her worries to move to the back of her mind. She shouldn't, she should think of nothing but the Earl of Chelfham right now, and so should Jack. But she was so weary of thinking about their problems, and Jack certainly did seem to have a convincing argument. And magnificent green eyes that seemed to narrow in a special way when he looked at her. And perfectly wonderful hands, that cupped the small of her back, that moved so expertly over her breasts. And his mouth. He seemed to have magic in his mouth. . . .

She clung to him as he lifted her, their mouths fused together, and carried her to his bed.

Yet again, she allowed him to be the aggressor, but this time she understood — she was *allowing* him to be the aggressor. He didn't take anything she wasn't more than willing to give him. Eager to give him.

He kissed away her clothing, and she let him.

He shrugged out of his own clothing, and she watched. When she realized that the chamber was lit well enough for her to see him — for him to see her — she only smiled, not at all concerned, but actually happy.

His kisses were long, drugging, extremely intimate, even more intimate when he used his hands on her to mimic the thrusts and soft swirls of his tongue as he eased her legs apart and moved his hands between her thighs.

She let him inside.

He was so gentle. He'd been gentle from the beginning, from their very first time . . . her very first time. As if she were fragile, as if she might break, as if he didn't want to frighten her, take the chance of harming her.

Her teeth ached with his gentleness, her every muscle screamed from his gentleness. . . .

"Eleanor, what's wrong?" Jack asked as she brought her hand down on top of his, moved him away from her.

"Nothing's wrong," she heard herself say, as if she was speaking from far, far away. Somewhere high above, looking down at the woman lying on the bed, wanting more, not knowing what that was. "I won't break, Jack. I promise."

He smiled, suddenly nervous. "I know that, Eleanor. But we have time for —"

"No. No one ever knows how much time there will be for anything. I'm a woman, Jack. I adore what you do to me, but I'm convinced there's more. I want to *feel* like a woman. I want to lose my mind with wanting you, and I want you to lose your mind with wanting me. Not be careful. Not be considerate. I need to *want*, Jack, and I need you to *want*."

"I do want you, Eleanor," Jack told her, amazed at the raw passion, the frustration, in her voice. His Eleanor. His quiet lady. "But you're so small, so — hell, I just don't want to hurt you."

"If I promise not to break, will you stop . . . stop being so damn careful? Please?"

"You're amazing," Jack said, moving his hands up to cup her breasts. "And I'd be an idiot to say no." He bent over her, gently pushing her breasts upward so that he could grasp her nipples between his thumbs and forefingers, then lightly rub back and forth.

Eleanor moaned softly, low in her throat, and arched her head back into the pillows.

He touched his tongue to her nipples; one, then the other, and felt them harden into small, perfect pebbles. And when he covered one nipple with his mouth, laved her with his tongue, and she stabbed her fingers into his hair, pulling him closer against her, he forgot to be gentle.

He pushed down on her hip bone, outlining her form with his hand as he rhythmically rocked her pelvis, guided her against the leg he'd slid between hers, drawn up so that his thigh was tight against her sex.

And then, somehow, he was on his back. With strength he didn't know she possessed, she had risen up and pushed at him, so that she could . . . *dear God.*

It had seemed so obvious to her earlier, when she'd first thought of the thing. Even logical. If Jack was afraid his weight and size were too much for her, then why not simply . . . *reverse* things. Would that be too bold? And did she care if it was? No. She really didn't.

Eleanor slid a perfect, creamy leg over Jack while balancing herself with one palm pressed against his stomach. Her blood roared in her ears as she found Jack and captured him. Then, her bottom lip caught between her teeth as she concentrated, she guided him toward her . . . and lowered her body onto him.

"Sweet Jesus," Jack breathed, putting his hands on her hips as she braced her arms behind her, on his thighs.

And then she began to move, riding him, tentatively at first, but as he held on to her hips, mimicked the pumping action she'd begun, she fell into a rhythm that seemed to echo throughout her entire body, sending wave after wave of pleasure crashing over her, lifting her higher, higher.

Eleanor threw back her head as Jack touched his fingers to her nipples yet again, teasing, pinching, sending silken threads of desire arrowing toward her very center.

With a cry of mingled pleasure and frustration, she launched herself forward, unable to go another moment without holding him, feeling his hard body against hers, and together they rolled over on the bed, until she was effectively pinned to the crisp white sheets that felt cool against her back.

Her eyes tightly closed, Eleanor reached her arms up and around Jack's neck, pulling him down to her. "Love me," she breathed into his ear. "Love me."

"I do," Jack said, taking up the rhythm once more.

Plunging deep.

Moving faster.

Losing control.

Eleanor held on tight, her arms and legs wrapped around him, and gave in to the overwhelming urge to bite at Jack's neck, lick his skin, seal her open mouth to him and suck his salty taste into her mouth.

Faster.

Deeper.

Higher.

Give to me, give to me.

Take from me, take from me.

Always one, one made from two.

Now.

Forever . . .

CHAPTER
TWENTY-TWO

"Eleanor?"

Eleanor mumbled something unintelligible and curved her body more closely against his.

"Eleanor."

"Mmm . . ." she breathed on a contented sigh, sliding a hand across his chest, bending her knee over his leg.

"Eleanor, I'm hungry," Jack said, stroking her hair. "And, much as I'm feeling both amazed and gratified at this moment, there is no possible way I can —"

She raised her head slightly, squinting at him through the darkness, and not at all ashamed of her grin at his expense. Goodness, she barely recognized herself . . . but she liked how she felt, and she wouldn't undo a moment of the hours they'd spent here, in this bed. "Oh. Did you say you're hungry?"

"You mentioned a trifle several lifetimes

ago. What sort of trifle?"

"Hmm . . . strawberry, I believe. I was too worried about you to agree to a dessert course."

"Strawberry," Jack repeated, wondering if Eleanor would still consider him to be loverlike if his stomach were to begin growling. "Do you think there's a chance any of it is still in the kitchens?"

"Well, I don't know, but we could go downstairs and see, I suppose," Eleanor said, throwing back the covers, to realize that she was quite naked. She had, in her opinion, come a long way tonight in freeing herself from her self-made strictures, her idea of what constituted ladylike behavior — at least the way it was described in the books she'd read. But, even taking that new freedom into consideration, she was not about to go prancing about the bedchamber, naked. There were limits, and she would set them!

Dragging the coverlet with her, she slid out of the high tester bed, retrieved her night rail and dressing gown, then disappeared behind the screen in the corner of the room.

Leaving Jack to bury his face in one of the pillows, so she wouldn't hear his laughter. His Eleanor. His *lady.*

He supposed she was expecting him to also be clothed when she reappeared from behind the screen, so, still chuckling, he made quick work out of locating his pantaloons and shirt.

He picked up a bedside candle, then called out, "You can safely come out now, Miss Becket. I'm decent."

Eleanor poked her head out from behind the screen, her mop of dark curls having asserted themselves at some point in the evening. "You are the most *annoying* man."

"Yes. I apply myself," Jack said, then took her hand as the two of them left the bedchamber and crept down the hallway to the servant stairs.

The fires were banked in the kitchens and the only inhabitant was a large, overfed orange cat that opened one eye when they entered, holding hands and laughing like guilty children, then stood, turned its back, and lay down again.

"I rather like this, you know," Jack told Eleanor as she motioned him to a chair, then provided him with a spoon and the bit of trifle she discovered in the stillroom. "And why are we whispering? This is my house. Why shouldn't I be in the kitchens?"

"Because you're only a man, and you're afraid of Mrs. Ryan?" Eleanor offered, sitting down across the thick, scarred wooden table and resting her chin in her hand. "Is it good?"

"Delicious," Jack told her, then held out the spoon to her. "Here. Try a bite."

Eleanor leaned forward and allowed Jack to feed her, giggling when a bit of strawberry clung to her bottom lip, and he reached across the tabletop to lick it away.

Once the trifle was finished, they began poking about the kitchens for more substantial food. Jack was using an enormous knife to slice some cheese when a yawning maid entered, still rubbing the sleep out of her eyes; the first up, with the job of refurbishing the fire and refilling the kettle.

"Here now," she said, blinking rapidly in the early-morning dimness. "What are you doin' thinkin' you can come in here and — Mr. Eastwood? Oh, laws."

"It's all right, Maisie," Eleanor assured the girl, who looked ready to cry. "Mr. Eastwood was hungry, that's all. Would you care to bring some meat and cheese and what's left of yesterday's loaves up to his study in a few minutes? We don't want to be in your way."

Maisie bobbed her head and curtsied with more alacrity than grace as Eleanor led Jack back toward the stairs. "Poor thing. You must have frightened her half out of her mind."

"Ah, now you see it, do you? Yet, strangely, not when *you* first went marching down to the kitchens, General Becket."

Eleanor pressed her head against his arm. "A true gentleman would forget that, you know," she said as they paused at the top of the steps and Jack took advantage of the moment to draw her into his arms, kiss her.

There were worries in their world, danger, but it all melted away when he kissed Eleanor Becket, and Jack's world became a wonderful place.

"You taste like strawberries," he whispered against her ear after they broke the kiss and he pulled her in closer. "Yet I'm strangely more hungry for you than I am food. Let's go back upstairs."

Eleanor pushed back slightly and shook her head. "No. You said you were hungry, and Maisie is bringing a plate for you. Besides, we really must talk about our plans for tomorrow . . . today."

"I know. Coward that I am, I'm simply trying to delay that conversation. But, Eleanor, I meant what I said. There will be no coach riding out of town later today to see if Chelfham truly recognized you and wants you dead. The plan was insane from the beginning, and I won't allow it."

"You won't allow it?" Eleanor closed her eyes, took a deep, steadying breath. "All right, Jack. I understand. You're worried about me, and I appreciate that. You're certain you have enough to bring him down, and that's wonderful. Now, tell me another way to do this, because I *will* speak with him. I will *know*."

"I know you want to personally confront the bastard, Eleanor, and you have every right. I kept trying to find a way that you could, but in the end I realized it's just impossible. We needed this done, and we needed it done now. Yesterday. Chance agreed with me."

"Chance?" Eleanor felt an anger she'd never experienced before well up inside her, nearly choking her. "He's here? First Rian, and now Chance? Papa did this, didn't he? He didn't trust me — he didn't trust you. How dare he not trust you!"

Jack quickly considered his recent confession to Chance Becket, and the fact that Ainsley had known all about him from the very beginning. He understood why Ainsley had sent two of his sons to watch him. He'd explain all of that to Eleanor, and she'd understand; he was confident of that now, and there really should be no more secrets between them. Although he was fairly certain that he'd be wise not to mention Treacle's presence in the household.

"Ainsley is a prudent man, Eleanor. I don't mind that your brothers are here, and I appreciate their help. Besides, I enjoyed meeting your oldest brother. He's an interesting man."

Eleanor began pacing up and down the hallway in her bare feet. "Interesting? Oh, yes, they're all extremely *interesting.* Wonderfully *protective.* Morgan always went her own way. Fanny goes her own way. But here I am, the oldest, and I'm being treated as no more grown-up and responsible than Callie." She stopped directly in front of Jack. "It's insulting, that's what it is, and I will not stand for it."

"And you shouldn't," Jack agreed, because that was probably safest while Eleanor was in her current mood. Besides, she was no longer thinking about confronting Chelfham, and that had to be a good thing. "I'm meeting your brother this morning, in just a few hours, and I'll be sure to bring him back here with me, so you can tell him that yourself."

Eleanor nodded her head sharply. "And I

will tell him." She was bringing herself back under control, because she'd immediately realized that she *liked* feeling in control, not screaming like some banshee — which never did anyone any good anyway. "And then I will explain to him that, even though you seem to have settled everything else between you, *I* still need to speak with the Earl of Chelfham. And I *will* speak with him."

"No, Eleanor, you won't," Jack said, his hand on the latch of the door to his study. "I told you that we have the journals, and that's true. I put them directly into Chance's hands just before coming home last night. I didn't tell you this yet, but we also have Eccles as our witness. Chelfham's done, finished. By nine o'clock this morning, before he has a chance to miss them, Chance will have delivered the journals to one of his acquaintances at the War Office, and Chelfham will have been arrested."

"Arrested? Then I'll never be able to ask him anything. Oh, Jack, how could you do that? You should have told me this last night."

"I know, and I'm sorry. I would have, but when I saw you, when I kissed you — nothing else seemed important. But it's over, and I can't be sorry for that. You will be driving out in the coach today, sweetheart, but I'll be riding in it with you as we return to Becket Hall, where I will ask — no, *tell* — Ainsley that we're going to be married as soon as the banns can be read. That is what we're doing today."

"Married? But you haven't even asked me if I — *married? Really?*" Eleanor's world was suddenly rosy, wonderful beyond all imagining. The Earl of Chelfham and her questions for him suddenly seemed insignificant, unnecessary. Why look back, when there was suddenly so much to look forward to? It was true, what she'd read. When a woman loses her heart, often her mind is not far behind! "Well, um, *thank you.* Thank you very much."

Jack shook his head, laughing, his heart full. "God, I adore you." He depressed the latch and pushed open the door, elaborately bowing so that Eleanor could precede him into the room. "The drapes are drawn. I should have brought a candle up from the kitchens," he said as he moved past Eleanor. "You stand still, and I'll — *what in hell?*"

Jack landed on whatever he'd tripped over, and it only took him an instant to realize that it had been Cluny's body that had cushioned his fall.

"Eleanor, *run!*" he yelled just before he heard her scream, a scream abruptly cut off. He was halfway to his feet when something hard slammed against the side of his head.

When he awoke he was on the couch in his study, with Treacle looking down at him, and the maid, Maisie, weeping in the corner.

"Eleanor?" he asked, struggling into a sitting position, the pain in his head almost nauseating.

"Not here, sir," Treacle said, attempting to hold a cold wet cloth against Jack's temple. "I've sent for Mr. Chance."

Chance. Yes, that was good. Chance had the journals. Chelfham had checked, seen that they were gone, and come after them. That was the only explanation. "What time is it?"

"Not quite seven, sir," the butler answered, and Jack pushed away the cloth, struggled to his feet. "Sir, you really should be lying down."

Jack didn't so much agree to sit down again as fall down. "Seven. Chance still has them then. Good. He wants a trade, she'll be safe until then." Another thought struck him as he fought to clear his head. "Cluny. Where's Cluny?"

Maisie's weeping grew louder, and Treacle

told her to leave the room. "Pardon her, sir, she's upset, finding you and all. Mrs. Hendersen is with him, sir. Someone cut him rather badly, but Mrs. Hendersen feels sure he'll recover. They . . . um . . . they painted his face, sir."

"Painted his face?" Jack wondered how hard he'd been hit, because that didn't make sense.

"Yes, sir. With his own blood."

"A calling card. I've seen it before," Chance Becket said as he entered the room, tossing his hat and greatcoat onto the desk. "It's the Red Men, Jack, no question, or at least Chelfham's pale imitation of the men who do the actual work. If whoever was here had really been one of the Red Men, your Irish friend would be very dead." Then he looked to Treacle. "How bad is Mr. Eastwood? Can he be of any use?"

"*He* is perfectly capable of answering for himself," Jack said tightly, pushing himself to his feet, willing himself not to fall down again as the edges of his vision turned black. "Give me a minute," he told Chance. "Let me think."

"Take your time, Jack. You know the man better than I."

"Yes. Yes, I do. Eleanor and I discussed

him, at length. Chelfham doesn't want her, you know. He came for the journals, and we stumbled over his plot — literally. He has no plan now. He couldn't. And that makes him dangerous, unless indecision paralyzes him, keeps him from thinking clearly. He probably still has her here, in London, possibly even in his own house."

"Ainsley says it's always comforting to know you're smarter than your enemy, as long as you don't make the mistake of becoming overconfident," Chance told him quietly.

Jack summoned a small smile. "Yes, I remember hearing him say exactly that when we first discussed Chelfham. But he also said that it's important to always remember that even idiots are successful at times, if only by mistake."

"So we proceed, but cautiously."

"That's the answer, at least." He squinted as he looked at Chance, the candlelit study now too bright rather than dark, his head pounding with pain. "The question is, how do we get her back? We can't just go charging in there, or Eleanor could be hurt."

"I thought about that when I read Treacle's summons. My guess is there'll be a note, telling us where and when we'll meet for the exchange. Eleanor for the journals.

After all, we're dealing with a man who considers himself elegant, sophisticated. Even with Phelps and Eccles, he didn't personally dirty his hands, remember? Bloody hell! This was my idea. I was so sure we could loose the War Office on him before he even knew the journals were gone. They've only been missing from his desk for a few hours."

Treacle held out the wet cloth again, and this time Jack took it, pressed it against his head, pushed himself to think clearly. "My fault, as well, Chance. I agreed with you. Anything to keep Eleanor from insisting we use her to draw him out. And now he's got her. He'll at least pretend he's willing to release her unharmed, if I return the journals, bow to his superiority. He's arrogant. He still thinks he controls me."

Chance looked at Jack and saw his ashen complexion, his slowly swaying body. "Good point. Just for God's sake, sit down, stop trying to prove you're all right. Because you're not. No, wait, don't sit down. Treacle, take the man upstairs and get him dressed, get him something to drink. And tell Rian I need him down here."

"Don't do that," Jack protested as Treacle tried to take his arm. "I want to be here when Chelfham's note arrives with his demands. Do you suppose he's got her in his own house? It wouldn't surprise me. He'd feel safest there."

"Jack, you're not dressed. Your head's not clear. I appreciate your feelings, believe me. Elly's my sister, remember? But in times like this, it's first things first. Put your heart away, Jack, and think with your head."

"Damn! But you're right. And I need to see Cluny." Jack looked to Treacle, then turned to Chance once more, his expression bleak. "It's just . . . it's just that this is Eleanor. I'm used to thinking of myself first, thinking like a soldier. But it's Eleanor, Chance. Everything's different. All I can think about is Eleanor. *She's* my life now."

"I know," Chance said quietly, watching as Jack left the room, Treacle at his side, supporting him. "God, man, I know. . . ."

CHAPTER
TWENTY-THREE

Eleanor felt unnaturally calm. She was sure it was unnatural to be so calm, at any rate.

Perhaps it was because she felt so certain that Jack would come for her.

Or perhaps it was because the Earl of Chelfham, this man her mind and memories had made into a monster, looked anything but intimidating at the moment. When she'd been carried into his study, and dropped unceremoniously onto a couch, the blanket over her head removed, the man had actually blanched in front of her.

"The journals, damn you! I said the *journals!* What in Hades do I want with her?"

The man Eleanor believed must be Beatrice's supposed suitor had explained in fits and starts that he'd been taken by surprise in Jack's study, first by Cluny. He'd taken care of the Irishman, even did that thing the Red Men Gang did, smeared the man's face with blood.

But he still couldn't find the journals anywhere, and then Eastwood himself came into the study. Before daybreak! Did no one sleep in that household? He'd heard him talking, in the hallway, and grabbed up a brass candlestick and hidden himself behind the door. Knocked him down.

Still with no journals to be found, and with Eleanor screaming to wake the dead, he hadn't really thought about much more than getting her shut up, and getting them out of there.

"I thought . . . I thought you could maybe *trade* the lady for the journals, my lord?" Gerald ended hopefully, looking apologetically toward Eleanor.

"A man with initiative. How pleased you must be with your henchman, my lord. And a plausible solution, as well. But only if I'm unharmed, of course. Otherwise, I would imagine Jack will feed both of you your own eyeballs," Eleanor warned in polite tones, carefully checking her neckline to be sure she was modestly covered. Outwardly calm, her mind was tumbling over itself in its search for solutions, and had already come up with that threat about eyeballs, remembering Jacko saying something very like it one time in jest, when Spencer had done something to annoy him.

In any case, she was establishing herself as a force, even as she remained a captive. It was important that Chelfham understand that she was not intimidated, not powerless. Not afraid.

Her sister Morgan would be attacking, verbally and physically, her anger overwhelming her. But she was not Morgan. She did not have Morgan's strengths, her blind courage.

So what did she have? What were her weapons? Her cool head in a crisis? Her supposedly ladylike, demure appearance? Her quiet air of command that had worked wonders on her brothers and sisters over the years? Those, some would say, were her virtues.

And then, hiding her smile behind her hand, Eleanor thought of something she had read in one of Montaigne's essays. "I find that the best virtue I have has in it some tinture of vice."

She did have a weapon. She had *herself.*

Her mind raced on, seeking solutions. She and Jack had spoken of their conclusions as to how Chelfham's own mind worked, how he approached problems.

He'd make a plan and not deviate from it, not expect the unexpected or prepare for it. Clearly, he'd planned to take back his journals by breaking into Jack's study. Safe in his own house, he'd sent someone else to do the real work, believing he'd soon have his property back where it belonged.

But now the unexpected had happened, and Eleanor saw the panic in the man's eyes, the uncertainty. The weakness.

So she would graciously deign to help him, give him a new plan. Set his feet down another path, and pray that Jack would come to the same conclusion she had come to — that Chelfham wasn't capable of thinking much beyond his mission, that of recovering the journals. Consequences. Chelfham didn't expend a lot of effort on thinking of possibly adverse consequences, preferring rosy scenarios in their place.

"What a fine mess, my lord Chelfham," she said conversationally, as if they were guests at a dinner party, discussing someone else's problem. "You're really not all that proficient in the finer points of skulduggery, are you? I'm surprised you've lasted so long in this dangerous game."

"I could gag you," Chelfham threatened, pacing the carpet in front of her. "I could have you killed."

"Not if you wish to continue living," Eleanor told him, folding her hands in her blanket-covered lap, keeping her posture rigid. "But I'll be quiet, allow you to think. You really do need to think, my lord, find a way to make the best of what is certainly a rather embarrassing debacle for you. And so unfair, that a gentleman like yourself should be so badly used. Oh, wait, I have an idea. Compose a conciliatory note to my husband and ask him to come here to fetch me, my lord — effect that trade your man spoke of. Although I do believe Jack, his constitution being much more rough-and-tumble than yours, may wish to renegotiate your partnership. Therefore, a slight hint of humility in the note might be advisable."

Chelfham glared at her, actually took one menacing step in her direction. But then he stopped, turned and sat himself behind his desk, still glaring at her as he pulled paper and pen in front of him.

Eleanor inclined her head slightly, and then composed her features as she pretended to inspect a rather inferior hunt scene hung behind the earl's head.

Yes. Calm. She was unreasonably, unnaturally calm. Right here, in the presence of her nightmare, her boogeyman. And he was only human, and more than fallible. How liberating!

Jack would come for her. He had been moving on the floor even as the man who could be no one other than Beatrice's Gerald had picked her up, thrown her over his shoulder. She'd even heard him groan.

She wasn't as sure about Cluny, however, and that did worry her. She didn't really know the man that well, but he was important to Jack. And what was important to Jack was important to her.

For nearly a half hour, there was nothing but silence in the earl's study as Eleanor watched the man pace, pause, look at the mantel clock, then begin to pace once more.

The note had been written and dispatched to Portland Place. Jack would be here soon. To "correct an unfortunate error on the part of one of my overzealous servants." Chelfham had actually read the note to her, as if seeking her approval, and she had assured him that Jack would be most forgiving. ". . . as there is fault on both sides, isn't there, my lord? There will be these little *bumps* at the outset of any new association."

Calm. So wonderfully, mercifully, eerily calm . . .

"Thank you. Gerald, isn't it?" Eleanor said a few minutes later as that man placed a silver tea tray on the table in front of her. He'd already brought her a shawl that smelled of Lady Chelfham's perfume. "I see that the burn on your hand is healing nicely.

Beatrice is also well on her way to mending. You've acted badly, Gerald, but you've also been kind. I'll be sure to mention that kindness to my husband."

"Yes, ma'am, thank you," Gerald said, hiding his burned hand behind his back, then crying out as a small silver paperweight bounced off his shoulder.

"Idiots. I'm surrounded by them," Chelfham spat from behind his desk. "Who told you to bring her tea?"

"Oh, for goodness sake, your lordship, there's no need to be so outraged," Eleanor scolded. "It's only tea. I highly doubt I've corrupted the man. Again, Gerald, thank you. I had begun to take a chill, being dragged through the streets before dawn in my nightclothes."

"Get out of here now, you fool! Eastwood's due within the hour. Let me know when you hear him at the door. Be of some damn use to me after the mess you've made," Chelfham ordered tersely to the now nervously bowing Gerald, and the man quickly exited the study, leaving Eleanor alone with the earl once more.

He leaned his elbows on the desktop littered with a brace of silver-handled dueling pistols and glowered at her. "You're a piece of work, aren't you? Sitting there, so much the lady, acting as if butter wouldn't melt in your mouth."

Eleanor didn't respond until she'd replaced the small teapot on the tray and was reaching for the tongs for the sugar cubes Gerald had provided. Less than an hour. If she was going to act, it would have to be now. "What else is there for me, my lord? I can scarcely overpower you, physically — even if you are old enough to be my father."

Chelfham sprawled back against his chair as if shoved there by an unseen hand, one arm dangling over one of its leather arms, the other bent, the back of his hand to his mouth as he concentrated on Eleanor. "I wanted to believe it all a horrible coincidence. But you know, don't you."

Eleanor willed her hand steady as she dropped a single sugar cube into her cup. Years. She'd waited years for this moment. "Who I am? Who *you* are? Yes. Yes, I do."

The earl bit on his knuckle for a moment, then sat forward once more. "Who *I* am? How would you know that?"

"An answer for an answer, my lord? As long as we're merely attempting to pass the time?"

He didn't say anything, but simply made a small circular motion with his hand, as if inviting her to speak.

"Very well. First allow me to say that my husband is aware of what I know, but we decided not to act upon that knowledge, feeling it more profitable to become your partner than to try to prove my . . . parentage. Secondly, I know who you are because I overheard my mother admit as much to your brother, just before she had him thrown overboard. Now, my first question. Were you planning to have me murdered as I left London for Jack's estate?"

Once again, Chelfham looked genuinely shocked. Or perhaps Eleanor wanted to believe he was genuinely shocked. He'd been so malleable, she had to guard against becoming overconfident. "Murder you? Why would I do that?"

"Isn't that obvious? Because you know who I am."

"And you think, knowing who you are, that I'd order you killed? I just wanted you gone. You look too much like her, remind me of a time I want to forget. I'm going to give you back, remember, just as soon as Eastwood gets here with my journals. I'm *civilized,* damn it. None of this was my idea — it was all forced on me. We live in a civilized country. We're not a bunch of . . . of *pirates.*"

"Yes, pirates," Eleanor said, her heart pounding now. "Let's speak of pirates for a few moments, shall we, leaving the idea you might want me dead for another time? How, exactly, did you arrange your brother's death? How much does it cost a civilized gentleman such as yourself to buy an entire crew, and their captain, as well, I would suppose?"

The earl's face had begun to flush an unhealthy red. "I should have ordered you bound and gagged. It was her idea, not mine. Your whore of a mother. And look where it got us. Her dead, me enslaved." He got up from his chair and strode over to a table littered with crystal decanters. "No more questions."

"Oh, my lord, you can't stop now. *Enslaved?* You hardly look enslaved. I suppose I should thank you for not wanting to see me dead? You're the civilized gentleman, so perhaps you can help me here. Does a daughter thank her father for something like that? Does a daughter apologize for even thinking a father capable of such a thing? Ah, but you've murdered flesh and blood before, haven't you? My mother wasn't acting alone. Surely you can understand my concern."

411

"Shut up! Just shut your mouth!" Chelfham turned about so quickly, his arm caught one of the decanters and sent it crashing to the floor, the smell of brandy quickly permeating the small room and instantly reminding Eleanor of the night Jack had given her brandy to drink. Just the thought of Jack lent her strength to keep pushing this man.

"Certainly, *Father.* A bit of silence may be just what we both need. Time to reflect on all we've learned, perhaps?"

Eleanor picked up her teacup and brought it to her mouth, sipped some of the still rather hot contents. Calm. She was still so amazingly calm, almost as if she was an actress in a play. How could that be? Then she deliberately smiled, put down the cup, and folded her hands in her lap.

And waited for Chelfham to fill the silence. She had no "lines" right now. It was time to be quiet. Papa had always told her that her greatest weapon was her silences.

And, eventually, with only the sound of the clock on the mantel audible, Chelfham succumbed to that weapon.

"It's been so long. What? More than fifteen years since I last saw her?" Chelfham said, retaking his seat. "I didn't recognize you. Not at all, even though you look just like her. It took my slut of a wife to comment on the resemblance to a portrait that still hangs somewhere in this house. God, how I loved your mother. And how I loathe her now. *She* did this to me. She did it all."

Eleanor was careful to remain very still, keep her expression as close to neutral as possible, even as his every word sliced into her.

He pointed one shaky finger at her. "Yes, she looked like that, too. Just like that. Like butter wouldn't melt in her mouth. We couldn't marry, you know, even with Robert dead. But that didn't matter to her. It would be enough that we had the money, that we had each other. Her, the dowager countess, me, the bachelor earl, both of us living under the same roof. Anything to get that dull as ditch water Robert out of her life. I was so young, so stupidly flattered. I've often wondered, over the years, how long I would have survived my brother."

Eleanor's memories of her mother, the man she'd believed to be her father, were only vague, never clear. Still, it hurt to hear Chelfham speak about either of them this way. "You believe now that she was only using you for her own purposes? Is that how you salve your conscience, by seeing yourself as a victim? Surely not everything that happened was terrible for you. After all, fratricide gained you an earldom."

Chelfham retrieved his glass of wine, still intent on his own thoughts, his own memories. Clearly, his mind was a good fifteen or more years in the past. "My father used to say, when you sup with the devil be careful to use a long spoon. I forgot that. I paid him to be rid of Robert, and he paid me back by attacking the ship for its cargo."

He gave a short sniff of wry amusement. "We hired her own killer. Amazing, isn't it? And then he came back three years ago, holding *my* crime over my head, my signed note to him telling him what I wanted him to do about Robert, and he forced me into doing business with him. His minion. His slave."

He looked into his wineglass, raised it to his lips. "That's what I did. I forgot my father's warning. When you sup with the devil . . ." he repeated, then downed the contents all at once.

Eleanor was reeling now, as all the pieces slammed into place at one time. Chelfham was only half right. It wasn't Ainsley who had picked a ship, a crew, and then, knowing its course, devised a plan to attack that same ship that carried the woman Rawley

414

Maddox coveted enough to want his brother dead. Attacking that ship as it traveled in a well-protected, heavily armed phalanx of ships had been left to Ainsley — that was true enough — but everything had been set into motion by Ainsley's partner, Edmund Beales.

Edmund Beales, who supposedly had been dead these past fifteen years. Edmund Beales, the monster who had destroyed so much, who was responsible for so much pain.

But he wasn't dead. Not if Eleanor could believe what Chelfham was saying — which she did. Her breathing became more rapid, shallow, as she realized she now knew something no one else knew: it had been her mother, her father, who had been the catalysts that had helped to bring such misery to Ainsley Becket, to all of them.

She couldn't wait for Jack and her brothers to respond to the note the earl had sent, demanding the return of the journals. She couldn't sit here and pretend she wasn't in any real danger, that this man who was her real father would live up to his announced plan to turn her safely over to Jack in return for those journals.

No, she no longer had that luxury. Nor could she afford the time necessary to carefully guide Chelfham into revealing more secrets.

There may not be much time left for anything at all.

Because Edmund Beales was here.

When you sup with the devil . . .

And now the devil had come to London.

Eleanor got to her feet, which brought a frown to Chelfham's face. "Sit down," he told her. "You'll be there, with your tea, and I'll be here, behind the desk. All very civilized as we await the exchange. I said, *sit down.*"

She ignored his order. She walked over to the desk, put her palms flat against the surface. "That's enough of your self-pitying lies, and enough of me pretending to believe them. Did you tell him? When you discovered that the journals were gone, did you tell him?"

"Tell whom? And why am I even talking to you? Sit down before I forget you're my daughter. You've caused all of this. You and Eastwood."

"Yes, nothing is *your* fault, is it? First my mother, and now Jack and me. Never you. What a pitiful, disgusting creature you are."

"You have no right to —"

Eleanor lifted one hand and brought the

side of her fist down hard on the desktop. "Answer me. Edmund Beales. Between the time you discovered the journals gone and now — *did . . . you . . . tell him?*"

Her air of quiet command, even as she stood there, barefoot, a shawl over her dressing gown, seemed to have impressed on Chelfham that something was very, very wrong. His mouth moved several times before he made any sound. "I . . . I don't know that name. Was that the name he used, all those years ago? And how would you know that? I only remember the face. That smug, smiling face as he told me how I would introduce him to society, to my friends. Told me how I would be the one to take all the risks, while he took most of the money. I thought I was done with him fifteen years ago . . . and then he came back."

In this small, closed room, Eleanor suddenly felt overwhelmingly exposed. Dangerously vulnerable. "What name does he use now? No, never mind, there's no time for that now. Please," she said as calmly as possible, "answer the question. Did you tell him someone had taken your journals? And remember this, your life may hang with your answer."

"I . . . I didn't have to tell him. One of his

men was here, last night, waiting in this room when we returned home from the theater." Chelfham drew his hands into fists on the desktop. "He and his men are everywhere, like a bad rash. This one, a damned Frenchie, had come for the journals. They're always doing that, checking on me, making sure I'm not trying to cheat them, I suppose. But the records were gone."

He looked up at Eleanor, fear in his eyes. "I knew who had them. I told the man I'd get them back. He . . . he asked me when I'd last looked at the journals, how long it had been, how long they might have been missing. That's when I remembered showing them to Eastwood, yesterday morning, but I couldn't tell him that. No one is to know about my arrangement with your husband. So I said a day, they might have been gone for a day, no longer, that my idiot brother-in-law must have taken them. He just looked at me as if I was dirt beneath his feet and told me that was too long. *C'est beaucoup trop long, vous dupent.* He said that — called me a fool, as if I don't know the Frenchie tongue — and then he left. But I can get them back, and everything will be all right again. I know I can fix this."

Eleanor looked over her shoulder, at the

mantel clock. If Jack and Chance decided to play by the rules set down by Chelfham, Jack would be knocking on the front door in less than ten minutes, with Chance nearby, ready to help. She couldn't let that happen, couldn't let them be seen by whoever might be watching.

Because Edmund Beales might be watching. Edmund Beales, who might even recognize Chance. Fifteen years of hiding, of rebuilding, of rebirth — all of it could be gone in an instant.

"The man was right, you are a fool. And we have to go," she told Chelfham, her decision made. "Rouse your wife, everyone. We have to get out of here."

"Leave here? No. I told you, I've taken steps. I've got everything under control," Chelfham said, picking up the pistols, getting to his feet — and at last showing her she'd been right to fear him, woefully wrong to believe he possessed a single redeeming quality. "You surprised me, Julianna. I didn't think you knew. You took me off my guard for a few minutes, I'll grant you that, but I'm thinking clearly again now. I'm in charge here. I said I'd get the journals back, and I will. He'll be fine with that, he'll understand when I tell him who you are, how this all happened. After all, he's at fault, too — he let you live. He'll understand, I tell you, especially when you and Eastwood are both dead. He'll be pleased that I killed you. He doesn't like loose ends, you understand."

"You said . . . you said you didn't want to kill me," Eleanor reminded him, slowly backing away from the desk.

Chelfham smiled. "I say a lot of things. Ask my dear brother-in-law. No, wait, you can't do that, can you, Julianna?"

"Don't call me that. My name is Eleanor now."

"I'm sure that's the name they'll put on your headstone. Now, go back where you were. Sit down, have some more tea, my dear," he told her, motioning with one of the pistols before he took up his place behind the desk once more, the pistols hidden on his lap. "As I said before your hysterical outburst, we need to appear very civilized when your husband arrives."

Eleanor stood her ground. "No, we can't do that. You're deluding yourself. You're *not* in control here, Chelfham, for all your lies and bravado. Don't you understand? What *you* are is a loose end. Jack and I aren't the enemy any longer, not with Beales here. We may be your only hope. Please, summon

Gerald, have him wake everyone. The servants, too. Everyone has to get out, now. Or do you really want your wife and unborn child to be here when Edmund Beales sends someone back to snip any remaining loose threads?"

"He wouldn't dare," Chelfham said, but his complexion had gone quite white.

"Please don't make me waste time reminding you that he knew my mother and I were on that ship. Women, children, even unborn babes. You said it — he's the devil. *He doesn't care.*"

At last, Eleanor seemed to get through to the man. A pistol in each hand, Chelfham ran toward the closed door, already calling for Gerald. But when he opened it, Jack was standing there, more than happy to relieve the earl of his pistols while Chance held another one pressed against Gerald's back.

"Well, thank you, Chelfham," Jack said sarcastically. "I was wondering how we'd disarm you."

"Jack! Oh, thank God you aren't civilized!" Eleanor called out as Chelfham backed up into the room, his hands now raised in the air. Then she saw her brother. "Chance! It's Edmund Beales. He's the real head of the Red Men Gang. Edmund

Beales, Chance! He's here in London. He's *alive.*"

Chance shot a quick look at Chelfham and Jack before saying, "You're certain? It's really him?"

Eleanor nodded her head emphatically. Chance didn't seem overly surprised at her news, but she'd think about that later. There was no time for anything else now but getting themselves out of here. She'd heard the stories. She knew the danger. "It has to be him. And he knows the journals are gone, he's known for hours and hours. You know what he's like, what he's capable of doing. We have to get everyone away from here, *now.*"

But Chance wasn't listening to her anymore. She should have known as much. Yes, she'd heard about the island, what had happened there, but she hadn't seen it, seen the carnage. She'd been a child left behind onboard the *Black Ghost,* unconscious, her ankle mangled. She hadn't seen what Chance had seen. She'd never laughed, and drunk, and broken bread with a fiend like Edmund Beales.

Chance let go of Gerald, who immediately turned on his heels and fled, already yelling for everyone in the house to wake up, get out. "An obedient sort, isn't he? I suppose you've been working your magic again, Elly," Chance said, then advanced on the earl of Chelfham. "Now it's your turn. Where is he? Where does he live? What does he call himself?" He leveled his pistol at the earl. *"Answer me."*

"B-B-Beatty," Chelfham mumbled almost inaudibly. "He calls himself Nathaniel Beatty, and . . . and he keeps a town house in Grosvenor Street. Number . . . number forty-five. Is it true? What she says — is it true? Would he really kill us all? My wife. She carries my heir. I have to get her out of here!"

At last Jack spoke, his head still pounding, his knees still weak. Hell, they'd been delayed in arriving at Chelfham's town house because he'd had to stop twice, lean out of the town carriage to throw up in the gutter. "His heir, but not his only child. Bastard. I have an idea, Chance. I say we let him find out what this Beales is capable of. Get everyone else out of the house, and leave him here, tied up with a bow."

Eleanor should have agreed. The man might be her father, but he was evil, and even wanted her dead. But he *was* her father. "No, Jack," she said, stepping toward him. "We agreed. We turn him over to the Crown."

But she'd gotten too close. Over their heads, behind them in the hallways, the sounds of a rudely awakened household filtered down to them, the sound of running feet may even have distracted them. Whatever the reason, Chelfham was quick to take advantage of it, grabbing one of the pair of pistols out of Jack's hand at the same time he roughly threw his other arm around Eleanor's neck, dragged her backward with him, the pistol pressed into her side.

"Son of a bitch," Jack bit out, taking a single step forward before getting himself back under control. "Chelfham, don't be an ass. Let her go. I don't know this Edmund Beales, but I've heard enough to believe it's time we were all shed of this place. We'll settle our own arguments later."

Rian Becket appeared in the doorway, his young face flushed with anger. "There's an idiot woman upstairs who refuses to budge until I fetch a servant to pack her clothes and jewels. What do I do with her, Chance?"

"A good question, Rian. Chelfham? Would that be your wife?"

Jack watched as the earl backed up another two steps, Eleanor nearly falling as she tried to maintain her balance with the man's forearm pressed hard across the front of her throat. "Carrying your heir, you said? Shall we just leave her to your partner's tender mercies?"

"You're all just trying to confuse me," Chelfham shouted, drawing his forearm tighter, so that Eleanor couldn't hold back a painful wince. "He'll understand. Once I have the journals. Once I explain to him. He's a reasonable man."

Jack and Chance still held their pistols pointed at the earl. "What do you say, Chance?" Jack asked, his eyes intent on Chelfham. "Do we all wait here, to find out if he's right?"

Chance shook his head. "Not me, thank you. If I thought he'd show up personally, then yes, I'd stay. But I won't knowingly remain here to meet with his hired assassins. We're none of us prepared for that sort of battle. Rian, is everyone else out of the house?"

"We sent them out through the kitchens. Treacle and that Gerald fellow. They're probably scattered over half of London by now. There's only the woman left. Is Elly going to be all right? I know I'm not in charge, but don't you two think it's time you did something about that, rather than just standing here? There's three of us and only one of him, you know. Or don't you think he's figured that out yet?"

"Rian," Chance said without a trace of emotion in his voice, "shut up."

Jack didn't know what Chance was thinking, or what Eleanor feared, but his imagination was running wild. A band of armed men. A fire. A cask of gunpowder hurled through the window, carrying a lit fuse. It would be hours before anyone except servants and a few delivery wagons were awake and about in the fashionable Square. They were isolated here, as if they were in a house in the middle of a sleeping woods. Here, in the midst of Mayfair, in the center of supposed civilization, it would appear that they all could soon be under attack, with no one to see, no one to notice until it was too late.

"Order the woman at gunpoint if necessary, Rian," Jack instructed the younger man, never taking his eyes from the pistol now aimed at Eleanor's head. "Get her out, hide her in Chelfham's stables, then send Treacle to the closest watchouse for help."

"No!" Chelfham shouted as Rian turned to leave the room. "Nobody moves. Leave my wife where she is. Nobody goes anywhere. This is all a hum meant to confuse me. Where are the journals? Bring me the journals or she dies. That's what he wants, and that's what I demand."

"Amateurs, you can't reason with them. We need an end to this, Jack," Chance said quietly. Then, to Chelfham, he said, making a great business out of lowering his pistol, "My lord, I have the journals at my house in Upper Brook Street. If I promise to turn them over to you, will you agree to adjourn there now? You have my word that nothing will happen to you."

Chelfham pressed the muzzle of the pistol hard against Eleanor's temple. "*You* have the journals?" he asked Chance. "I don't even *know* you!"

Jack's head was splitting and his stomach was turning again. He feared he might pass out. But the weapon in his hand never wavered, and his gaze never left Chelfham's cocked and ready pistol. "Let her go, Chelfham. Let her go and we'll do anything you say."

"I can't," Chelfham said, backing up yet again, until he was stopped by the edge of his desk. "Pirates. Smugglers. Hooligans! This isn't the way it was supposed to be. Why couldn't you have just brought me the journals? It's not too late. He said it was too late, but it's not. It's not! *Get me the journals!*"

Hard on the heels of Chelfham's demand came the sound of breaking glass. Everywhere, upstairs and down, the sound of breaking glass, including in the study, where everyone stood as if frozen into a tableau, staring at the fire that had blossomed in the middle of the room.

Rian ran out of the room, but was back in seconds. "Everywhere, Chance. Fire everywhere. I'll get the woman."

"He can't! He can't do this! Barbarians! My house! This is *my* house!"

With his every word, Chelfham tightened his grip on Eleanor, until she felt lightheaded from lack of breath. She clawed at the earl's forearm, but he was past understanding what he was doing to her. She couldn't swallow. She couldn't cry out.

"Eleanor!"

She pulled on Chelfham's arm hard enough that she was able to draw in another breath as she looked to Jack, to the growing fire between them.

But was she really here? Or was she on the ship? In the cupboard, Mama holding her tight, too tight. *No!* She was here, in London, and Jack was . . . Jack was . . . *oh, God!* Everything was different. Everything was the same. The terror. The fire. The pistol. She was going to die.

Again.

"Eleanor," Jack said, his voice low, commanding, as she seemed to look at him without seeing him. He had to get her back, rouse her from whatever nightmare had seized her or, failing that, he had to use what he knew. The ship. Jacko.

Could he do it, break through her terror? Would she understand? Chelfham couldn't understand what he was about to say. Jack. *Jacko.* No, Chelfham wouldn't understand. But Eleanor might. *Please God, let her understand.* "Eleanor? It's me, Jacko. Do you hear me, Eleanor? It's your Jacko. *Jacko.* Eleanor, understand? You remember what you're going to do, don't you, Eleanor? Stay still for Jacko. Stay very, very still."

"Jacko?" Eleanor mouthed the name, unable to actually speak. Then, suddenly, she knew. The child inside her knew what would happen next.

Six-year-old Julianna Maddox ceased her struggles to be free, closed her eyes, and braced for the sound of the shot. . . .

CHAPTER
TWENTY-FOUR

"Are you certain you're all right?"

"No, Chance, I'm not," Eleanor said in a resigned voice, for this was not the first time she'd heard the question. "Although I probably would be absolutely fine . . . if you'd stop staring at me as if I might dissolve into a puddle at any moment."

"She's got you there, Chance," Rian said as he walked into the drawing room, dressed for travel. "Elly coddles us, remember? Not the other way round. She likes it best that way. Now, Elly, ask me if I believe I'm dressed warmly enough, if I have enough money in my pocket, and if I'm sure I know how to find my way home. Then I'll be on my way."

"Cheeky, isn't he?" Chance said, getting to his feet to clap his brother on the back. "Remember, halfling. I'll be following you in two days' time, and I expect you to keep that mouth of yours shut until I can speak directly to Ainsley."

"Tell Papa? I'm not that much of a looby. I'll leave that to you. It's enough that I'm going to have to tell him why *I* disappeared without telling anyone but Jacko. Who won't defend me, you know."

"I think you should stay, Rian, and ride to Becket Hall with Chance," Eleanor said, putting aside her embroidery, that she hadn't really been attending to in the first place. "I simply don't understand this rush to be gone. You've barely seen London as it is."

"I've seen enough," Rian told her, bending to kiss her cheek. "And somebody has to go prepare the family for the news about you and Jack. Our Jacko will probably take to his bed with the shock — then meet Jack at the door with a list of demands to prove he's worthy of you."

Eleanor felt her cheeks flushing. "That's not true."

"Oh, it is, Elly, it is," Rian promised her. "Not to mention how I'm going to tell them about the way you've been shorn. Fanny's going to go green with envy, as she's always complaining about her masses of hair. We'll have to hide all the scissors in the house. Well, I'm off," he said, extending his hand to Chance.

"Not so much as a hint about Beales," Chance warned yet again, holding tight to his brother's hand.

"Not a word about any of it. Mostly because I still can't believe the half of it."

"He'll be fine," Eleanor said once Rian was gone and Chance returned to his seat. "Now, as I've been waiting patiently for hours — tell me."

"Tell you what, Elly?"

Clearly Chance didn't yet quite realize what she knew — that the past fortnight had changed her, that she felt a new assertiveness, a new strength, and the daring to say what was on her mind. "No coddling, Chance. You've been gone all day and I saw your face when you came in just before luncheon, and before you realized I was at the head of the stairs. What's happened?"

"I should leave that to Jack," Chance said, rising from the chair to walk over to the drinks table. "You might want to hear it from him, rather than me."

"You've told Jack? Honestly, Chance, do you really think he's up to hearing distressing news? And it is distressing news, isn't it?"

"You're coddling him just as Rian says, and he's letting you, the rotter." Chance returned to his chair, a glass of wine in his hand. "He'd be out of that bed now, if he wasn't enjoying himself so much. It's been three days, Elly, and the man has an incredibly hard head. I don't think I could have managed such a delicate shot even without first being conked half-senseless with a candlestick. If it hadn't been for the fact that he then promptly fainted while Chelfham screamed and the house burned down around our ears, I'd say the man was extraordinary. What I'm trying to say, Elly, is that I completely approve of your choice. If that matters to you at all."

"It does. Thank you, Chance." Eleanor smiled in quiet pride — and a bit of definitely misplaced humor — at the memory of how Jack had shot the dueling pistol straight out of Chelfham's hand. "He still swears he aimed to kill and missed, but I don't believe him. He'd promised me, you know — that he'd avoid personally dispatching anyone if at all possible. Now, tell me what's wrong. What's happened?"

"All right, although I will say you're reminding me very much of my inquisitive wife at the moment," Chance said, putting down his wineglass. "It's Eccles."

"He's confessed? He's said something about Edmund Beales?"

Chance shook his head. "No, Elly. That

433

would have been much too easy. Beales was gone from London before we so much as heard of his whereabouts from Chelfham, remember. An entire house, cleared to the walls. Only the devil knows where he is now or what he plans next. Since we already had Eccles, he couldn't know where Beales has gone, either. But it would seem the bastard has very long arms, tentacles that even reach over prison walls, as they found Eccles dead in his cell this morning, his throat neatly sliced. I can tell you, this is causing a good deal of turmoil, since no one except a few people in the War Office supposedly even knew we had him."

"But . . . but Jack and I both believed Eccles to be a very minor entity in all of this. I doubt he even knew anything of any real importance. I rather feel sorry for him." Then another thought struck her and she sat up very straight. "Chelfham. Is he dead, too?"

"No. He's been moved under heavy guard, to a place I, a lowly former member of the Minister's staff, am not privileged to know. I do know they offered him promises to keep him safe from the hangman if he agrees to cooperate, answer each question put to him. The fool wrote everything down, every name, and now he's going through the journals with the Minister himself."

"Because the journals are written in some sort of code."

"Yes, but one not difficult to break. I deciphered the copies I made with very little trouble before turning the journals over to the Minister. Names of leaders of the different smaller gangs up and down the coast that all operated as a part of the Red Men. Places where contraband was stored before being moved overland. Even landing sites."

"He was very thorough, wasn't he?"

"Yes. He explained that he never knew what his superior — the man he calls Nathaniel Beatty — could ask for, so he wrote down everything. Dragoons are already on the move, making arrests. There are also quite a few members of the *ton* who are going to be rusticating at their country estates for a while, to reflect on their involvement in freetrading."

"They won't be taken to prison? Why?"

Chance sighed, because he wasn't particularly happy to know that, once again, justice was far from fairly applied. "Because, Elly, they are peers. They have titles that go back for centuries . . . and they all have very powerful, influential friends. Eccles would have hanged, certainly, to serve as a warning — but no one is about to line up two dozen peers and throw nooses around their necks in some public display of punishment. Think of the embarrassment."

"So it was all for nothing?" Eleanor held out her hands to stop Chance from answering. "No, I'm sorry. I didn't mean that. The Red Men Gang is in a shambles, and that's certainly a good thing, both for England and for our friends in Romney Marsh. But Edmund Beales is still out there. I can't imagine what Papa will do when he finds out."

"I can," Chance said, shaking his head. "He'll go straight back into whatever hell he was mired in for so damn long. Remembering. Regretting. Blaming himself. He was so much better, Elly, these past few years. We all were. We were all beginning to feel safe." He slammed his fist into his palm. "Damn! We don't even know where to begin to look for the bastard!"

Eleanor folded her hands in her lap, wondering how many times she and Chance would have this same conversation before he finally left for Becket Hall. She hated that Edmund Beales was back in their lives, seemed to be taking over their lives, even in his absence. "Yesterday, you thought France. Chelfham did say that the man who came looking for the journals was French."

"I know. Beales wouldn't blink at working for Bonaparte. His only real loyalty is for himself, and I doubt he'd have any problem changing sides to whoever was winning at the moment. The only good thing right now is that we know he's still alive, while he believes we're dead. He won't know we're after him until we're in his face — and that's the last thing he'll ever know."

The prospect of that eventual confrontation was frightening. Terrifying. And it was time she went upstairs to check on Jack, made sure he was still resting, as the doctor had ordered.

But she didn't want to leave Chance alone in the drawing room in his present mood.

"I . . . um, I received a note this morning from Miranda Phelps."

Chance looked at her in curiosity. "I beg your pardon, Elly. Who is Miranda Phelps? Oh, wait a moment. Would she be the widow of Chelfham's brother-in-law? The one he poisoned with brandy?"

"Yes, poor woman, although I will say that her note was generally quite . . . cheerful. She's home with her family, who welcomed her even though she arrived without so much as a farthing or a bit of clothes other than what she stood up in — those are her words. She wished to thank me for arranging transportation for her. And, she told me, Lady Chelfham has barricaded herself in the country at Chelfham Hall, fearful the Crown will dare to take her home from her. Do you think that will happen?"

"I suppose it's possible. Why, Elly? Do you want the place?"

"That's difficult to answer, as I'm not sure what I'd do with it if the Crown strips Chelfham of his title and properties," she said, then sighed. "I think . . . I think I would like to know her child has a home."

"The child who will be your blood relative," Chance pointed out needlessly. "That must be sobering and exciting at the same time."

"It's troubling, actually. What if Beales decides to take some sort of revenge on the countess?"

"No, I don't think he'll bother. It's too late for that. He has to know that Chelfham is out of his reach."

"If that's true, Chance, how and why did he arrange for Eccles to be murdered? I don't think either of us needs to be reminded just how vindictive the man is, do we? Chelfham was discovered, and all the money — and you tell me it was substantial — that had been flowing to Beales is now cut off. He has to be very angry."

Chance rubbed at his chin as he looked at Eleanor, considered her argument, which was unfortunately sound. "What do you want, Elly?"

"I don't know. But we probably should be doing something, shouldn't we? Mrs. Phelps is most likely safe, at home with her parents, but the countess is very easy to find as long as she resides at Chelfham Hall. At least until Edmund Beales finds something else, and someone else, to occupy his mind."

"Very well," Chance said, getting to his feet. "It would seem I'll be leaving you sooner than I thought. I'll arrange for guards on the woman — for what? Six months? Does that seem sufficient to you, General?"

Eleanor smiled. "Jack calls me that from time to time, and not always to flatter me. But, yes, six months seems sufficient. Thank you, Chance. And it all could be for nothing. Beales may never come back to England."

"Then we'll find him where he is, won't we?" Chance said, his expression determined. "No matter how long it takes. Now, while I go tell my valet to pack for me, you go tell that slugabed upstairs that the two of you leave for Becket Hall in the morning.

London has seen the last of the Beckets for quite some time."

"I don't know if the doctor believes Jack can travel yet, Chance," Eleanor protested. "And we were none of us ever known to Beales, so it isn't as if we aren't safe here."

Chance smiled knowingly. "You're not ready to share him yet, are you, Elly?"

Eleanor got to her feet. "We'll see you in the morning, Chance, before you leave," she said, employing her quiet but firm tone, and then lifted her chin as she left the drawing room, Chance's knowing chuckle following her.

With each step she climbed on the broad staircase, Eleanor's worries dropped away.

The Earl of Chelfham was out of her life, having been a part of it in only the most unfortunate of ways.

Edmund Beales was gone, at least for now, and perhaps forever. And, contrary to what Chance feared, she believed Ainsley Becket was now strong enough again to deal with whatever might happen in the future.

She knew who she was, once and for all, and she was the person she had made. Anything else had been out of her control — the circumstances of her birth, what had happened on that ship so long ago. None of that was her. Julianna Maddox was a dream now long in the past. She was Eleanor Becket . . . soon to be Eleanor Eastwood.

Together, she and Jack would look to the future, because the past no longer held any danger, any pain.

And that was fine with her.

She knocked lightly on the door to Jack's bedchamber, then depressed the latch and stepped inside, to see that the heavy velvet drapes had been drawn against the afternoon sunlight.

She began to back out of the chamber, believing him to be asleep, only to cry out in shock when a strong arm wrapped about her waist.

"You wouldn't dare leave again now that you're here, would you?" Jack asked, his mouth mere inches from her ear. "The disappointment might set back my recovery for days."

Eleanor turned in his light embrace, moving against him. "What are you doing out of bed?" she asked, touching a hand to his cheek. "And you've been shaved."

"No one else is allowed to put a blade on my neck, madam. I shave myself. I also bathe myself, and may never forgive Treacle and my valet for that rather ignominious experience the other day."

"You would rather have been put to bed

in your dirt? You were covered with soot by the time we could drag you to safety. Like some heavy lump of coal," she added, smiling.

"I'll never be able to live that down, will I? Fainting like a woman."

"This woman did not faint," she reminded him, then laid her cheek against his strong chest. "This woman was much too grateful to her rescuer to do any such thing. The doctor said you're lucky to be alive, that another inch lower and your skull would have cracked like an egg, and he's still amazed that you'd actually not gone unconscious long before you did. Worse, I imagine, is that Mrs. Hendersen now refers to *you* as *that poor dearie.* Are you really feeling well enough to be up and dressed, you poor dearie?"

"Possibly not, imp," Jack said, lightly stroking Eleanor's back, reveling in the feel of her. "As a matter of fact, now that you've reminded me of my physician's concerns, you should probably undress me and put me back to bed as quickly as possible."

Eleanor smiled as he cupped her bottom with both hands and drew her more closely against him, to feel his arousal hard against her belly. "Really? I don't know, Jack. I'm beginning to think you're quite prodigiously well . . . recovered."

He scooped her up into his arms. "Shall we test that theory?" he asked, carrying her over to the bed, his mouth locked on hers as they tumbled, together, onto the silken coverlet.

A few days ago, Jack had been terrified that he'd never be able to hold Eleanor again. Never kiss her. Never look deeply into her eyes as he took her to the pinnacle, and beyond. Never see her swollen with his child growing inside her. Never hold her hand and talk of Latin proverbs and ancient strategies. Never grow old with her, loving her more each day of their lives.

He turned onto his back, pulling Eleanor along with him, so that her face was above him as he studied her delicate, finely drawn features, felt his heart swell as she smiled down at him. "Now, my love, where were we before we were so rudely interrupted? Ah, I remember, although it's all still a little hazy. I believe I was telling you that I adore you."

Eleanor leaned down, kissed his cheek. "I think I much prefer a slightly earlier conversation. One where you were declaring rather forcefully that we were to be married. Do you remember that?"

Jack raised one speaking eyebrow. "What? I'm sorry, but I've sustained an injury to my head, you know. I actually don't recall that. Marriage, you said?"

"No," Eleanor told him, her fingers busy on the buttons of his shirt. "Marriage, *you* said."

"Oh, wait. I think it's coming back to me now." His own hands were busy on the row of small buttons that marched down the back of her simple muslin gown. "You thanked me, didn't you? I was extremely flattered, although, now that I consider the thing, a simple *yes* might have been the preferred response."

"It would, if I wished to marry you," Eleanor teased as he rolled her onto her back, her gown already lowered to her waist — he really, *really* was very good at this. "I may, however, have decided that I should be happier being a fallen woman and living in sin. In my effort to no longer be so very proper, you understand. Shouldn't every virtue be tinged with just a little vice? *Mmm, that's nice.*"

Jack had captured one exposed nipple between his thumb and forefinger, and was enjoying watching as she seemed to flower beneath his touch. "Nice, but no longer decadent, I suppose? And you'd enjoy feeling decadent?"

Eleanor would enjoy it if Jack would simply shut up and love her, as this newly discovered passion had been missing from her life for three entire days and nights, and his simplest touch had enflamed her senses with a swiftness that was very nearly frightening. She wanted his touch. Needed his touch. Longed for him to be inside her. Moving in her. Touching all the places he already knew to touch, even as she, in her turn, began to learn more of him.

He'd somehow pushed her gown and undergarments to her hips now, and was lightly teasing the rim of her navel with his tongue even as his fingers worked their magic on her breasts.

"Jack . . ." she breathed, her eyes closed as she reached down to him, slid her fingers into his hair. But he eluded her, sliding lower, kissing her belly, licking her highly sensitive skin. "Please. I want to hold you . . . Jack? No . . . what are you . . . ? I didn't mean it. I wouldn't really even know *how* to be deca — *oh, Jack.*"

He gently spread her, exposing her most private secrets to his fevered gaze. "Beautiful," he whispered hoarsely, hoping to reassure her, gain her trust. "So very beautiful . . ."

He softly blew on her exposed center, marveled as she reacted involuntarily, as the small, sensitive bud swelled, lured him closer.

Eleanor's exquisitely honest moan of pleasure as he sealed his mouth over her filled him with the need to take her to heights the maiden she had so recently been could never hope to imagine.

He suckled on her, drawing her sweetness into his mouth, teased that small bud with his tongue until he felt her raise her hips to him, inviting all that he desired, offering all that she could give.

Eleanor's world centered on this one small, most vitally alive part of herself, any reservations or thoughts of modesty scattered to the four winds as Jack moved his tongue swiftly, deftly, her every nerve ending sending out a sweet, burning blush that enveloped her, lifted her, and at last burst into a shower of light and color as her body seemed to return his most intimate kiss.

He stayed with her as the storm he'd ignited slowly passed in a series of pleasurable pulses of her now highly sensitized flesh, before at last allowing her to hold him, bury her head against his shoulder as he soothed her with words of love.

But she couldn't be content, not yet. She needed him still, needed him deep inside her, needed to feel his pleasure. Given so much, all she wanted was to give in return.

Jack felt the tension in her, in her quick, shallow breaths, in the way she began to strain against him once more, in the way she dug her fingertips into his back.

In a matter of moments he had shed his clothing and hovered above her, his heart swelling as he looked down at her, as he slowly eased himself into her.

"I'll never let you go," he whispered. "You're my life, Eleanor. My beginning and my end."

Eleanor smiled as she raised her arms to him, gloried in the feel of his weight against her as they held each other close. "My forever . . ."

EPILOGUE

"Oh, there he is! Look, Jack — do you see him?"

"Eleanor, my love, my wife, my own," Jack said, amused, "there are at least fifty gulls on the beach right now. How on earth do you suppose I should *recognize* one particular bird?"

"You'll see." Eleanor took Jack's hand and led him over the shingle to the small spit of sand that led into the Channel. As they approached, the gulls reacted as one, gracefully lifting into the air, wheeling as one as they voiced their disapproval at being chased from the beach.

All the gulls, that is, save one that remained where it was, jerkily cocking its head from side to side as it observed the approaching humans.

"Hello, Ignatius," Eleanor said, careful to approach the large white gull slowly. "Have you missed me?"

"Ignatius, is it?" Jack said, taking his cue from Eleanor, and speaking quietly, moving slowly. "How do you know that's — my God, it's only got one leg."

"One of the village dogs, I'm afraid," Eleanor said, opening a twist of greased paper she'd pulled from her pocket, exposing several strips of fresh fish she'd taken from the kitchens. "Callie rescued him and Odette healed him, but he'd only feed if I fed him. We have a special bond. Isn't that right, Ignatius?"

Jack shook his head in amazement as the gull hopped sure-footedly on its single leg, approaching Eleanor as she held out a strip of raw fish. "He actually feeds from your hand?"

Eleanor let go of the strip of fish and Ignatius deftly snared it in his beak. "I told you. We're friends. Ignatius has been at Becket Hall for five years now. We take in all strays." She turned to smile at Jack. "Even you."

"Yes, thank you. And if Jacko would stop grumbling under his breath every time he sees me, I might feed out of his hand, too."

Eleanor laughed, her heart free, her happiness so thorough that each day seemed a new adventure, a whole new opportunity to enjoy life to its fullest. "Poor Jack," she said, then quickly finished feeding Ignatius, as some of the other gulls had begun to gather, wanting their share of the delicacy.

Jack took the empty greased paper from her hand and squeezed it into a ball, tucking it in a pocket of his greatcoat before taking Eleanor's hand. "Look, sweetheart. Over there."

She looked where he pointed, to an outcropping of wet, dark boulders that were more exposed now that the tide was low. At the very end of the natural pier, spray from the breaking waves lapping at his booted feet, stood Ainsley Becket, his dark head bare, his black greatcoat flapping around his knees in a fairly stiff sea breeze.

He was looking out to sea. Not moving. This tall, spare man, this strong, tortured soul. Oblivious to his surroundings. Clearly suffering.

Eleanor blinked back sudden tears as she leaned against Jack and he slid an arm around her protectively. "It's been a month since Chance told him about Edmund Beales. I can't even imagine what he must be thinking, what he must be feeling," she said quietly.

"Because there's nothing he can do, is there?" Jack said, understanding the deep frustration Ainsley must be harboring, as he had suffered the same feeling of impotence when he'd realized that Chelfham had taken Eleanor from him. "Chance says it could be years before Beales surfaces again."

"If he ever does. And he could be any-where. France. Russia. Even America. We may have crippled him somewhat by losing him the revenue from the Red Men Gang, and denied him the place in English society he seemed to covet, but that doesn't mean he's beaten. Courtland told me that Papa believes we need to follow the winners, for that's where Beales will be."

"I know, sweetheart. He said much the same thing to me. But Court also said *years*. Ainsley may have to wait years for his re-venge."

"Justice," Eleanor corrected quietly, look-ing at Ainsley Becket as he stood, his face into the wind, his entire being seemingly etched in suppressed agony. "Papa deserves justice. We all do."

Jack leaned down and kissed Eleanor's windswept curls. "I know, sweetheart, and we'll have it. Do you know what Ainsley said to me the other night after you'd gone up to bed? He said that we live in an often ugly world."

"Oh, Jack, that's so sad."

"It is, I'll grant you that. But that's not all

he said. He told me that what makes life bearable — even lifts life into the realm of the extraordinary — is love. He said that when you find love, you must guard it with everything that's in you, because that love is the only worthwhile thing in this world. And that, my love, is exactly what I intend to do."

"We will guard our love, Jack, both of us." Eleanor wiped at the tears that had spilled onto her cheeks, then looked toward Ainsley Becket one last time before Jack slid his arm more firmly around her and led her away from the beach. . . .

ABOUT THE AUTHOR

USA Today bestselling author **Kasey Michaels** is the author of more than ninety books. She has earned three starred reviews from *Publisher's Weekly,* and has been awarded the RITA® Award from Romance Writers of America, the *Romantic Times* Career Achievement Award, the Waldenbooks and BookRak awards, and several other commendations for her writing excellence in both contemporary and historical novels. There are more than eight million copies of her books in print around the world. Kasey resides in Pennsylvania with her family, where she is always at work on her next book.